Detective
AUNTY

ALSO BY UZMA JALALUDDIN

Ayesha at Last

Hana Khan Carries On

Three Holidays and a Wedding (with Marissa Stapley)

Much Ado About Nada

Detective AUNTY

A Novel

UZMA JALALUDDIN

HARPER PERENNIAL

NEW YORK • LONDON • TORONTO • SYDNEY • NEW DELHI • AUCKLAND

HARPER PERENNIAL

Simultaneously published in 2025 by HarperCollins Canada Ltd.

HarperCollins books may be purchased for educational, business, or sales promotional use. For information in the U.S., address HarperCollins Publishers, 195 Broadway, New York, NY 10007, U.S.A. In Canada, address HarperCollins Publishers Ltd, Bay Adelaide Centre, East Tower, 22 Adelaide Street West, 41st Floor, Toronto, Ontario, M5H 4E3, Canada.

FIRST US AND CANADIAN EDITIONS

Library of Congress Cataloging-in-Publication Data has been applied for.

Library and Archives Canada Cataloguing in Publication information is available upon request.

ISBN 978-0-06-343487-5 (US pbk.)

ISBN 978-1-4434-7284-5 (Canada pbk.)

25 26 27 28 29 LBC 5 4 3 2 1

For my mother-in-law, Fouzia, who loves a good mystery, and my mom, Azmat, who introduced me to Agatha Christie.

And to all the "aunties" launching their second act—I see you.

PROLOGUE

Every soul shall taste death.

Imran remembered the line from a childhood lesson with his mother; the words, quoted from the Quran, had meant nothing to him as a six-year-old boy. Back then, his thoughts had only fixed on the idea of tasting death as if it were a flavor, and from there had wandered to what snack he might sneak from the kitchen. Now, nearly fifty years later, far from his childhood home in India, he knew death did have a taste, and that it was metallic and harsh in his mouth. It was accompanied by panic, desperation, and, finally, a preternatural calm.

He knew where he was and what was happening. He had tried to save himself in those last, final moments when movement and action were still possible. Now he lay awkwardly sprawled on the floor, body heavy and numb, as darkness dimmed the edges of his vision. There was a sudden flash of pain, as something shifted in the center of his chest, replaced by another, duller sensation.

Imran wanted to roar, to rail against the unfairness. His father had died an old man, surrounded by family. Didn't he deserve the same?

More footsteps nearby, and then a weight pushed against him. It wouldn't be long now. Already the darkness had grabbed hold, and he sensed a shadowy figure waiting for him, trailing ghostly fingers on his face and over his body.

He had never believed in an afterlife, despite his mother's stories. For the first time, he thought of the judgment he had been taught to expect in the grave, the angels who would sit on his chest and mete out punishment, pain, or peace. His body spasmed, and the cold made him shiver one final time. He knew what he deserved, and the thought made him rage, made him long to hurt.

With his last breath, he spoke his final words. The footsteps stopped abruptly, rooted to the spot. Finally, the captive audience he'd wanted.

Imran Thakur died with a faint smile on his lips, pleased he had left the world a slightly worse place than he had found it.

CHAPTER 1

The second-worst phone call of Kausar Khan's life came in the middle of an ordinary morning, knocking her world into a new direction entirely.

Sixteen months had passed since Hassan's pancreatic cancer diagnosis, nearly a year since her husband's death, and she woke with no premonition of the chaos to come. But if there was one thing Kausar had learned in her fifty-seven years, it was to beware moments of tranquility.

She was on the phone for twenty-three seconds and afterwards sat staring at nothing. The familiar, solid furniture in her neat sitting room faded into the background: the plush recliner where Hassan had spent the first few weeks after his diagnosis; the stone fireplace they vowed to use every winter but never had; the cream-colored fabric couch she had slumped back into; the solid wood coffee table where her rapidly cooling chai sat next to a stack of Agatha Christie paperbacks, her and her late husband's favorite, though he had complained she always guessed the identity of the murderer too easily.

The large airy room, which Kausar had decorated in beige and deep blue when they had first moved into the tidy bungalow seventeen years ago, now felt oppressive as she tried to make sense of what had just happened.

"*Ammi.*" Kausar's eldest child, Sana, her voice carefully calm, had said over the line. "I need you in Toronto. Now."

Kausar hadn't responded, frozen in the crossbeams of two contradictory thoughts—that she couldn't return to Toronto, and that her daughter would never ask unless something had gone terribly wrong.

Sana continued in that strangely calm voice, as if her words were nothing more than a commentary on the day. As if this moment, too, were inevitable. "I'm in trouble. There's been a murder, and I'm the prime suspect."

"S*ana, a suspect in a murder? I can't believe it.*" May Kildair, Kausar's best friend in North Bay, repeated. Her friend had arrived at her house promptly, in response to the text Kausar sent one hour prior. *I'm flying to Toronto. Can you drive me to the airport?*

Her friend, a white woman born and raised in the Northern Ontario town, was dressed in her usual uniform of yoga pants and an oversized shirt that dwarfed her petite frame, short blond bob motionless despite the warm April breeze and the wide-open windows of her fifteen-year-old forest green Jeep. May's children had jokingly gifted her with a novelty two-foot-tall bottle of hairspray for Christmas last year.

May's eyes were trained on the road now, her speed steady at fifty kilometers an hour—ten under the official speed limit, twenty under the unofficial one. An SUV honked and cut her off, but she didn't pay any attention. At least May had waited until they were on their way to the airport before she probed into the reason for Kausar's last-minute flight. It had taken Kausar several tries to get the story out, still unable to believe what was happening.

Suspect in a murder investigation. My daughter, Sana Khan, age thirty-six, resident of Toronto and married mother of two, is at a police station, waiting to be arrested and charged for murder.

Who had been murdered? When? How? Kausar had no answers for May. It was all she could do to tick her mental checkboxes as she prepared to leave North Bay for the first time in almost two decades: Book a flight to the one place she had never wanted to see again—check. Pack a bag—check. Don't panic—unchecked, but she was trying.

It was only a four-hour drive to Toronto, but Kausar hadn't sat behind the wheel of a car in seventeen years. May knew the reason why. As a result, her friend had played chauffeur during their entire friendship with no complaint. They had become friends when Kausar thought herself broken; May had helped her pick up the pieces and build a new life. She felt a rush of gratitude for her friend—even now, May knew to let Kausar sit in silence as she contemplated her next steps. As soon as she got to Toronto, she'd go straight to Sana's house to take care of her granddaughters; Sana had made it clear that Kausar was not to go to the police station.

"After she said there had been a murder, my mind went blank," Kausar said now. "If only Hassan were with me. He would know what to do."

May's reassurance was immediate. "Hassan is happy you're here to take care of the children when he can't. Which you are more than capable of doing." She was ten years older than Kausar, with four children and twelve grandchildren (and counting). They had met at the local library the first week Kausar moved to North Bay and had bonded over a shared love for Louise Penny. "It might even be good for you, to go back to the city," she added, with a sideways glance at her friend.

Toronto was full of ghosts for Kausar. Every year, she made plans to visit Sana and her granddaughters. And every year, after

Hassan had arranged the details, she canceled. *Perhaps in the spring. In the summer, when Maleeha and Fizza are on school holidays. In Ramadan, when we can break fast together.*

Then Hassan was diagnosed, and travel became impossible. Now Sana, the child who had never caused her a moment's worry, was under suspicion of committing murder.

Kausar made a quick *dua*: Let this all be a misunderstanding. The thought of her Sana committing a violent act was unthinkable. The idea of her daughter in jail, beyond the realm of possibility. The most unexpected thing to have happened to her daughter was her decision to open a desi fashion boutique last year. But the business was a good fit for her organized, stylish daughter. The grand opening was held last fall; Kausar had not attended.

"I could drive down, in a few days," May offered, breaking into Kausar's reverie. "In case you need help."

Kausar smiled at her friend. "I appreciate that," she said. "But I've booked a return ticket for one week's time. I'm sure there has been some mistake. Besides, Jenny needs you."

May blinked. "How did you know that?" She grinned. "I can see why Sana called you first. She knows her mother will be able to figure out what really happened, probably even before those Toronto cops."

Kausar shook her head, lips twitching in a smile. "I think she just wants her mother there."

May shook her head. "Regardless, it always amazes me when you know things about my children before I do."

Kausar spoke carefully. "I am happy for Jenny, though she didn't seem quite herself when I saw her."

May didn't seem ready to dive into her youngest daughter's troubles and deftly changed the subject. "I expect daily updates. Will you be okay on your own?"

Kausar glanced down at her large, black leather purse, where she had carefully tucked two small photographs—one of her and Hassan on their wedding day, nearly forty years ago; the second of her youngest son, Ali, frozen forever at fifteen, his cheeky smile promising endless mischief.

"Inshallah," Kausar answered. May was familiar with the versatile word, which meant "God willing" in Arabic, but could also mean "I hope so" and "fingers crossed" and "send positive vibes!"

May pulled into the small parking lot at Jack Garland, the municipal airport that served as the gateway to remote Northern Ontario communities, as well as the city. It had not changed much since Kausar first arrived, after Hassan had reached out to an old army friend in the Canadian military and was put in touch with Wing 22 North Bay when he knew his wife needed to get away from all the things that had happened in Toronto.

The Canadian Forces base had once been a bustling hub for NORAD, the North American Aerospace Defense Command, which monitored Soviet activity during the Cold War and continued to monitor all aircraft entering North America. The original building, with its unique helix underground headquarters capable of withstanding a direct nuclear attack, was a marvel of engineering. The base had been decommissioned in 2006 and replaced by a smaller, modern building, but budget cuts eventually reduced military personnel to a shadow of its former capacity. As a result, Wing 22 was the only Canadian Air Force base without any planes. But the surrounding town needed a doctor, and so Hassan got the job. The couple moved, leaving Adam and Sana behind in Toronto to finish university, and Ali in his final resting place. As heartbreaking as it had been to leave her children, as well as the city that had been home for most of her adult life, Kausar knew that moving to North Bay had saved her life.

Hassan had been quickly engulfed by his new medical practice serving veterans, retirees, and the small population that made up the community of North Bay, including a growing Muslim community. Kausar spent her days taking care of the small home they purchased, trying her hand at gardening, visiting the library, and trying to heal from her loss. It had taken almost a year for her to get out of bed before noon, and another year before she could take joy in simple pleasures without feeling guilty. But slowly, she and Hassan rebuilt a semblance of a new life.

When Hassan passed away last year, nearly the entire town had turned out for his funeral, and Kausar's freezer was stocked with casseroles she couldn't bring herself to eat.

May nosed into a parking spot near the airport entrance. At this time of day, the lot was empty. She reached into the back seat for a small paper bag and handed it to Kausar. Inside was a notebook, the cover textured to resemble leather, a bold pattern of yellow, purple, and orange flowers spilling across the buttery surface.

"It made me think of your garden," May explained. "My students think paper is antiquated, but I always need to write things down. It might help you solve the case, Detective Aunty."

Kausar had once explained to May the use of honorifics in desi culture, where every older person was an aunty or uncle, even if they were only thirty years old, while blood relations were acknowledged with specific titles for their role in the family. May had been charmed and taken to calling herself *Teacher Aunty*, and sometimes *Overworked, Exhausted Aunty*. But Kausar had quickly been christened *Detective Aunty* whenever May wanted to tease her.

Kausar smiled, touched at the gift. "I'm not a detective. I simply notice things."

"For your noticings, then," May said, and pressed the book into her friend's hand. She hesitated. "How *did* you know about Jenny?"

Kausar placed the gift in her purse, and a feeling of déjà vu hit, making her dizzy. As if she had already lived through this moment, perhaps in another life, perhaps in a dream. *I simply notice things.*

"I remembered how much she craved snack food the last time she was pregnant. I saw her in the grocery store with two bottles of salsa and three bags of chips. I will pray for her, and for your lucky number thirteen."

A cloud passed over May's face, and Kausar wondered if she had misread the situation. Hassan had been alternately amused and annoyed by what he called her "party trick." Kausar could not help noticing things others did not, from people's moods, words, and behaviors, and then extrapolating from her observations. It felt as natural as breathing to notice the local imam had stained his sleeve a particularly vibrant orange hue and to figure out that his sister, who made homemade achar chutney, was visiting. Or years ago, when she realized her eight-year-old daughter was being bullied at school. Not everyone appreciated her observations, however. When she asked the imam to pass along her salaams to his sister, he had been surprised and even disturbed. What came naturally to her, others—even her children—seemed to find intrusive or embarrassing. Eventually, she had begun to simply file her observations away in a corner of her mind and feign surprise whenever someone confided a secret she already knew.

It was different with May. Her friend usually enjoyed her "noticings." Except something was wrong this time. Kausar resolved to call her friend later and find out if her suspicions were correct and there was more going on with Jenny than a long-awaited and very welcome pregnancy.

"I know it's only been a year since Hassan passed," May started, changing the subject again. "And that there's no timeline for grief and loss. But while I'm sorry for the circumstances, I'm glad you're going to Toronto. You've been hiding yourself away up here for a long time." Her friend's eyes were full of empathy, understanding, and something else. May had raised her four children on her own after her husband left her for the Alberta oil fields. She had worked as a high school teacher and after-school tutor, taught summer school and night school to support her family. It wasn't until she retired a few years ago that she finally took a break. "There's life in you yet, and don't you forget it. You're only fifty-seven. This is your second act. You get to decide what to do with it." May handed her the overnight bag from the trunk.

Her friend meant well, but Kausar knew they had been raised with different expectations. She'd married Hassan at seventeen, shortly after completing high school in Hyderabad, India. Hassan had been thirty-two, already a medical doctor and a retired soldier in the Canadian Armed Forces. Though his family had moved to Canada when he was a child, his parents wanted him to marry a girl from "back home," and a mutual friend arranged the *rishta* proposal. After two brief meetings, where her father made conversation with Hassan's father and Kausar and Hassan only looked at each other shyly, the *nikah* date was set. Despite the age difference and her parents' reluctance to send their only daughter to Canada, Hassan's family had a good reputation, and every reference checked out. Besides, a doctor who didn't ask for an outrageous bride gift was rare.

Yet, it hadn't been easy. Hassan was kind, but they were strangers. And though a deep and abiding love had grown between them eventually, one that stayed steady over decades of marriage, the birth of their three children, and even devastating loss, Kausar had always understood her place. She was a wife and mother; her domain extended only as far as the household, the children, her social and community obligations. To their friends, she would always be Mrs. Dr. Hassan Khan, her husband's accomplishments and identity conflated with her own.

Kausar had no complaints and knew she lived a comfortable life. After the children started school, she had finished a degree in psychology part-time, knowing she would never use her qualifications, but still enjoying the academic rigor. The idea of a second act was something people like May could look forward to. Kausar accepted that the best she could hope for was a few quiet decades. The dreams she couldn't even acknowledge to herself—for adventure, for intrigue, to contribute to her community in her own right and not only through her role as wife and mother—had long ago withered to dust.

Kausar hefted her small bag and hugged May. "*The pens have been lifted, and the pages have dried*," she said, quoting a well-known Muslim idiom.

May shook her head. "I don't know what that means, Kausar Khan. But there's more to life than sitting alone in your house surrounded by ghosts and memories."

CHAPTER 2

The flight was delayed by an hour, and Kausar spent the time worrying. Had Sana been arrested? Was she in a jail cell right now, and would she need money for bail? Kausar had no idea how the Canadian criminal justice system worked; she'd never had any direct involvement with it. Everything she knew came from watching American and British crime shows and reading detective fiction.

The last time her family interacted with the police, Hassan had handled everything. Kausar had not been in any shape to talk with law enforcement, lawyers, the coroner, or the journalists who had called the house. But now Hassan was gone, and Sana needed her.

The colorful yellow swirl of May's gift caught Kausar's eye, and she pulled the notebook from her purse and flipped to the first page. *Kausar Khan Investigates* was written across the top in May's neat handwriting, the *K* of her first and last name a flourish. May's optimism made her smile.

When they had first met, May was still teaching history at the local high school. Once their friendship was firmly established and May stumbled upon her observational talents, Kausar had helped out with a few incidents: random thefts at school, a case of plagiarism and another of mistaken identity involving criminally minded teenage triplets.

"We all have a superpower," May told her once. "I can motivate a reluctant learner and make Canadian history seem interesting to teenagers. You were born to solve mysteries."

The plane finally began to board, and she flashed her driver's license at the attendant, who carefully studied the picture, comparing it to her face. Kausar kept renewing it, though she hadn't driven since Ali's death.

The queue for cabs at the Toronto airport was short, and her driver was desi and polite. He smoothly merged onto the habitually crowded Highway 401, heading east towards Scarborough, the suburb where Sana lived.

Ramadan had ended a few weeks ago, and even in late April, evidence of Toronto's construction season was everywhere. Cranes dotted the landscape and condominium towers sprouted like glass-fronted redwoods, reaching towards the sky and battling for the best view of the busy metropolis.

They exited the highway and turned onto a main street, where Kausar's gaze was drawn to the many people on the sidewalks, some waiting for the bus, parents pushing strollers, teenagers hanging out, so many faces that looked like her own.

The driver navigated the small streets of the densely packed suburb, coming to a stop in front of a large two-story detached home before jumping out to help with her bag. Kausar handed him a hefty tip.

After retrieving Sana's house keys from her purse, Kausar walked up the drive. Sana had pressed the keys into Hassan's hands the last time he visited, and Kausar recalled his expression of delight when he recounted the story of their daughter asking him to consider the house his own. In a way, it was—he had paid for most of it.

It was a large home with a generous three-car driveway. The

spacious foyer, where Kausar took off her shoes, opened into a large sitting room with twenty-foot ceilings and floor-length windows that let in cheerful sunlight. The house felt empty, but Kausar heard running footsteps.

"*Ammi*. You came," Sana said, and launched herself into her mother's arms.

At first, Kausar was confused. What was Sana doing here? Kausar had spent the flight worried Sana was being interrogated at the police station, or detained. Sana explained that she had beat her mother home by fifteen minutes and led Kausar into the large, open-concept kitchen, all chrome fixtures, white marble countertops, and a massive kitchen island. She paused to admire the open space, decorated in Sana's minimalist style. Everything looked shiny, well-maintained, and expensive.

"The detective on the case wanted to keep me longer, but I told him my husband was out of town and my kids are young," Sana explained, taking a seat at the kitchen island, her legs dangling from a sleek but uncomfortable-looking chrome bar stool.

At thirty-six, Sana was a beautiful woman with large, dark eyes fringed with thick lashes; her nose, like Hassan's, was slightly beaky but the rest of her features mirrored Kausar's almost exactly: lips a small bow, eyebrows thick and dark against blemish-free light brown skin. Her face had filled out over the years, and Kausar thought the new curves suited her daughter's tall frame of five foot eight, which Sana emphasized by favoring heels and platform shoes, though she also had a large collection of *qusay*, embroidered and sequined slippers. Her daughter had always loved pretty, well-made things and often paired tunic tops and pants in cotton, linen, or wool, even when she was running errands or cooking dinner. Her need for order extended to the house—there wasn't a single dirty dish in the sink, no mess of plastic containers on the counter, no smear of something sticky from the children's breakfast.

Today Sana was dressed in a bright orange and blue kurta top with gold embroidery and matching capri pants. The clothes looked incredibly fresh, which was strange for someone who had spent the day being interrogated in a police station. As if reading her mother's thoughts, Sana pulled at the fabric and made a face.

"They wanted my clothing. There was a lot of blood," she explained, voice trembling only slightly. "I didn't even realize how dirty my clothes were until the police arrived. I grabbed the first outfit I could from one of the racks, though I would never wear this color . . ." She was in shock, Kausar realized. There was a brittleness about her daughter, a shakiness to her movements. Instinctively, Kausar began opening drawers, searching for a small pot in which to brew chai.

"Take a shower, Sana *beta*," Kausar urged, placing the pot on the stove and adding two cups of water before hunting for tea bags and whole cardamom pods. "The children will be home from school soon, and we must talk. I will take care of everything."

Relief passed across Sana's face, shifting to curiosity when she caught sight of the floral notebook Kausar had dropped on the kitchen table. Before Kausar could protest, Sana picked it up and studied the first page, with its bold proclamation: *Kausar Khan Investigates*. Sana's eyes narrowed as she placed it back on the table without a word and moved towards the stairs to follow her mother's direction.

T*he perfect cup of chai takes at least twenty minutes to* brew, which was why Kausar usually stuck to the quick method of a tea bag and boiled water. But she wanted to give both Sana and herself time to process what had happened. She added three tea bags to the small pot, throwing in whole cardamom once the water started to bubble, and let her thoughts wander. Her usually unflappable daughter was rattled, far more than she would have thought possible. Her granddaughters likely had no idea what was going on—and where was Hamza, Sana's husband of nearly sixteen years?

She pushed away the other thought crowding her mind, the long-repressed memories from the last time she had been in Toronto. She could feel Ali's presence more strongly here than in North Bay and felt a prickle at the back of her neck as she bent over the stove, certain that if she turned her head, Ali would come strolling downstairs to ask what was for dinner, before trying to wheedle her into making him a snack.

The tea was boiling now, a furious churn of dark water, fragrant with spice. Kausar reached for milk and poured a generous amount, instantly cooling the brew and turning it a rich golden brown. She set the pot to simmer, and by the time Sana returned downstairs, hair damp and some of the exhaustion washed from her face, the chai was ready.

Kausar set two steaming mugs on the table and motioned for her daughter to join her. "Tell me what happened."

Sana gripped her mug, plain white porcelain with an etching of an elaborately lashed eye, staring straight at her. "My landlord, Imran Thakur, was murdered. I found him inside my store this morning around five a.m. He had collapsed by the register. He was lying in a pool of blood." Sana swallowed, then took a sip of chai to steady herself, though her next words wavered. "He had been stabbed. There was a . . . knife in his chest."

Kausar closed her eyes and breathed deeply. She could imagine the horror of the moment. She also knew this wasn't the first time Sana had stumbled upon a dead body. The clock ticked in the kitchen, a heavy ornate piece that looked like a long-ago wedding gift, and Kausar counted to fifteen alongside the second hand, sifting through her thoughts rapidly. "That must have been awful," she said quietly. "*Beta*, can I ask what you were doing in the store so early?" Her use of the endearment *beta*, "my dear child," was automatic.

Sana's eyes flew to her mother. "My store is nearby—you remember the old Golden Crescent Plaza? It's there—sometimes I go in early, for an hour or so, to take care of things I didn't get to the day before. Then I come back home to get the girls ready for school." Kausar waited. She sensed there was more, and she wasn't wrong. "I called the police right away. They questioned me for hours, and it wasn't until later in the morning that I realized they were treating me like a suspect and not a witness." A tinge of bitterness entered her voice, but also something that sounded like fear.

"Why would they suspect you?" Kausar asked, trying to keep her voice mild.

"I don't know!" Sana cried out, knocking over her remaining chai. The brown liquid spread quickly across the glass surface of the table, and she jumped up in search of a cloth, mopping aggressively. "I found the body, he was in my store. They jumped to conclusions when they realized the knife was from my display window." She cut herself off abruptly, as if she had said too much.

Kausar contemplated her daughter's erratic movements in silence. Sana was not easily frazzled, but her actions now were clumsy. A result of shock and leftover adrenaline, most likely. Kausar rose to refill Sana's mug with the remaining chai on the stove. "Where is Hamza?" she asked, careful to keep her voice casual as she placed the fresh cup of tea in front of Sana. She had noted his absence in the house when she walked in: no shoes in the foyer or on the shoe rack, no bulky men's jacket on the coat stand.

"Traveling," Sana said shortly. "He's on his way home now."

Kausar counted another ten seconds by the clock. "Why would Imran have been in your store? Were you expecting him for some reason?"

Sana froze, her mug midway to her mouth. "No," she said shortly. "Landlords aren't allowed inside tenant units unless we're there, and even then, they need to give prior notice. Not that Imran was one to follow rules."

"What do you mean? Had he entered your store without permission before?"

Sana considered this, and Kausar could practically see the calculation in her mind, whether to tell the truth, or deny.

"I suspected he was entering my unit when I was absent," she said finally. "One time Maleeha caught him sneaking out. We share a back entrance with his office and another unit. I've asked him not to enter without me there, but he always denied it."

Kausar considered this careful response, certain she had uttered no lie, but also sure she had left something out. The reason for this subterfuge was less clear. Why had Sana asked her for help if she wasn't going to be honest?

"Do you have security cameras in the store?" Kausar asked.

"Of course I do," Sana snapped. The strain of the day was wearing on her, and she took a long swallow of chai. "I gave the footage to the police already. There's nothing to see, though. The camera malfunctioned sometime last week and hasn't worked properly since. I meant to get it fixed."

"That's unfortunate. Did you get along with Imran?" Kausar asked, voice gentle.

Sana shrugged. "I didn't really know him. Hamza knew him better. He seemed decent enough, I guess. I certainly didn't know him well enough to want to kill him," she added caustically. "The police will figure that out soon enough."

"Can you tell me about the plaza? Do you know your fellow

shopkeepers well?" Kausar asked. Surely, if the landlord had been murdered on his property, there was a good chance all the business owners would be suspects, not just Sana.

Sana sighed but answered readily. The largest unit was a grocer, run by Mr. Jin, a beloved plaza staple for decades. There was a Tamil bakery run by Luxmi, a bubble tea place, a cell phone and computer repair shop whose owner had just changed hands, and a roti take-out shop run by Lisa. She wasn't particularly close with any of the other shopkeepers, though they were all polite. No vendettas or blood oaths that she was aware of, if that was what Kausar was thinking.

"Were you home last night?" Kausar wasn't sure why she asked this, except something about this story was starting to trouble her, and she couldn't figure out why. It felt as if she and Sana were talking at cross-purposes, as if Kausar were the interrogator and Sana the reluctant witness, which made no sense. She was there to help.

Her daughter's response to this question was steeped in irritation. "Where else would I be? I came home right after I closed the store, cooked dinner, and helped Maleeha with homework. Fizza had an art class, and afterwards we stopped for groceries. We got home around nine p.m., and I put Fizza to bed and told Maleeha to get off her phone, pray her namaz, and head to bed, too. It was lights out at ten p.m. I can barely keep my eyes open later than that these days, especially when Hamza is traveling and everything is left to me."

Kausar remembered what it had been like when her three children were in school: the endless loop of drop-offs, pickups, school lunches, and extracurricular activities. Combined with starting a new business and a spouse who traveled for work, no wonder Sana dropped from exhaustion every night.

"I will call Nasir and get some recommendations for a lawyer," Kausar said, decisive now. Nasir Hafeez was a popular community figure who handled legal trusts and wills, and had expanded into a thriving commercial real estate law practice. He was also a close friend of the family; he had made the drive to North Bay last year for Hassan's *janazah* and told Kausar to call on him if she ever needed help. This situation definitely qualified. Except Sana was shaking her head, and Kausar recognized the stubborn look in her eye.

"I don't need a lawyer. I couldn't pay for one, in any case. I didn't call you to play detective, Mom," Sana said.

"Then why did you call me?" Kausar asked, stung. She hadn't missed Sana's protestation about her finances, either, especially considering the large house they were sitting in, located in one of the most expensive cities in the world. She avoided making an obvious show of looking around the kitchen at the high-end appliances and designer cutlery.

"I was scared," Sana admitted. "Hamza wasn't picking up his phone, and the police had been questioning me since six a.m., when I called them."

"You said you found the body at five a.m., and called the police immediately," Kausar interrupted. "And why wasn't Hamza answering?"

Sana's annoyance flared once more as she leveled a hard-eyed stare at her mother. "Forgive me, I was a bit distracted by the *dead man in my store* to pay attention to the exact time!"

Noting the sidestep of her second question, and not entirely satisfied with Sana's answer to the first, Kausar broke their standoff first and nodded at Sana to continue.

A sheepish expression replaced Sana's earlier frustration. "I called you because . . . yours was the only other number I have memorized. The police had my phone."

Kausar sat back, her mind spinning. She recalled her frantic movements that morning, the adrenaline that had flooded her system upon hearing Sana's shaken voice, throwing her clothing into a bag with little consideration, and buying a last-minute plane ticket to Toronto, the one city she hoped never to see again. All because Hamza hadn't picked up his phone, and Sana didn't have anyone else's number memorized. It hurt Kausar a bit to hear that Sana had only called her because she had no other option, and not because she wanted her.

"I wasn't sure you would come." Sana's softly spoken words were not an accusation, yet they felt like a slap in the face. She hurriedly added, "But I really want you here. You've already made everything better." Sana reached for the chai and took a long swallow. "The truth is, I've been wanting to ask you for months. I could use your help, with the girls and the house, with cooking. Ever since I opened the store, it's been hard to stay on top of everything. Can you stay? At least until I sort through this trouble? It shouldn't take too long, maybe a few weeks."

So Sana wanted her mother here as domestic help, and nothing else. Suddenly, the notebook on the kitchen table filled Kausar with embarrassment. The worst of it was, she couldn't blame her daughter: Sana was simply navigating the barriers Kausar had put up years ago, when she had left Toronto. Helper, cook, child minder—that was who she was, all she had ever been, and all she ever would be.

Kausar swallowed her disappointment with the remainder of her chai. "Of course, *beta*. Whatever you need."

CHAPTER 3

"The case of the convenient caretaker," Kausar said into her cell phone. "The mystery of the cleaning grandmother. The curious incident of the naan-i."

At the other end of the line, May laughed heartily. "Our children's words are sharpened daggers, and they aim straight for the heart," she said.

Kausar winced at May's unfortunate choice of words, Sana's description of Imran's death still vibrant in her mind. "I suppose I should be grateful my phone number is still lodged in Sana's long-term memory, or I might never hear from her again," she joked.

She looked around the guest bedroom, where she had settled shortly after the unsatisfying conversation in the kitchen. The room was generously proportioned but sparsely furnished with castoffs, as befitting a rarely used space. An older double bed with a plain white duvet took up most of the room, a sturdy but dated cherrywood dresser tucked into the corner. The large window had a clear view of the main street that served as an artery into the neighborhood. There was a small closet, filled with boxes of old clothes and the children's school mementos, while another door led to a shared bathroom.

"I'm sure she didn't mean to be cruel," May said, reassuring. Kausar supposed this was true. She also knew she had disappointed Sana again and again over the years, too consumed by her own deep grief. They had coped in very different ways to Ali's death: Kausar retreated, while Sana had thrown herself into a new life, first by marrying Hamza only months after meeting him as an undergrad, and then by quickly starting a family. Sana had never asked Kausar for help, not even when she had two children under the age of five and a husband who was never home. Perhaps she had understood Kausar was in no condition to help anyone, not even herself.

Things were different now. Kausar was different, and with Hassan gone, she hoped to rebuild some semblance of a closer relationship with Sana and her grandchildren. Perhaps that was why a small part of her had dared to hope that Sana had called for help—just not of the domestic variety.

Then there was the bigger problem of Sana's story. Kausar wanted to believe her daughter, but even their brief conversation left her with questions. There was the timing inconsistency, for one, and Sana had never been a particularly early riser. What had she been doing at her store so early, especially when it meant leaving her daughters at home alone? She also claimed she entered the store at five a.m. and immediately called the police, but later contradicted herself. Then there was the issue of the security cameras. It was almost too convenient that they would fail when a murder was committed on the premises, especially when combined with the slip that the murder weapon came from Sana's own window display. No doubt the police had taken all this into account when they had cautioned Sana not to leave town. Maybe it was the shock of finding a body that had led Sana to muddle things and dissemble, but Kausar suspected there was more to the story. The thought frightened her, even as a small part of her quickened at the possibility of proving useful in a way her daughter had never anticipated.

May interrupted her thoughts. "What are you going to do? I can hear you thinking."

"My daughter asked for my help," Kausar said. "I plan to do as she asked."

"Good thing I gave you that notebook, eh?" May teased.

"I'm not investigating. I will simply notice things for Sana." Even to her ears, the distinction sounded weak. But that was all she intended to do, Kausar promised herself. She would simply look around and perhaps ask a few questions. Only to clear up her own confusion and confirm the details of Sana's tale.

"Just so long as you call me with updates," May said. "This is better than *Murdoch Mysteries*." Her friend was a fan of the long-running police procedural set in early twentieth-century Toronto, and they'd sometimes watch it together.

With a promise to call again soon, Kausar hung up and considered her options. Sana had instructed her not to call Nasir. Stranger still, she had said she couldn't *afford* a lawyer. Kausar wondered about that. Did she mean it, or was she downplaying the trouble she faced? Likely the latter—Hamza had a lucrative job as the director of marketing for a well-known telecom company, while Sana had inherited a comfortable sum from Hassan's estate only a year ago. Surely the family had enough financial security to retain legal counsel when possibly facing a murder charge. In any case, even if Sana couldn't afford legal counsel, Kausar could pay.

Mind made up, she dialed. A familiar voice picked up on the second ring.

"*Bhabhi*, I'm so glad you called," Nasir said, using the honorific for the wife of a brother, or in his case, a good friend. "Please, tell me you have agreed to catch up over a meal. I can drive up to North Bay this weekend. Old friends are best, after all." The lawyer's voice was warm and charming. His admiration of Kausar had always been clear in every interaction. Hassan had even noticed it, calling Nasir a shameless flirt.

"There's no need to drive to North Bay, as I happen to be in Toronto," Kausar answered lightly.

For once, Nasir was at a loss for words. When he spoke again, he sounded worried. "What has brought you back?" The question was a testament to how well he knew her. Quickly, Kausar filled him in on Sana's situation.

"Of course, Sana is innocent," Nasir said without hesitation. "The Toronto police are simply following the formalities. I know a few criminal lawyers. I will get back to you with names and recommendations right away."

Kausar thanked him and promised to arrange a visit soon, before hanging up and contemplating her next steps. Sana had left to pick up ten-year-old Fizza from school, pulling her keys out of a black pouch that resembled a sunglasses case. Fifteen-year-old Maleeha walked home from the nearby high school. In half an hour, she would see her granddaughters for the first time since Hassan passed, and as eager as she was for that meeting, she was also curious about the plaza and—if she were being honest with herself—the crime scene. Sana had mentioned her shop was within walking distance. Surely, she could travel there and back before the girls returned.

It wasn't simply curiosity to see where Imran had died that pulled her downstairs or eased her feet into the sturdy loafers she had brought. Kausar knew little about Sana's life in Toronto. Though her daughter had studied accounting and finance in school, she had married during her second year, and when Maleeha had come along shortly after, it had made sense to take a break from her studies, despite Kausar's protests. When she tried to broach the subject once, Sana had shut her down.

"I don't want to send my kids to day care and work all day, then return home exhausted. Hamza makes enough money to keep us going. It's not like I have family in town I can rely on," Sana had added pointedly, and Kausar never brought up the subject again. Yet her fears had been realized: Sana never returned to school.

Kausar wanted to see where Sana spent her life, wanted to walk through the neighborhood and look into the faces that passed her daughter and granddaughters every day. She needed to do something, to move. Sana had settled near their old neighborhood, and Ali's ghost was everywhere

Hesitating only a second, Kausar scooped the notebook into her purse and left the house, inputting the plaza into her maps app as she went. It was only a fifteen-minute walk from the house, down Escola Avenue, and then west.

At this time of day, the streets were slowly filling with students on their way home from school and parents, grandparents, and caregivers doing pickups, and traffic was heavy. One thing Kausar already missed about North Bay was its relative calm. Even in this residential neighborhood, Kausar felt the thrum of energy, of barely repressed impatience in the surrounding vehicles. She hurried across the road at an intersection with her head down, trying to calm herself while an SUV edged past.

Ali had stood at one of these intersections. He had crossed a street, had turned down another, confident despite the late hour, young and invincible and ready to take on the world. And then—she squeezed her eyes closed, and when she opened them, she could make out the plaza ahead.

The neighborhood was part of the Golden Crescent, nicknamed for the crescent shape the area made on a map. A large sign—*Golden Crescent Plaza*—welcomed visitors. She knew Sana's clothing store was in the far corner, sandwiched between the roti takeout and the admin office—even though she hadn't attended the opening, she'd pored over the pictures Sana had sent her. But Kausar couldn't make out the details from where she was approaching, not even the name, because of the crowd gathered in front and the yellow caution tape everywhere.

Kausar spotted two people who seemed to be shopkeepers standing near the stores, watching the activity: an older Asian man with silver hair who must be Mr. Jin, and beside him a younger Black woman in an apron, her long hair in tight braids, perhaps Lisa from the roti shop. A white man in plainclothes, his hair blond in the bright afternoon sun, directed the uniformed officers with a quiet confidence. Kausar itched to approach, but instead walked carefully down the grassy embankment towards the parking lot to examine the plaza from a distance.

Golden Crescent Plaza was a squat, brown brick building, emerging from the center of a bowl-shaped area, and surrounded by plentiful parking. Stairs around the commercial building led up to the crumbling pedestrian sidewalk, from which Kausar now surveyed the scene. From her vantage point, she was nearly eye level with the low-hanging roof. Kausar was surprised Sana had settled on this location. The gawking crowd notwithstanding, the parking lot was mostly empty. Or perhaps most of the patrons walked from the surrounding neighborhood. Even so, there was a tired, neglected air about the plaza, evident in the weeds that sprouted from the paved frontage, the dated storefronts, and the awning so low that she still couldn't read the name of Sana's shop. Uniformed officers milled around the walkway, and Kausar saw one walk out of the bubble tea shop with a tray of drinks. He seemed familiar but soon disappeared into the huddle of police. Before she could place him, a voice called from one of the cars in the parking lot.

"Kausar Aunty?" A tall man with dark brown skin and sharp features, bits of gray scattered among the black of his close-cropped fade, stood in front of an older, silver-colored sedan, looking at her uncertainly. It took her a minute to recognize him—the last time she had seen Siraj Bajwa, he'd been a skinny teenager, the son of her then best friend, Fatima. It was a shock to see the boy she had known in the familiar brown eyes of the man before her, a reminder of how much time had passed. She caught sight of the large, black insulated bag in his hands. When she looked back up at him, a red tinge suffused his cheeks.

"I didn't know you were back in town," he started.

Taking his cue, Kausar ignored the food delivery bag. "I'm here for Sana."

Understanding dawned. "I heard something happened at the plaza. I didn't know Sana was . . . involved."

"She's not," Kausar said firmly.

"Of course. My mistake."

They lapsed into awkward silence, Siraj shifting his weight from foot to foot.

"How is your mother?" Kausar asked finally.

"*Alhamdulillah*," he said, carefully neutral.

"Please pass along my salaams," she said, inwardly cringing at the banal words. At one point, Fatima had been her closest friend in the world. Kausar had left too many things behind when she fled Toronto; her friendships had been another inadvertent casualty.

Siraj considered this. "Her number hasn't changed," he said quietly. "In case you wanted to pass along those salaams yourself." He hefted his bag and headed towards the roti take-out shop without another word.

Kausar stood staring after him, smiling ruefully. Canada's largest city, the sprawling Greater Toronto Area, was a metropolis of six million souls—but sometimes it felt no different from a small town. No doubt, news of her arrival would soon circulate among her former friends, the ones she had cut off abruptly when she left. Fatima was probably angry and hurt at her long silence, and though Siraj's suggestion to call was a good one, she knew she wouldn't follow up. She was here to help her daughter, and then head back to her quiet life in North Bay.

With that, Kausar continued her perusal of the plaza from the parking lot. She spotted a young woman facing the street with her back to the plaza, outstretched arm holding a mobile phone and speaking in a lively voice that traveled.

"What's good, fam? This is your girl Brianna Chen-Malik. I'm parked here in front of the OG, the Golden Crescent Plaza in Scarborough, where the police pulled in and set up this morning. Detective Drake—yes, fam, that's his real name—won't say more, but I'm hearing something serious went down. I'll keep watch like I always do. In the meantime, keep your eyes open and your cameras on." She flashed a peace sign at the screen and held her smile. Looking up, the young woman caught Kausar's eye. "How'd I do, Aunty? Salaams."

Kausar approached the friendly young woman. "Brief but riveting," she complimented. Then, thinking fast, she explained that she was new to the neighborhood and had come by to pick up a few grocery items. Did Brianna know what was going on?

"Someone got themselves killed," the young woman said, with a certain amount of relish. "I've been here all morning. According to Mr. Jin, they arrested that poor woman, the one who runs the new desi clothing store with the pricey 'fits." She motioned towards the older Asian man, who now stood alone. The younger Black woman had disappeared. "He runs the grocery store, and Mom says he keeps his prices low, unlike the capitalist thugs overcharging for bread in these streets."

Kausar agreed the price of bread was shameful and carefully took in the young woman. Brianna's pronunciation of salaams and desi was authentic, and she had smooth, dark skin, with large eyes that slanted in the corners and were fringed with thick, dark lashes, while her natural curls fell in a halo around her head. She was dressed in a cropped top, track pants, and colorful sneakers, an unzipped hoodie sliding down bare shoulders.

"Are you a reporter?" Kausar asked, and Brianna's eyes crinkled as she laughed, revealing large, very white teeth.

"I'm a community activist. The aunties from the masjid used to call me a troublemaker." Brianna paused, waiting for Kausar to process that nugget of information, perhaps to ask if she were Muslim, too, or about her ethnicity. Kausar suspected that Brianna had frequently been asked who she was and where she fit in, which likely made her feel like she fit in nowhere.

Kausar only smiled. "Have you managed to learn anything else? Such as who was killed?"

Brianna sized up Kausar but only shrugged. "The cops won't talk to someone like me, but they're also not quiet, and my hearing is fantastic. It was Imran, dude who owns this place. Don't feel sorry for him, though, the man was trouble."

Kausar perked up at this. "Why would you say that?"

"My dad used to have a store here, but when Imran took over, he got out. Too much drama, and Imran was always up to something. Latest rumor is the plaza is up for sale. Some developer who wants to build condos no one in this 'hood can afford." She smiled crookedly at Kausar. "You got a whole lot out of me today, Aunty, without even trying. I should try to be more like you. You have yourself a blessed day." She put her hands together in a namaste, and Kausar smiled back, charmed by the young woman's irrepressible energy.

Kausar glanced towards Sana's store and drifted closer, trying to look as unobtrusive and harmless as possible. The crowd had thinned somewhat, and she could make out two large, square planters filled with bright floral arrangements standing sentry in front of her daughter's store, the name emblazoned in a curly sans serif font on the tasteful yet striking entryway: *Muhabbat Designs*. *Muhabbat* was "love" in Urdu, a whimsical name for her sensible daughter. Her gaze moved to the front window display, where instead of faceless mannequins, there was a stylized scene: vibrant and ornate desi clothes pinned to a black, starry backdrop, an outfit positioned so it was hanging from the ceiling with sleeves outstretched, and another laid out on the ground, each with matching accessories—bangles, chandelier and *jhumpka* earrings, ornate necklaces, a thick choker with delicate silver filigree. One of the silhouettes was an Indian groom, complete with brocade sherwani, cream-colored turban, and curly-toed shoes. Kausar's eyes lingered on the bejeweled ceremonial sheath on a jeweled belt, the sort a long-ago maharajah might wear. With a sinking heart, she saw that the dagger inside was missing.

"Excuse me, ma'am, you'll have to step away," a female police officer said brusquely. "This is an active crime scene."

"That's my daughter's store," Kausar blurted, and instantly wanted to take the words back. She could feel a shadow looming, and then the blond-haired detective—Drake, Brianna had said—addressed her.

"Ms. Khan said she didn't have family in town." Detective Drake frowned at her, and she realized he was older than he had first appeared—in his late forties at least—loose skin heavily freckled, hair more white than blond, with deep-set hazel eyes that regarded her with suspicion. When he shifted position, she could make out the bulge of a handgun by his hip.

This was the detective who had intimidated Sana, who had wanted to keep her at the precinct all day. With a spark of defiance, Kausar lifted her chin.

"I flew down this morning only, Detective Drake."

He raised an eyebrow at her, but whether it was because he was impressed or indifferent that she knew his name or because she had not backed down, she wasn't sure. "If you flew down to help your daughter, why are you here and not with her, Mrs. Khan? Or were you just curious, like the rest of them?" He looked contemptuously at the lingering crowd.

"My daughter has gone to pick up her children from school," Kausar said carefully. "I was out for a walk, and yes, I was also curious. I have never been here before."

The detective's eyes sharpened on her now. "Never visited your daughter's store? Live overseas, I suppose. You got to Toronto quickly, in that case."

"I live in North Bay, Detective," Kausar said.

"From the look of things, Sana could have used your help earlier. It's a shame you weren't here for her. Maybe then she wouldn't be in this mess." Drake's eyes were trained on her, watching for a reaction. He was baiting her, Kausar realized. An intelligent man, he wanted to see if she would grow angry at his questions. Perhaps angry enough to answer in haste.

She inclined her head. "My living in Toronto or elsewhere could hardly have prevented a man dying in my daughter's store," she said evenly.

"Plenty of grandparents live with their adult children in this neighborhood," he remarked. "Raising grandkids while the parents work. It's long hours, starting a business from the jump. From what I've heard, that Imran fellow wasn't too good at understanding boundaries, either. I'm sure things couldn't have been easy for your daughter." Detective Drake's eyes glittered at Kausar. "Did Sana confide in you about what *really* happened?"

Kausar didn't appreciate this man's clumsy attempt at catching her out. Perhaps she had led a sheltered life, for the most part, marrying young, having Hassan to guide and protect her for much of her life. But Kausar was also a survivor from a community of survivors. She had moved to a new country with little understanding of Canadian culture. She had raised three children far from family and friends. She had endured terrible loss, regularly managed nosy, intrusive community gossip, and was too clever to fall into the detective's obvious trap. Once more, she raised her chin and looked squarely at the younger man. "I hope you find the criminal responsible for this terrible crime. My daughter and I are eager to help in any way we can."

To his credit, Detective Drake didn't grind his teeth in frustration. Instead, he nodded curtly and handed her his card. "In case Sana happens to remember anything else," he said. "Remind her not to get too comfortable in that big house of hers. I'll be in touch soon."

Kausar risked one more peek inside the store. The interior was masked in shadows, but she could make out a dark stain near the door and a heavy-looking black phone knocked to the ground, cord and receiver separated. The body had been removed, thankfully, but the store was in disarray, clothing and accessories strewn about. She wasn't sure how much of that was the police or a result of the terrible crime that had taken place here only hours before. Kausar shivered at the thought. How would Sana ever rebuild after this?

Kausar didn't know what sort of man Imran had been, and from what she'd learned so far, she suspected he would not be mourned for long, but no one deserved such a death. With one last glance at the shops and near-empty parking lot, she turned towards Sana's home. Her curiosity had been stoked, not banked, and she knew she would be back soon to speak to the shopkeepers and form her own conclusions, no matter what Sana said. In the meantime, she could look forward to the pleasurable business of greeting her grandchildren and then perhaps writing up her initial observations in the yellow floral notebook. May would be pleased; it was proving to be a useful gift, after all.

CHAPTER 4

Her granddaughters were in the kitchen when Kausar returned, and Sana shot her a worried look. "I went for a walk," she explained, but didn't have time to elaborate; ten-year-old Fizza had caught sight of her grandmother, and her delight was immediate.

"*Nani!*" she cried, using the Urdu word for maternal grandmother, and launched herself into Kausar's arms. Behind her, fifteen-year-old Maleeha rose slowly from where she was sprawled on the large sectional sofa, her expression more reserved. But she dutifully hugged her grandmother, and Kausar breathed in the sweet smell of the girls: light floral mixed with sweat and sunshine. Despite the tragic circumstances that had led her back to the city, her granddaughters remained the light of her life.

"You grew," she mock-admonished Fizza. "I thought we agreed you would stop doing that. It makes me feel old."

Fizza giggled. She was tall for her age, on track to take after her mother, and almost reached Kausar's shoulder now. The baby roundness on her face had started to melt away, revealing cheekbones and a sharp jaw, but she was still very much a child, dancing to her mother to accept a bowl of apple slices before bargaining for a cookie, too.

"If Fizza waited to grow only when she saw you, she'd be three feet tall," Maleeha said, accepting a separate bowl of cut-up apples from her mother. Her older granddaughter had entered her teens with a vengeance; the cheerful, perky child she had once been was replaced by a quiet, brooding young woman who embraced sarcasm as if it were her new religion. Her hair was thick and dark, and swept down her back in lush waves. She was only a few inches taller than her little sister, despite the five-year age difference, her body spare and compact. Kausar smiled at the older girl's words; she reminded her of Sana at that age, though her daughter now seemed embarrassed by Maleeha's rudeness.

"Be nice to your *nani*," she admonished. "She came all this way, and she's going to be staying with us for a while."

Both girls were surprised by this news and reacted in predictable ways—Fizza by breaking into a cheer, Maleeha by crossing her arms and looking at Kausar with new, appraising eyes.

"What's going on?" Maleeha asked, and Kausar had the feeling that not much escaped her granddaughter.

"Nothing. Eat your snack," Sana said. The exhausted look was back, and Kausar remembered what Detective Drake had mockingly asked: *Did Sana confide in you about what* really *happened?*

His words had stung more than the detective could possibly know, reminding Kausar that Sana would never feel comfortable confiding in her about anything. It was equally clear that Sana had carried this tendency into her relationship with her own daughters, and this realization filled Kausar with an even greater determination to help.

"What's for dinner?" Fizza asked now. Kausar remembered this question from when her children were young, especially her sons. Once they had hit their teen years, it felt as if she were always cooking for them, and that they were never full.

"How does pizza sound?" Sana said.

"Not *again*," Maleeha muttered, her fingers flying across her phone.

"Let me cook," Kausar said. She needed something to do. "You look like you could use a nap."

"Gee, thanks," Sana said, but accepted the offer. "Nothing too spicy. The girls won't eat it."

An hour later, a steaming pot of basmati rice was ready, alongside a simmering *miti dal*, garnished with caramelized onion and paired with a simple tomato chicken curry. The *dal* had been Ali's favorite, and Kausar could see the flicker of recognition on her daughter's face. Sana glanced over at the mantle, to a framed photograph of the three siblings; Kausar had noticed it earlier. In the picture, Sana stood in the middle, frowning slightly at the camera, while Adam and Ali struck a pose on either side of her, both grinning. They had been on vacation in Florida, and Hassan had somehow managed to corral the children together, sand at their feet, blue ocean and sky behind. She looked away, a wave of grief causing a lump to rise in her throat.

"I don't like basmati rice," Maleeha announced once she had taken a seat at the large kitchen table.

Fizza, who apparently did like basmati rice, as well as everything else Kausar had prepared, loaded her plate and took her first bite. She blanched and reached for the water glass. "Spicy!" she said, fanning her mouth.

Kausar tried to hide her dismay. "I haven't cooked for anyone besides myself in a long time," she said, apologetic. "I'm out of practice."

"Eat your food," Sana instructed her daughters. "Your *nani* made this for you, and if you don't like it, there's nothing else."

Mutinous, Maleeha poured a tiny helping of *dal* on her plate and an even smaller ladle of the offending basmati rice, before taking a careful bite. "Are you going to tell us what's going on now?" she demanded.

"What do you mean?" Sana said. She shoveled food automatically into her mouth, mind clearly on other things.

Maleeha's plate was clear in minutes, and she reached for more. Kausar smiled to herself. "Everyone was talking about what happened at Golden plaza today. The school even went into lockdown. They said someone died. Is that why we had to go to school on our own this morning?"

Fizza stopped eating—her mother had added yogurt to the chicken curry to ease the sting of spice—and stared at Sana. Kausar recognized that look. The younger girl was bracing for something. Once more, Kausar wondered what secrets Sana carried.

With a quick glance at her mother, Sana turned her attention to her daughters. "Yes, someone died. When I went to the store this morning, I found Imran Uncle. He was collapsed inside by the cash register."

Kausar noticed Maleeha's grip tighten on her spoon, turning her knuckles white. "How did he die?" she said.

Sana's voice was gentle, steady. "He was murdered."

Fizza blinked, looking from her mother to her sister, and then to Kausar. "Who killed him?" she whispered, and then her eyes filled with tears. She buried her face in her hands and started to sob.

"You didn't even know him, dummy," Maleeha snapped, which did nothing to calm her little sister. Sana stroked Fizza's back and pulled her onto her lap, whispering soft words of comfort into her ear.

"Does Dad know?" Maleeha asked, and the tension in the room instantly spiked up.

"He's traveling and will be here as soon as he can," Sana said, but there was an edge to her voice that Kausar picked up.

"How was Imran killed?" Fizza asked in a small voice.

"That's not something you should worry about—" Sana started.

"He was stabbed," Maleeha said. "All the kids at school said so." Fizza resumed crying. "They think you did it, don't they?" Maleeha asked, her tone flat. "The cops think you killed him."

Fizza sobbed louder, and Sana looked at her mother for help. Kausar rose and started to gather plates. Keeping her voice brisk, she said, "This is a terrible tragedy, but Sana had nothing to do with it. There is nothing to worry about."

Maleeha looked hard at her mother, before shoving the chair back roughly as she got up. "I have homework," she announced, taking the stairs two at a time.

Fizza stopped crying, but her cheeks were flushed and tear-stained when she looked at Sana. "What will happen if you go to prison? Will *Nani* take care of us?"

Kausar reached across to squeeze Fizza's arm. "Your mother isn't going anywhere, and neither am I," she promised, even as she wondered why the young girl had not mentioned her father.

It was strange, sleeping in a new house after all these years. Kausar had not slept anywhere but her bed in North Bay in so long, and this mattress was not as firm. After half an hour of restlessness, she rose to open the window, hoping the cool spring air would help. It was only half past ten, but the house was settled for the night, the girls tucked in early as it was a school night.

She looked out her window and thought about dinner. She didn't even know what her granddaughters liked to eat, and Fizza's enthusiasm, contrasted with Maleeha's wariness, only emphasized how much of a stranger she was in her own family's life.

Which was entirely her own fault. It was she who had stayed away, who had refused to visit Toronto and insisted Sana bring the girls to visit her in North Bay every summer. The few weeks they spent together wasn't enough time to form the sort of lasting bonds she had once imagined she would have with her grandchildren.

Yet it was more than that. Hamza's absence felt stranger with every passing hour. When she asked earlier where he was traveling from, Sana had made vague noises about Europe. It was possible he was still in transit, but Maleeha's dismissive reaction coupled with Fizza's anxiety hinted at another story. Where was he, and what was really going on?

As for the murder, the girls' reactions had at first seemed consistent with their personalities, but there had been an air of unreality, too—Fizza's tears too passionate for someone she barely knew, and Maleeha's anger too volatile.

She thought about Brianna's theory that the entire plaza was about to be sold. Was the murder related to that, perhaps a business deal gone deadly wrong? Was Sana's store simply a case of wrong place, wrong crime?

Lost in thought, Kausar became aware of flashing blue and red lights outside her window. A police cruiser was parked across the street, and a young man in a white hoodie stood next to an officer. If it hadn't been for the streetlamp illuminating the scene, Kausar wouldn't have been able to see what was happening. Her heart started to pound as the officer leaned close and roughly grabbed the young man's arm, yanking hard. Before she knew what she was doing, her feet were nosing into the *chappals* by her bed, and then she was running down the stairs, out of the house, and hurrying across the street.

"What's going on?" Kausar called, breathless from her sudden dash, startling both the officer and the person he was apprehending. The officer had by now clamped a second arm around the young man—he was a boy, really, his frame slight, barely taller than Maleeha.

"Excuse me, ma'am," the officer said, his tone polite but the warning clear. “This is none of your concern. Please return to your place of residence.”

“It is my concern, that’s my nephew!” Kausar said loudly, and reaching out, she removed the officer’s hands from the young man’s arm. A part of her was shocked at her boldness, while another part, frozen for years, flickered to life. *My Ali, you were alone, all alone.*

The officer, skepticism clear in his voice, repeated, “Your *nephew*?”

“Yes,” Kausar repeated. Surely, she didn’t look that old? Perhaps she should have gone with grandmother. She risked a glance at the young man in question and quickly realized her mistake. For one, he was Black. For another, now that she could actually make out the youth’s features, they were distinctly feminine.

“I think you mean your *niece*,” the officer said.

“I wouldn’t presume if I were you,” Kausar said primly, which forced a stifled laugh from the youth at her side. She wondered what they had done to attract the officer’s attention, and more importantly, why no one had come to their aid when it was clear they were being harassed in the street.

Just then, another squad car joined the first, and Kausar prepared for things to get a lot worse. Instead, a familiar voice called out, “Kausar Aunty? Is that you?”

The Golden Crescent was truly the world’s smallest fishbowl, because for the second time that day, she bumped into an old acquaintance from her past.

Ilyas Marjani had been twenty years old when Kausar and Hassan moved to North Bay, a lanky young man with dark eyes that tilted up at the corners, a legacy from his Afghani father, along with high cheekbones and a light tan complexion. An intimate friend of both her sons despite being a few years older, he had grown up playing street hockey in front of their house and joining intense, neighborhood-wide games of hide-and-seek. He had also been half in love with Sana from the age of twelve. It had taken Sana a few years to notice and then return his interest. Kausar remembered hearing that Ilyas joined the police academy after graduating from university, but she had not seen him in almost two decades.

The man who greeted her now was almost unrecognizable. The curly mop of hair he had cultivated as a young man was replaced with a neat fade, cut close to his skull. His lanky form had filled out, broad shoulders and powerful-looking arms obvious even beneath his blue uniform. But his eyes were the same: sharp and watchful, flickering with recognition and something else.

"You were at the plaza today," Kausar said, thinking of the uniformed officer holding the tray of bubble tea, and Ilyas nodded. The shock of seeing him again loosened the grip Kausar had on the young woman in the white hoodie, who immediately took to her heels. With a shout of dismay, the trio watched her disappear onto a side street.

"This is your fault," the original officer spluttered, pale face crawling with angry red. He took a step towards Kausar, and Ilyas raised a hand in warning.

"Cool it, Colin. I'll handle this," Ilyas said, and the cold formality in his voice made the other man pause, uncertain. Deciding to salvage what was left of his dignity, and with a final disgusted look at Kausar, Colin strode to his car and drove away.

Kausar turned back to Ilyas, expecting an official reprimand. Instead, his eyes were soft, a note of pity in their depths.

"I was sad to hear about Hassan Uncle. He was always kind to me. I'm sorry I couldn't make the *janazah*."

Kausar nodded, accepting his condolences. "I heard you had gone into law enforcement, but I didn't know you were keeping an eye on your old neighborhood."

"I started here a few months ago. I used to work with the OPP," he explained, referring to the Ontario Provincial Police, which served the province. "I took this job to be closer to my mother. She hasn't been well." He turned in the direction of where the young girl in the hoodie had fled. "You really shouldn't have interfered," he started, and Kausar bristled.

"Your *colleague* was manhandling that young person, and from what I could tell, with little to no provocation," she said sharply.

Ilyas sighed. "I'll talk to Colin. But, Kausar Aunty, the neighborhood has changed since you lived here. We've had a spike in car thefts in the area. It's practically an epidemic. Cars are stolen from people's driveways, from mall parking lots, everywhere. We had a report of someone loitering on this street the past few nights. Plus, with the murder at the plaza this morning . . . Promise me you'll be careful?"

Though she knew he meant the words kindly, Kausar bristled. "Things have never been safe in this neighborhood. Not for people like us, or for that young girl."

Ilyas said nothing, but the pitying expression was back on his face. Kausar could picture him now as she had seen him last—pale, trembling, stumbling over his words as he offered his condolences during the worst day of her life. "Of course, you're right, Aunty."

It was the last remark, spoken with a hint of condescension, that pushed her over the edge. "How could you stand by and allow them to arrest Sana? You used to be close."

Something dark moved behind his eyes, and his demeanor stiffened. "Sana wasn't arrested, there were no handcuffs or perp walk. She was questioned and then released. Detective Drake is only doing his job." His words were automatic, as if he were used to sticking up for his superiors. Kausar wondered if he believed them himself.

"Sana didn't do anything. She found a body in her store and called the authorities. For that, the detective suspects her? It makes no sense," Kausar said, keeping her gaze pinned on his face. She saw a flicker of something behind his eyes.

"You can hardly blame the detective for questioning the person who found the body. If Sana did nothing wrong, she has nothing to worry about," Ilyas said.

Except they both knew the world didn't work like that. Perhaps he had forgotten that fact, or more likely had been forced to take a side if he wanted to survive in his profession. Ilyas reached into his pocket for a card, which he handed to Kausar after scribbling his personal cell number on the back.

"If you hear anything you think could be of interest to us, or have concerns, or just want to talk, please give me a call. Assalamu alaikum, Aunty." Peace be with you.

Aunty. There had been a time when Kausar assumed Ilyas might call her by another name one day. When Sana told her they had broken up, Kausar had put that dream aside, among others. There were worse things, and her grief over Ali had been fresh back then. Now she looked at Ilyas and wondered.

"Are you married, Ilyas? Do you have children?" she asked impulsively.

Ilyas shook his head, sidestepping her question. "It's good to see you again. Sana will need your support."

Kausar watched him return to his cruiser. A rustle of movement behind a large hedge, and the flash of a white hoodie, caught her eye.

"I'm fine, child," Kausar said to the hedge. "Go home and sleep easy." Smiling to herself, she returned to Sana's house.

CHAPTER 5

When Kausar returned to the house, the digital clock in the foyer read 11:07 p.m., and she noticed a pair of hand-tailored Italian loafers abandoned in front of the door. Hamza had returned. As she climbed the stairs to her room, she heard muffled voices from the master suite. Muffled, but angry. The door opened, and Hamza stalked out.

Her son-in-law was a handsome man, his features symmetrical and pleasing. In his late thirties now, he kept himself fit, and with his broad shoulders and trim waist, he could pass for a man in his late twenties. Despite this, Hamza had a sullen pout to his mouth that Kausar had never entirely trusted. His brown eyes blazed with anger, and behind him, Sana stood framed in the doorway, fairly vibrating with frustration and impatience. With her hair tied back in a braid, she looked young and vulnerable. They both stopped short upon seeing Kausar. She hoped they wouldn't think she had been eavesdropping.

"I was downstairs getting water," she lied. She didn't want to answer any questions about where she had been, or who she had just met, at least not yet.

Hamza rearranged his features, slipping into the easy, slightly ingratiating expression that had always given Kausar pause. "We're so happy to see you, Mom. What do you think of the house?"

It was a strange question, considering the circumstances. She made complimentary noises, which Hamza accepted with faux humility. Kausar made to return to her room, and to her surprise, Hamza followed, closing the door behind him, his brow furrowed in concern.

"I'm so relieved you're here. I feel terrible that I wasn't able to get back sooner," he began, leaning against the door.

Kausar examined Hamza closely. He was dressed in dark pants and a loose-fitting T-shirt, his long hair pushed back from his face, but his eyes were alert and clear, no trace of jet lag or exhaustion from a transatlantic flight.

She inclined her head. "Sana tried to call you but you didn't pick up. I'm glad she thought to call me next. There is nowhere else I would want to be," she said.

Hamza passed a hand through his hair. "I couldn't believe it when Sana told me Imran was dead. Who would want to kill him?"

"That is the question," Kausar replied. "The police questioned Sana for hours." She hoped Hamza would pick up on her disapproval of his absence, for not being there when his family needed him.

Hamza again passed a hand through his hair. Kausar remembered that when they were newly married, Sana had teased Hamza about the gesture during a card game, calling it his "tell." Was he nervous?

"Did you like Imran?" Kausar asked now, watching her son-in-law closely.

"He wasn't my favorite person," Hamza started, then stopped, shaking his head. He took a seat on the bed beside Kausar and reached for the extra pillow, burying his face in it. "It's my fault Sana is in this mess," he said, voice muffled. Alarmed, Kausar patted his arm. They weren't, as a rule, a physically affectionate family.

Hamza raised his face, and the anguish in his eyes was the first genuine emotion she had seen from him tonight. "I introduced Sana to Imran. He's an old family friend. He said he could give her a deal on the rent because one of his tenant's broke their lease early. I knew how badly she wanted to open a store."

"No one could have predicted what happened," Kausar said. "Sana had nothing to do with the murder. The police will realize soon enough."

Hamza nodded, rising swiftly. "Of course, you're right," he said, embarrassed at his outburst.

"What sort of man was Imran?" Kausar asked.

Hamza's hand was on the door. "Let's just say, his manner of death doesn't entirely surprise me."

He was gone before she could ask any follow-up questions. It only occurred to her after he left that Hamza had taken the extra pillow with him, and she wondered if he were sleeping downstairs tonight.

Her suspicion was proven correct the next morning. Her extra pillow and a few quilts were piled on the large sectional couch. Sana was folding them when Kausar joined her.

"Hamza had an early meeting downtown," Sana explained. After glancing down at the bedding in her arms, she then admitted, "We had a fight."

"It has been a stressful time for you, *beta*," Kausar said, careful to keep her voice mild. "Can I make the girls breakfast while you put those away?"

For the first time since she'd arrived, Sana shot her mother a grateful glance. It was clear she didn't want her daughters to see the blankets, and they would be downstairs momentarily. "There's fruit in the fridge. I'll be right back." She hurried away, and Kausar busied herself gathering breakfast supplies—bowls, cutlery, milk, fruit. The girls' lunches had already been packed. Clearly, Hamza wasn't the only one who rose early, a change from when Sana was younger. Her daughter hadn't gotten much sleep the previous night, either. She must be exhausted.

Once breakfast was assembled, Kausar wandered to the fireplace mantle, where pictures of the girls at various ages took precedence, alongside the framed picture of Sana with her siblings. Kausar admired shots of a smiling Maleeha on her fifth birthday, the girls beaming in front of Kausar's bungalow in North Bay, Fizza hoisting a trophy for a junior basketball league championship. There were no pictures of Hamza and Sana, not even from their wedding day. Something pricked at the edges of Kausar's attention, and she examined the objects by the fireplace again, reflecting on her daughter's marriage.

Sana met Hamza during her first year at university. He had been a couple of years ahead of her, but they kept bumping into each other on campus. Finally, Hamza found the nerve to strike up a conversation, and they quickly realized they knew many of the same people from the large Muslim population on campus. They started dating, and a year later, Hamza proposed.

Both Hassan and Kausar had their apprehensions about the union, for very different reasons. Hassan worried that Hamza, at twenty-two, wouldn't be able to support a family, while Kausar was more concerned for her daughter's future. Entering into a lifelong commitment at the age of twenty had not been part of Kausar's dreams for her only daughter. But Sana had been adamant. When Maleeha arrived almost exactly one year later, Kausar and Hassan were overjoyed, even though her predictions proved correct. Sana never finished her undergraduate degree, and until she opened *Muhabbat Designs* last year, she had never worked outside the home.

Hamza, on the other hand, had quickly found his niche in telecom sales, and flourished. Every year the family went on expensive vacations to Disney World, Europe, high-end Caribbean resorts, or cruises. Their cars were always brand new, replaced every two years, and Hamza had recently floated the idea of purchasing a cottage. Whenever the family met, Hamza would boast about his latest expensive hobby, trip, or bonus commission. For her part, Kausar wondered if her daughter was happy. Combined with Sana's strange comment yesterday about not being able to afford a lawyer's consult, something wasn't adding up.

The girls thundered downstairs and fell on their breakfast like hungry wolves. Sana returned from putting the bedding away to hand out lunch bags and hustle Fizza out the door. Maleeha, whose school started twenty minutes later, dawdled, double-checking the contents of her bag, snagging an extra granola bar, filling a large metal water bottle, and casting glances at Kausar.

"Are you really going to stay for a while?" she asked abruptly.

Kausar thought over the question. Maleeha wouldn't appreciate a reassuring answer, only an honest one. "I have a flight booked for next week, but I plan to extend my stay. I think your mother could use my help right now." She waited while the young girl absorbed this.

Maleeha nodded. "I'll see you after school," she said, grabbing her bag. Kausar was sure Maleeha wanted to say something more, and she wondered again about her granddaughter's reaction to Imran's death yesterday. If she were anything like her mother, Maleeha would only speak when she was ready.

Sana returned just as Kausar finished putting the kitchen to rights. Her daughter looked around the space, pleased. "The morning rush usually takes it out of me. Thanks for helping out, Mom. It's a two-person job."

"Hamza doesn't help?" The question slipped out, and Sana snorted.

"He's about as helpful with the kids as Dad was with us."

"Your father was very busy with his medical practice," Kausar said, the excuse coming naturally.

Sana flopped into a chair at the kitchen table and fiddled with a napkin. "Dad was part of a different generation. I get it," she said. "As for Hamza, he knows I'll do it if he stays away. He's always waiting for me to pick up the slack. It's called the 'invisible load,' and it's exhausting. Now that I'm busy with the store, he's resentful at having to pitch in more."

Sana had cracked open a door with this revelation, and Kausar wondered how to proceed without coming across as intrusive. "I thought Hamza was happy about the store," she said, recalling what he had confided last night about finding the space at the plaza for his wife.

When Sana first announced her intention to open a South Asian clothing boutique, it had taken Kausar and Hassan by surprise. They knew their daughter was interested in desi fashion, but she had always been a purchaser, not a retailer. The sort of curated collection Sana had in mind was a gamble. She wanted to stock designer products and deal directly with locally sourced fashion ateliers in India, Pakistan, and Bangladesh, with their accompanying higher price points. Kausar remembered asking what Hamza thought of the enterprise, but Sana had been determined.

"Hamza isn't happy about having to pitch in more around the house. He isn't happy about how busy I've been." Sana stood up, restless. "To be honest, he hasn't been happy, period." Cupping one hand, she brushed a few crumbs from the table and carried them to the kitchen sink.

Kausar considered this. "Was he worried about the money it would take to open the store?" she asked instead.

"It wasn't his money to worry about," Sana said shortly. She had been upfront about her intention to use her share of the inheritance after Hassan's death for her new business.

While the bulk of her late husband's wealth—various real estate properties and a robust investment portfolio—had transferred to Kausar for use during her lifetime, both Adam and Sana had been given generous settlements in the mid-six-figures. Adam had used his share for a down payment on a flat near central London.

Sana continued. "The girls are growing up, and I never intended to be a stay-at-home mom all my life." Her eyes flicked to her mother. "No offense."

"I never wanted that for you, either," Kausar said. Hassan was open-minded in many ways, but he had never wanted her to pursue a career or job outside the home. To people of his generation, and especially among their friends in the same social class, such a move would imply he could not provide for his family, and his pride would never have allowed for that.

"Where did you really go last night? I know you weren't downstairs. Hamza would have seen you when he came in." Sana's question was casual, but the glance she threw her mother was not. "I hope you're not getting yourself in trouble already."

Kausar raised an eyebrow at this. She could ask questions, too. "Speaking of getting into trouble—yesterday, when you were telling me your story about what happened with Imran, I noticed a few inconsistencies."

"Oh, did you now," Sana muttered.

"Why do you think Imran was in your store to begin with?" Kausar continued, ignoring her remark.

Sana shrugged. "I don't know."

"How did he get in?"

"He's the landlord. I assume he has a key. Besides, we share a back entrance. I told you all this already."

Kausar decided she would check out this shared entrance the next time she visited the plaza. "Did Imran make a habit of entering your store after hours?"

For the first time since they began to talk, Sana seemed to falter. "I told you before, I'm not sure. Maybe."

"Had you seen him on camera, before?"

"No," she conceded. "But sometimes when I came back to the store in the morning . . ."

"Yes?" Kausar encouraged.

"It felt like someone had been there. A few items moved around, little things like that. He always denied it. I got my own security system soon after. The one before was supplied by the plaza, and it only focused on the front entrance, so I installed my own."

"And this second alarm system happened to fail on the night of Imran's murder," Kausar said evenly.

Sana stared at her mother. "You think I'm lying."

"I think you were in shock yesterday and might have forgotten a few things. That can happen, after trauma," she said carefully.

"Did you learn that from the one time you tried therapy?" Sana snapped. Silence stretched between them. "I'm sorry," she mumbled.

"*Beta*, it feels like you are concealing something from me, and I only want to help," Kausar said.

"You're already helping," Sana said stubbornly. "I feel better with you here."

Did she feel better because her mother was here to cook and clean and mind the children, or because Kausar could contribute in other, more meaningful ways? Kausar was afraid to hear the answer to that query and so didn't ask.

"Hamza said he wasn't surprised Imran ended up dead," she started, and Sana threw her an impatient look.

"Hamza says a lot of things. Can we drop this, please? It's bad enough Detective Drake wants to speak to me again today. I don't need a pregame interrogation at home." And just like that, the fragile truce they had forged was broken. Still, Kausar persisted.

"Did you confront Imran about entering your store after hours?" she asked.

"I told you, he denied it. That's why I installed the camera, and why I went there so early that morning. I wanted to catch him in the act." Sana picked up a cloth and started to wipe down the stainless steel front of the Sub-Zero fridge.

"I'm confused. Did you go to the store early to do work, or because you saw something on your security camera?"

Sana's hand slowed, and the look she sent her mother was both exasperated and something else. Was she wary? "There's always more work at the store than I can get through during the day, especially with customers around."

"And when you arrived early, you found Imran's body," Kausar said. "It's a shame the camera was not working."

"I should have gotten it fixed, but things have been so busy with the store, and the girls, and with Hamza always traveling. It just felt like one errand too many."

Kausar mulled this over. It was a likely explanation, perhaps even a true one, if not for one fact: Her daughter was one of the most efficient people she knew. If the camera were malfunctioning, it would have been immediately fixed or repaired. She decided not to press this point, at least not yet.

Sana eyed her mother. "Are you going to answer my question now? Where were you last night?"

Kausar decided to keep the details about her confrontation with Officer Colin to herself, but she could share the other person she had met. "I went out to get some fresh air and saw a police cruiser parked across the street. It was Ilyas." She watched her daughter's face for a reaction.

"I heard Ilyas had joined the Toronto Police Service," Sana said with careful indifference. After a final wipe of the fridge, she turned to go. "Detective Drake doesn't strike me as a patient man, and he wants to see me first thing this morning."

"I also need to get ready," Kausar said. "I have an appointment with an old friend." Sana had told her not to consult with a lawyer, but the more she thought about the situation, the more she suspected her daughter would need expert legal advice soon, perhaps even today if the police were already asking her back for more questioning.

"I was hoping you'd be home when the girls came back," Sana said. "Maybe you could cook dinner again if it's not too much trouble?"

"I'll be back with plenty of time," she reassured Sana.

Sana turned to go, then hesitated. "If your errand won't take long, you can take my car. I can take the bus to the police station. Just be really careful about locking it. A few of my neighbors have had their cars stolen recently. It's becoming an epidemic."

Ilyas had used the same word. Kausar wondered how big a problem the car thefts were in the city. "I can take the bus," she said.

Sana shrugged. "Suit yourself. The keys are always in the pouch by the door, if you ever need it." She hesitated. "I hope this goes without saying, but please don't even think about involving yourself in the investigation. This isn't like the little problems you helped solve when I was younger." She didn't wait for a reply, climbing the stairs to change.

Kausar was about to follow, when she caught sight of the luggage at the foot of the stairs and the tags on Hamza's suitcase. Her eyes narrowed, considering. Clearly, Sana wasn't the only one keeping secrets. Kausar made a mental note to speak with her son-in-law and find out where he had really been when his wife was being interrogated about a murder.

CHAPTER 6

The bus was at half capacity, and Kausar found a seat easily. It had been a long time since she'd taken public transit, but Sana had lent her a Presto card for the red, black, and white TTC bus. Once seated, she reached in her purse for mints and her fingers closed around the yellow floral notebook. She remembered Sana's bemused expression when she read *Kausar Khan Investigates* scrawled at the top of the page. What a joke. The most she could do was tap her contacts and quietly arrange a meeting with an old family friend.

Your superpower is solving mysteries, May had said to her once. Perhaps it was; maybe she did have the ability to read people's expressions, to pick up on minute details in conversation and connect the dots into a verifiable conclusion, but what did that really amount to? A few problems solved, but trouble gained, too. Besides, Sana said she didn't want her mother's help—at least not beyond the domestic sphere. After she'd spoken with Nasir and found her daughter a good criminal lawyer, Kausar resolved to respect Sana's wishes.

Except all her instincts were clamoring to do otherwise. How could she simply cook and clean while Sana and her granddaughters grappled with this enormous crisis? *One I would never have known about had I not been the only number Sana remembered*, a voice needled her. Perhaps that was it. She felt guilty.

She transferred to a bus going north once she got to Kennedy Station, and after twenty minutes, it dropped her across the street from Nasir's place of business. His offices took up most of the third floor in a modern-looking business complex that also included a doctor's office, an independent pharmacy, and a physiotherapy clinic. The building was in much better condition than the Golden Crescent Plaza. The receptionist, a pretty, young South Asian woman, took her name, and Nasir did not leave her waiting long. He greeted her with a booming voice and wide smile.

"Kausar *bhabhi*! What a pleasant surprise. Razia, please prepare chai and biscuits for my old friend," he said, addressing the receptionist, who nodded and rose at once, even as Kausar demurred that she did not want to be any trouble and said how kind Nasir was to help her family.

"It is Hassan *bhai* who was kind. He helped me set up right out of law school, and I will never forget it. Everything I have now, it is because he took a chance on me all those years ago." He twinkled at her. "I suspect you had some influence there, yes?"

Kausar felt herself blushing. "It was a loan, only. I had a feeling you would be good for it. You have a way with people, and we needed more family lawyers in our community."

Nasir laughed again. "I always knew you were the numbers person in that marriage. Just like my wife. *Ex*-wife," he corrected.

Kausar was surprised. "I'm sorry to hear that," she started, as Nasir waved her into a conference room with a large table and swivel chairs surrounding it. She had liked Zahida, a round-faced woman with a cheerful disposition and a killer right hook; she had boxed in university.

Nasir shook his head, no trace of hurt or rancor on his broad, handsome face. "Relationships end when they are meant to, though it wasn't easy when we first split. It's been five years now, and I'm quite used to being on my own. I've even learned how to cook. Isn't it funny how being single makes you learn new skills?" He paused, looking at her. "I know how hard it can be in the beginning. I am glad you called, *bhabhi*."

"You never remarried?" Kausar asked.

"Who would marry me, with the hours I keep? Besides, all the best women are already taken." Nasir smiled, and looking into his handsome face, Kausar couldn't help thinking, *Many, many women would marry you.* The thought made her unexpectedly blush, and Nasir grinned, mischief radiating from his dark brown eyes. With his salt-and-pepper hair and strong features, Nasir Hafeez could have attracted another wife quick enough. He was in his early fifties, but he looked younger. But perhaps he was charming as a friend, and incorrigible as a husband. She knew plenty of men like that. She bet he snored, hogged the covers, and insisted on buying brand name electronics he didn't know how to use.

They were interrupted by a tap on the door, and then Razia entered, bearing a tray with three cups of steaming hot chai and a plate of chocolate digestive biscuits. The chai looked like it had been homemade, a perfect warm brown. To her surprise, Razia took a seat at the table and reached for a cup of chai for herself.

"Razia has interned with us these last three months. She graduated from law school recently," Nasir explained, taking an appreciative sip of his chai. "I tasked her with finding the best criminal lawyers in the east end, who are both available and willing." From the way his assistant was looking at Nasir, it was clear that she was more than happy to help her boss with anything he liked. Kausar smiled to herself and nodded at Razia.

The young woman reached for a printed sheet of paper from a folder she'd brought in with her and rattled off some names. "Nasir didn't tell me what area of criminal law, so these are general practitioners. I would suggest you get in touch with Ms. Kaur first." She handed Kausar the paper and took a dainty sip of her chai.

Nasir beamed at his assistant. "Razia has been a marvelous addition to our staff. Kausar *bhabhi*, we must find her a good match. Or am I not allowed to say that these days?"

Once more, the smile Razia shot him was warm, a hint proprietary. "With my hours, who would have me?" she said, parroting his own words. Kausar had to bite her lip to keep from laughing; the young woman must have been listening at the door. Nasir seemed startled for a moment, then laughed heartily at his assistant's teasing. Kausar reflected, not for the first time, that Nasir was kind as well as a shrewd businessman, just as she had suspected all those years ago.

"Young women have better things to do than get married," Kausar said. "Not like in our day."

"Nonsense. Women can have it all, just as you did, *bhabhi*. Marriage, children, plus a brilliant mind capable of anything," Nasir said gallantly.

Razia shot Kausar a more considering glance. "Do you work, Aunty? Outside the home, I mean," she said, a trace of condescension in her voice.

"Kausar *bhabhi* is one of the most intelligent and wise women I have met in my life," Nasir said, answering for her. His brown eyes were filled with genuine admiration, which only made Kausar uncomfortable. She had never enjoyed praise, even when meted out with such sincerity.

"Oh, I don't know about that. I was a homemaker. I looked after my family. In my day, that was all a woman was expected to do."

Razia's smile was cool. "You remind me of my mom. She kept herself busy, driving me and my brothers around, trying new recipes for dinner, and starting a new home renovation project every few months. Raising a family is the *most* important job. Good for you, Aunty."

Feeling as if her head had been metaphorically patted, Kausar rose, taking her cue. "I wish you all the best, Razia. Thank you for the chai. It was delicious—please share the recipe."

Razia rose, too, looking slightly offended at her words. "Oh, I didn't make the tea, I ordered it on a delivery app. I've always been too busy to learn how to cook."

Smiling slightly at the idea of equating chai with cooking, Kausar made her way to the front door, Nasir following at her heels. She suspected he had only followed about a tenth of the subtext in the conversation between the two women. Give the man a contract and he would tear it apart; emotional currents were harder to follow.

"Now that you are in town, we must make dinner plans," he said. "There are so few people left who know the old stories. I'll take you to one of those hip new halal spots, and you can complain about your children."

"Or perhaps you wish to complain about yours," Kausar teased. "How old are they now?"

"Hadiyah just turned eighteen, and Faisal is sixteen. Lights of my life, but don't tell them that. I still live in the old neighborhood. Zahida and I share custody and I wanted to stay close. She remarried, of course. Had her pick of the lot once she kicked me to the curb. Not that I didn't deserve it; she was well rid of me." He smiled, but the slight tightness around his eyes hinted at deeper feelings. Despite Nasir's easy manner, he still carried some scars from the breakup, she diagnosed. She also suspected he wouldn't appreciate if she tried to poke his wounds. In that way, they were similar. Both of them were about as likely to post their feelings on social media as they were to walk around the Golden Crescent in their underwear.

"I don't mind telling you, I was concerned when I first heard that Sana had opened a store at the Golden Crescent Plaza," Nasir said now, keeping his voice low, and Kausar understood this was the real reason he had followed her outside, away from the eavesdropping Razia. "I almost picked up my phone to call you a dozen times. But you were still grieving Hassan's passing, and I thought perhaps I was overstepping."

Kausar was touched by this solicitude and reached out to pat Nasir's forearm. The gesture made them both freeze. She removed her hand swiftly, but his eyes lingered on the place where her hand had been, and he rubbed it absently.

"Why were you worried?" she asked, and Nasir shrugged.

"I've been in this business long enough to know when things are starting to smell. And that plaza was starting to develop a distinct stench, detectable to those of us in the real estate world. There were rumors. A wink and a nod only, you understand."

"I'm afraid I don't," Kausar said.

"I know Imran was flirting with selling the plaza, and I suspected it was because he needed the money. I also know there was a very interested buyer."

"Who?" Kausar asked, still puzzling over his last comment about rumors.

"A company called Platinum Properties."

"A developer?" she guessed. Perhaps Brianna's accusation was true, and the plaza was destined to be sold off and rebuilt into another expensive condominium project. People did need a place to live, though with the sky-high price point that went along with any residential property built in the Greater Toronto Area these days, the local middle- and working-class residents would be unlikely to benefit. She briefly thought of Siraj, her friend Fatima's son, and his embarrassment at working in food delivery. Perhaps that was his extra job, because he had found one alone not nearly enough to cover his bills and support his family.

"I don't know much about Platinum Properties, only that the

company was keen to purchase. I also heard Imran was stalling on selling."

"Why, if he needed the money?" Kausar asked, but again Nasir shrugged.

"Who can tell in these circumstances? Perhaps he was nostalgic. He inherited the plaza from his father not long ago."

"Thank you for telling me," Kausar said. "I'll see what I can find out."

Nasir shifted his weight from one foot to the other. "I was afraid you would say that. I know it is none of my business, *bhabhi*, but do you think that wise? Hassan *bhai* mentioned a few times that you had . . . a habit of involving yourself in things." Nasir backtracked at the expression on her face. "I only mean, things can get quite nasty when it comes to commercial real estate. And now there's been a murder. You do not have experience in this sort of thing, to my knowledge."

"You mean with involving myself in matters that do not concern me?" Kausar asked coldly. "Hassan apparently told you I have plenty of experience with that."

Nasir ducked his head. "I've stuck my foot in it, haven't I? Zahida always said that when others remained silent, I blundered ahead."

"A man has been murdered and my daughter is at the center of the investigation," Kausar said. "I will not simply stand by helplessly."

"Of course, you're right," Nasir said. He caught her eye and held it. "You will be careful?"

Nodding, Kausar accepted his quasi-apology. "Please thank Razia for her research," she said stiffly. Then, wondering if she should drop a hint, decided it was better for the lawyer to be warned. "She's quite fond of you. Perhaps as more than a mentor or boss."

For a moment, Nasir didn't understand, but then comprehension dawned. "Thanks for the warning," he said, looking sheepish. "I'll do my best not to encourage her, but it will be hard, what with my movie star good looks. Did you know someone once called me the desi Tom Cruise?"

"Yes, I've seen your business cards," Kausar joked, the mood between them once again genial. She left the office, feeling lighter than she had in a long time. She had a lead now, however tenuous. She spent the bus ride home googling Platinum Properties.

H*amza was home when she returned. Kausar was* exhausted—she had forgotten how long everything took when one had to rely on public transportation. The girls weren't back from school yet, and her son-in-law lay sprawled on the couch, fingers flying across his screen as he texted. He startled when he caught sight of her, jumping to his feet and quickly turning the phone over.

"No work today?" Kausar asked.

Hamza shrugged. "It's all virtual appointments and paperwork with my job, ever since the pandemic."

"And yet Sana complains you're always traveling," Kausar observed, taking a seat on an armchair.

"Some clients prefer face-to-face meetings," he explained, fidgeting. He was the sort of man who was always on the go and rarely stood still. His vitality had likely seemed energizing to Sana when they first married. She wondered if her daughter felt drained by it now.

"I noticed your luggage downstairs," Kausar said, after allowing the silence between them to stretch uncomfortably.

"I was too tired to take my bags upstairs last night."

Kausar nodded. "Where were you flying in from? Sana mentioned the UK."

Hamza hesitated slightly. "I met with potential buyers in

Romania. Transited through London. Heathrow is a disaster, so many people and no one knows where they're going. We're grateful you got here so quickly. Sana was beside herself with panic."

Kausar lifted an eyebrow. Too many details, the hallmark of a bad liar. "She seemed quite collected when I arrived. You can always rely on Sana to keep her head, even when her world is falling apart." She leveled Hamza with another pointed look, and he nearly lunged for his car keys.

"I should get Fizza from school. Sana is still at the police station. She just texted me."

Another lie. Whomever Hamza had been texting with when she had walked in, it wasn't Sana. Her daughter said the police had held on to her cell phone. But she let it go, rising with Hamza.

Now her son-in-law stood uncertainly, shifting from foot to foot. "How are you doing, otherwise?" The question carried a trace of the man Kausar remembered from when he and Sana were first married, kind and loving.

"*Alhamdulillah*. Some days are more difficult than others."

In five days, it would be the one-year anniversary of Hassan's death, and she wasn't sure how to mark the occasion. Some families planned elaborate memorials; Kausar had assumed she would have a quiet day of reflection in North Bay. Now that she was in Toronto navigating a crisis, she was too busy to plan anything.

"Are you managing financially?" he asked. "It must be a burden to suddenly be responsible for everything. Paying all the bills on time is something I keep forgetting to do." He smiled at her, but Kausar said nothing. She had never paid a bill late in her life, but Hamza spoke like a man who had a point he wanted to make, and she had an unpleasant feeling she knew what it was.

"I'm handling it just fine," she said evenly.

"I imagine Dad left you quite comfortable," Hamza said, his tone casual.

There it was. The real question he wanted to ask: *How much?* It was a question she had managed to avoid. No one in North Bay knew their family well, and beyond May, she hadn't made any other close friends who would pry. She was fortunate that May couldn't care less about money matters. Her friends and family in Toronto, however, knew that Hassan had been uncannily good at picking stocks and investing in real estate—or rather, that Kausar was, though that had been their little secret. She waited, hoping Hamza would get to the point.

"If you ever need help or advice on managing it all, I'm here for you," Hamza said. "I've got a great financial planner, Ahmed Malik, and he's taking on a few new clients. Naturally, I thought of you. It might help take the burden from you, Mom."

Kausar smiled thinly. "I'll keep that in mind. Thank you, Hamza." She felt uncomfortable discussing her financial situation with her son-in-law, or anyone else. The truth was, Hassan had left her a very wealthy woman. While their children would eventually inherit, Hassan had wanted to ensure Kausar had control over the bulk of their assets. He had teased that since she had been responsible for their extensive portfolio in the first place, it was better off in her hands.

Perhaps Hamza was curious about the real state of her affairs. Or did he think that he and Sana deserved a larger share of the inheritance?

Kausar remembered the first time she had met Hamza. Her daughter had not been happy about her parents' plan to move to North Bay. They had been arguing about it for months, and Kausar knew her daughter felt abandoned and resentful. When Sana first approached them about Hamza, it was a relief to talk about something normal—a new relationship—instead of the grief and depression that had driven them to sell their belongings and make plans to leave the city. Kausar was so relieved to have Sana speaking to her again that she had swallowed up most of her objections about the early marriage.

Hamza had been different back then. Kausar wondered where the earnest young man had gone. Standing before her now was a man who had grown into his handsome features, and who had also developed an ingratiating manner that rang false with every word.

"Yesterday you said you weren't surprised Imran was murdered," she said.

Hamza blinked at this change in topic, keys still in his hands. "He wasn't well-liked," he agreed, tone cautious.

"And you let your wife open a store in his plaza?"

He considered her words. "He was offering a good price on rent for six months. And I didn't realize a few things, when she signed the lease."

"What things?" Kausar pressed.

The keys jangled in his hand, a reminder that this conversation had a time limit. "Imran wasn't honest, and he wasn't above taking advantage."

Kausar's tone sharpened. "Did he mistreat Sana in some way?"

Hamza seemed alarmed at the suggestion. "He was an opportunist, that's all. It would take too long to explain." He glanced at his watch. "Fizza's waiting for me. Sana said you would help with dinner today?" Kausar nodded, and Hamza left.

The suddenly empty house made her feel restless, so Kausar opened the patio door to the backyard and dialed her son Adam, calculating the time difference as she did. Her middle child lived in central London with his family, where he worked as a barrister. Adam picked up on the second ring.

"Assalamu alaikum, Mom. Is everything okay?"

Adam always started every conversation like this, as if the

only time Kausar called was when she was in crisis. Still, hearing his warm voice, which reminded her so much of Hassan's, soothed her immediately. "*Alhamdulillah*, just calling to talk. How is Joy? And little Aneesa?" she asked, referring to Adam's wife of four years, Joy Lee, and their two-year-old daughter.

"Everyone's good. Joy is putting Ani down for the night. She's been giving us a hard time lately, but we think we hit on the right combination. Bottle of milk, two books, and three lullabies. Or was it three books and two lullabies? Joy will know."

"I hope you're helping out at home," Kausar admonished. "Why aren't you putting Aneesa to bed and giving your wife a break?"

Adam laughed. "It wasn't my turn. But we're sharing the work, I promise. As if Joy would let me bunk off. How are you enjoying being at Sana's? Isn't the house massive? Big enough to stroke Hamza's ego, I guess."

"Why would you say that?" Kausar asked sharply.

Her son seemed taken aback. "I was joking, Mom. You know what Hamza's like—always has to have the best house, the newest car, the biggest piece of pie. How is Sana holding up?"

"I spoke with Nasir, and got some recommendations for criminal lawyers," Kausar admitted.

"That's brilliant! I knew you'd take care of things." Adam had spent nearly a decade in the UK and had picked up some slang and a vague British accent that his mother still had a hard time getting used to hearing.

"Hamza told me he was in transit through the UK when Sana was arrested. Did he reach out to you?" she asked now.

"No," Adam said, considering. "But if he was here on a work trip, he wouldn't call me, would he?"

"I think he's lying. I don't think he left the city."

"Mom, don't jump to conclusions," Adam warned. "That's between Hamza and Sana. Let them sort it, okay? Every marriage has its own issues."

So there was something to sort out, Kausar thought. For a barrister, Adam wasn't always discreet. She knew her daughter and son were very close, which was part of the reason she had decided to call him in the first place.

"I'm not interfering," Kausar said. "I only want to find out what's going on."

"That is the literal definition of interfering, Mom." Adam sighed. "I take it back. Sana could probably use your help. We both know Hamza can't be bothered, plus he's got his own troubles. Maybe it's good you're there to hurry things along."

"What troubles?" Kausar asked, feeling secretly pleased at her son's words. She hadn't realized how much she needed to hear the note of support from someone in her family until Adam had given it.

A murmur from another voice in the room, then the sounds of a toddler's giggle. "Uh-oh. Looks like the first bedtime attempt failed. I'll see you soon, yeah?"

"Are you planning a visit?" Kausar asked. But Adam quickly said goodbye, leaving Kausar to wonder. Hearing voices from the driveway, she hurried around the side of the house. On the porch, two women stood on the stoop, the younger dressed in a familiar white hoodie.

CHAPTER 7

"That's the lady," the girl in the white hoodie announced. Beside her, an older Black woman, hair in a neat bob and dressed in pink scrubs beneath a wool coat, peered at Kausar.

"Do you know my granddaughter?" the older woman asked in a melodious Jamaican accent.

Kausar smiled warmly at the girl in the white hoodie. "I've never seen anyone run as fast as you," she said.

At her side, her grandmother gave the girl a push. "Go on, Cerise."

Cerise held a card in her hand, which she sheepishly handed to Kausar. "Thank you, Aunty," she said. "You didn't have to get involved last night. I appreciate you."

Kausar took the card, which said *Thank You* on the cover, and read the simple message inside. She reached out and embraced the young girl. Cerise froze for a moment, then hugged her back.

"I'm Beatrice," the older woman said, holding out her hand to shake, explaining she was an emergency room nurse who lived with her daughter and grandchildren a few streets over. Her daughter would have come, too, but she was at work—she ran a take-out shop nearby.

Kausar introduced herself, adding that she had lived in the city years ago and was back to visit family. "Is your daughter's name Lisa?" she asked, thinking of the woman standing beside Mr. Jin at the plaza.

"Do you know my mom?" Cerise asked.

"My daughter owns a desi clothing store in the same plaza as your mother's roti shop," Kausar said.

"You're Maleeha's grandmother?" Cerise seemed delighted by the coincidence.

"Cerise and Maleeha used to be good friends," Beatrice explained. "I couldn't believe it when Lisa told me what happened to Imran. That plaza is cursed."

"Why would you say that?" Kausar asked. Beside them, Cerise had started to fidget. No doubt she had heard this story many times before.

"Run along, Cerise. Make a snack and then get started on your homework right away," Beatrice said. "I'll be there soon, after I finish talking to Aunty." She waited until Cerise had disappeared around the corner before turning back to Kausar. "She's a good girl, but school was tough for her last year. All that online learning. Not good for anyone. She's smart but needs someone to keep an eye out, or she'll spend all her time on that YouTube." The women commiserated on the trials of technology before Beatrice returned to the topic of curses and the plaza.

"Lisa's been running her shop for nearly ten years, and that plaza has gone downhill, let me tell you," Beatrice said. "It was fine when the old man was alive. Then Imran took over and it went to hell."

"What old man?" Kausar asked.

"Afzal Thakur, Imran's father. Bought the plaza for nothing in the seventies, back when nobody thought much of Scarborough. Used to call it 'Scarberia'—remember that? Not that anyone thinks much of Scarborough now, either. Too many colored folks. Makes white people uncomfortable." Beatrice laughed, and Kausar smiled. She remembered when Hassan and she had first moved to the suburb in the early nineties. Her children had faced some racism, but soon made friends. The suburb had appealed because of the many different cultures and the growing Muslim community. They had been happy here. Until they weren't.

"The old man was so proud of the plaza. Lisa signed her first lease with him, and he gave her a deal because he loves Jamaican food," Beatrice said, a fond smile playing about her full lips.

"What sort of landlord was the old man—Mr. Thakur?" Kausar asked. She already had a portrait of Imran forming in her mind, but this was turning into a family affair.

"Afzal had what Cerise calls rizz." Beatrice smiled. "That means charisma, apparently. He was a big personality, always laughing and making jokes. Everyone loved him. Imran was his little shadow: standing right behind his dad, but usually ignored. I think he resented how much everyone loved his father. It goes that way sometimes."

Kausar nodded, thinking of friends she had known who always seemed to suck up the oxygen and attention in the room. As beloved as they were, it could be exhausting for the people who had to live with them.

"Everything changed after Afzal had his first heart attack and Imran took over the day-to-day operations, according to Lisa," Beatrice added. "He treated the place like his own fiefdom. Everyone hated him and missed his father, and he knew it. Made him even meaner, especially after Afzal died. There was some trouble back then, too, some financial issues. And now Imran's dead. Maybe his son will take over, except Mubeen takes after his father and isn't one for business, not like his older sister,

Anjum. The family is traditional, though. They'll want the son to run it, or maybe sell the place." Beatrice looked at Kausar with sympathy. "I heard your daughter found the body, and the police are giving her a hard time."

"She is innocent. I only hope the police realize that soon," Kausar said, and the women exchanged a knowing glance.

Beatrice looked curiously at Kausar. "Why did you help my Cerise last night? I'm grateful, but most people wouldn't bother."

Kausar hesitated. Beatrice was a stranger, but they shared a kinship of sorts. They had both raised their children in the east end of the city, and now their daughters were doing the same. Their individual experiences differed, yet a bond existed. She knew, instinctively, that Beatrice would understand.

"I have three children," Kausar started, brushing her hand down the sweater she had thrown on that morning. This story was not easy to share. "Sana, my eldest, followed by Adam, and then my youngest, Ali." She took a deep breath, and Beatrice stilled beside her, as if bracing for what was coming. "When he was fifteen years old, my Ali was coming home from his friend's place. It was late, but not that late. He was walking home, just like your Cerise was, when he was hit by a car. The driver fled the scene, and my son died alone. Nobody helped him. If someone had, then maybe . . ." she trailed off and struggled to control her breathing.

A warm hand settled on her shoulder. "Do you like cake?" Beatrice asked. Startled, Kausar nodded, wiping her eyes. "I'll bring you by a pound cake next time I visit. Somehow, I don't think you'd like my rum cake too well." She said it with a kind smile.

Something in Kausar's heart eased at the older woman's gentle understanding, at her kindness coupled with a lack of pity. "I'd like that," she said.

S*ana still hadn't returned from the police station by the* time dinner was ready at six p.m. While the girls ate the pasta and green salad she had prepared, Kausar made small talk with Hamza about his job, the weather, and local mosque news, both of them glancing at the clock every few minutes. Where was Sana?

Finally, at eight p.m., an exhausted Sana let herself into the house. Fizza and Maleeha, who had been watching Netflix in the sitting room, flew to their mother instantly. In the kitchen, Kausar wiped her hands on a tea towel—she had cleaned up the meal as well as cooking it—and joined them.

"What happened?" she asked.

"Everything takes a long time at the station," Sana said, shooting her mother a warning glance. "I'm going to take a shower, and, Fizza, you should get ready for bed. Maleeha, did you finish your homework?"

The girls obeyed without complaint, as if they could sense that something was wrong. Hamza followed Sana upstairs, and after a while, Kausar heard the shower turn on. Hamza came back downstairs, his expression grim.

Kausar had put a pot of water on the stove for chai, more for the soothing comfort of the action than because she wanted a cup. "Did Sana tell you what happened at the station?" she asked. Hamza was nosing into shoes and reaching for a jacket. Where was he going at this time of night?

"No, she won't talk to me. Not that that's new. Maybe you'll get something out of her," he muttered, and shut the door behind him with a slam.

She turned around to see Maleeha halfway down the stairs, a witness to the scene. For an instant, their eyes met, and Kausar recognized the emotion she saw there. Maleeha was worried. About her mother, her parents, or something else? Kausar was sure her granddaughter had wanted to tell her something that morning. Then she blinked and the angry teenager was back. She ran back to her room before Kausar could say anything.

Sana joined her mother thirty minutes later and accepted without a word the cup of chai Kausar had prepared. She didn't speak until the mug was half drained. "They didn't lay charges," she said, voice steady. "Detective Drake said they're waiting on some evidence. I went over my story again and again. I think it might be time to call a lawyer."

Kausar reached across and squeezed her daughter's hand. It was freezing cold, despite the hot chai. "I know you're innocent. There is no question in my mind. We just need to make sure the Toronto police understand this as well." She passed her the information Razia had gathered.

Sana looked down at the numbers. "Is that where you went today, to talk to Nasir Uncle?"

Kausar nodded. "His assistant suggested we start with Jessica Kaur. Do not worry about cost. I will cover it, if needed."

Sana nodded, looking distracted, and Kausar resisted the urge to probe deeper or ask why funds were so tight right now. The shadows under Sana's eyes looked more pronounced tonight, and under the glare of the pendant lights above the kitchen island, the fine lines and hollows of her cheeks stood out starkly. Her daughter seemed hollowed out.

"Hamza said he tried to talk to you," Kausar started.

Sana snorted and looked away. "He suggested I try to get legal aid. Helpful, as always."

Kausar was shocked at Hamza's callousness. "*Beta*, what is going on?"

Misinterpreting her question, Sana continued bitterly. "He blames me for everything. For opening the store in the first place, even though he was the one who introduced me to Imran. For installing the alarm that took me there in the morning, even though I did it because Imran kept lying to me." Sana's head dropped into her hands. "I don't know what to do," she whispered.

"Let me help you," Kausar said, even as she clocked her daughter's inconsistency again. Sana had insisted this morning that she had gone early to the store to catch up on work, and yet she was contradicting herself once more. If she had done this during her interrogation, no wonder the police were suspicious. "You don't have to deal with this alone. Talk to Hamza. He loves you. Think of your daughters."

Sana looked up, and her eyes were dry. "I only ever think about the girls," she said. "You're already helping by being here, by taking care of the house, by cooking dinner and keeping an eye on Maleeha and Fizza. You found me the number for a lawyer. You've already done so much."

"I can help in other ways, if you'll let me," she started. "I can speak with people at the plaza. Maybe even Imran's family. Perhaps they will talk to me. No one wants to speak with the police."

"Mom, *no*." Sana's voice was sharp and urgent now. "This is my problem, not yours. I don't want you to get involved like that. Just be there for my family and let me handle this. Okay?"

Be there for my family. Not hers, but Sana's. It was a slip of the tongue, Kausar knew. She was being sensitive. And yet. After a moment, Kausar nodded. Satisfied, Sana stood, and on impulse, hugged her mother. Sana's body felt fragile, her bones delicate.

"Dad's death anniversary is this weekend." Sana's voice was muffled against Kausar's shoulder.

"I know," Kausar said.

Sana pulled back, and hesitated before speaking. "I organized something. To mark the one-year anniversary. Adam is flying in, just for one day. He was going to drive up to North Bay and convince you to attend. Then everything with Imran happened, and I almost canceled . . . Adam convinced me I should go ahead."

Kausar was shocked. "You planned a party for Hassan's death anniversary without telling me?" This explained Adam's slip during their call. He had known he would be in town but hadn't wanted to spoil the surprise. Or perhaps he was scared of her reaction.

"I knew you'd say there was no point, but I was missing Dad so much. I wanted to do something. For me, I guess. For you, too. I wish he were here right now."

Kausar's smile grew shaky. "He always knew what to do in a crisis."

"You're not angry with me?" Sana asked. "You don't think this is a bad idea?"

She was hurt, and she did think it was a bad idea, but that wasn't what Sana wanted to hear. "Thank you for arranging it. I don't think I could have done it myself," she said truthfully, adding, "it will be good to see Adam."

"You saved him a trip by showing up in the city. He thought he'd have to kidnap you from North Bay. He was going to get May involved." Sana smiled a real smile, the first one since Kausar had arrived in the city. It brightened her face.

Upstairs in her room, Kausar replayed the conversation with Sana as she tried to get comfortable on the too-soft mattress. Sana was not capable of murder. Kausar knew that. And she ignored the voice in her head that whispered she barely knew Sana now, and that given the proper motivation, anyone could be driven to violence.

The truth was, every time she spoke with Sana, or Hamza, or even Nasir, she was left with more questions. Sana had asked her to stay out of it—but she had been wrong about not needing a lawyer. Surely it couldn't hurt to pay a visit to the plaza and ask a few harmless questions? They were running out of groceries, in any case, and Sana *had* asked Kausar to help out. Buying groceries, and perhaps picking up some roti take-out, was definitely helping.

Feeling happier with this plan, Kausar fell asleep and dreamt of Hassan. He was sitting on the bench in the park they loved, a five-minute walk from their home in North Bay. He smiled when she approached, patting the seat beside him. She breathed in his familiar scent of starch and sandalwood cologne. Wordlessly, he took her hand, and they sat together in silence.

CHAPTER 8

Sana slept in the next day, at Kausar's urging. The shop was closed due to the ongoing investigation, and her daughter needed rest. Kausar's offer to wake early to help the girls get ready for school was not entirely altruistic, however. She planned to leave the house as soon as the girls left and didn't want to answer any questions about where she was going.

There were no blankets on the couch this morning, and Kausar wondered where Hamza had slept. She shouldn't worry; she was sure both Fizza and Maleeha were aware that things were not as they should be in their parents' marriage. Besides, she was angry at Hamza for the way he was dealing with his wife's crisis—that he had actually suggested Sana find a lawyer through legal aid still rankled—and she resolved to do fewer chores or favors for him in the future, until he made amends.

With the girls out of the house and Sana still fast asleep, Kausar called Ilyas. He didn't pick up, and she left a message requesting a meeting. Then, after a quick breakfast of toast and chai, she set off for the Golden Crescent Plaza in search of answers.

It was just past ten, and the roti shop was closed. The sign said it would open in an hour, and Kausar contemplated her options, settling on the grocer. It was the largest unit in the plaza, a neat maze of vegetable bins, with the back shelves full of nonperishables and spices. In deference to his diverse clientele, Mr. Jin stocked cans of sardines, mango pulp, fresh coconut, an array of Asian spices, and a frozen food section that carried halal cold cuts and frozen parathas, alongside dim sum wrappers and fresh noodles. The store was relatively empty, with only a few shoppers in the aisles. Kausar picked up some tea and fruit before heading to the checkout where Mr. Jin stood by the sole cash register. She recognized him from her first day in the city, though she took careful stock of him now. Mr. Jin looked to be in his late sixties, with thinning silver hair, and though he was no taller than Sana, his frame was stocky and solid from decades spent lifting boxes and restocking grocery shelves. He was dressed today in a button-down white shirt and dark pants, a strangely formal combination, though the clothes seemed worn and dated. Reading glasses dangled from his chest on an ornate silver chain that looked expensive. Kausar wondered if there was a Mrs. Jin, and whether he had any children to help him at the store.

She approached the register and placed her purchases on the counter. "What a terrible tragedy, the other day," she said casually. "Did you know the man who was killed?"

He was soft-spoken, and there was a strong accent on his English, his diction clipped and direct. "My old landlord's son. Didn't come to my store often. Sometimes his wife did when she needed vegetables. But they mostly shopped at the Superstore," he said, referring to the large chain store nearby.

Kausar nodded. "It was strange he was inside that clothing store when he died. I wonder what he was doing there."

Mr. Jin didn't answer, only indicating for Kausar to pay.

"Did he often do that, enter stores out of hours?" Kausar pressed, tapping her card on the point-of-sale machine.

Mr. Jin shrugged, and Kausar felt foolish. She wasn't used to asking strangers questions; she had been raised to be polite and accommodating. Pressing an older man for details in his place of business felt wrong, but Kausar persevered. This was about Sana's future, her safety. She decided to explain her relationship to the crime, hoping that would loosen the older man's tongue.

"Sana, the woman who owns the store where Imran was killed, is my daughter," she explained. "I want to help her. I'm worried."

Mr. Jin looked at her, his face impassive and arms folded. Finally, he said, "I know who you are, Mrs. Khan. I have nothing to say about what happened. Imran is dead, and I'm sorry for his family. That is all."

"Do you know who might have wanted Imran dead?" she pressed.

Mr. Jin tilted his head, thinking, and his gaze drifted behind her, to the parking lot. "You should leave now," he said quietly. "I have customers." The store was empty, but she took the hint—even though she would have bet her entire grocery haul that Mr. Jin knew something.

L*isa's store still wasn't open, but next door, an older* woman flipped the *Closed* sign to *Open* at the Tamil bakery and waved at Kausar through the window.

"I saw you go inside Mr. Jin's store. Are you Sana's mother?" the woman said when Kausar entered. She was shorter than Kausar and at least ten years younger, with thick, black hair pulled back in a long plait and clear, unlined brown skin. Her large dark eyes were friendly but inquisitive.

"How did you know?" she asked, and the other woman, who had yet to introduce herself, smiled in delight.

"Same eyes as Sana. More importantly, same eyebrows. You can always tell family from the eyebrows. I'm Luxmi. Would you like a fish bun? Made fresh just this morning. My mother's recipe."

Kausar accepted and reached inside her purse to pay, but Luxmi waved her away. "Sana said you couldn't make it to her grand opening. Illness, was it?"

"I'm afraid I don't leave my home in North Bay very often."

Luxmi nodded. "Very wise. At your age, travel isn't easy."

Kausar's lips tightened. She wasn't even sixty, but perhaps Luxmi assumed she was older. Even among her generation, it wasn't common to have had children as young as she had, barely out of her teens.

"I appreciate your concern," she said. "You seem like you keep an eye on things around here."

"I'm the longest tenant in the plaza. Well, except for Mr. Jin, but he keeps to himself. I like to know what's going on." Now a shadow passed across her face. "I don't know what will happen now, with Imran gone."

Kausar leaned close, in a confiding gesture. "I heard the plaza might be sold to developers."

Luxmi nodded. "His son Mubeen will want to sell. I wouldn't be surprised if we are all kicked out." She motioned with her chin towards Mr. Jin's store. "I don't know what the old man will do. Running that store is his entire life." She tutted in disapproval.

"Are you worried about yourself if that happens?" Kausar asked.

Luxmi drew herself up stiffly. "My customers are loyal. They say no one makes bread and *aloo bonda* and fish curry like me. They will come to wherever I am."

It wasn't an answer, Kausar noted. "Your fish bun is the best I've had," she said, not adding that it was the first one she had sampled. The other woman accepted the flattery as her due, and Kausar could practically see her feathers settle. Time for a more pointed question. "Did you get on with Imran?" she asked.

"He only cared the rent was paid on time," Luxmi said. Avoiding the question again, Kausar noted. Luxmi continued, leaning close. "I know he had problems with Sana. They argued, you know, the day before Imran was killed. I'm afraid I had to tell the police about it. I hope you won't be upset with me, Aunty, but it was my duty to share what I knew."

Kausar gritted her teeth. She might be a grandmother, but Luxmi wasn't young enough to call her Aunty. *Didi* or *Apa*, maybe. "How do you know they argued? Your store is not very close to either Imran's office or my daughter's store," she observed.

Luxmi seemed to bristle at the idea that something could happen in the plaza without her knowledge. "I heard it from Lisa, whose store is right next door to Sana. The night Imran died, Lisa was at her store late. She's a single mother and works very hard. She heard them clear as you're standing in front of me, Aunty." Luxmi's breath was cinnamon spice and her eyes were gleaming with the fervor of a born gossip. "Sana threatened to kill Imran. And he was stabbed that very night!"

I*t didn't appear as if the roti shop would open today. Eleven* o'clock had come and gone, and the storefront remained dark. Perhaps Lisa had an appointment, or maybe she had decided to stay closed, out of deference for Imran's death. Kausar fished a card from her purse and dialed 42 Division again, asking the reception to put her through to Ilyas.

"Officer Marjani," a familiar voice answered.

Kausar greeted him with salaams. "I called earlier and left a message. I was hoping you'd have a few minutes to talk about the investigation."

From the long pause that followed her request, she knew he was hesitating. "Please, Ilyas. I only want to help Sana."

"I'll be at Elliott Lake Park this afternoon canvassing the neighborhood," he said with some reluctance. It wasn't an invitation, but she would take it.

Feeling pleased, Kausar decided to do some canvassing of her own. Walking from one end of the plaza to the other, she made careful note of each store and its location relative to *Muhabbat Designs*. The grocer took up the largest unit in the middle of the plaza, beside Luxmi's bakery, followed by the roti shop, Sana's store, and the admin office. On the other side of the grocer was a bubble tea shop next to a computer and cell phone repair shop that was also closed today. Kausar stood in front of Sana's store, considering. The plaza felt dead, but perhaps it came alive later in the day, when shoppers were looking for a quick meal or a new desi outfit to wear to a party, or they needed to pick up groceries or a bubble tea treat.

Once more, Kausar wondered why Sana had decided to open a shop in this plaza, and why Hamza had encouraged it. She would have assumed her son-in-law would want a newer, flashier plaza for his wife's business venture. And considering his reluctance to hire his wife a lawyer, she'd have to assume he wouldn't have wanted her opening a store at all. Retail was always a gamble, and Sana's plans were ambitious. She half wondered if she should note down license plates of the cars in the lot, before dismissing the idea.

Kausar was starting to feel foolish again; Mr. Jin and Luxmi had easily identified her and guessed at her motives. After all, who was she? Not a cop. Not even a community member. She was a widow and a mother with too much time on her hands. What could she do that Ilyas or Detective Drake, with the resources of the entire Toronto Police Service behind them, couldn't do? She was only playing at detective. Sana was right; she should cook and mind the children only.

Her phone rang, and Kausar saw that it was May. She walked to the other side of the empty parking lot, far away from anyone who might overhear, before accepting the call.

"Do you need rescuing yet?" May's cheerful voice chirped from the other end. "I'll be your getaway driver any day."

"Am I the criminal in this scenario or the damsel in distress?" Kausar asked, eliciting a laugh from her friend.

"Heaven help us if you decide to embark on a life of crime," May said. "As for being a damsel, we're both a few decades beyond that, I think. Now, tell me what you're up to. On the case, I hope?"

Kausar smiled, despite her glum thoughts. Her friend's faith was cheering. May was a retired high school teacher, someone who dealt with dramatic teenagers. She would tell Kausar if she were being delusional, surely.

She explained what had happened so far—Hamza's behavior and Sana's insistence that she stay out of the case, as well as her conversation with Nasir and the descriptions of Imran from Beatrice and Luxmi.

"I am at the plaza right now and feeling out of my depth," Kausar said. "What business do I have, asking questions of strangers?" She knew she sounded needy, but what were friends for, other than to give you a lift, or to tell you off, depending on which you needed in the moment?

"Two days in the city and you're ready to give up?" May asked, with more than a little bit of the severe teacher in her voice. "That's not the Kausar Khan I know. Look what you've managed to accomplish in only forty-eight hours! You've gotten information from the shopkeepers, realized your son-in-law is a liar, cooked dinner for your family, found Sana a lawyer, and been asked to dinner by a handsome silver fox. I assume he's handsome—all the flirty ones are. Do you have a picture you can share?"

This elicited a shocked laugh from Kausar. "No, I do not have a picture of Nasir!"

While she talked, her pacing feet brought her to the back of the plaza. A large garbage bin blocked her path, and she maneuvered around it to scrutinize the back door, where *Units 1–3* was engraved on a small grimy sign. Walking forward, she spotted another door: *Units 4–6*. This must be the shared back entrance Sana had mentioned.

May was still talking. "Make sure to get a picture to share, next time you meet the handsome lawyer. Just pretend you need to use the camera to check your hair. That's what my daughter does. She's got a thing for men in uniform. Sent me a picture of a security guard only last week. He had dreamy eyes." Kausar laughed; she was positive Nasir would find her friend amusing, and the thought cheered her. May continued. "As for your other worries, even if you don't really get anywhere with your inquiries, I can tell you one thing. People open up to you. They'll talk to you over the police any day. And what's more, you know how to listen and then make the exact right connection. It's a gift. These are your people, after all, even if you haven't lived in the community for a while."

Her friend's words were a much-needed boost. "Thank you, May. You're right, I understand this neighborhood in a way no police force ever could." As she spoke, she caught sight of a pretty Black woman walking purposefully towards the plaza from the parking lot, her long hair wrapped in a silk scarf. Making her excuses, Kausar made her way to the roti shop. Lisa was back.

L*isa was arranging pineapple tarts and a selection of beef* patties in the display window when Kausar entered, and she straightened with a professionally friendly smile. That smile faded slightly as she looked at Kausar, then brightened into a more genuine one. She started to pack a box of treats.

"You must be Mrs. Khan," Lisa said. "I wanted to come to the house with my mom and Cerise, but when you run a business, it always comes first. I was hoping I'd get a chance to thank you for looking out for my girl. She's at a tricky age." The younger woman was attractive, her skin a dark rich brown, the hair under the wrap a cascade of small braids that fell to her waist. She wore a plain, fitted blue shirt and black trousers, and her large inquisitive eyes were fixed on Kausar. Cerise had inherited her mother's nose and eyebrows, Kausar noted.

Lisa handed her the box of patties and tarts and assured her the food was halal. She waved away payment.

"Cerise said she used to be good friends with my Maleeha, when they were younger," Kausar started.

Lisa hesitated before answering. "Yes, when they were in elementary school. I used to see Sana at play dates. I was sorry when the girls drifted, but it happens sometimes."

"You don't see Sana here, at the plaza?"

Lisa busied herself wiping the spotless counter. "The store is busy. Some days, I look up and it's time to close. I don't see Sana as often as I'd like."

"But you hear her?" Kausar asked, her eyes sharp on Lisa's face. "Luxmi said you heard Sana argue with Imran the night he was killed. She told the police all about it."

Lisa's face fell. "I shouldn't have said that to Luxmi. I had no idea she would share with the police, Mrs. Khan."

Kausar considered this. She had clocked the baker as a gossip within moments of meeting; surely Lisa knew that whatever she shared with Luxmi would soon become public knowledge. "Did you actually hear my daughter threaten Imran?" Kausar pressed.

Now hesitation warred with something else on Lisa's face. Finally, the younger woman nodded. "I couldn't hear clearly at first, but their voices kept rising. Sana started yelling. She said that if Imran didn't stop, he would regret it. There was something about a dead body." Lisa looked miserable. "I'm so sorry."

Kausar's heart sank at these words. Lisa didn't seem the sort to exaggerate. "If Imran didn't stop what? What did Sana mean?"

Lisa shook her head. "I don't know. Sometimes people lose their tempers. It's been tough here for the last few months. Business has been slow since the pandemic. Maybe she was blowing off steam."

"Except Imran was murdered a few hours later," Kausar said.

Lisa's shoulders rose in a shrug. "Sana wouldn't hurt anyone. I feel terrible the story got back to the police. I shouldn't have told Luxmi."

Sensing an opening, Kausar pounced. "My daughter's store is closed for the next few days, while she sorts out this business with Imran's death. I worry the police have settled on her as their main suspect. But then, they so often hassle our people."

She was laying it on thick, considering what had happened with Cerise the previous night, but it seemed to be working; Lisa slowed her vigorous wiping to listen. Thinking of the shared back entrance, Kausar continued. "I did not attend the grand opening for Sana's store. It has been . . . hard for me to visit Toronto. Sometimes it feels like the city is haunted. Perhaps your mother shared with you the reason why," Kausar hedged. Waiting till Lisa had nodded, she continued, "I wish there was a way I could see my daughter's store and Imran's office." She waited for Lisa to make up her mind, which didn't take long. The younger woman put down her cloth and motioned for her to follow.

The kitchen in the back room was cluttered but tidy. Beside the pantry was a locked door, an industrial freezer pushed in front. With some effort, Lisa pushed the freezer to the side and took a key from her pocket, which she carefully placed on the steel table behind her.

"This is an old plaza. Some of the units share a joint exit at the back, plus an adjoining door, like in a hotel. I share a door with Sana's unit. We never used it, and the police made sure to check it out when they were here. Sana's store has an adjoining door to Imran's office. I've got some things to do in the front of the store, which should take me about fifteen minutes." She looked meaningfully at Kausar and left.

Not wasting any time, Kausar unlocked the door and stepped inside her daughter's store. Or rather, into a storage room at the back of the store. Another door led to the back of the plaza, no doubt the same back entrance Kausar had spotted when talking to May.

The first thing she noticed was a drop in temperature. A small storage room beside the door that led to Sana's store gaped open, a window broken inside, haphazardly covered with tarp. Shivering, Kausar made her way through a narrow corridor towards the store. She stepped inside the main space, careful to stay at the periphery. The large display windows faced the parking lot, but thankfully the lights were off, the interior gloomy and not easily visible to a passing customer, not unless they stopped to take a good look.

Kausar moved to the front of the store. It was still an active crime scene—a few yellow markers were scattered to indicate points of interest. She carefully stepped around them and started taking pictures from different angles, using her phone. She paused, thinking. If Imran had been stabbed with the dagger from the display window, why had he staggered towards the center of the store, and not outside, where he could have easily called for help?

She noticed a yellow marker beside the glass display counter, which also held the cash register, and stepped closer. Nothing seemed to be missing, though the display was in some disarray, the point-of-sale system overturned, a monitor tilted to the side, and a heavy black phone knocked to the ground. The chaotic state of the store would have made her organized daughter's fingers itch to clean it up, but Kausar touched nothing. She returned to the shared corridor, hurrying towards the door at the other end of the storage room, the one Sana's unit shared with Imran's office.

The door was unlocked, which made Kausar pause. She opened it and stepped inside.

At first, Imran's office looked as if it had been trashed. But upon careful inspection, it became clear that chaos was simply the normal state of things. Kausar was not as neat as her daughter, but the mess in this office made her wonder how Imran could run a business, let alone find anything among the carnage. The office overflowed with files and junk, virtually indistinguishable. Boxes were piled everywhere. There were at least three filing cabinets with more paper piled on top and falling to the side. A tower of newspapers and another of magazines were teetering near the door. There was no place to sit and only a narrow space to walk. Kausar took pictures from the door, before chancing a few steps inside, searching for Imran's desk. She found it on the other side of the door. Strangely, the desk was the only space in the cluttered office that was clear. The table had a few file folders stacked in neat piles, but it was otherwise bare. Even the chair had been tucked in. After taking more pictures, Kausar carefully made her way back to Lisa's kitchen.

She placed the key on the counter, before flipping through the pictures on her phone, wondering what to make of them. There was something here that might be the key to what had really happened the night Imran died. But the more she stared at the pictures, the more confused and overwhelmed she felt.

"I hope that was useful," Lisa's voice cut in, making Kausar jump.

"Thank you. I should get going," Kausar said, and the relief on Lisa's face was immediate. "I just have one more question. Did you like Imran?"

Lisa's features tightened. "Not really," she said, and held the kitchen door open. "Does anyone like their landlord?"

"Your mother seemed to think you liked his father, Afzal," Kausar said.

"Afzal actually cared about his tenants. Imran just saw us as a means to an end. He was like that about a lot of things. He didn't have a lot of compassion for anyone who didn't matter."

"You didn't matter to him?" Kausar asked. She had clearly struck a nerve. Lisa's jaw ticked and it looked as if she were grinding her teeth.

"No one did, in the end."

Kausar wasn't sure what Lisa meant with that final remark, but she could take a hint. Thanking the young woman again, she left the store.

CHAPTER 9

Elliott Lake Park was neither a lake nor much of a park. Located on the other side of the neighborhood, it was a twenty-minute walk from the Golden Crescent Plaza. Kausar could have taken the bus, but walking helped organize her thoughts and consider questions for Ilyas. As a police officer, he was taking a risk in even speaking with Kausar. On the other hand, she had known Ilyas since he was a child. Surely some of his loyalty was still tied to their community, to Sana, and to the truth.

The truth was the issue here, Kausar reflected as she walked. Though she was convinced her daughter was not capable of committing murder, she knew Sana was not above dissembling. She had told Kausar that someone was entering her store after hours, and it couldn't have been Lisa—the freezer blocking their adjoining door looked like it hadn't been shifted in years. But why would Imran enter her store? Perhaps his office had become too untidy to work inside? In any case, if Sana were so eager to catch him in the act, wouldn't she have made sure her camera system worked? And if she had erased the surveillance footage, as the police no doubt suspected, was that a confirmation of her guilt?

Also, what had she argued with Imran about, hours before his death? Then there was the broken window in the storage room—perhaps there was a third party, someone who had broken into the unit and unleashed this chaos. She wondered if the police had followed that line of questioning, or if they were looking for the easy answer—her daughter.

Ilyas waited near a bench in the tiny parkette, which seemed to be popular with dog walkers because of the abundance of trees, and less popular with children because of the lack of playground equipment. This early in the afternoon, the grounds were nearly empty. Ilyas was on the phone with someone when she approached, and she heard him hurriedly say salaam, muttering something in Pashtun. He was talking to his mother.

“Thank you for meeting with me,” Kausar started, and Ilyas smiled crookedly at her.

“I wasn’t aware I had a choice,” he joked. “I hope you understand that I can’t tell you any details about an active police investigation.”

“I was wondering why you were allowed to be part of this investigation, considering your past relationship with Sana,” Kausar said, deciding to go on the offensive.

Ilyas stiffened. “Sana and I knew each other when we were kids. It doesn’t make a difference to the case,” he said, his tone cool. “Detective Drake knows that my expertise here is invaluable. I was hoping *you* could help our investigation, which is why I agreed to meet. Have you learned anything helpful? I have no doubt you’ve already been asking questions to other folks in the neighborhood. I remember how easily you could get us all to spill our secrets as children.” This last comment coaxed a smile from her. He was right—she had always asked a lot of questions, and if she expected Ilyas to share information, it was only fair for her to offer him something in return.

“I noticed there is a shared back entrance into the plaza, and that several shopkeepers would have had access to the one behind Sana's unit. I also noticed a broken window in Sana's storeroom, which was also unlocked," Kausar said.

"How observant of you," Ilyas said, and Kausar narrowed her eyes at his sarcasm. He looked contrite. "Sorry," he muttered, and she bit back a smile. At his core, Ilyas was still a polite desi boy, raised not to sass his elders.

"I've also had a few casual conversations with . . . concerned neighbors," Kausar added. "The consensus is that Imran was not a popular figure, unlike his father. There was some concern about him selling the plaza to a developer."

Ilyas sighed, deeply. "All of this might be true, Kausar Aunty, but none of it explains why he wound up stabbed through the heart in your daughter's store."

Kausar decided to try a different tactic. "Sana said her clothes were confiscated for evidence. Was that because there was blood on them?" she asked him now.

"It would be strange if there weren't," he said, not entirely answering her question. Kausar was starting to realize that Ilyas was determined to be as unhelpful as possible, and she wondered why he had agreed to meet her in the first place.

As if he could read her mind, he admitted, "I was hoping you might have some information for me. People are more likely to talk to you than me, even if I was born and raised in the neighborhood. They see the uniform and clam up."

"Can you blame them?" Kausar asked, and she couldn't keep the sharpness out of her voice. "Cerise certainly has reason to be wary. So did my Ali." Hassan had shielded her from the worst of it after Ali was killed, but she'd sat through more than one conversation with a police officer who had insinuated that Ali was up to no good, or that his death had been a targeted hit, that her son had deserved to die. She had never forgotten.

Ilyas sighed and rubbed a hand over his eyes. He looked

tired, Kausar noted. Perhaps this case had kept him up late last night, as it had her. Maybe he was worried about Sana after all. She decided to ask one final question. "Are there other suspects besides Sana?"

He hesitated. "We're speaking with everyone involved. The plaza has been the subject of a fair number of rumors lately."

"What sort of rumors?" Kausar asked.

"I'm sure you'll hear them all soon enough, knowing you," he said, smiling slightly, and Kausar recognized a trace of the young man he had been, the boy who had been in and out of her house, always joking with Adam and Ali and only fumbled to silence when Sana came into the room.

"I only want to help my daughter," she said quietly. "The way I couldn't help Ali." It was a low blow, and Ilyas inhaled sharply at the reminder of his long-ago best friend. "When Ali died, you know what the police assumed. They took one look at him and jumped to the wrong conclusion. I can't let the same thing happen to my family again."

Ilyas was silent for a long moment. "What happened to Ali is what made me want to be a cop," he said in a low voice, not meeting her eyes. "After he died, I was so angry. I saw what it did to your family, to Sana. I thought, if I was on the other side, maybe I could help. Maybe I could make things better for the next family."

"You can help *this* family now," Kausar said, pressing her advantage. "What do you know about Imran and his family? What is happening at the plaza? I understand this is your job, *beta,* but this is Sana's life."

Ilyas stood up from where they had been seated on a bench, and the look he gave her was gentle, but wary. It must be difficult to know the neighborhood as intimately as he did and yet be responsible for policing everyone's actions at the same time. Lonely, too, Kausar thought.

"You know I can't answer those questions, Kausar Aunty. But I'm sure you've heard by now that Mr. Thakur's body has been released to the family. I've been told they're planning to hold the *janazah* tomorrow afternoon at the mosque." He paused, holding her gaze. "Maybe I'll see you there. His widow, Parveen, and his two children, Anjum and Mubeen, will be there, of course."

Kausar stood, matching Ilyas's thoughtful expression, and recognized his helpful tip for what it was. "Thank you, *beta*. Please pass along my salaams to your mother."

She had asked Siraj the same thing, to convey her salaams to her long-ago best friend Fatima when they had met that first day she arrived. It was only two days ago, and yet it felt like a lifetime. Perhaps she would meet Fatima at the *janazah* as well. Funerals were considered community events, though part of her wondered how she would bring herself to attend this one.

Ilyas must have been thinking the same thing, because his next words, though placidly delivered, seemed designed to spur her. "Detective Drake is under enormous pressure to wrap up the case quickly." He hesitated, then added, "I don't think it will be too long before there is an arrest."

"There's only one suspect, isn't there?" Kausar asked, realizing what he had been hinting at all along.

Ilyas couldn't meet her gaze. "Take care of yourself, Aunty. Your family will need you."

"He *told you something useful, at least. I think he's trying* to help, without jeopardizing his job," May said on the phone. Her voice competed with the sound of chopping—May was in the middle of dinner prep, though it was only three in the afternoon. Her friend cooked when she was nervous; the sounds Kausar heard revealed more about her anxiety than her words.

Kausar had returned home to a blissfully empty house. The children would be home within the hour, and Sana was out, presumably running errands before she picked Fizza up from school. Hamza still hadn't returned, but Kausar noticed the luggage was gone from the hallway. She had made herself a strong cup of chai and called her friend.

"The *jan*-azaah is open to anyone who happens to be at the mosque, right?" May asked, mispronouncing the word. "I remember that from Hassan's funeral. Most everyone came to pay their respects, but a few had just wandered into the mosque for prayer time. It will be a good way to talk to Imran's family, and maybe pick up some gossip. I know we're not supposed to speak ill of the dead, but funerals tend to be chatty places. As my granddaughters say, there might be a *vibe*."

"That's true," Kausar said. She hesitated. "I haven't been to the Toronto Muslim Assembly in a long time." She didn't add that the last time had been for Ali's *janazah*.

"With some luck, you won't be recognized. From what Ilyas said, you don't have much time. It was kind of him to warn you."

Kausar agreed. Ilyas had been forthcoming in some ways, though not in others. He had also—mistakenly—assumed that if she learned information relevant to the investigation, she would pass it along to the TPS. She vowed that would only happen if it helped Sana's defense.

May continued. "At the funeral, you can keep your ears open and ask questions. Everyone will assume you're just being a nosy aunty, and they'll be too polite to tell you to buzz off."

Despite her gloomy mood, Kausar smiled. "Maybe you should be asking questions," she teased. "You're the one with the good ideas."

May huffed. "I would stick out at the mosque, though I do look pretty good in *salwar kameez*. I'm afraid it's down to you. Isn't that always the case, though? No, you'll blend right into the crowd, in a way Detective Drake and even Officer Ilyas could never do. You always know how to get people to talk."

"You make me sound like a mob enforcer," Kausar joked.

"Even better—you're a friendly face, and if you'll forgive my saying so, you seem entirely harmless. Most people aren't very good at looking below the surface, are they?"

"Are you implying I'm a dangerous person?" Kausar asked, chuckling.

"You're the most dangerous sort, my friend: the one everyone underestimates."

The women laugh, the moment of levity lightening the mood.

"Ilyas didn't come out and say it, but Detective Drake thinks Sana is guilty. I'm afraid Sana is in denial about the real danger she is in," Kausar said. Murder, even in the second degree, came with a life sentence, with the earliest chance of parole only after ten years. Kausar had googled it last night. If Sana were found guilty of first-degree murder, her children would be adults by the time she was released, and Hamza seemed unlikely to step up as a parent, given his track record so far. The damage to the family would be incalculable.

On the other end of the line, May's voice was firm. "Your daughter is not a killer." But Kausar noticed the chopping had sped up.

"What if she is?" Kausar asked softly. The idea had lurked in her mind from the start, and she couldn't shake it loose. How much did she know about her daughter, after all? They had barely spoken in the past fifteen years, beyond updates about the grandchildren. She hadn't even known about Sana's store until Hassan told her, and though there were times that she suspected Sana's marriage was not a happy one, her daughter had never confided in her. Sana had even arranged a one-year death anniversary party to mark Hassan's passing without consulting her mother.

None of that meant she was capable of murder, of course. But she was more than capable of keeping secrets.

"I don't know what to do," Kausar said. A note of despair had crept into her voice.

The chopping stopped abruptly, and May's voice filled her ear, firm and unwavering. "You figure out what really happened. You talk with everyone, you get their story, you move like an invisible force, and you find out the truth."

"And if I discover that my daughter is guilty of murder?" Kausar asked.

May didn't hesitate. "Then you help her get away with it."

CHAPTER 10

Sana returned home laden with grocery bags shortly after Kausar had hung up the phone. Not from Mr. Jin's store, Kausar noticed, as she helped sort through vegetables and place them in the crisper. Her daughter had bought pantry staples, cleaning products, and more fruit and produce than the girls could eat in two weeks.

"It's for the party. The death-iversary, I mean," Sana explained. "I thought I'd make a few things, instead of having it all catered. I don't have anything else to do, the police closed the store until the end of the week." She gently pushed Kausar to the side, taking over rearranging the vegetables. "I like it done a certain way," she explained.

Kausar watched her daughter move swiftly around the kitchen. When she was younger, Sana had shunned all household duties. Now she moved with a quiet competence, the result of years of practice.

"Did Hamza come home last night?" Kausar asked, watching Sana carefully for a reaction.

"He stayed over at his friend's place," she said, as if this wasn't the first time. "He'll come home when he calms down. He can't resist a party."

"Death-iversary," Kausar corrected.

"Same thing, for Hamza," Sana said. Her eyes briefly met her mother's before turning to unload boxes of cookies and bags of chips.

"Are you going to tell me what's going on?" Kausar asked. May's parting words were on her mind, and she didn't know if she were asking about Sana's marriage or about what had really happened at the store. It was obvious her daughter was lying about both.

Sana chose to answer the most obvious question. "Hamza and I are going through a rough patch. Nothing we haven't survived before," she said. Her movements were jerky as she spoke, and Kausar worried the potato chip bag might burst from the forceful way Sana shoved it into the pantry.

"Are you having money troubles, *beta*?" Kausar asked cautiously.

"Every couple fights about money. It's practically the law. Well, money or in-laws, and you're not around enough," she added. It was a joke, but it struck home.

Kausar changed tracks. "You said your security system was malfunctioning. How did you know someone had entered the store?" She had been wondering how the system worked.

Sana sighed heavily. "The camera was broken. The alarm worked just fine. I knew someone had entered the store, I couldn't see who."

"Is that why you rushed to the store?" Kausar asked.

Sana hesitated. "Why are you asking me this?" she asked, suspicious.

Kausar decided to come clean; Sana would find out anyway from her fellow shopkeepers. "I went to the plaza today, to pick up a few things. While I was there, I spoke with your neighbors. You're not the only one who hated Imran."

Sana's arm froze at her mother's words. "I asked you to stay out of it," she said, her voice deadly calm.

Kausar continued, ignoring her daughter's words. "Lisa said she overheard an argument between you and Imran, the night before he was killed. I'm afraid she shared that story with Luxmi, who felt compelled to tell the police."

Sana's eyes fluttered closed. "Gossip and hearsay," she said, but her voice sounded faint.

"Did you argue with Imran the night he was murdered?" Kausar asked. Sana hesitated, then nodded.

"I told him to stay out of my store. He denied everything, as usual. I might have lost my temper."

"Lisa heard something about a dead body," Kausar said.

Her eyes widened a fraction. "I can't remember what I said, exactly. Imran knew how to make me angry."

The two women stared at each other, Sana daring Kausar to ask the question: *Angry enough to kill?*

"In any case, I wouldn't trust anything Lisa said," Sana added. "Our girls used to be friends, but they had a falling out this year. I stayed out of it; you know how teen girls can be. But Lisa said some hurtful things about Maleeha. We haven't spoken since."

"She seemed sad about the girls drifting. What did she say about Maleeha?"

Sana shrugged. "That Maleeha was a bad influence on Cerise. It was all nonsense. I told her we should let the girls figure it out. Unlike my neighbors, I don't get involved in things that don't concern me. Lisa and Luxmi should learn that lesson, before they stick their noses in the wrong person's business."

Alarmed, Kausar stared at Sana. Her daughter had an ugly glint in her eye.

"I'm only going to say this one more time: Stay out of it, Mom. I know you enjoy digging into people's business and making up theories, but this is dangerous. Promise me you'll drop whatever it is you're doing. I can't worry about myself, the kids, Hamza, and you, too," Sana said, and for the first time, her voice wavered.

Instantly, Kausar went to her, embracing her daughter. Sana regained control quickly. “Promise me,” she repeated.

Kausar didn’t hesitate. “I will do what you need.”

Back in her room, Kausar pulled the notebook from her purse and stared at it. Her last question to May echoed in her mind, along with her friend’s answer:

And if I discover that my daughter is guilty of murder?

Then you help her get away with it.

Ilyas was right to worry about Sana. She was the most obvious, and most likely, suspect. She had been on the scene, had possibly tampered with the video surveillance in her store, and may have had a motive to kill Imran. But her daughter was wrong to think that Kausar would simply sit idly by while Sana set her world on fire. If Kausar was wrong and Sana was guilty, then she could help her daughter by finding a few viable suspects to throw the police off her trail. And if she was innocent, then Kausar could find out who had really killed Imran.

Ilyas had said Detective Drake needed to close the case, but Kausar was after the truth. How she behaved once she learned it would depend on who was guilty.

She opened her notebook, thinking. It all came down to one question, really: Who wanted Imran dead and why? She wrote at the top of the page: *Questions and Action Items.*

1. Who broke the window in Sana’s storage room? Did this happen before or after Imran’s murder?
2. Speak with Imran’s family and find out their plans for the plaza. Does Mubeen plan to sell or run it himself?
3. Talk to the other shopkeepers—bubble tea owner, cell phone repair shop—and find out what they know or suspect.

4. Track down citizen journalist Brianna and find out what she knows—is she a possible ally?
5. Hamza—where was he when Sana was arrested? Why did he want her to open a store in the Golden plaza?
6. Who runs Platinum Properties, and what happened to the development deal?

The list was a good start, and it was comforting to have it all down on paper. When her phone rang, she saw that it was Nasir and her heart gave an unexpected skip as she answered.

"Assalamu alaikum, *bhabhi*. I was just thinking of you." Nasir's voice was warm and friendly. "Jessica Kaur said your daughter has been in touch," he said, referring to the lawyer he had recommended.

Another thing Sana had not bothered to mention. "So she does listen to her mother," Kausar said. Nasir was too sharp not to pick up on her tone, but too polite to comment.

"I also have some gossip for you. It was passed through the grapevine, and the moment I heard it, I thought you might find it interesting." He paused, waiting, and Kausar wondered if he was flirting with her.

"Are you going to tell me?" she asked.

"I was hoping to tell you over dinner tonight," Nasir said. "You could bring along one of your granddaughters, if you felt you needed a chaperone."

Kausar smiled. He was definitely flirting. She considered his words, and his offer. It would be pleasant to go out for a meal. She had spent the past two nights cooking for her distant daughter, mercurial son-in-law, one surly teenage granddaughter, and one admittedly delightful Fizza. On the other hand, she didn't want to give Nasir any ideas—at least, not until she had thoroughly considered them for herself first.

"Perhaps you should just tell me over the phone," she said.

To his credit, Nasir didn't hesitate or try to cajole her to change her mind. "I learned the *janazah* for Imran will be held tomorrow at the mosque, and they expect a large crowd. I'm sure you've already heard about that, of course. But I've also discovered the name of the CEO of Platinum Properties, the one interested in purchasing the plaza: Patrick Kim. And he isn't the only one eager to put down an offer."

"That is interesting," Kausar murmured, wondering how Mubeen fit into this mix.

"Worth the price of admission?" Nasir asked, laughing. "Platinum Properties specializes in rezoning older commercial real estate in the city, and I heard his investors are nervous about the deal falling through. I wouldn't be surprised if Patrick showed up to the *janazah* to ingratiate himself to the grieving family."

"Do you know the name of the other company?" she asked.

"I can find out through my WhatsApp groups. Someone will know, I am sure."

"Thank you, Nasir. You're a good friend," Kausar said, making a note of this information in her notebook.

Nasir hesitated, considering his words. "I know Hassan *bhai* only recently passed. I always considered him a friend and mentor. But I confess, I also wondered how he managed to find such a charming, intelligent wife."

On the other end of the line, Kausar blushed, unsure how to respond. She had married so young, she was unused to such flattery and attention. "The mysteries of arranged marriage," she said, laughing weakly. "All matches are fated."

Nasir sighed. "And some are not meant to last. I will convince you to have dinner with me yet, *bhabhi*."

He really was a charming man. "Inshallah," she said.

CHAPTER 11

Kausar spent a few hours that night looking up Patrick Kim. It was a popular name, but once she had narrowed it down to the Patrick Kim who was also a property developer in Toronto, there were plenty of pictures. He was a handsome man who looked to be in his early thirties, tall and slim with broad shoulders, sharp cheekbones, and dimples when he smiled, which he did frequently—presumably in an attempt to distract from his intelligent eyes, but Kausar was not fooled. This was a man who noticed everything. She also noticed that Patrick was only ever photographed with other men in business suits, at gala dinners, charity functions, and corporate events. No partner or children by his side, and his social media was set to private.

When she looked up Platinum Properties, she noted an event for prospective investors at their offices tonight. Checking her watch, and then Google Maps for the best route on public transit, she decided she could just make it.

A quiet voice urged her to call Nasir. He would no doubt be pleased to escort her to the event and serve as an excellent co-conspirator. But another part of her wanted to do this on her own, if only to prove that she could.

Fizza's excited voice floated up the stairs—apparently, basketball practice at school had gone well. Kausar was glad Sana had a young child at home still; there was no better distraction than a young person's enthusiasm for life. She would text Sana once she was on the bus, she decided. She could keep secrets, too. Unfortunately, she was too old to be shimmying down drainpipes or leaping from windows, and so would have to take a more direct route out of the house.

She passed Maleeha, curled up in bed and scrolling on her phone. Pausing, she asked her teenage granddaughter how her day had been. Maleeha shrugged. Kausar waited a beat, but the teen's eyes only flicked back to her cell phone.

"I met Lisa today," Kausar said casually. "She mentioned you used to be friends with her daughter, Cerise."

Maleeha shrugged. "We're still friends."

"Your mother says otherwise. Why did you and Cerise stop speaking?" Kausar pressed.

Maleeha's brows drew together—in confusion or annoyance, Kausar wasn't sure. "We still talk, it's not like that. Could you close the door, *Nani*?"

Suitably rebuked, Kausar continued downstairs. Fizza was in the middle of a dramatic replay of a flawless pass during basketball practice when Kausar slipped on her shoes.

"Where are you going, Mom?" Sana called.

"I have an evening engagement. An investment opportunity Nasir Uncle told me about," she said, the lie coming easily.

"I thought you would cook dinner again," Sana said.

"Not tonight, *beta*. You're on your own." *Just the way you like it*, Kausar thought uncharitably. The two women stared at each other.

"You can take the car, if you like," Sana said, her suggestion laced with only a trace of mockery. "The keys are in the pouch by the closet."

"I prefer the TTC," Kausar said.

"No one prefers public transit," Sana pushed back.

"It's better for the environment," Fizza piped up behind them, oblivious of the tension between the two women. "Our science teacher, Mrs. Ko, said that when parents drive their kids everywhere, they're increasing the carbon footprint for everyone."

"And how does your teacher get to school?" Sana asked her daughter.

"She has an e-bike. It's gray and purple," Fizza said brightly.

Kausar used the distraction to slip outside, walking swiftly towards the bus stop. Sana was goading her, but the idea of getting behind the wheel of a car still filled her with panic. The therapist Hassan insisted she see after Ali's death suggested she would never truly recover until she drove again. She hated that therapist.

Ninety minutes and three buses later, she stood across the street from Patrick Kim's office. The tall, glass-fronted building in midtown Toronto was a sprawling space with an enormous marble lobby. After explaining her purpose to the attendant behind the reception desk, she was waved towards a bank of elevators, the floor preprogrammed for added security.

The presentation was half finished by the time she arrived, and an attentive assistant pressed a prospectus into her hand as she settled into a padded chair at the back of the reception area. The room held about two dozen people, mostly men, though it was a diverse crowd. Patrick stood in the front by a podium, walking investors through a curated and highly polished presentation. From his practiced delivery, Kausar guessed he had made this same pitch many times before. There were charts and graphs, forecasted sales and projected growth, all neatly laid out on the screen behind him as he talked. Even a cursory analysis of the prospectus in her hands revealed that Platinum Properties had ambitious goals and several projects on the go.

From her seat at the back of the room, Kausar examined Patrick. He was dressed in one of the habitual dark business suits she knew he favored from her Google search, but he appeared more reserved than she had thought. His glance had noted her presence when she walked in; she knew the simple printed *salwar kameez* and *dupatta* shawl she had thrown carelessly over her head made her stand out among the drab sea of black, blue, and gray business casual.

The presentation concluded, and the catering staff came around with drinks and snacks while the small crowd mingled. More than a few curious glances were thrown her way; she assumed that most of the people here knew each other and that an older desi woman in this world was an unexpected sight. A few of the South Asian men automatically straightened at the sight of her; some even trying to hide their drinks, perhaps wondering if she were an aunty spy planted to report back to their mothers. The thought amused her, and if she had more time, she might have asked them a few intrusive questions just for fun, but her sights were set on Mr. Kim. She waited until he was alone before approaching, smiling as if they were old friends and holding out her hand.

"What an interesting presentation," Kausar said.

"You missed half of it, Ms. . . ." He paused delicately, shaking her hand.

"Call me Mrs. Khan. I recently returned to the city after many years, following the death of my husband, Dr. Khan. We own a sizable real estate portfolio in the city and I've been considering how best to grow his legacy. For my grandchildren, of course."

Patrick relaxed. A wealthy widow looking to inflate her assets—he must have assumed he was on sure footing here.

"My daughter lives in the Golden Crescent neighborhood in Scarborough. Have you heard of it?" she asked.

"I'm familiar with the area," he said. Unlike so many other business types she had encountered over the years, he kept his gaze focused on her and not roving the crowd to see if there was someone more interesting to talk to.

"Then you are also familiar with the Golden Crescent Plaza. Someone mentioned that it is up for sale. That, in fact, *you* were involved in the deal."

A flicker of surprise mixed with caution sharpened Patrick's gaze. "Platinum Properties is interested in several older commercial plazas in the inner-city suburbs. Many of them are struggling, and we are keen to rezone and repurpose."

"I'm sure you're aware that the owners of the Golden Crescent Plaza recently suffered a tragedy?" Kausar asked, eyes wide, as if she were imparting gossip only.

"I did hear about Mr. Imran Thakur's unexpected death, yes. Are you a friend of the family?" he asked politely, eyes sharp on her face. He was familiar with this dance, Kausar realized, of saying nothing and staying on your toes for the crumbs your conversational opponent accidentally dropped, examining each for hidden razors.

Kausar pulled her *dupatta* up over her head and tried to look old and harmless. "As a community elder, I consider it my duty to stay informed," she said piously.

"I thought you said you had only recently returned to Toronto," Patrick said, raising an eyebrow. "And if you'll forgive me, Mrs. Khan, you don't seem that old to me." He twinkled at her.

"My heart never left the city," Kausar said sweetly, ignoring the compliment. "Which is why I'm so eager to invest in the same suburb where my grandchildren live. Do you have a similar connection to the area?" In her deep dive last night, Kausar noticed that Patrick had attended more than a few Scarborough-specific charities and events. He said nothing, only looked at her, waiting her out, she realized. "I don't mind sharing that the sale of the plaza might cause some community uproar," Kausar said, taking on a confiding tone and leaning close to the young man. "The neighborhood would become a bit of a food desert, as they say. There is one grocer in particular who is frequented by many of the locals, and not everyone has a car."

Patrick's eyes seemed to harden at her words. "People also need a place to live, Mrs. Khan," he said evenly.

"That is very true, though I would imagine the local inhabitants would hardly be able to afford the new condos you hope to develop. Though perhaps Imran's death has complicated things . . ." Kausar said, trailing off suggestively. Part of her was amazed at her cheeky behavior. The Kausar of even a week ago would never have had the temerity to attend an investor's meeting and ask the CEO such bold questions. It was a wonder what a person could accomplish, given the right motivation.

"Mr. Thakur's death has indeed complicated matters," Patrick conceded. "I'm still very interested in the purchase, though there was some trouble even before he passed." He paused, weighing his words. "There was a competing interest, I believe. There often is, when the question of price comes up." Patrick smiled at her, his expression suddenly wolfish. This was not a man who easily backed down from what he wanted, Kausar thought.

"Imran was an opportunist, I imagine," Kausar said.

Patrick took a drink from a water bottle, eyeing her. No alcohol for him, either, she noted. Perhaps he needed to keep his head clear in case another nosy aunty accosted him. "In more ways than one," he agreed.

"You must have been angry when Imran threatened to sell to someone else," Kausar suggested.

Patrick considered her words, a smile playing about his lips, revealing those deep dimples. He was a good-looking man, Kausar realized. And he was enjoying their sparring conversation. Perhaps he found these pitch presentations boring.

"It can be a frustrating business. But if I murdered everyone who went back on their word, I wouldn't have anyone left to do business with, Mrs. Khan."

There it was, out in the open. Patrick was no fool, and he knew exactly what she had been getting at. He eyed her now more thoughtfully. "Are you perhaps related to one of the shop owners?"

Kausar felt herself blushing. She thought she had kept up during this conversation, just to realize that Patrick was only humoring her. "Sana is my daughter," she admitted. "Naturally, I am concerned with the recent turn of events."

"I thought so," he said quietly.

"Did you like Imran?" Kausar asked. She figured she had one more question before he ended the conversation.

Patrick inhaled sharply, as if the question had caught him off guard. "I liked some aspects of him," he said carefully. Then he straightened, as if he had said too much, and the formal mask was back. "I hope you will consider Platinum Properties for your real estate portfolio, Mrs. Khan. Please contact my office if you have any investment-specific questions. My manager would be only too happy to assist in any commercial real estate inquiries."

Kausar thanked him for his time, then watched as Patrick worked the room, shaking hands and flashing those dimples at clusters of people. He was good at this, Kausar thought. Though she had come here on a fact-finding mission, she made a note to have her accountant look into Platinum Properties. If the company was clean, she might actually consider investing. If not, then she might have found another likely suspect to present to Ilyas and to distract Detective Drake.

As Kausar scanned the crowd, she met the gaze of a young South Asian woman in the corner, nursing a club soda. She was wearing a dark sheath dress that hugged her generous curves, hair loose and flowing down her back, attracting more than one appreciative glance from the people around her. However, the expression on her face kept them away; it was carefully controlled, a mirror of Patrick's polite mask. Kausar nodded at the woman, who only stared back. After a final glance around the room, Kausar left.

It was late by the time she returned home, and the kitchen was clean. An empty pizza box was balanced on top of the recycling bin, and Kausar found a few slices on a plate inside the oven. Forgoing the trouble of warming them up, she ate her dinner cold. Feeling emboldened by tonight's relative success, she decided that tomorrow, she would attend Imran's *janazah*, and hopefully learn more about the dead man's family. She had a feeling they held the key to everything.

CHAPTER 12

When Sana asked Kausar if she could walk Fizza to school the next day, she agreed readily, partly because she wanted to spend more time with her younger granddaughter, and partly because she knew that young children noticed everything.

Fizza was practically skipping with glee on the way there—she couldn't wait for after-school basketball practice, she told Kausar as they walked.

The school was a fifteen-minute walk away, the neighborhood streets busy with school traffic. Kausar weaved around scooters, bikes, and herds of meandering teens, their backpacks forming a slowly moving wall of chatter and laughter. Beside her, Fizza swung her bright blue lunch bag, backpack low on her shoulders. Hamza had returned last night, and the remnants of another night spent on the couch greeted Kausar when she descended the stairs that morning. She wondered if Maleeha and Fizza understood what was going on between their parents, and whether she should ask.

"Why didn't you ever visit us before?" Fizza asked, before Kausar could figure out how to steer the conversation to Hamza.

"I wanted to," Kausar said. "I thought about you and Maleeha and your mom every day, *jaanu*." The term of endearment—"my life"—fell naturally.

"Then why did we always have to come visit you in North Bay?" Fizza's gaze was fixed on the sidewalk in front of her, her voice curious, not judgmental. Kausar forced herself to relax her shoulders and to think about the question.

"I suppose I was afraid," she said after a moment of silence.

"Because of Ali *mamu*?"

The term *mamu* made Kausar pause. It was the Urdu term for "mother's brother." Of course, Fizza would refer to Ali as her *mamu*, even though they had never met.

Fizza continued. "Mom gets sad about Ali *mamu*, too. Sometimes she shows us pictures, and she has tears in her eyes. She tries to hide them, so I pretend I don't notice." She stopped to look at Kausar. "Maybe you can tell me some stories about him? I've heard all the ones from Mom already."

"I'd like that," Kausar said. She told Fizza one of her favorite Ali stories, the time he went into the guerrilla shoe-shining business. He had relieved her friends of everything they had in their pockets after he polished their shoes, unasked, during a dinner party, and then extorted payment after dessert.

At the school gates, Fizza hugged Kausar before running off to join her friends. Turning to walk back to Sana's house, Kausar was glad that she hadn't asked the young girl about Sana and Hamza. Fizza was a naturally joyful child, and she didn't want that to change if her granddaughter hadn't yet realized what was happening between her parents. She wondered if Maleeha, being a bit older, would open up to her instead, and whether she would ever learn what really happened between Cerise and her elder granddaughter.

T*he* janazah *was scheduled for early afternoon, following zuhr* prayer. After spending twenty minutes trying to choose between two virtually identical outfits, Kausar admitted to herself that she was stalling. The last time Kausar had been to the Toronto Muslim Assembly, the largest mosque in the east end of the city, was on the day they had buried Ali.

Kausar remembered every moment of that day as if it were etched in glass. She remembered feeling cold. Even as well-wishers and friends hugged her and offered their condolences, she had been racked by whole-body tremors. She couldn't get warm, despite the heat of the day, not even after someone handed her chai in a disposable cup, not even when Hassan wrapped his arms around her body and held her close, his tears soaking into her shoulder as they watched Ali's coffin being loaded into the hearse, for transportation to the cemetery.

Her own tears had been spent the nights preceding, and she couldn't muster any for Ali's funeral. Of course, the tears had returned, again and again, every day for the next few years.

Kausar finally chose a dark blue *salwar kameez*, paired with a beige *dupatta* she used as a hijab. She had worn the hijab full-time for a few years after Ali died. Eventually she returned to her usual practice, which was to pull a *dupatta* shawl over her head on occasion, but leave it around her shoulders at other times. Sana and her daughters had never adopted the veil, though many of their friends wore it full-time. The ability to choose was the important part, Kausar believed. Hassan hadn't cared one way or another, claiming that she looked beautiful both with and without hijab.

The mosque was a short bus ride away, and though her heart beat fast as she crossed the street to the large, white stucco building with its distinctive copper dome and white minaret tower, her steps didn't falter.

She was early, but Imran's family and friends had already gathered inside a small side room set up to greet guests. For an instant, she hesitated on the threshold of the room, overwhelmed by memories. She almost expected to see Ali's body wrapped in clean white cotton when she approached the coffin. Instead, a diminutive man in his early sixties with thinning gray hair and thick, black eyebrows was inside. His jaw had been shaved, and though he had deep frown lines bracketing his mouth, his expression was relaxed, as if something had made him smile, even as his life ended.

Muslim burial rituals were simple. The body was first washed in a ceremony called *ghusl*, then wrapped in a white cotton shroud. Usually, this ritual was performed by volunteers or friends and family of the deceased; Adam and Hassan had both helped prepare Ali's body, and afterwards, Adam had been pale and shaking, while Hassan looked as if he had aged five years. The funeral ceremony itself consisted of a brief communal prayer beside the simple pine coffin, followed by burial.

What had haunted Kausar for weeks after Ali's death was leaving the gravesite. Muslims believed the soul remained tethered to the body even after death, and for weeks after Ali's *janazah*, she had woken every night gasping, certain that she, and not Ali, was trapped beneath six feet of dirt; wishing over and over again that she was the one who had died and not her son. Hassan had eventually convinced her to take sleeping pills.

Kausar shook her head now and forced herself to breathe, slowly and evenly. It wouldn't help anyone, least of all Sana, if she had a panic attack in the middle of the mosque. She needed to focus on her goal—to speak with Imran's family. She scanned the crowd, trying to identify them based on the circumstances and the information she'd gleaned from her conversations with Nasir and Beatrice.

An older woman dressed in a dark gray abaya dress, hair covered by a wrinkled white hijab, sat sobbing in a folding chair beside the coffin. Kausar recognized the anguished expression on the woman's face: She must be Imran's widow, Parveen. Beside her, a young man dressed in black pants and a charcoal polo shifted impatiently, not even attempting to comfort the older woman—Kausar took him to be Imran's son, Mubeen. He had the same thick, dark brows as his father, though his chin was weak. He leaned over to an attractive, capable-looking woman—his sister Anjum, who was murmuring something comforting to her mother. Kausar considered the young woman; she had an air of quiet competence about her as she observed the crowd and assessed what needed to be attended to next. When she caught Kausar's gaze, they both blinked in surprise. It was the same woman from Patrick Kim's investor meeting the night before.

Leaning against the back wall, Kausar spotted another familiar form—Patrick Kim himself. He caught her eye just as the *adhan*, the melodious call to prayer, started over the loudspeaker and the crowd shuffled to the door. The *janazah* would be held immediately after the afternoon *zuhr* prayer, as was customary. Mubeen took the opportunity to exit, leaving his mother and sister alone together. Kausar seized her chance and approached.

"Can I get you something?" Kausar asked, approaching the duo and addressing Anjum. "Water for your mother, perhaps?"

Anjum roused herself and smiled wanly at Kausar. "You're very kind. Did you know my father?"

"He knew my son-in-law," Kausar explained vaguely. She addressed Parveen: "My husband died recently. May Allah grant you patience, sister. *Inna lillahi wa inna ilayhi raji'un.*" It was the condolence every Muslim offered—"To God we belong, and to Him we return." Kausar continued: "I know how difficult this must be, Mrs. Thakur. I will keep you and your family in my *duas.*" Then she turned to Anjum. "You look familiar. Were you at an event last night at Platinum Pro—"

Anjum's face shuttered as she quickly interrupted. "No, I wasn't. You must be mistaken."

Parveen looked curiously at Kausar. "My daughter has not left the house since my husband passed."

A quick glance at Anjum silenced Kausar. "Of course, I can see now I was mistaken. Please excuse me, I don't want to keep you with the prayer about to begin."

Kausar knew she had not imagined the flicker of recognition in the younger woman's eyes, and she wondered why Anjum was hiding her attendance. Distracted, Kausar stumbled over a water bottle, bumping into the person ahead of her. The woman turned around and Kausar found herself staring at her long-ago best friend. "Fatima?"

CHAPTER 13

"What are you doing here?" Fatima asked. Her friend, who was dressed in a dark abaya dress and matching hijab, had aged, but despite new wrinkles and softened features, she was still an attractive woman. Her light brown eyes were fixed on Kausar, as if making sure her eyesight wasn't failing her.

"I'm here for Imran's *janazah*," Kausar said, gently placing her hand on Fatima's arm. "It is good to see you again, my friend."

The women embraced, and Fatima led the way towards the prayer hall, where they joined the congregration for *zuhr*, after which the imam led the brief funeral service.

Fatima had been Kausar's closest friend in the city for years before she moved to North Bay. They were both part of a larger social circle but had grown especially fond of each other. Fatima's son, Siraj, was the same age as Sana, and her daughter, Khadijah, was a few years younger. Kausar had suspected that Ali had a crush on her and used to joke with Fatima about arranging their marriage when they were older.

After Ali's death, Fatima came around with food every day for a month, but Kausar couldn't bring herself to talk with her friend; sometimes she had not even emerged from her bedroom. When Kausar and Hassan decided to move to North Bay, she hadn't told anyone—not even Fatima—leaving it instead to her husband to inform their social group. Fatima had visited that last day to give Kausar a hug and present a black wool shawl embroidered with orange flowers as a going-away gift, explaining that she had picked it up from a trip to Kashmir the previous year.

"For the Northern Ontario chill," Fatima had said with a smile. "Call me, when you can."

Kausar never called, not even when she heard Fatima's husband had died from a sudden heart attack a few years later. She still felt guilty about her behavior, but anything from her old life in Toronto had become too painful to navigate, and so she had simply set it all aside. Seeing her old friend again brought the memories rushing back, along with the guilt and shame over her breakdown following Ali's death. But ever a friend, Fatima seemed only happy to see her.

"I heard you were back in town," Fatima admitted. "Siraj mentioned he bumped into you in the parking lot of the plaza. I'm only sorry to meet again under such circumstances."

Kausar wasn't sure what Fatima knew, but she assumed gossip about Sana had made the rounds. "I felt compelled to attend the funeral," she said cautiously. "I thought, perhaps, I could speak with Imran's family."

Fatima squeezed her hand in understanding. "I should have reached out. I wasn't sure if you wanted to hear from me."

Instantly, Kausar was filled with regret for all the years that had passed without a word. "I was so sorry to hear about Umar," she said, referring to Fatima's husband.

"I know you were. And Hassan *bhai* called. He used to call once or twice a year. I always asked after you." She nudged her gently with her shoulder. "You could have called."

Kausar nodded, and another wave of grief climbed her throat. Her husband had done his best to shield her, always. "I'm so sorry—" she started, but Fatima shook her head.

"There is no need to apologize. I know you did the best you could. I missed you, that is all. Perhaps we could have chai sometime?"

They had drifted towards the exit, where Imran's coffin was being loaded into the hearse as his children and widow watched. Impulsively, Kausar turned to Fatima. "Sana is hosting a small gathering to mark Hassan's one-year death anniversary this weekend. Please come. I'd like to catch up."

Fatima agreed, and Kausar wrote down the address on the back of a receipt fished from her wallet, along with her phone number.

"I wanted to drive up to North Bay for Hassan *bhai*'s *janazah*," Fatima said quietly as they watched. "But Siraj couldn't get the time away, and I don't like to drive that far alone."

"It's all right. Almost the entire town came to the funeral. I had many to keep me company."

"Wherever Hassan *bhai* went, he was loved," Fatima said, and Kausar's eyes filled with tears. They stood in silence, watching the parade of mourners get into cars. A smaller contingent would follow the hearse to the Muslim cemetery, where a longer prayer would be read before Imran's coffin was lowered into the ground.

Siraj joined them and nodded at Kausar. He seemed pleased to see his mother reunited with her old friend.

"You've grown into a handsome man, *mashallah*. You must have had your pick of *rishtas*," Kausar teased.

A shadow moved behind his eyes, and Fatima was quick to interject. "You'll never be able to get any good gossip out of him. He still doesn't talk too much, nothing like your Ali. What a chatterbox he used to be."

"I used to hide in the washroom sometimes, when he was younger. He would stand outside and keep talking," Kausar joked. She had forgotten that story and was grateful to be reminded. Her memories of Ali were starting to fray at the edges, and it felt good to talk to someone who had been there when Ali was a baby, toddler, child, and teen. Before their lives imploded.

Siraj told Fatima he would wait in the car. As he walked away, Fatima lowered her voice. “He has been going through a hard time. He got divorced last year and had to sell his business and move in with me to cover the costs. The worst part is not seeing his children every day. He’s been doing odd jobs now, delivering food, some handyman work in the neighborhood and in the plaza, until he gets back on his feet. Children always need you, don’t they? Khadijah lives in the United States now, and only calls every few weeks, after I send her a dozen texts.” Fatima hugged her. “Give Sana my salaams. I know things have been difficult for her, too; she must be grateful to have you here.”

“I’ve been doing my best to help with the children and the house, and trying to pay attention to anything that might be useful. Perhaps you can let me know if you hear anything?” Kausar asked.

A mischievous smile lit up her friend’s face. “When Siraj said he saw you in the plaza, I had a suspicion you were asking questions. Some things never change.” With another hug, Fatima left her.

Kausar watched the hearse drive slowly out of the mosque parking lot, followed by a dozen other cars in procession to the cemetery. Ali had been laid to rest in the same cemetery, and Hassan had joined him last year, after the *janazah* in North Bay. Perhaps someday she would have the strength to visit them both while she was in the city. Sana had arranged the funeral and burial here for Hassan last year. She wondered if her daughter felt resentful about this as well.

Guilt was a familiar companion to Kausar. It was hard to exist as a desi woman, as a mother and wife, without guilt and its companion, shame, stalking her life. Yet, for the first time in her life, she was free to figure out how she wanted to spend her remaining years. Trying to keep her daughter out of jail seemed a good place to start.

I*t was almost three p.m. when she returned home, and she* was surprised to see Maleeha in the kitchen. She was even more surprised that her granddaughter wasn't staring down at her phone, but seemed to be waiting for her.

"I came straight home," Maleeha explained. "*Nani* . . ." she started, then stopped, looking awkward. "I wanted to ask . . . that is, I was hoping . . ." she trailed off again.

Kausar took a seat at the kitchen table and motioned for her granddaughter to continue. Maleeha, nervous, passed a hand through her thick, straight hair, loose about her shoulders. A smudge of eyeliner remained at the side of her eye, and her eyebrows had been combed so they appeared even more full.

"You can tell me anything, *beta*. I will keep what we speak about private, unless you are in danger," Kausar said.

"It's not that," Maleeha said, impatient. "I want to help."

"Help with what?"

Maleeha spoke in a rush. "Your investigation. Don't deny it—I saw the notebook in your room and took a peek. It said *Kausar Khan Investigates*. Mom told me the stories from when she was young, about how you always knew everything but pretended you didn't."

Kausar leaned back in her seat. There was no such thing as privacy in this house. "What stories?" she asked, stalling.

"Like the time you found out Adam's friend was stealing from him and then Adam didn't believe you, so you set up a sting operation."

"I simply asked Ali to plant a recording device in his brother's room," Kausar said.

"Or the time you got my mom's bully suspended by framing

her for dealing drugs. Where did you find all those prescription medicines, anyway?"

Kausar flushed. She was not especially proud of that incident, but Sana's bully had been relentless, and the school administration little help. "I'm not sure your mother should be sharing such stories."

"Please let me help you," Maleeha said. "I can't stand by and do nothing. Mom didn't call you here only to cook dinner and do the laundry." The stubborn cast to her jaw reminded Kausar of Sana.

"I'm sure you are more than capable of doing your own laundry," Kausar said, buying time. Maleeha's expression was a mix of grim resolve and frustration, and she sighed. "Your mother made me promise to stop any inquiries I might have started," she said carefully.

"And did you?" Maleeha asked. "Because I'm pretty sure you just came back from Imran's *janazah*."

Kausar blinked. "How did you . . ."

Maleeha indicated Kausar's dark clothing. "Funeral clothes. Please, let me help," Maleeha said, and the simple plea was impossible to ignore. Perhaps it would be useful to have her young granddaughter around, to talk over ideas and gain a fresh perspective. Besides, a curious child could avoid suspicion as easily as a nosy aunty. In any case, it couldn't hurt.

"If we are to work together, you must promise to do everything I say," Kausar started.

"Of course!" Maleeha said eagerly.

"You are not to put yourself in any danger. That will only make things worse for your mother."

"I promise."

"And you must tell me everything you discover."

"Send me in, Coach." Maleeha's smile was brilliant, the first genuine one she had given to Kausar since she arrived three days ago.

"If you have read my notebook without my permission"—Maleeha had the grace to blush at that—"then you have seen my list of questions. Do you know Brianna?"

"She's a few years older than me, but sure. She's a legend."

Kausar considered this. "I spoke with her the morning your mother was first questioned. She was recording herself while talking to the internet."

Maleeha smothered a smile. "You mean live streaming?"

Kausar inclined her head. "She mentioned that she would keep an eye on things at the plaza and that she had witnessed your mother's apprehension. Can you find out what she knows?"

Maleeha nodded, eager. "She lives nearby, plus her little brother is in my grade. I think she'll talk to me. She's really involved in local activism."

"Is that why she is a legend?" Kausar asked.

Her granddaughter shook her head, a look of awe creeping over her face. "She graduated last year but didn't go to university, even though she got a full-ride scholarship and won all the academic awards. Said she wanted to make a difference now, while she was young and had the time, and before the planet burned. Total legend."

Kausar wondered how Brianna's parents felt about this decision but then remembered what the girl had said about her father, who had left the plaza when Imran took over. She shared this thought with Maleeha. She wasn't used to having someone else to run ideas by, except for May, who mostly just listened and cheered Kausar on.

"I'll ask about her dad," Maleeha confirmed, making a note on her phone. "She's super into social justice issues. I mean, she's Blasian and her mom's Muslim, from Malaysia I think, so it all tracks."

Kausar hesitated, thinking. There was another thing she wanted to ask Maleeha, but it might backfire. "You're a smart girl, someone who observes and notices things. Your mother is a private person, but I can't help her if I don't have the full picture."

"What do you want to know, *Nani*?" Maleeha asked, and this time there was a wariness to her tone.

"Do you know what is going on between your parents?"

Maleeha froze, and the look of betrayal she shot Kausar made her conscience prick. When she answered, her voice was several degrees cooler. "I only know they're not getting along. It's happened before but this is the worst it's been."

"What are they fighting about?" Kausar asked.

Maleeha shrugged. "Money. I thought it would get easier once Mom got that inheritance from *Nana*. But it only made things worse, especially with the store opening."

"Your mother used the inheritance to open the store, I believe," Kausar said, hoping she wasn't revealing too much about the family finances, but Maleeha only nodded.

"Mom got so busy, and Dad had to do more around the house. It made him angry."

"Were your parents fighting about money, or about the change in the domestic load?" Kausar asked, and Maleeha blinked at her. "Because Hamza had to help with laundry, grocery shopping, and cooking?" she added.

"I don't really stick around when they get into it," Maleeha explained, looking uncomfortable. "Seems like they can't talk about anything lately without it turning into an argument. It started getting really bad after *Nana* died. I remember once, Dad told Mom she would ruin everything." Now Maleeha looked away, the hurt on her face plain.

"Thank you for telling me, *beta*," Kausar said. She wasn't surprised to have her initial suspicions confirmed, but she was sorry her daughter and her granddaughters had been going through such a difficult time. Something wasn't quite adding up about this business with Hamza and the store.

As she contemplated this, there was the sound of the key in the lock, and Hamza stepped inside the house. Maleeha immediately rose from her seat, shooting her grandmother a panicked look. She didn't want to be caught talking about her parents. "I'll see what information I can get for you, *Nani*," she said, and hurried from the room.

Hamza filled a glass with water and took his daughter's place. He seemed so relaxed and at ease, it made Kausar's blood boil. How much of his ease was due to the hard work her daughter had put into building a home and taking care of their children? Yet when Sana needed him after Hassan's death, when she had opened her store, and even now, when she was fighting for her very life, he abandoned her. Anger simmered in Kausar's chest as she looked at her handsome son-in-law. What had happened to the affectionate man her daughter had married? Had he been a phantom all along?

"What were you and Maleeha chatting about?" Hamza asked. His knee bobbed, and Kausar wondered if he was nervous.

"I was asking her about school and how things have changed since Sana opened her store. It was a surprising thing for her to do, after all these years," she said, watching Hamza closely. Did he seem relieved at this line of questioning?

"I wasn't a fan at first, but I came around. Especially when Imran said he could give us a deal on rent." Hamza's words sounded reasonable, but his knee continued to bob. Kausar decided to pick at another loose thread she'd noticed since she'd been there.

"Sana said you suggested she try for legal aid," Kausar pressed. "Are you having money troubles?"

Hamza seemed startled at the suggestion. "I only wanted her to explore her options. Sana is innocent, so why bother paying expensive lawyer fees when this will all be sorted out soon?" He stood up, leaving the glass on the side table for someone else to carry to the sink, and reached for his phone. Scrolling through it, he asked, "Have you thought some more about what we talked about? Ahmed would be happy to talk over your investment plans and portfolio. I could drive you over, any time you like."

"That's very kind," Kausar said, her mind working furiously. Maleeha said her parents fought about money, confirming what Sana had admitted herself. Perhaps this Ahmed person could be convinced to share more details about her daughter and son-in-law's financial picture. She wasn't sure what this had to do with Imran's murder, except that Hamza's behavior was strange, and she wanted to know why. Perhaps they were separate issues, but they both warranted investigating.

"Would you like me to set up an appointment?" Hamza asked. His tone was carefully neutral, his expression bland, and suddenly Kausar felt a rebellious spirit rising.

"Text me the contact. I will make an appointment for tomorrow," Kausar said sweetly. "But don't worry about driving me. I'm sure you will be very busy helping Sana get ready for the memorial for Hassan. Oh, and I hope you won't mind figuring out dinner for tonight? Sana is busy, and I have plans. Thank you, Hamza. What a gem you are."

CHAPTER 14

"I have over twenty years' experience as a mortgage broker and financial advisor, *Alhamdulillah*, and it has been my very great pleasure to serve our community," Ahmed Malik assured Kausar after she had been ushered into his office in a nearby suburb. It was much smaller than Patrick's setup, Kausar thought, and not as polished as Nasir's office. The thought of the gregarious lawyer gave Kausar a pang. She had considered calling him before heading to Ahmed's office. It was a little disturbing how often her mind bent in Nasir's direction lately. She wondered what he would make of her actions, and whether he would be tickled by her latest plan.

The man who sat before her now could not be more different from her friend. Ahmed was dressed in a cheap suit, his belly straining against the shirt buttons. He was sweating, even though the office was cool, and he swabbed at his forehead with a handkerchief as he spoke. His pungent body odor, mixed with strong cologne, lay heavy between them, and she longed to open a window to let in the fresh spring air. The things she did for her family, Kausar thought wryly.

She pasted an interested, but slightly overwhelmed, expression on her face, one Ahmed was no doubt familiar with when he spoke to "members of the community." Most people were easily confused when talking about their finances. She wanted Ahmed to assume that Hamza's clueless mother-in-law, a housewife and recent widow, was no different.

"Hamza said you are good at the investing?" she said, infusing her voice with a slight quaver. Ahmed smiled with a condescension he didn't even try to mask.

"We offer a range of products and services, Aunty, and we are happy to take over the management of the accounts your husband left you. I'm sure it has been quite difficult to keep track of them all."

Not really—Kausar had both a capable accountant and a family solicitor on retainer, but Ahmed didn't need to know that. "The banks and the investment people, they keep sending me paperwork. It has become too much. I don't even open the envelopes anymore. What a relief it will be to have someone I can trust." Kausar threw him a grateful glance, wondering if she was laying it on too thick. Judging by his smug grin, he was lapping her words up. Clearly, no one had told Ahmed to never trust an aunty.

"I consider helping the elderly in our community a collective responsibility," Ahmed said piously.

"I'm barely older than you, *beta*," Kausar said sweetly, baring her teeth. At Ahmed's startled expression, she pulled her *dupatta* over her hair and tried to look meek. It was time to get this conversation pointed in the right direction. "My son-in-law Hamza says you have helped him enormously. I was so sorry to hear about their financial trouble."

Ahmed didn't even hesitate. "Yes, he was in quite a bind when he came to me. I helped him rearrange a few things. He lost a fair bit on a few bad decisions." He leaned forward and mouthed, "*Crypto.*"

Kausar's heart sank, even as she shook her head helplessly at Ahmed. "Hamza started a cryptic crossword?" she asked, her mind working furiously. Had Hamza invested in a volatile market he hadn't understood? She recalled her son-in-law's arrogance, his evasiveness and inability to accept responsibility. Of course, he had.

Ahmed chuckled. "No, crypto*currency*. It's a complicated concept, Aunty, one not everyone can understand. Essentially, people invest in internet money that can only be bought and sold online, and there is an unlimited supply."

Wrong, Kausar thought. She had invested early in bitcoin and a few other cryptocurrencies. All pocket change, of course. The bulk of her portfolio was in real estate holdings and dividend-paying stock. She followed Warren Buffett's advice and invested in things she actually understood. "How very interesting. And poor Hamza lost money on the internets, did he?"

"More than he'd like, but thankfully he came to me before it was too late. I think he might have lost some of his wife's money, too. Women aren't used to looking after the finances. Too busy taking care of the children and buying things for the house. Especially their closets!" He chuckled.

"Where is the money now?" Kausar asked, trying to keep the simmering anger from her voice. Ahmed was an idiot, and his face was so very punchable.

Ahmed seemed surprised at this. "He invested in my company, Silver Star Holdings. I thought that was why you came to see me, because Hamza recommended our services. He has been very happy with his returns, and of course, we have a long wait-list of clients, but we can make an exception for family. Let me run you through the presentation."

With a click of his mouse, Ahmed pulled up a prospectus with pictures of happy couples and families and began his pitch. Kausar only half listened. Her own financial literacy was largely self-taught through trial and error and picking things up over the years. At first, it had been a challenge to grow their small savings, but Hassan had encouraged her interest in investing. He had no head for numbers, and no time, either, but he had gotten a kick out of his wife's proficiency in following the markets.

Kausar tuned back into Ahmed's pitch just as he started to list the properties Silver Star Holdings owned.

"Did you say the Golden Crescent Plaza? Imran Thakur owns that. Or he did. I'm sure you heard he died recently," Kausar said.

Ahmed didn't enjoy being interrupted. "We were in final negotiations with Imran before his death. I have already connected with his son, Mubeen, to finish the paperwork on the plaza."

"What do Parveen and Anjum think about this?" Kausar asked. Ahmed looked blankly at her, so she clarified: "Imran's widow and daughter?"

Ahmed took on a fatuous expression. "Imran would have wanted us to deal with Mubeen, as the man of the house. His daughter will soon be married, in any case."

"I didn't know Anjum was engaged," Kausar said. There had been no fiancé hovering by her elbow at the funeral.

Ahmed leaned forward confidentially. "Imran told me a few months ago that he was planning to marry off his daughter as soon as possible, and I'm sure that will be his widow's priority, now that he has passed. I heard rumors that Anjum had brought a highly unsuitable match home, but Imran forbade it, and of course his daughter obeyed."

"One wonders if she still has reason to obey, now that her father is dead," Kausar said.

Ahmed seemed shocked at this suggestion. "A good girl will listen to her parents' wishes. They know best, after all."

Kausar looked at Ahmed. "Do they?"

"Imran was a good man," Ahmed said piously. "May Allah have mercy on him."

"That's not quite what I've heard," Kausar said mildly. "*Ameen*," she added to his prayer.

Ahmed's face grew almost purple when he was angry, Kausar noted with some amusement. "Kausar Aunty, you have no *right*—" he started.

"Please, call me Mrs. Khan. We're practically the same age, remember?" The smile she threw him was filled with daggers.

"Imran Thakur was my friend. I won't have his reputation muddied by rumor and gossip, especially when he is not here to defend himself," Ahmed said tightly, and now Kausar felt badly. Even villains had friends, apparently.

"You're right, of course," she murmured. "I'm sorry for your loss. You must miss him."

Mollified, Ahmed accepted her apology. "These last few months, we had started to work on a project together. That's actually how I met your son-in-law. Imran introduced me to Hamza. In my line of work, it's all about referrals, you see, Kausar Aunty . . . er, I mean, Mrs. Khan."

Kausar nodded, thinking about Anjum and Mubeen. If Imran had left the plaza to his wife and children, then surely all three would get a say in what happened to it? She wondered if Anjum wanted to sell to Ahmed from Silver Star Holdings, and if so, what she had been doing at an investor event for Platinum Properties.

Ahmed interrupted her musing. "Can I put you down for an initial investment in the low six figures?"

Kausar considered. It might be worth pretending to go through the motions, if only to find out more about his company and what Silver Star Holdings actually did—especially if it was another bad financial decision on Hamza's part, which she suspected it was. The prospectus would be a good place to start.

One of the reasons why Kausar had been so successful as an

investor was because she had a good instinct when it came to people and business opportunities. It was how she had known to trust Nasir when she first met him as a young law school grad. The instinct had failed her a few times, but for the most part, she trusted her gut. And her gut was saying that there was something troubling about Ahmed's company.

"Next time we meet, I will bring a check," she promised, standing.

"A wire payment or bank transfer would be easier," he started, but she waved his words away.

"Thank you so much for your time, Ahmed," she said. "I will take a copy of that prospectus and be on my way." Ahmed pressed Print, beaming. *It will be a pleasure to trip this little man up, and wipe the smirk from his face,* Kausar thought as she left his office.

Kausar Khan, you are a menace," May said, chuckling. Kausar could hear the TV on low volume in the background. She was once again on the bus, on her way home. "I think the fate of the plaza might be the key to solving who murdered Imran. Looks like Hamza actually did you a solid by introducing you to Ahmed. At least you've solved one mystery—the name of the other buyer."

"Yes, I'll be sure to thank Hamza for being useful for once," Kausar grumbled.

May laughed. "I'm sure you would have figured it out in due course. Look at how much you've learned in only five days. It's diabolical. Are you sure you're not a witch?"

"I simply observe and ask questions."

"And I love that you share those observations with me. It's so entertaining." May unwrapped something, and seconds later, Kausar heard the unmistakable sound of microwave popcorn.

"Well, I observed that Ahmed is sexist and a liar. Plus, he has terrible taste in friends. He said he and Imran shared a similar outlook. Based on what I've heard about Imran, I shudder to know what that would be," Kausar said.

"Making their wives and children miserable is high on that list, I would wager. What are you going to do next?" May transferred the popcorn into a bowl. Kausar was familiar with her friend's routine—May was about to watch a *Jeopardy* rerun; she enjoyed calling out the answers to questions she had heard before.

"Next is Hassan's one-year death anniversary," Kausar said.

"How are you feeling about it?" May asked.

"I hadn't planned to observe it," Kausar said, sighing. "But Sana was close to her father. She misses him. I understand why she wants to hold the memorial, but part of me wishes she had canceled. I did invite my old friend Fatima. We were close, when I lived in the city. It will be nice to be in her company again."

"Replacing me already," May joked.

"Impossible," Kausar countered.

As she hung up on her friend and settled back into the durable felt of the TTC seat, she could only imagine the chaos surely taking place at Sana's home, cooking and cleaning and everyone having to endure Hamza. He'd made his irritation at being left to fend for himself and the children last night clear, and Kausar didn't know if she'd be able to hold her tongue if she had to watch him sit around while Sana did everything to prepare for the party. A confrontation between the two of them certainly wasn't going to lessen the stress on her daughter. Picking up her phone, she dialed another number.

"You wouldn't happen to be free for an early dinner?" Kausar asked.

"I can pick you up in twenty minutes," Nasir said.

S*ince Kausar was already heading back to the Golden* Crescent, they decided to meet at a South Indian restaurant on the way. Nasir was seated in a booth when Kausar arrived, two steaming cups of chai and two mango lassis in front of him. He beamed when she approached, standing to welcome her. He really was a good-looking man: tall, with striking features and thick hair. A veritable silver fox, as May had guessed. More importantly, he had kind eyes and a generous mouth bracketed with laugh lines. Though he had always been a slim man, he had filled out in the last decade, and the extra weight suited him. Nasir seemed comfortable in his skin, the restless energy of his youth tempered by experience, though he retained an interest and curiosity for life. Too many men his age were bogged down by responsibilities and trials, or they had turned cynical and grumpy. Despite his hectic work schedule and the personal difficulties he had endured, Nasir managed to maintain a zest for life.

"I wasn't sure which one you preferred, so I got both," he said, smiling. Kausar reached for the chai first, taking a seat across from her old friend. "Dare I ask what prompted you to call me?" he asked, eyes twinkling in amusement. "Or is another family member in trouble with the law? Perhaps little Fizza requires the services of a commercial litigator. I know you didn't ask me to dinner simply for my stellar company."

Kausar laughed. She enjoyed Nasir's self-deprecating humor. For all his many good qualities, Hassan had never been able to laugh at himself. Not that she should be comparing the two men. This wasn't a date, after all. "I wasn't ready to go home," she confided.

Nasir leaned forward. "Always happy to distract a friend," he said. He reached for a mango lassi and took a long sip. "My kryptonite. When I was a boy in Karachi, my *mamu* would treat me whenever we went out."

"Mango is the most popular fruit around the world," Kausar said, not sure if it were true. Her opinion was it should be. She finished the chai in its steel tumbler and reached for her lassi, taking an enjoyable sip. Nasir watched her intently, though he looked away when she caught his eye. They ordered their dinner from a bored-looking server.

"So how is work—" she started.

"How long will you be—" he said at the same time.

They both stopped, and Kausar laughed awkwardly. Had this been a mistake? Ever since she had returned to the city, she'd been making one impulsive decision after another. It was entirely unlike her but also something she was coming to enjoy, if she were being honest with herself. As if reading her mind, Nasir leaned back in his seat.

"I'm glad you called," he said. "Even if you simply needed a reason to delay the inevitable."

"What do you mean?" Kausar said.

"Sana invited me to the one-year death anniversary, too. I declined, as I have a case coming up," he explained.

Kausar flushed. "You're busy. We didn't have to meet today."

But Nasir was shaking his head. "*Bhabhi*, I am always busy. It's the reason why Zahida left. I was never there, even when I was. I focused only on growing my law practice and left everything else to her: our children, our life. The day she packed her bags, she said she would be surprised if I even noticed her absence. But she was wrong. I noticed."

Kausar waited, trying not to fidget with her glass. She had a feeling she knew where he was going with this, and it made her want to bolt from the booth. She had always suspected he noticed too much.

"Marriage was something expected for us, wasn't it, *bhabhi*. I moved to Canada when I was a teenager, with my parents. When it was time to settle down, they helped me find a good bride, a local girl. We settled into married life, we had our children. Never once did I ask myself if I wanted any of it. I don't think you did, either." Nasir's voice was soft, contemplative. "It wasn't until Zahida left that I wondered whether we should have married at all."

"Hassan was a good man," Kausar started, then stopped. She didn't need to defend her late husband. Nasir already knew all this.

"He was one of the best men I knew," Nasir agreed. He paused, picking his words carefully. "But perhaps the best of men are not always the best of spouses? While marriage is presented as an inevitability, the outcome is never supposed to be in doubt. And yet it so often is."

Their dosas arrived then, crispy savory crepes filled with masala potato for her and paneer curry for him, and Kausar enjoyed her food while she gathered her thoughts. This night should be devoted to the memory of her husband, to the man she had nursed through his last illness, the person she had built her life around, had children with, survived tragedy alongside. Yet it was true that her thoughts also included other, darker questions she had long ago pushed to the bottom of her subconscious. Questions like: Had she been happy with him? Was happiness in marriage even possible, when their union had been, as Nasir put it, presented as an inevitability? Perhaps that was the real reason she had called him. Old friends were best, as he put it.

"My parents never forced me to marry Hassan," Kausar started. She couldn't quite meet Nasir's keen gaze.

"And my parents did not force me to marry Zahida. They simply presented options and told me to choose. The idea of choosing no one never even occurred to them, or to me." Nasir's voice was wry, and Kausar chanced a quick glance. He looked sad, the charming flirt of their previous interactions taking a momentary rest. "So, you see, I know Hassan was a good man. I know that he treated you well. I suppose I just wanted to tell you, Kausar *bhabhi*, that I understand if you are also feeling some other, more complicated feelings. Even the best marriages demand a compromise of our very self. It can be a hard thing to reconcile when a marriage ends."

Kausar dipped her crispy dosa into the *sambar* curry that came with her dish, savoring the sharp tangy heat on her tongue. "My marriage was not bad, but perhaps also not everything it could have been," she said quietly. "But I was content. And perhaps it is time you called me by my name."

Nasir took another long drink of his mango lassi, draining it. "As you wish, Kausar."

CHAPTER 15

The rest of the meal was pleasant, two old friends catching up. The lawyer soon slipped back into his usual charming persona; the only indication their conversation had taken a more serious turn was his use of her first name, without the *bhabhi* honorific.

Over dosas and another round of chai, he regaled her with stories of his single fatherhood, of learning how to cook, and his failed attempts at *dal*. "The simplest desi dish and I burn it every time, Kausar!" he crowed, to her laughter. "But I have mastered biryani. I would be delighted to host you, one day. And your family, too, of course."

It was strange for her, having dinner with a man without her children or Hassan present. It was not how things were done in her circle. If her mother, God rest her soul, caught sight of her now, she would be shocked. Yet once they started chatting, the awkwardness melted, and she realized that spending a few hours with someone who had known and liked Hassan felt like a more respectful way of honoring her husband's memory than accepting the condolences of strangers at Sana's party. At least Fatima had promised to attend, so she'd have one friend there.

It was after seven p.m. when Nasir dropped her off, and she returned to a house transformed. Furniture had been pushed back to make space for standing room, the periphery lined with a dozen folding chairs. In the center of the sitting room, a large, framed picture of Hassan had replaced the other pictures on the mantle. Next to it was a box collecting donations for the Canadian Cancer Society.

Hamza walked past, fingers flying on his phone. "You're back," he said, appearing distracted. "Ahmed said you had a productive chat."

"Very informative," Kausar said. She wondered if he was texting Ahmed—or perhaps someone else. She hadn't forgotten about the luggage tags, but those questions could wait until tomorrow. After the conversation with Ahmed, she had even more queries for her son-in-law.

She approached the large, black-and-white picture of her husband placed on the mantle, set in a simple silver frame. She remembered this picture; it had been taken when he was in his late fifties, the same age she was now. Her husband had been a handsome man, and in the picture, his hair was still salt and pepper. His eyes twinkled warmly, the barest ghost of a smile on his lips. He was dressed in a collared long-sleeve shirt and sports jacket, his stomach starting to round, though with his large frame, it was barely noticeable. She remembered how she had used to tease him about his belly. She reached out a finger to follow the curve of his jaw, his thick eyebrows and long face.

Remembering her conversation with Nasir, a spasm of loneliness and grief hit her. Kausar was not a romantic person; she had long ago accepted that Hassan was not the love of her life. But perhaps he had been the best friend of her life. She still missed him—his handsome face, his heavy tread around the house, his soft laughter at her stories, even his deeply unfunny jokes. As Nasir had said, marriage was complicated at the best of times.

She made her way to the kitchen, where Sana stood sentry over the stove, watching a large pot of rice, another of *haleem*, a fragrant meat stew made with lentils and barley, and a third of *karahi* chicken curry.

"You've been busy," Kausar observed, swallowing her sadness. Sana had gone to a lot of trouble and likely could have used her help.

"I helped!" Adam said as he jumped up from the kitchen stool and engulfed his mother in a bear hug. "Hi, Mom. Did you have fun terrorizing Hamza's finance guy?"

She smiled, pulling back to look at her middle child's face. His eyes were clear, but he looked thin and tired. Approaching his mid-thirties, Adam was starting to resemble Hassan more and more with each passing year. Her late husband's lopsided smile was aimed at her now.

"I did not terrorize Ahmed. We had a good chat," she said.

"That's a shame. Last time I was in town, he tried to sell me on a condo. I told him, mate, I live in the UK, what do I need a condo in Toronto for?"

At the stove, Sana rolled her eyes. "Ahmed might not be the sharpest knife in the drawer, but he's solid. A lot of people have invested with him. And it isn't as if he's in charge. Silver Star Holdings has a board," she said, stirring the *haleem.* Kausar raised an eyebrow at this. Ahmed made it sound as if he were the head of the company. Perhaps he meant that he was in charge of finding new investors.

"Explain to me again why you invested with this gem of an advisor?" Adam asked, and Sana shrugged.

"He's Hamza's friend. The company itself is sound. Besides, we don't have that much with Ahmed. The bulk of it is in index funds, just like Mom always suggested."

Kausar wondered if that were true, or if Hamza had diverted those funds into more volatile stock, as Ahmed had hinted. Now was not the time to ask, but she made a mental note to do so soon.

Adam shrugged and changed the subject. "Isn't Sana's house

ridiculous? I've been trying to convince her to sell and pocket the cash, but she won't hear of it. It's certainly big enough to host a memorial, I guess."

Sana made a face at her little brother before opening the oven, where a large tray of tandoori chicken was almost done baking.

Kausar smiled. It felt good to have her children here with her, despite the circumstances. The last time they had all been together was during Hassan's *janazah* in North Bay. Adam had stayed for a week, while Sana and the girls had returned to Toronto the next day, where Sana had arranged Hassan's burial in the same cemetery where Ali had been laid to rest. Hamza had missed all of it, away on an important business trip. Looking back, Kausar wondered how she had accepted the excuse so readily. It was obvious, now, that her daughter and Hamza were having serious problems, the sort that might lead to the end of their marriage.

Adam filled them in on his latest news while Sana busied herself in the kitchen: A case he had spent six months preparing for had been settled out of court; Joy was thinking of quitting her stuffy law firm and setting out her own shingle; their toddler, Aneesa, was perfect in every way. After Adam showed off a few dozen pictures of his daughter, they fell into a comfortable silence. Kausar knew her children were thinking of the two people who weren't in the room with them.

"He would have been thirty-two this year," Sana said softly, referring to Ali.

"I wonder what he would have thought of this house," Adam added cheekily, and Sana swatted his arm. The doorbell rang with their first guest, and Kausar wished she had suggested they mark this sad occasion with just the three of them, those who had known Hassan best and loved him the longest.

People brought flowers and cake, samosas, *mithai* sweets, even a box of mangos. The kitchen island quickly grew crowded with food, and still the doorbell kept ringing.

"How many people did Sana invite?" Kausar asked her son after an hour. Hassan had been a popular figure in the community. Unlike Kausar, he'd made regular visits back to Toronto and kept up with his friends, many of whom had not been able to drive to North Bay for his *janazah*, or the burial in Toronto. This was their opportunity to pay their respects, to him and his widow, since Kausar had never returned to Toronto after he passed.

Part of her was touched to see so many familiar faces. Another part wanted to run away; the gathering reminded her of the nightmarish days following Ali's death, when many of the same people had poured into her home. She had spent most of that time locked in her bedroom, alternately numb or sobbing.

Now, she embraced old friends; everyone was older, and though their smiles were genuine and their reminiscences fond, too much time had passed to pick up where they had left off. It was a relief to spot Fatima by the entrance. Maleeha and Fizza joined the crowd on the main floor, and Kausar motioned them near.

"My granddaughters," she said proudly. The girls were dressed in dark-colored *salwar kameez*, likely from their mother's collection. "Fatima was my closest friend when I lived in the city," she explained to the girls. "Her son, Siraj, and your *mamus* would hang out and play street hockey."

Fizza greeted Fatima with enthusiasm, but Maleeha only frowned. Luckily, Fatima paid no attention, squeezing the girls' arms and smiling.

"I knew your mother from when she was a baby. And I've known your *nani* since before she was a mother!" she said to them.

Fizza grinned. "Do you have any stories? I heard my Ali *mamu* used to get into trouble all the time."

Fatima put her arm around Fizza. "My dear, he was a foot soldier only. It was your mother who was the mastermind. One time, I had a basket of *gulab jamun* I made for a party, and by the time it was time to serve dessert, there were only three left. Guess who organized the theft? There's one in every family, I'm afraid."

Fizza giggled at the anecdote and asked for another, which Fatima was happy to provide. Beside her, Maleeha now seemed bored and disinterested, her arms crossed over her chest. Kausar leaned close, inhaling her granddaughter's sweetly floral perfume. "Are you all right, *beta*?"

Maleeha nodded. "I spoke with Brianna. Can we go somewhere to talk?"

"After the party. We will talk then," Kausar assured her.

Maleeha hesitated, her eyes roving through the crowd. "I think we should talk now. *Nani*, there's something I want to . . ."

Following her gaze, Kausar spotted Sana tucked into a corner with Hamza. From the unhappy expression on her daughter's face and Hamza's gesticulations, it was clear they were fighting again. As she watched, her son-in-law turned abruptly away from his wife, accidentally jostling Adam and Siraj, who were chatting behind them.

"It's nice that so many people turned out," Kausar said to her granddaughter, attempting to comfort her. "Your mother will be happy, and she could use the distraction. Now, what did you want to tell me?"

Except the moment had passed. Maleeha only shook her head and, tight-lipped, took the opportunity to slip from under Kausar's arm and run upstairs.

"She left her phone in her room," Kausar lied to Fatima and Fizza. She pasted a smile to her face with effort, making a note to press Sana more firmly on what was happening in her family. Things must be bad if Sana and Hamza were unable to keep the peace even at Hassan's memorial. She recalled now that Maleeha had also disappeared upstairs as soon as her father had come home yesterday. At least Maleeha was starting to feel more comfortable with her. Perhaps after the guests left, she would be willing to talk to her about the true state of affairs at home.

For the next hour, Kausar circulated, encouraging people to replenish their plates, accepting their condolences, and listening to stories of Hassan. It made her realize how hidden away she had been in North Bay all these years. At the time, it had felt necessary to escape the constant reminders of Ali's death, the pitying glances of her friends, and the whispers that followed her everywhere: *Her son was killed. The police never found out who did it.* As well as the darker insinuations: *What was Ali up to? Why was he out so late? Did the police know something?*

In many ways, the move to North Bay had saved her life. It gave Kausar time to break through the fog of her grief. She realized now that it had also stopped her from living. The injustice of it all hit her with the force of a blow, and she had to take a seat on one of the folding chairs, near a group of chatting women who were all vaguely familiar.

The doorbell rang once more, and a guest standing nearby answered, welcoming Ilyas. He was even more striking out of uniform, dressed in a plain, gray button-down shirt and dark pants, hair neatly combed. He stepped inside, smiling tentatively at the people near the entrance, before bending down to remove his shoes and add them to the pile by the door.

Beside her, the circle of women murmured: "Is that Raisa's son? He's a police officer, you know. He never married, though she brought him many *rishtas*." This comment was followed by a discussion of how better off all their children would be if only they listened to their mothers.

Kausar watched Ilyas greet Adam, and the two men embraced, before joining a circle of chatting younger people. If Ali were here, he would have been in the thick of the loudest group, joking even at his father's memorial. Her heart gave a pang, but the thought was more wistful than painful. Surrounded by family and old friends, her youngest son's loss felt more bearable, as if his memory, buoyed by the presence of loved ones, felt lighter somehow, alongside their remembrance of Hassan.

Fatima took a seat next to Kausar just as Sana walked past. At the sight of their host, a few of the women nearby quieted, and with a wary glance at Kausar, leaned their heads together and lowered their voices.

"They eat your food, give you their *poorsa*, but can't resist a good scandal," Fatima said with a sigh.

"If our community were as good at investigating as we are with sharing gossip, Imran's murder would be solved by now," Kausar joked.

Siraj and Ilyas came up to them, two tall, good-looking men with serious expressions. They greeted Fatima and each gave their condolences to Kausar; in return she urged them to eat.

Ilyas assured Kausar he was full from dinner and that dropping in had been a last-minute decision. "Adam invited me," he explained, the unspoken apology in his words. "I hope it's okay I came."

Kausar and Fatima exchanged glances. Of course, it was strange for Ilyas to be here, but he had been close to her family when he was younger.

"I am glad you came, *beta*." She realized she meant the sentiment, adding, "Hassan loved both of you." Siraj and Ilyas demurred, embarrassed, but Kausar waved away their words. "You were good friends of my children. If my Ali were here, he would have stood by your side, made inappropriate jokes about the guests, and teased you mercilessly, no doubt."

Ilyas grinned in agreement, but Siraj seemed lost in thought. "He was the funniest person I knew," he said quietly. "I think about him a lot."

Sana walked past them, and Kausar noticed Ilyas's eyes lingering on her face. Sana gave the group a distracted nod, but she was moving too quickly to make conversation. Kausar watched her slip outside the patio doors. A few moments later, the men made their excuses: Siraj heading towards the door, while Ilyas drifted to where Adam chatted with a few of Hamza's friends.

"He has to pick up his children from his ex-wife. He has them on the weekends," Fatima explained after her son left. "How messy divorce can be. But then, our marriages were no easier."

The women around them had dispersed to grab dessert and chai, leaving them alone. Kausar settled into the cushions of the couch, meditative. "I wonder, sometimes, if I was ever truly happy with Hassan," she said, recalling her earlier conversation with Nasir. The moment the words were out of her mouth, she wanted to grab them back.

But Fatima only looked at her with understanding. "What did we know of happiness or love? We were taught duty, honor, and expectation," she said. "When Umar died, he left us with nothing. I took any job I could find, those first few years. Eventually, I went to school at night, finished my early childhood education training. I was lucky to find a job in a city-run day care. Our parents never prepared us for any of this."

Kausar shook her head. If Hassan had died early, as Umar had, before he had managed to save up a significant sum, what would she have done? She looked at her friend with understanding. "Our parents did what they thought best. No doubt, we have done the same for our children."

Fatima stared after her son. Siraj was chatting with friends by the door as he eased into his shoes. "I used to worry his divorce was my fault. His wife never liked me. She said I interfered. When they first got married, I thought, good thing he married a desi girl. She would be more understanding of our family. But it made no difference, in the end." Kausar squeezed her friend's hand, and Fatima turned to her with a smile. "Of course, you loved Hassan. Just as I loved my Umar. No one can tell us what that love should look like." The friends were silent. One of the guests had brought them both chai, and they sipped the hot brew in silence, each lost in their remembrances. It felt peaceful. From her vantage point, Kausar watched as Ilyas quietly slipped out the patio door. Sana still had not returned to the party, she noticed.

Fatima roused herself and turned to her friend, the familiar spark back in her eyes. "Now, tell me everything you've been up to since I last saw you. Spare no detail, we have decades to cover."

Kausar filed away her observations and was happy to oblige.

CHAPTER 16

Maleeha was in the kitchen when Kausar came downstairs. Hamza had already left with Fizza for Sunday morning basketball practice, while Adam had caught an early-morning flight back to the UK.

She greeted her granddaughter with a wary smile. Maleeha hadn't returned to the party until much later, after most of the guests had left, and Kausar wasn't sure how to proceed. It had been a long time since she'd had a teenager at home, but she remembered her children only opened up on their own schedule, no matter how hard she pushed.

Perhaps she should have spoken with Maleeha last night, like she had wanted, but a full house was no place to discuss a murder investigation, or whatever else had been bothering her granddaughter. She hoped Maleeha would feel comfortable now.

"We raised nearly eight hundred dollars last night for the cancer society," Maleeha said, taking a sip of her herbal tea. She had yet to develop a taste for chai.

"Was the donation box your idea? How clever of you. Your *nana* would have been proud." She turned the kettle on and waited for Maleeha to decide where she wanted the conversation to proceed next.

"Mom never mentioned Fatima Aunty before," Maleeha started. "I've seen her around the mosque and stuff, but I didn't know you used to be close. She seems nice."

Kausar nodded, reaching for a slice of bread to toast. She knew from experience that it was sometimes easier to speak of other people's challenges before addressing your own. "Fatima has had a difficult life. Her family always struggled financially. Her husband died when her children were teenagers. I regret I wasn't there for her as I should have been," she said, looking meaningfully at Maleeha. "Your *nana* and I had moved to North Bay by then, and I wasn't in any condition to think about the friends or even family I left behind."

"Because of your depression," Maleeha said.

Kausar stopped short, her hand still on the toaster dial. Her depression. That was what it had been, of course. "Yes," she said quietly.

Since she had refused to see a therapist more than once, Kausar had never been officially diagnosed. But Hassan had known. Depression, following the death of her child. Depression, which had blocked the sun from her life. It only started to lift years after their move to North Bay, and only because she had finally agreed to try antidepressants. The ease with which her granddaughter spoke about this amazed her; when she was younger, such breakdowns were considered a moral failing, evidence of a deficiency in one's character—as if heaping shame on top of grief did any good. She was grateful to see that this new generation didn't share those same feelings and were more open to naming and talking about such challenges.

"I was depressed for a long time," Kausar said, testing out the words.

"It would have been strange if you weren't," Maleeha said, her tone matter-of-fact. She hopped down from the counter where she had been sitting and reached for the cereal cabinet, sticking her hand inside a box of Froot Loops. The crunch of the cereal was the only sound in the kitchen as Kausar prepared her chai and buttered her toast. "Brianna has depression, too. She blames the pandemic."

Kausar was relieved they had moved on. As much as she appreciated Maleeha's candor, she was not used to discussing her mental health with a fifteen-year-old. "When did you speak with her?"

"Yesterday. That's what I wanted to tell you last night. Her brother gave me her number, and after I introduced myself, she was happy to talk. She said that her dad used to run a shop in the plaza but moved out after Imran took over. His unit was where the bubble tea place is now."

Kausar nodded, remembering that Brianna had told her the same thing when they met. "What sort of business did Brianna's father run?"

Maleeha shrugged. "Jewelry. His parents had a shop back in Guyana or something. He ended up in a better location for almost the same rent. The reason Brianna is so interested in the plaza is because she thinks it will be sold and torn down, and she wants to launch a campaign to save it. She says if condos go up, it'll change the neighborhood, and we have to hold the line." Maleeha stopped munching the cereal to think. "Her videos about the shady things she's heard around the neighborhood have gotten a lot of likes. She even made it onto 6ixBuzz."

"Is that a good thing?" Kausar asked, not sure what her granddaughter meant.

Maleeha made a face. "I guess it's like a local tabloid? 6ixBuzz is an online company that reports on stuff around the city, like breaking news, but also weird things. Anyways, it got me thinking that maybe Brianna was live streaming for the likes. Which is fine," she hastened to add.

"It is good she has an abundance of passion for the community and an interest in local events," Kausar agreed.

Maleeha nodded. "That video about the plaza got, like, nearly five thousand likes, and the comments weren't all bots, either. She's hustling." Again, her granddaughter hesitated, and Kausar intuited what she meant.

"You are worried her interest in the plaza is not only motivated by concern for the community?" Kausar suggested, and Maleeha looked relieved at not having to spell it out.

"Yes. Maybe. I don't know. In her latest video, Brianna said she's been watching the plaza, and that she's noticed a lot of cars parked after hours and delivery trucks at strange hours. It could be true, or . . ." Maleeha trailed off.

"Or it could be a good story that attracts more viewers to her Facebook page," Kausar finished.

Maleeha's lips twitched. "To her TikTok and Insta, but yes." She shrugged, sealing the cereal box and returning it to the shelf. "I'm sure her intentions are good. At least I hope so, but I can't be sure. People will do mad things to build their platform, and sometimes it's easy to get caught up."

"Thank you for looking into this, *beta*. Every new bit of information helps," Kausar said, and Maleeha's face brightened.

"What else can I do? You never told me what you learned at Imran Uncle's *janazah*. Do you have any leads?"

Kausar smiled at her granddaughter's eagerness. "We are simply having conversations that may assist your mother," she said carefully. "At this point, I know very little. I did meet Imran's widow and his children at the mosque. I don't think much of Mubeen, though Anjum seemed competent."

An expression of distaste crossed Maleeha's face at the names, gone before Kausar was sure she had clocked it. "Do you think his kids might have done it?" Maleeha asked.

"We must not jump to conclusions, as the police seem to be doing," Kausar admonished. "We do not have their power or their resources, and we must proceed with caution."

Maleeha shifted her weight from one foot to the other. The sugar boost from the Froot Loops had clearly given her excess energy she needed to burn. "I'm worried about Mom. I feel so helpless."

A feeling of sadness filled Kausar, and she wanted to press her granddaughter, to ask her to open up more. Instead, she kept her tone mild. "We are doing our best. And you have other responsibilities, such as school."

Maleeha nodded. "That reminds me, I'm going to meet some friends at the library to study for a math test. Can you tell my mom? I'll be back in a few hours."

Kausar nodded, lost in thought. "Of course, *beta*. Will Cerise be there?"

Maleeha shook her head. "No, we don't really hang out like that anymore." Her granddaughter was now rummaging in the pantry for study snacks, before reaching for one of the oversized reusable water bottles Sana kept on the drying rack and filling it with water.

Kausar tried to broach what had happened last night. She remembered that her children were more likely to open up when they weren't facing her. "*Beta*, last night, you disappeared and did not return to the party for a long time."

Maleeha had finished filling her water bottle, tightening the top as she turned back towards her grandmother. "I'm fine, *Nani*," she said, her tone light. "Just not a party person, I guess."

"I noticed your parents arguing last night," Kausar said.

"What else is new," Maleeha answered, the words resigned. Snacks in hand, she walked quickly out of the kitchen before Kausar could ask more questions, leaving her to wonder if they would ever be close enough to have a full conversation. She hoped she hadn't missed her chance by hiding away in North Bay. By *healing* in North Bay, she corrected herself. Maleeha had been right about that, at least. She heard the front door open and close.

Kausar made her way upstairs, pausing in front of her elder granddaughter's bedroom. The bed was unmade, clothes were strewn around the floor, and the desk was piled high with binders and books. One caught her eye—a math textbook shoved beneath a science text, alongside a spiral graphing notebook and calculator. Kausar took a seat on her granddaughter's bed, thinking. How could Maleeha study for a math test without her textbook or calculator? Which meant she had lied about where she was really headed. Maleeha was a teenager, with the accompanying poor judgment and underdeveloped frontal lobe, but the casual—and convincing—way she had lied to Kausar was worrisome.

Without realizing what she was doing, Kausar started to straighten the bed, feeling around the edges of the mattress as she did so. With a guilty sigh, she gave up any pretense of innocence, closed the bedroom door, and gave into the urge to do some thorough snooping. She checked under the bed, rummaged through drawers, peeked inside the air vent, even unscrewed the light bulb and checked inside shoeboxes piled inside the closet. She didn't find an incriminating diary, no empty bottles of alcohol, no bong, not even a vape pen.

There was a small cardboard box full of cash, however.

Kausar tried to steady her breathing as her hand sifted through twenties, fifties, and hundred-dollar bills, all haphazardly shoved inside a shoebox at the far end of Maleeha's closet. There must be thousands of dollars in here. Far more than could be accounted for by Eid, birthday, or allowance money.

The sound of running water jolted her from her reverie, and she shoved the box back into its hiding spot, before returning the bedspread to its former messy state and slipping out of the room. Her first instinct was to speak to Sana, but wouldn't this only add to her burden? Perhaps there was an innocent explanation. She should speak with Maleeha first.

At least there was one thing she could do while she waited for Maleeha to return from wherever she was. She went to her room and dialed Ilyas. Seeing him in Sana's home last night had been a reminder that despite everything, he still had ties to the community, and to her family. He picked up after a few rings.

"It was good to see you last night, Ilyas," Kausar said after they exchanged salaams.

"The *haleem* alone would have been worth it," Ilyas joked, referring to the savory meat and lentil stew made with cracked wheat and served with fried onions, lime wedges, and plenty of green chilies. "You haven't lost your touch, Kausar Aunty."

"Actually, Sana made everything. I was like a guest at the party. She wanted to do it all herself. To remember her father."

"He loved *haleem* almost as much as me," Ilyas agreed. They lapsed into silence, each lost in their thoughts. "How can I help you today?" he finally said.

"I know you cannot talk about the investigation, even though I have known you since you were in diapers," Kausar started, and Ilyas huffed out a laugh. "But I thought I might pass along a few things I have learned."

"Learned how?" Ilyas asked, and the change in his tone was clear—he had put on his "investigating officer" voice.

"I am an easy person to talk to, *beta*."

This time Ilyas laughed out loud. "Yes, you appear entirely harmless, until one gets to know you."

Kausar liked the sound of that, even if it was half insult. "Nobody seemed to like Imran much," she said. Then, thinking of Ahmed Malik, she added, "With rare exception." The financier had been almost on the verge of tears when speaking of his friend's death.

"I can confirm that," Ilyas said dryly.

"Did you also know that the plaza was for sale and had two competing offers? One from Platinum Properties—"

"And the other from Silver Star Holdings. Yes, the TPS prides itself on asking questions as well, Kausar Aunty." A small note of impatience had entered Ilyas's voice now. "If there's nothing else . . ."

"One last thing," Kausar said. "Some people mentioned suspicious activity in the plaza late at night."

Ilyas was quiet. "Where did you hear about this?" he asked.

Kausar thought about Brianna, and what Maleeha had implied. Perhaps admitting that her source was a local activist eager to grow her social media following would not be a good move. "I can't reveal my sources," she said primly, and Ilyas sighed.

"Can you reveal what the suspicious activity involved?" he asked, exasperation clear in his voice. Kausar reminded herself that Ilyas was a busy man.

"There have been cars spotted in the parking lot after hours, and delivery vans coming and going at odd hours."

Again, Ilyas was silent, and Kausar allowed herself to hope she might have provided another possible lead—one that led the investigation as far away from Sana as possible.

"Your unnamed sources are worried about cars parked in a parking lot, and delivery vans making deliveries?" Ilyas said evenly.

"Yes," Kausar said firmly. "I definitely think the investigation should look into this tip."

Another deep sigh, but when Ilyas spoke again, his voice was kind. "Thank you for sharing, Kausar Aunty," he said. Then, hesitating, he added, "When I came over yesterday, as much as I enjoyed the *haleem* and the company, there was another reason."

Kausar's mind instantly flew to Sana slipping into the backyard, followed by Ilyas a few minutes later.

"I spoke with Sana last night. I shouldn't have, but it didn't feel right, not letting her know. Detective Drake is waiting on some final results from the lab, and . . . it doesn't look good. Especially considering Sana's criminal record."

Kausar's heart stopped at these words. *What criminal record?*

"If you haven't already, I think it's time to find Sana a criminal lawyer. That's all you can do now." The line went dead.

CHAPTER 17

A criminal record. *Did Kausar know her daughter at all? A tentative* knock on the door, and Sana peeked her head inside the guest bedroom.

"Where's Maleeha?" she asked, still dressed in her pajamas.

"I can't help you if you keep secrets from me, *beta*," Kausar said abruptly. Sana's eyebrows rose, and she stepped into the room.

"Did she tell you where she was going?" Sana persisted, but Kausar's mind was spinning from what Ilyas had just said. *Her daughter had a criminal record.* Was she guilty after all, and had Kausar been summoned to step into Sana's shoes while she dealt with the consequences of her actions?

Kausar met her daughter's questioning look. Dressed in sleep shorts and a tank top, her hair in a loose plait that fell down her back, Sana looked well rested, the worry lines around her mouth smoothed out, the faint blush of sleep still on her cheeks. Her eldest child looked no more guilty than a toddler.

"Do you have a criminal record?" Kausar asked abruptly, and Sana's face instantly shut down. She turned to go, hand on the doorknob, but Kausar was faster. She shut the door closed and turned to face her daughter.

"Maleeha said she was going to the library to study with friends," she said carefully. "The house is empty, your store is closed, and there is no death anniversary looming. Perhaps you can do me a favor and be honest for once."

Her words must have loosened something in Sana, because her daughter's eyes flashed mutinously, a familiar expression from when she was younger.

"I've told you what I think you can handle, Mom. I know how easily you get overwhelmed," Sana said deliberately. The words stung, a whiplash memory to the years she hadn't been there for her daughter and the rest of the family.

Except she was here now. Kausar squared her shoulders. "I want to help you, Sana," she tried again. "But you're keeping things from me. I spoke with Ilyas. He said he talked to you last night, that he warned you an arrest was on the horizon."

This got Sana's attention, and she shifted so her back was to the door, facing her mother squarely. Sana was a tall woman, and she had a good six inches on Kausar. "He had no right to tell you that," she said, a sliver of anger entering her voice. "And if the cops think the actions of a nineteen-year-old child nearly twenty years ago have anything to do with my behavior as a thirty-six-year-old mother of two, they're even more incompetent than I thought. What happened to innocent until proven guilty?"

Kausar's mind worked quickly. "Nineteen? Was this after Ali died?"

The look Sana shot her was withering. "I did something stupid. Dad bailed me out. You weren't in any condition to help, and we thought it best not to add to your worries. I was given community service. That detective must have dug it all up after I found Imran. Or maybe Ilyas told him," she said, her pitch rising at this last thought.

"What did you do?" Kausar asked, but Sana waved her words away.

"It's all ancient history and doesn't have anything to do with this."

"*Beta*, you should have told me—" Kausar started, but Sana interrupted, her tone harsh.

"Mom, *drop it.* I don't like to think about that time in my life. If you can't see that, maybe you should go back to hiding in North Bay." The words hung in the air between them for a moment, Sana's stare angry, Kausar's stricken.

"That's not fair," Kausar said. "I lost my son."

"*And I lost my brother*," Sana shot back. "I'm the one who found him, remember? When you sent me to look for him. I called 911. I tried to do CPR, even though there was so much blood . . ." Her breath hitched, voice breaking as she fought back tears. "*I* was the one who had to call you and tell you what happened."

Kausar's mind was dragged back to that night, seventeen years ago. Ali had gone out with friends, promising to return by *maghrib* for dinner. It was summer, and sunset fell late. It wasn't the first time her son had come home later than expected; he was high-spirited and popular, and for the first hour, she had assumed he'd lost track of time, or grabbed something to eat at a friend's house. But as the minutes ticked by, she couldn't shake her unease. When she called Hassan, who was on shift at the Emergency Department at Scarborough General Hospital, he had reassured her as usual: Ali was a teenager, he was out having fun with his friends and had lost track of time. There was nothing to worry about. By ten p.m., her worries had boiled over, and when Sana offered to drive around looking for him, Kausar was grateful. They knew his usual haunts—the school basketball court, the park behind the library, the nearest Tim Hortons. Kausar stayed home in case Ali returned.

Sana found Ali curled up by the side of the road, only a few streets from home. Her voice on the phone had been frantic, and the rest of the hellish night Kausar recalled in flashes: reaching for her shoes—reaching Ali's side—the flashing lights of the ambulance—the crowd of neighbors—Hassan's haggard, disbelieving face in the hospital. *A hit and run*, one of the paramedics called it, but she couldn't understand, couldn't make sense of the words. Someone had hurt her son, and then left him to die by the side of the road. Something broke inside Kausar that night and had never healed.

Looking at Sana now, Kausar felt the jagged pieces of her heart stabbing inside her chest. "How can you stand there and judge? I wouldn't wish what I went through on anyone."

"I'm not blaming you," Sana said. "I'm just reminding you that you're not the only one who lost someone. We lost Ali, and we lost you, too. And I never really got you back, did I?"

Kausar shook her head. "You're hiding things."

"Do you think I killed Imran?" Sana asked, her voice cold now. Kausar shook her head no. "Then be there for me. Just be my mom. That's all I want."

There was nothing more to say. Sana left the room, and a few minutes later, she heard the car backing out of the driveway, as Sana escaped the house. Kausar slumped back on the bed.

Just be my mom.

Sana was right, but she was wrong, too. Kausar knew she hadn't been the present, supportive mother her surviving children needed after Ali's death. Hassan was the one who had kept the family functional, or at least tried.

The truth was, Sana didn't trust her not to fall apart now, as she had after Ali's death. She didn't trust her mother to stay calm during a crisis and do what needed to be done, and she couldn't blame her. But she would prove her daughter wrong this time. And to do that, she needed to find out what really happened the night Imran was murdered. She wasn't going to fail her daughter again.

Kausar remembered the pictures she had taken a few days ago, when Lisa had let her into the two adjoining units, and started to flip through them. The first one took in Sana's entire store at a glance, and she tried to imagine what might have happened on that fateful night. What if Sana was at the store late, and Imran had entered for some reason? Perhaps Imran made it a habit to steal from his tenants. Caught in the act, he might have argued with Sana and grown aggressive. Fearing for her safety, Sana may have reached for the first weapon at hand, a dagger from the display window, and then—Kausar closed her eyes at what she saw next: blood, death, remorse. No, she couldn't believe it. If Sana had acted in self-defense, she would have admitted as much.

Also, the dagger was on the other side of the store from where Imran's body had fallen. Trekking to the display and back didn't make any sense, because it would have given Imran time to flee. Which meant that either the killer had held the dagger in their hand and lain in wait for Imran, or there had been a struggle right in front of the display window.

If that were the case, why hadn't anyone come forward as witness? Even if it was early morning, with bakeries and restaurants in the plaza, someone must have been there preparing for the day, not to mention the surrounding residential neighborhood.

So then why had her daughter insisted on the relatively complicated explanation of stumbling upon the body when she arrived early to the store and of the malfunctioning security camera? How was this related to what Kausar had discovered about the possible sale of the plaza, to Silver Star Holdings or Platinum Properties, and where did the money lead?

Speaking of money, what was her granddaughter up to? Then there was Sana and Hamza's alarming financial situation, plus their crumbling marriage, none of which seemed to have anything to do with Imran's death. Or did it?

Kausar's head was starting to hurt from all the loose ends she couldn't tie up. Her phone buzzed with a WhatsApp message from an unknown number.

Assalamu alaikum, Kausar, this is Fatima. I hope it is okay to message rather than call. If you are free, come over for chai today. I can pick you up if you need a ride.

Tea with an old friend was exactly what she needed.

F*atima lived in a bungalow set well back from the road, a* twenty-minute bus ride away from Sana's house and in an older part of the neighborhood. Houses here made up the original development in the Golden Crescent and were close to fifty years old, though her friend had moved in during the past decade. When Kausar used to live in Toronto, Fatima's family had rented a townhouse with too many stairs. Now Kausar admired the postage stamp garden made up of a lilac bush and neatly trimmed fern beside a bed of flowers just starting to bloom.

Her friend must have been watching from the bay window at the front of the house, because she opened the door before Kausar could ring the bell. Fatima was dressed in a simple cotton *salwar kameez*, hair in a tight bun and almost entirely gray.

"I would have picked you up," she scolded while simultaneously hugging her and taking her coat. "Siraj is at work, otherwise I would have sent him out for samosas. I hope you don't mind chai and biscuits instead, and I have some bhel puri—the prepackaged stuff is quite good these days."

Kausar was ushered into a large living and dining room and settled onto a plush, cream-colored couch. She looked around the comfortable space, adorned with framed Quranic verses and a large picture of the holy mosques in Mecca and Medina. Plants lined the bay window in large and small pots, vines climbing the wall, and her eyes lingered on one particularly lush specimen, its trunk thicker than a child's leg.

"My little hobby," Fatima said, twinkling at her friend. "Siraj claims they make him sneeze, but his children like to help water them when they come over. We all must have our little outside interests. Otherwise, there's not much to fill the day, is there?" Fatima had told Kausar she recently retired from her job, and since then had been at a loose end. "I loved working at the day care, but chasing after four-year-olds requires young knees," she joked.

It was easy to slip into conversation. Kausar couldn't believe she had allowed nearly two decades to pass without speaking to Fatima. They chatted about their children, about old friends and the changes to the neighborhood.

"I know people keep telling me things are worse in the neighborhood, but we had problems here even when our children were young," Kausar said.

Fatima agreed. "This is a good place to live, with the mosque nearby. Siraj thinks so, too, though his wife moved to the west end after their split. It has been hard." She sighed.

Kausar hummed in sympathy, but didn't want to pry. After what Fatima had confided in her at the memorial, she didn't want to poke a wound. "Marriage is difficult at the best of times," she said gamely.

"And my son did not have the best of marriages," Fatima said sadly. "He works all the time and has lost so much. He was telling me only yesterday that he doesn't know if he will ever be able to buy a house again."

Kausar recalled Brianna's concerns, that people in their middle- and working-class neighborhood would be unable to afford even a condominium in the Golden Crescent. "Are things that bad in the city?" she asked, though she knew the answer.

Fatima snorted. “If I had not bought this place years ago, I would be renting for the rest of my life, too, Kausar. I told Siraj he will always have a place with me, and that, inshallah, things will get better. It already is better. Siraj and his wife were miserable. We never had a choice to leave, if things went badly. The scandal would have brought shame to our families, plus how would we have survived?” Fatima added. “What you said at the party—about wondering if you had ever been happy—I’ve been thinking about it ever since.”

“Me, too,” Kausar admitted.

“Your Hassan and my Umar, they were men of their time. They could never imagine a world where their wives might want something more than they could provide,” Fatima said, again in that meditative voice.

“I blamed the age difference,” Kausar said. “Hassan was fifteen years older than me.”

“It was the time, not the years. Umar always wanted a wife who was content to be a mother and homemaker, and I wasn’t raised to want anything more,” Fatima said. “Even though in my heart, I did.”

“I did, too,” Kausar said. She reached for the chai, served in delicate floral china cups, and helped herself to a Peek Freans jelly biscuit.

“A woman’s ambition is always limited by her circumstances,” Fatima remarked. “And now that we have freedom, we’re too old to enjoy it!”

The women laughed, but Kausar felt a wave of unease. Was she truly too old? She was not yet sixty. May had encouraged her to make the most of her time. She had called this her “second act” and encouraged her to be selfish. But Fatima was like her; they shared a similar background and had lived with the same family expectations; they were part of the same community and social group. Fatima seemed to pick up on Kausar's thoughts, and she hurried to explain.

"We still have plenty of options. Especially you. Hassan left you comfortable, and your children are independent. Once Siraj gets back on his feet, you and I can really get into some mischief." Fatima's smile faded. "If you plan to stay in the city, that is."

Kausar didn't want to promise something she wasn't sure about herself. "I am here for now," she said.

"I'll take it. Now, tell me all you have been up to in Toronto. I know you've been helping Sana."

"Yes, she needed help with her children and with the cooking . . ." Kausar started, but Fatima only laughed.

"I know you have been doing a lot more than that! I saw you speak to Imran's family at the *janazah*, and you didn't miss a thing at Hassan's memorial. You forget, we are old friends. I remember years ago, you were the first to suspect Haneef had stolen his wife's gold jewelry, though he tried to blame it on the contractor who renovated their bathrooms."

"A lucky guess," Kausar said modestly.

"What about the time you told Maysoon her daughter was writing essays for her bully?"

"Sana helped with that."

"And our surprise when the bully turned out to be Haneef's daughter! Not a good family," Fatima said.

"Rotten to the core," Kausar agreed. "That last dinner party was quite awkward." The women laughed at the memory. "Hassan never liked when I made my little observations," Kausar said quietly. "I think he was embarrassed. He thought I was causing trouble."

"More fool, him," Fatima said, taking a decisive bite of a chocolate wafer. "You stopped more trouble than you caused."

"I don't think he understood. Perhaps part of him, the superstitious part, thought there was *jadoo* at work," Kausar said. "He never really understood that I simply noticed things and remembered."

"He was the doctor, you were just his wife," Fatima said, and Kausar nodded. "Umar was terrible with money. Not like you, with your investing. Oh, don't deny it, I always knew you were the one who held the purse strings in your family. What a terrible contradiction our husbands were."

"I'm worried about Sana and Hamza," Kausar said quietly.

Fatima reached forward to pat her friend's hand. "I saw them arguing at the memorial. When there's something to tell, they will let you know. Until then, you must do the most difficult thing. Stay out of it."

"Not something I'm good at," Kausar agreed. "What would you have done, if you hadn't married and had children so young?"

Fatima thought. "I would have started a business, like your Sana. I think I could have run a company. Perhaps even an empire." She laughed at the thought. "I rather like being in charge of things. What about you?"

Kausar thought for a moment, then shook her head. "It's hard to imagine. A teacher, maybe. Sometimes I think I would have made a good police officer. Overall, I don't think I would have changed a thing."

Fatima raised her chai in a mock toast. "A woman who has made her peace with the past is wise, indeed. Now, are you going to tell me about your investigation? Spare no details."

Kausar started to share what she had learned so far, when her phone buzzed with an incoming call from Maleeha.

"*Nani*, where are you?" her granddaughter asked. She sounded out of breath, as if she had been running. Instantly, Kausar's heart sped up.

"What's wrong? What has happened?" she asked. Beside her, Fatima looked alarmed.

"The police are here. They're arresting Mom for Imran's murder."

F*atima insisted on driving rather than having Kausar* take the bus back and fished the keys from the same black pouch Sana had. Kausar had learned that they were meant to prevent car thefts by blocking would-be thieves from disrupting key fobs inside the house.

The flashing lights in front of the house were the first indication that something terrible was unfolding, and the crowd of curious neighbors was the next. Kausar rushed from Fatima's car before it came to a complete stop. A few people tried to ask her what was going on, but she didn't stop to explain.

Inside, Detective Drake stood in the foyer, next to a crying Maleeha. Sana was silent, and Kausar stopped dead when she caught sight of the handcuffs on her wrists. Ilyas stood beside the detective. He didn't meet Kausar's eye. Fizza was huddled on the couch.

"Where's your father?" Kausar demanded of Maleeha, but she only shook her head.

"We tried calling Mr. Syed, but he didn't pick up," the detective said. The door opened and Fatima entered, taking in the scene in an instant. She went to Fizza and coaxed her into the kitchen.

Sana's gaze was fiery on the detective. "I didn't kill Imran. You're making a mistake."

He ignored her, only motioning to Ilyas with his chin. Ilyas turned to Sana and proceeded to read her rights in a robotic voice.

When he was done, Sana looked at her mother. "Call Jessica," she said, referring to her lawyer. The fine needle of panic in her daughter's voice nearly undid Kausar. She held her mother's gaze. "Keep the girls safe. Promise me."

Kausar nodded and pulled a sobbing Maleeha into her arms. Her body felt numb as she watched Sana led away. Her mouth felt like cotton, and when she blinked, she could see stars; she forced herself to breathe deeply, determined to stay standing, no matter how lightheaded she felt.

When the female constable pushed Sana outside roughly, Kausar's bleak gaze turned to Ilyas. Surely, he would put a stop to this. But his expression was carefully neutral, his "officer" mask firmly in place. He had done all he could already, when he warned Sana and Kausar about what was to come. From now on, they were on their own.

"Kausar, are you all right?" Fatima called from the kitchen, and she forced herself to reply, though every instinct demanded she *do* something: scream, throw a *chappal*, grab her daughter's arm and refuse to let go. Instead, she held Maleeha close to her body and reminded herself to breathe, reminded herself that this was not the same as what had happened to Ali. Her daughter was alive. Sana would be fine. Kausar would sort it all out. All she had to do right now was breathe.

The door closed behind them, and then there was silence.

CHAPTER 18

Fatima left soon after, with a promise to send Siraj with some food for the family. Kausar was too busy trying to keep Maleeha calm to walk her friend to the door, but to her surprise, Fizza stepped up. She could hear them conferring in the foyer, even as she rocked Maleeha's small form in her arms on the couch.

"Shhhh," Kausar soothed, straining to hear what Fatima had to say to her younger granddaughter. "Your mother and I knew this was coming. She has a good lawyer, and your father will be here soon."

Maleeha looked up at her grandmother, her face tear stained and eyes wild. "It's too late. No one can help her now."

Fizza joined them on the couch, silent and pale. "What happens next?" she asked, and Kausar knew from the matter-of-fact tone that her ten-year-old granddaughter had just left her childhood behind. This would be a delineating moment in Fizza's life, and Kausar's heart ached for her.

She made herself sound reassuring. The girls needed to feel there was a plan, even as the worst unfolded. "Now I call your mother's lawyer. Fizza *beta*, why don't you give your father another ring, to make sure he knows what's going on?"

"He won't come home," Maleeha said darkly. The tears had

stopped, but her voice was low and raw. "He's had one foot out the door for months."

Kausar reached out and stroked Maleeha's hair, which had come loose from her elastic. "No matter what's happened between your parents, your father will hurry home to make sure you are all right."

She wasn't sure she entirely believed her own words, but she wanted to comfort the girls. She stole away to the kitchen to call Jessica Kaur, the number on the card Sana had pinned to the corkboard by the fridge. The lawyer answered on the second ring. After-hours calls were probably a normal occurrence for criminal attorneys.

Quickly, Kausar explained what happened. Jessica didn't interrupt, listening intently.

"That happened more quickly than I thought," the lawyer said. "I'll head over to the station now, to see what they have on Sana that led to the arrest. Last time we spoke, they were waiting on more evidence." Jessica hesitated. "I'm afraid your daughter is looking at serious jail time if found guilty. Even just being arrested will have a significant toll on her reputation and mental health. I hope your family is prepared. Is Hamza around?"

"We are trying to locate him," Kausar said.

"A doting husband will help optics. Things often boil down to appearances, once things get underway."

"I'm not sure how doting he will be," Kausar said.

Another pause. "I understand. However, appearances are all we are interested in at this point. What the jury chooses to believe is key. We want the best possible outcome for Sana. I'll do everything I can to help her achieve that, Aunty."

The lawyer's words made Kausar pause: *Appearances are all we are interested in*. The words nudged at something in her subconscious, and she struggled to place it in the shifting puzzle that was Imran's death.

"When I locate Hamza, I will impress upon him what is expected," Kausar promised.

Jessica thanked her and hung up, promising to call back when she had an update. When Kausar returned to the sitting room, Fizza gave her a thumbs-down: Hamza still wasn't picking up his phone. Maleeha had disappeared upstairs, perhaps to throw cold water on her face. Knowing her teenage granddaughter, she was likely embarrassed at her breakdown, especially when contrasted with her little sister's calm.

"What do we do now?" Fizza asked, coming to cuddle beside her grandmother.

"Now I make you dinner, and we wait for news."

True to her word, Fatima sent a meal with Siraj a few hours later, but Kausar had already made grilled cheese sandwiches and cut up carrots and broccoli as a side, which the girls ate silently at the table. When Siraj knocked on the door with containers full of chicken curry, rice, and a simple *halwa* dessert, she accepted gratefully.

The tall man lingered in the doorway. "I'm sorry I took so long. I had to finish up my deliveries for Lisa first. Someone on this street has a jerk chicken addiction," he said in an attempt at humor. "Any news?"

Kausar shook her head. Behind her, she heard footsteps, and Maleeha peered over her shoulder. Siraj caught her granddaughter's eye and mustered a tentative smile.

"Maleeha is getting so tall," Siraj said to Kausar. "My eldest just turned nine. Fizza is ten years old now, right? I've seen her in the neighborhood sometimes."

"It goes by so fast," Kausar agreed.

When she turned back, Maleeha had disappeared. She returned to Siraj, wondering if he wanted to be invited in. She didn't feel like entertaining. This was how it would be, Kausar realized. Curious neighbors and friends, eager to hear the story of Sana's arrest, would knock on their door, call them, send messages, stop them on the street. She remembered how it had been in the weeks and months after Ali died. The crawling sensation of panic and despair she had felt watching Sana being led away climbed up her throat now, but she pushed it down. Sana and her granddaughters needed her now.

"Where's Hamza? He should be here," Siraj said, radiating disapproval.

"He will be back soon," Kausar said, hoping the words would somehow hurry her errant son-in-law along.

Siraj shifted his weight. "I'm very sorry, Aunty. Your family has been through so much. Please let us know if we can help. And don't worry, my mother and I won't tell anyone what happened here tonight."

Their silence wouldn't be much help; half the street had watched Sana being led away in handcuffs.

Jessica called soon after, her tone grim. "They said the results came back from the crime scene, and they had permission to act right away," she started, without saying hello first. "Detective Drake even argued Sana was a flight risk. Something about having a brother in the UK, which is ridiculous. There's no way she would leave her children behind." She said the rest quickly, all in one breath. "Essentially, Sana's prints were all over the murder weapon, which makes sense since the dagger was part of Sana's window display. They also found her DNA on Imran's body, and his on the clothes she wore. There are indications of a struggle."

It was worse than she had imagined. "Did Imran attack Sana?" she asked.

Jessica was quick to reassure Kausar. "Nothing like that, no. I'm going to work on getting her released. You'll have to act as her surety, Aunty. Sana said Hamza wouldn't be able to." Jessica's voice was carefully neutral. "Have you located him?"

"Not yet," Kausar said.

"When you do, tell him I need him to pick her up from the station, likely tomorrow afternoon. They want to keep her overnight, despite my protests. That's common in first-degree murder charges."

Murder in the first degree, Kausar thought dully. Murder committed with purpose and forethought, with an automatic sentence of twenty-five years and no chance of parole, according to her internet searches. Sana would be older than Kausar was right now when she was released, if she were found guilty. That couldn't happen.

"I'll be at the precinct first thing tomorrow," Jessica continued. "But we have to start building the case now. Sana is a mother of two young girls, a hard-working business owner, and happily married. She's not a flight risk and has too much to lose to have committed this crime. That's the angle I'm going to take, and I need everyone on board."

"Of course," Kausar said. A thought occurred to her. "You should know Sana has a criminal record. From when she was nineteen, I think. Something happened after her brother died, but I don't know what it was. My husband . . . my late husband, Hassan, handled it all. I wasn't there for her—" Kausar's voice broke, and Jessica hurried to reassure her.

"You're doing exactly the right thing, Kausar Aunty," the lawyer said. "Now you will have to let me do my job. I promise to take care of Sana as if she were my own sister."

"Thank you," Kausar whispered. She would have to remember to thank Nasir for the reference. So far, Jessica had been calm, competent, and assured, and it was helping to quell Kausar's own incessant worries.

Jessica hesitated. "I'll need payment, for tonight and for the work ahead," she said, matter-of-fact. "I'm afraid criminal defenses aren't cheap."

Kausar promised to arrange a money transfer, and after she hung up, immediately called Hamza. He finally picked up on the fifth ring. It was past seven o'clock now, and he sounded aggrieved.

"Where are you?" Kausar demanded.

"I had a meeting on the other side of town, and it ran late," Hamza said. "My phone died and I've been charging it. What's up?"

"Your daughters have been calling and texting repeatedly," Kausar said coldly. "Sana was arrested and charged with Imran's murder a few hours ago."

Hamza cursed. She heard the rustle of fabric and his low voice, talking to someone. The answering voice sounded distinctly female.

"Is someone with you?" Kausar asked. "Where are you now, Hamza?"

"Still at work. I'll be there as soon as I can," he promised. "Traffic is murder on the 401."

They both paused at his poor choice of wording. "Get here as soon as you can," Kausar said. "Your daughters need you."

It was past ten by the time Hamza finally came home, and both girls had gone to bed. When he unlocked the door to find Kausar seated on the couch, he didn't offer any explanation for the delay, only asking what there was to eat.

"Nothing," Kausar said, too angry with him to offer Fatima's freshly cooked food.

He was in a conciliatory mood, and when Kausar explained Jessica's plan and the role he was to play, he was eager to acquiesce. "Of course, whatever Sana needs."

"She needed you to be home tonight," Kausar said, furious. "Your daughters needed you to pick up their phone calls."

"I've been working on a big pitch. Sana knows I keep long

hours. That was part of our deal. She handles things at home, and I pay the bills. Just like you and Dad." Hamza's mask was slipping, his belligerence showing, but Kausar was done playing this particular game.

"Hassan never abandoned me or our children when we needed him. He never disappeared with no explanation. He certainly never fought with me during a moment of mourning, as you did during his memorial," Kausar snapped. She was on her feet now, hands clenched at her sides, not caring if her voice carried upstairs in the open-concept house.

"That's not fair," Hamza said. His surprise at her tone was evident, and his wounded expression made her hands itch. Kausar was not a confrontational person. She had been raised to be polite, soft-spoken, to always consider the emotional and physical needs of others before herself. But the growing anger she felt now for Hamza was about to turn into an inferno, and she struggled to rein in her emotions.

Kausar took one step closer to him. "What do you know about fairness?" she hissed. "Your *friend* Ahmed told me all about what you have been up to with my daughter's inheritance."

Hamza's eyes widened in panic, and his excuses stepped on one another in their rush to emerge. "Th-that's not . . . w-what do you mean . . . I didn't do anything—" he stuttered.

With some effort, she calmed herself down and took a step back. Hamza might be useless, but Jessica had stressed that they needed him now, even if only for show.

"Is it all gone?" she demanded. She really didn't want to do this, not now. They were both tired and stressed. Or perhaps they could speak openly because exhaustion had broken down the usual constraints of politeness. In the past, her reticence and natural tendency not to interfere in her daughter's business would have kept her mouth shut. Right now, she wanted Hamza to realize what he was about to lose, and the dangers his poor decision-making had put his family in, unable to support themselves financially in a time of crisis.

"Is all your money gone?" she asked again.

He stared at her, speechless. Then, he slowly nodded. Kausar's heart sank. "What about Sana's inheritance?" she asked.

Hamza couldn't meet her gaze, shame writ large across his blandly handsome features, and just like that, the fight went out of her.

"You haven't been honest since I arrived," she said dully. "You even lied about where you were the night Imran was murdered. You said you flew home from Romania, through the UK."

"I did. I was out of town on business," he said, irritation creeping into his voice.

She was so tired of his dissembling. "Did you know luggage tags have the date on them? The dates on your luggage tags are from months ago. You weren't flying home the day Imran died. I suspect you hadn't even left the city."

Hamza exhaled slowly. "Sana isn't innocent, either, okay? I'm not the one who was just arrested for murder, *Mom*. You're so desperate to ride to the rescue now. Where have you been for the last decade and a half?" He continued, his voice low and mean. The mask was fully off now, and it chilled Kausar to see what lay beneath. Something twisted and rotten looked out of Hamza's dark eyes. "You can't fix something this broken, and I think it's pathetic for you of all people to even try."

"I have made mistakes in my life, but never because I was heartless," Kausar said with dignity. "If anything, my mistakes were because I felt too much. *You* only ever cared about yourself. You've put your family at risk, again and again, through your selfish and irresponsible behavior. First, through your financial mistakes, and now through a complete disregard for your wife and children. Yet you refuse to accept any responsibility, instead heaping blame on me. Tell me, Hamza, how does it feel to burn your life to the ground?"

Kausar sat for a long time in the dark after her son-in-law stormed upstairs. Strangely, she felt better after their confrontation; it felt like a sudden summer storm after days of unrelenting heat.

Mindful of Sana's parting request, Kausar looked in on both the girls when she went upstairs. Fizza was fast asleep, sprawled in her twin bed, blankets kicked to the side. Kausar pulled the sheets up, smoothing a gentle hand over her granddaughter's baby soft brow. When she got to Maleeha's room, the bed was empty. Trying not to panic, Kausar texted her.

Where are you?

Maleeha instantly answered. *Couldn't sleep. I'm in the backyard.*

Kausar moved to the window in Maleeha's room. At the very edge of the backyard, near the fence, she glimpsed a familiar form hunched over her cell phone. She hadn't even heard Maleeha leave the house. Had her granddaughter overheard her argument with Hamza? She hoped not. She thought of the money she had found in Maleeha's room; she would have to confront her granddaughter soon. She texted, *Ten minutes and then back inside, please.*

It wasn't until Kausar had finished praying *isha*, the late-night prayer, and was sitting in the *jalsa* position with her legs tucked underneath, that her phone vibrated with another message, this one from an unknown number. When she read it, her clear-eyed resolve vanished, and she felt the cold fingers of fear fasten once more around her neck and begin to squeeze.

I hope you've learned your lesson. See what happens when you stir up trouble, Kausar Khan? Stop digging. Unless you want your daughter to join Ali.

CHAPTER 19

"You need to show that message to Ilyas." May's voice was firm over the phone. Kausar had called early the next day after a sleepless night, and her friend had picked up on the first ring. "You have many talents, my friend, but navigating technology is not one of them."

Kausar had transcribed the message into her notebook sometime during the night, and the hateful words stared back in her spiky handwriting: *Stop digging. Unless you want your daughter to join Ali.* Whoever had sent this message knew that her daughter had been arrested, knew that Kausar was looking into Imran's murder, and also knew about Ali's death. The thought of someone keeping tabs on them chilled her. She thought of how many people had witnessed her talking to Imran's family at the *janazah*, and the shopkeepers in the plaza. Their community loved nothing more than a developing story, and she had put herself in the center of Imran's murder investigation at every turn. Had she thought this was a game? If so, she was playing checkers, while the real killer had just revealed they were playing chess.

"Have you managed to make any enemies in the week since you've been down there?" May asked, only half serious.

Kausar thought about Patrick Kim, Ahmed Malik, and Imran's family, not to mention Hamza. "Maybe a few," she admitted.

"You're Jack Reacher in a *dupatta*," May said. "I've got to get going, I have a play date with Lexi and her friends," she said, referring to her three-year-old granddaughter. "Call me with any updates. Better yet, text. I'll be too busy making sure Lexi stays out of my makeup drawer."

With a promise to keep her friend posted, Kausar hung up and stared at the message once more. Hamza had taken Fizza to school that morning, and he would hopefully stay out of Kausar's way all day. Maleeha had left early for school, before anyone else was up. Which meant Kausar had the house to herself.

Heeding her friend's advice, she texted Ilyas about the message, copying the text from her phone. She also shared the phone number it had been sent from, but after waiting a few minutes, there was no reply. He was probably busy, hopefully following the other leads she had suggested the last time she called.

In the meantime, perhaps it was time to have another conversation with Imran's family.

She texted Fatima: *Imran's family will be taking condolence calls.* Visiting the bereaved family and giving *poorsa* would stir up no suspicions, considering her friend was an acquaintance. Tagging along with Fatima wouldn't raise any eyebrows, either.

Her friend replied immediately. *What time do you want me to pick you up?*

Jessica called while Kausar was changing for the poorsa. The lawyer's voice was raw, as if she hadn't slept much the night before. "They're holding her another night. Arraignment is set for tomorrow morning."

"Can they do that? Should I take her some food?" Kausar said.

"A fresh meal is the least of her worries, Mrs. Khan," Jessica said grimly. "I was present while they questioned her last night. They have a strong case."

"Do you believe she is innocent?" Kausar asked, wondering if she should share the text message with Jessica, whether it would help.

The lawyer answered carefully. "I'm confident we can mount a successful defense."

She hadn't answered the question, Kausar noted, and decided to keep the text to herself for now, at least until after she'd visited Imran's family. However, she did relate her plan to the lawyer, who hummed as she thought.

"Attending a funeral at the mosque is one thing," Jessica said. "Going to the family's home might come across as harassment. You said your friend Fatima knows them? Be careful. From now on, your actions could prejudice the judge against your daughter's defense. That has to be the focus now. Whatever happened before Sana was charged can be explained away, but now that the wheels of the justice system are in motion, there's no way to stop it."

"Until we find the real killer," Kausar said.

This time, Jessica's hesitation was unmistakable. "Of course, Mrs. Khan. Until then."

F*atima picked her up in her blue Acura sedan and didn't* ask any questions other than if Sana was okay. Kausar felt as if she owed her an explanation, but when she started to speak, Fatima held up a hand.

"When Siraj's life fell apart last year, everyone wanted to hear the story. People he had not spoken with since his *nikah* ten years prior called him up. So many of my friends tried to corner me, asking about the divorce and custody battle. Our people love to talk. Sometimes, that can be a good thing. But I think first you need to give yourself time to think, yes? Not simply to react, but also to plan."

"Sana is in a lot of trouble," Kausar said quietly.

"How can I help?" Fatima asked without hesitation, and in that moment, Kausar felt a floodgate of relief and gratitude for her old friend, who innately understood what she needed.

"I need to speak with Imran's family, especially his wife and daughter. Perhaps you think this is a terrible intrusion on their grief—"

"You want to find out who really murdered Imran. I think that might make you the most important visitor of all," Fatima said. "Though I wonder if you need a disguise. And perhaps a cover story? I brought a niqab," she said, referring to the face veil. "We could say you are my cousin, visiting from the United States."

"If they ask, I will tell them I used to live in the community, and that I am back to visit old friends," Kausar answered. Fatima agreed to the plan, and they pulled into a congested side street packed with cars.

Giving *poorsa* was a communal act. Instead of a formal reception, family and friends visited the grieving family after the funeral, to offer their condolences, often bringing food. Kausar held a container filled with some of the fragrant chicken curry Siraj had dropped off last night and a package of *roghni* naan. Her friend found a parking spot on the street half a dozen houses away.

"If you need me to cause a distraction, scratch your nose," Fatima joked. "I will start telling everyone all about my ex-daughter-in-law."

"You're a good friend," Kausar said.

Imran's home was a large two-story building with a double-car garage, set on a pleasant, tree-lined street, a half-hour drive east of the Golden Crescent neighborhood. The door opened to a large living space, and another to a spacious kitchen. Kausar noted with a sinking stomach that people were everywhere—milling about in the living room and in the hallway that led to the bedrooms, and she spotted half a dozen women in the kitchen, putting food away, washing up, and murmuring in soft voices.

She should have anticipated a crowd; it had only been three days since Imran's *janazah*, and people visited soon after the funeral. She exchanged a meaningful glance with Fatima as they entered, passing the open-concept kitchen, where a large pot of chai simmered on the stove. Imran's daughter, Anjum, dressed in a simple cotton navy-blue *salwar kameez* with her long hair pulled back in a demure braid, stirred the milky tea to make sure it didn't boil over. Her mother, Parveen, sat in the airy living room, dabbing at her eyes, surrounded by a group of middle-aged and elderly women seated on the too-formal furniture. Imran's widow was a tiny mouse of a woman, dressed today in a plain white and black *salwar kameez*, black hijab pulled low over her forehead. She had lines of fatigue around her eyes, and her mouth was a thin line.

Once more, Kausar felt the awkwardness of intruding on a mourning family. Then she thought of her daughter sitting in a jail cell and the threatening text on her phone, and she took her place among the circle of women, Fatima beside her.

"He was a good man," a woman sitting on her left said, eyes red rimmed. "Remember how he threatened to call the police on the children at the masjid playing basketball? He was tough, but fair."

More stories about Imran's life were shared, and then Fatima leaned forward. "What will happen to the plaza now?" she asked.

"My brother wants to sell," Anjum said, entering the sitting room holding a tray arranged with a dozen small mugs of steaming chai and freshly fried samosas. She put the tray down on the coffee table and methodically began passing out the food.

"My husband knew how to run the plaza, but we don't," Parveen said. Her voice was tremulous. Instantly, Kausar's heart went out to her. She remembered the first few days after Hassan died, how alone and isolated she had felt, even surrounded by her children and friends.

"I have an MBA, and I worked at the plaza for years when I was younger. We don't have to sell," Anjum said quietly.

"Mubeen is in charge. Leave it to him. He is the man of the family now," Parveen said sharply to her daughter.

Kausar shifted, wrestling between the urge to say something and her mission to observe the family. From a business perspective, it made no sense to sell a real estate asset simply out of fear, especially in Toronto's red-hot market. On the other hand, perhaps Parveen didn't feel her children were up to the task of running the business, despite what Anjum thought. When Anjum rose with the empty tray and disappeared into the kitchen, Kausar followed.

"I'm so sorry for your loss," Kausar said to the younger woman, who had started to load the dishwasher. "*Inna lillahi wa inna ilayhi raji'un,*" she offered, meaning *To God we belong, and to Him we return.*

"I remember you. You were at the *janazah*, right?" When Kausar nodded, Anjum added, "You were asking questions at Patrick Kim's investor event as well." She looked down, embarrassed. "Yes, I was there. I didn't want my mom to know. If I didn't know better, I would suspect you were following me."

The tinkling laugh that accompanied this statement made Kausar flush, but Anjum couldn't hide the watchful expression in her dark eyes, or the knowing tweak to her mouth; she was clearly a woman who noticed everything and knew how to keep her own counsel.

"I suppose I can't help asking questions," Kausar said, sidestepping Anjum's accusation. "If you will forgive the observation, as someone who has invested in real estate for years, I'm not sure your brother's plan to sell the plaza is the correct one."

Anjum looked her over carefully, and Kausar held her breath. After a moment, she shrugged. "Mubeen doesn't want anything to do with the plaza. And maybe he's right, it feels tainted now. It's been a very difficult time for my family."

She wasn't like her mother, Kausar realized, who wore her grief plainly. Anjum's grief, in contrast, was lit with a restless energy. After she loaded the dishwasher, no doubt she would start on dinner, or perhaps run a half-marathon. Anything to stay active and keep the sadness at bay. Kausar wanted to tell her it wouldn't work—the harder one ran, the harder the ghosts chased, until you collapsed in an exhausted heap.

"At least they caught the person responsible," Anjum continued. "I knew her. We went to the same mosque. I even taught one of her kids in Sunday school when I used to volunteer. I can't believe Sana would do such a thing."

"Perhaps she didn't," Kausar couldn't help answer, and Anjum's eyes narrowed.

"Detective Drake has been keeping us updated. Believe me, it couldn't be more clear that she is guilty."

Kausar's heart twinged at the matter-of-fact way Anjum delivered this verdict. If she didn't clear Sana's name entirely, she realized, this was how her daughter would be seen in the community for the rest of her life. It would be like the cloud that had hung over her family after Ali died. The questions and curious stares would follow the family everywhere. Those same whispers and stares had chased Kausar to North Bay.

"I hope your family finds a way through this difficult time," Kausar said quietly.

"Thank you. It was kind of you to come, Aunty," she said meaningfully. *And now it is time for you to go*, Kausar filled in the blanks.

"Where's the food?" a voice called from behind them, and Mubeen strolled into the kitchen, fingers poking inside the foil-wrapped trays stacked on the counter. Fatima's chicken curry was one of many dishes the guests and fellow mourners had brought.

"Nice of you to show up," Anjum said to her brother.

Mubeen shrugged. "It's not like I know how to make chai and serve cookies to boring old aunties. That's your job." He noticed Kausar. "No offense, Aunty."

"Plenty taken," she said tartly. She had no patience for entitled, lazy men today. Behind him, Anjum smiled slightly. "Your mother was just sharing that you plan to sell the plaza," Kausar added.

Mubeen popped a pakora in his mouth. "If you're interested in buying, you'll have to get in line," he joked. "I've already got two offers breathing down my neck." He turned to his sister. "Ahmed came back with an interesting idea. Instead of selling the place outright, we could take out a reverse mortgage on the plaza and invest the money we get with his company. We'd make a ton of returns, plus we get to keep the plaza and you could run it or whatever."

"Let's not talk about that here," Anjum said, with a significant glance at Kausar. "Dad just passed away. It's not right."

But Mubeen was just warming to his topic, and he ignored his sister's words. "Or I was thinking, we could pit Patrick and Ahmed against each other, try to get some more money. I know Dad hated Kim, but he was a racist—"

"I said *not now*, Mubeen," Anjum hissed.

Her brother shrugged. "Whatever. Mom is leaving it to me, anyway, so your opinion doesn't really matter." He wandered out of the kitchen before Anjum could respond.

The silence between the two women stretched. "Things are complicated after a death in the family," Kausar finally said. "I lost my husband only last year. We're all still recovering."

Anjum nodded, clearly embarrassed. This time, Kausar took the hint and left the kitchen.

Outside the sitting room, she could see Parveen surrounded by mourners. It would be useless to return right now when there were so many people who wanted to talk to her. Perhaps if she waited a few minutes, some of the guests would leave. Stalling for time, she tried the powder room, but it was occupied. Another door led to the basement, and acting on impulse, she ducked down the stairs. On the landing, a hand pulled her to the side, and she yelped in fright.

Fatima put a finger to her lips, eyes dancing with mischief. "Took you long enough," she said.

"What are you doing down here?" Kausar demanded.

"I gave you the signal!" Fatima said. "When we were in the living room. I raised my eyebrow."

Kausar shook her head. "You did no such thing. What is that a signal for, anyway?"

Fatima swept her arm wide. "Imran's home office is down here. Hurry, we don't have much time." She pulled Kausar towards a small room in the far corner.

"We should go back upstairs, before we're missed," Kausar said. She didn't like this.

"When else will we get this opportunity?" Fatima argued. "It's not like you can get access to Imran's office in the plaza," she said. Kausar was about to tell her about her visit to both Sana's store and Imran's space, when Fatima opened the door and they gaped at the mess before them.

Imran's home office looked as if it had been ransacked by a demented toddler. Boxes were everywhere and papers were piled on every surface. Two tall filing cabinets were stuffed to bursting, drawers nudged open. The two women looked at each other in dismay.

"This would take weeks to go through," Kausar said.

"We only have fifteen minutes or so. You take the filing cabinet and I'll look through the desk. Take pictures of anything that looks interesting," Fatima ordered.

Unsure of what constituted "interesting," Kausar obeyed. The women worked in silence. The filing cabinets were full of old letters, bank statements, and flyers, all thrown haphazardly into file folders. Tax documents were stuffed beside old bills and collection notices. Inside the top drawer of the second filing cabinet, she found a well-thumbed calendar diary for this year. Flipping through it, she saw someone had scrawled what looked like a list of initials and numbers: A.P., T.D., N.H., H.S., M.A.-B. Comparing the handwriting with the others in the file cabinet, she could tell it belonged to Imran. Had he even known where it was in this disorganized mess? Her eye caught a familiar name for two months prior: *Nasir H.*, followed by a time: 11:15.

She wasn't sure what this notebook was, but it was the first thing that seemed promising. She only wished she had brought a bag with her so she could smuggle it out of the house. She started taking photos, flipping pages quickly. At the desk, Fatima pulled out what looked like a ledger and was studying the contents.

"Any luck?" Kausar whispered.

"His account ledger is full of doodles and random reminders. Imran had a thing for drawing women's body parts," Fatima said, wrinkling her nose and closing the ledger. "No sense of proportion."

Kausar smothered a laugh, and Fatima joined her, peering over her shoulder at the calendar diary, with its random initials and numbers.

"Imran should have hired an accountant and an assistant to clean this all up for him," Kausar said. She finished taking pictures and replaced the notebook in the file cabinet.

"I'm sure he convinced himself he had everything under control. Men!" Then Fatima froze, an ear cocked towards the door. "I hear footsteps. Quick, the closet!"

The women scrambled into the small closet, pushing banker's boxes to the side and wiggling between loose papers and file folders, before sliding the door closed. Fatima peered out from a gap between the sliding door and motioned for Kausar to be still. They waited in the dark for one minute, two minutes, three.

"I don't hear anything," Kausar said. Her leg was starting to cramp. She flexed her toe, accidentally tipping over a pile of papers. A moment later, the closet door jerked open, revealing Anjum's deeply unimpressed face.

"We were looking for the bathroom?" Kausar tried weakly.

CHAPTER 20

Outside Imran's home, Fatima was bent over, laughing. "Did you see Anjum's face?" she wheezed. "She was so mad!"

Beside her on the driveway, Kausar felt an unaccustomed snap of temper. This was all Fatima's fault, and she didn't find the situation funny at all.

Anjum had not wasted any time kicking them out. Not only did the bathroom excuse not fool her for a second, but her fury at finding the two women snooping through her late father's papers led to a full-on rant while she escorted them out. The only silver lining was that Anjum had not yet realized who Kausar was, or her relationship to Sana. Instead, she had assumed they were both nosy aunties looking for gossip.

"Fatima Aunty, Kausar Aunty, I am shocked at this behavior," she lectured as they meekly followed her past the guests in the sitting room. "To show up at a grieving family's home and behave in this fashion is shameful. Were you looking for something to share on your WhatsApp groups?" Her eyes flashed as she opened the door.

"What is happening, Anjum?" Parveen's voice floated towards them from the sitting room.

"These aunties were just leaving, *Ammi*," Anjum said tightly, glaring at Fatima and Kausar in turn.

"I am sorry, *beta*," Kausar said again, contrite.

"Don't call me that," Anjum said sharply. "I'm not your child. I'm a grown woman, and if I see either of you near my house again, I'll call the cops. My family is dealing with enough without our business being shared online!"

Then she had slammed the door in their faces.

Beside her, Fatima was still laughing, wiping tears from her face. Kausar's temper boiled over.

"It's NOT funny!" she yelled, and Fatima's laughter halted abruptly. "Is this a game to you? My daughter is in jail, and you laugh! I said it wasn't a good idea to go inside Imran's office. I wanted to talk to Parveen, Anjum, and Mubeen. Thanks to you, none of them will talk to me ever again. I asked you here to help, and instead you've only made things worse!"

Kausar stormed down the driveway, ignoring her friend's pleas to stop, to come back. She made her way to a bus stop and refused to look at Fatima, even when she brought her car around and begged for her to get in, to at least drive her home. When the bus arrived ten minutes later, Kausar grimly boarded. She maintained her composure until she arrived back at Sana's street and spotted Nasir waiting on the front porch. At the sight of his worried expression, she finally broke down, tears of anger mixing with a profound sense of failure. She had messed everything up, again.

"A*s you know, Kausar, I have absolute faith that you can* do anything you want. But trying to solve Imran's murder inside of a week might have been too ambitious, even for you."

They had wound up sitting side by side on the uncomfortable stone steps outside Sana's house. To his credit, Nasir let her cry, only offering a few crumpled-up tissues and a half-empty water bottle from his car, which she had waved away, and he hadn't said a word until her tears had run dry. He'd even listened to her long-winded explanation—which felt more like a confession—of everything she had been up to since she had returned to Toronto. Truly, Nasir was a prince among men.

"I can see why you would be upset with Fatima, but I think she genuinely meant to help," he said now. Catching her frown, he rushed to add, "I take that back. She was entirely in the wrong and you would be well within your rights to throw eggs at her house."

Kausar laughed through her tears. "Would you help?" she asked, drying her eyes with the tissue he had pressed into her hands. She was starting to feel embarrassed about her breakdown, though he had accepted her tears as readily as he did her laughter: with no judgment, only understanding.

"I will drive the getaway car," he promised. "My aim is not so good. I was thrown off the mosque softball team, as I'm sure you've heard."

"It was the talk of the neighborhood," she joked, playing along.

"I threatened to sue them, naturally," Nasir continued.

"Of course," Kausar agreed.

"In the end we settled for a box of *mithai* and a promise that I would never play organized sports for the mosque again."

"Was the *mithai* any good?" she asked.

"Terrible, actually. Just like my softball skills."

Kausar chuckled, and they settled into a comfortable silence. She had not had much opportunity to observe Sana's street. Her daughter had picked a good location—the street was a quiet one, but even in the early afternoon, there was a steady hum of activity, with cars driving past, children on bikes and scooters, a few neighbors doing yard work or sitting on porch swings. The drama of the past few days had probably been the most exciting thing to happen here in a long time.

Nasir stood, groaning softly. "I'm getting too old to sit on stone steps for long." He held out a hand to help her up, and Kausar took it. His hand was warm and dry in hers, and she was grateful for the help; she was certain her knees were in much worse shape than his, but she hadn't been thinking clearly when she sat down.

"Thank you," Kausar said. Her hand lingered in his for a second, and when their eyes met, his gaze was steady and warm on hers. She let go first, flustered. "I didn't even ask why you came," she said, not sure where to look.

Nasir dusted himself off. "I wanted to check on you. I heard about Sana's arrest, and I was worried. No one was answering the door, and I was about to call when you came marching up, looking like thunder. I was worried there had been another murder."

Kausar shuddered. "Do not even joke about that. One murder is sufficient, I assure you." She fished in her bag for her keys, before asking if he wanted to come inside. Nasir hesitated.

"I should get going. Now that I know you're okay, I'm much relieved," he said with a smile.

"Let me make you some chai, at least," Kausar offered, and he agreed, following her inside.

"I'm worried about this threatening text you received," Nasir said as he sat down on a stool by the kitchen island.

"I've notified Ilyas, but he has yet to respond," Kausar reassured him, filling a pot with water for tea.

"The more you look into this matter, the more complicated it becomes. I suppose reminding you to be careful would not do much good?"

"You tried once before," she reminded him, and he looked abashed.

"I assume Hassan *bhai* would not have approved of you involving yourself in these inquiries, even though they concern

Sana," Nasir guessed, and Kausar nodded. He sighed. "How can I help?" he asked simply, and Kausar felt a rush of affection for her friend. What an unexpected gift he was proving to be, alongside Fatima. Despite her earlier outburst, she knew she would make up with her friend. Eventually.

Reaching for her phone, she flipped through the pictures until she found the one from Imran's calendar diary. She passed him the phone.

"I came across this in Imran's home office. Don't look at me like that. It was Fatima's idea to go rummaging around," Kausar said when Nasir raised an eyebrow. She pointed to his name, magnifying the picture. "Did you meet with Imran two months ago, at eleven fifteen?"

Truthfully, she had been almost afraid to ask. If Nasir were somehow involved in Imran's business, she wasn't sure where her inquiries would lead next, but his baffled expression was reassuring. "I know Imran, of course, from the mosque and the neighborhood. But I'm positive we never had a meeting." He opened the calendar app on his phone and scrolled. "I met with someone named Ahmed Malik on that day, not Imran."

Kausar sat still, thinking. Behind her, the water started to boil on the stove, and Nasir opened cupboards until he located tea bags. Dropping three into the water, he added a few whole cardamom pods before locating the milk in the fridge and adding it to the brew and lowering the temperature. Kausar watched all this in silence. She couldn't remember the last time someone had made her a cup of tea.

"What did Ahmed want?" she asked, once he returned to his seat on the kitchen island. The tea simmered behind them.

Nasir grimaced. "He requested I help him close on a few real estate deals. I declined."

"Why?" she pressed, and Nasir hesitated.

"I told you before that sometimes I get a feeling about people.

The same is true for business deals. There was something off about what Ahmed wanted. To be honest, I probably should have probed more based on my hunch, but I have enough work to keep me busy without looking into every shady deal I'm offered."

Kausar absorbed this. "Was there something you were worried about in particular?" she asked, and his brow furrowed. How irritating that Nasir only grew more handsome when he frowned, she thought.

"I suppose I was worried he was involved in mortgage fraud," Nasir said, his tone thoughtful. "It's been cropping up more and more, as the real estate market in Toronto tightens every year. Someone posing as a mortgage agent or real estate expert convinces an inexperienced investor to use the equity in their own home to purchase other properties the agent acquires on their behalf. Except there is no other property, and the money is squirreled away or sent overseas. The investor usually ends up losing their home and life savings, too. There have been a few high-profile cases recently."

With a pang of fear, Kausar thought of Hamza and what he had admitted only the previous day—that Sana's money was gone. She also recalled Mubeen's suggestion to Anjum earlier that day, to borrow against the equity in the plaza and use it to invest in Silver Star Holdings. An idea he got from Ahmed himself.

"That's terrible," she said, and Nasir nodded in agreement, his face grim.

"It's predatory, and even when these bad actors are taken to court, the schemes are set up in a way to skirt legalities. Their actions are unethical, even unlawful, but the money is gone and there is little recourse for the victims. In some cases, the victims resort to violence to get justice."

"And what made you suspect Ahmed was involved in this?" she asked, and Nasir shrugged.

"It was a feeling, only. I was aware of the rise in this particular type of con, and when he explained what he wanted to do, my gut instinct was to refuse. I may be a lawyer, but I don't want to ruin people's lives. I'll leave that to tech CEOs," he joked.

"Imran and Ahmed were friends, but that doesn't explain why your name was in Imran's calendar," Kausar mused.

Nasir shrugged. "It could have been a mistaken entry. Maybe he was following up on Ahmed's meeting, or they were trying to run something together? Any number of reasons, really." Kausar wasn't entirely convinced.

Nasir rose to prepare the chai, asking if she took sugar before adding two teaspoons to his own cup and serving them both. "Too much sugar, I know, but I have few pleasures in life," he said, smiling at her. "I should take up golf. Or perhaps I should marry again. What do you think?"

"I've heard good things about golf," she said, and he laughed.

CHAPTER 21

Sana's arraignment was early the next morning, and Hamza and Kausar drove to the courthouse in tense silence. The girls had been quiet at breakfast, Fizza casting nervous glances between her father and her grandmother, while Maleeha ignored them both, eyes fixed on her phone. Kausar made a note to speak with her older granddaughter about the money she had found in her room, once Sana was home and safe.

"And you're sure Mom will be home today?" Fizza asked, before leaving for the neighbor's, who had agreed to take over drop-off and pickup duties for the rest of the week.

"Inshallah," Kausar said, which seemed to satisfy the young girl.

Maleeha waited until her father had gone upstairs before sidling up to her grandmother. "Brianna agreed to talk tonight," she said abruptly. Kausar nodded her assent, and the girl hesitated. "Dad won't answer any of my questions about Mom's arrest. It's bad, isn't it?"

Kausar wondered what she should say. Fizza seemed pleased her mother would be coming home today, without thinking about what lay ahead. Maleeha was older and knew better.

"The lawyer is confident she can mount a successful defense,"

Kausar said carefully, repeating Jessica Kaur's words. "I would prefer that defense not become necessary. We must all do what we can, *beta*."

Maleeha lifted her backpack and left for school.

Jessica Kaur waited for them at the front of the courthouse, and from the thrum of barely contained energy in the lawyer's posture, Kausar got the feeling she was in a hurry—and that this was her usual state of being. Jessica was a tall woman, standing over six feet in her black pumps and dressed in a knee-length, gray wool skirt and tailored black cashmere blazer. With her brown skin, piercing dark eyes, and hair pulled back in a sleek chignon, she was a striking figure. She held her hand out briskly to Hamza, then turned to hug Kausar.

"This won't take long," she said, motioning for them to follow her into the courtroom.

Sana was dressed in the same clothes she had been wearing when she was arrested. Her hair was tidy, but she looked worn out and exhausted. Yet Kausar was happy to note the determined look in Sana's eye, her chin lifted in defiance when the charges were read out. The arraignment had already been negotiated, Jessica assured them, but Kausar couldn't relax until the judge made it official. A few moments later, Sana was released on Kausar's surety. Jessica pulled Kausar to a desk, where paperwork waited for her signature. Behind them, Hamza hugged Sana, who was stiff in his arms.

"I've met a lot of guys like that," Jessica said, her gaze on Hamza. "It's all about what other people think, about their status. My ex-husband was the same. They have two daughters, right?"

"Fifteen and ten years old," Kausar said, filling in the form.

Jessica made a sympathetic face. "Once this is all over, don't expect him to stick around; his type usually doesn't. At least he showed up today. It made a difference with the judge. He's one of those 'family values' types." She rolled her eyes. "As if families don't come in all shapes, sizes, and compositions. Sana is lucky to have you, Aunty."

"I'm not sure she would agree," Kausar said wryly, signing the final document. The surety was high, in consideration of the severity of the crime: Sana had been charged with first-degree murder. Kausar refused to think about how many years in prison that would mean if her daughter were found guilty. She couldn't be found guilty. Kausar wouldn't allow it.

Jessica flashed another warm smile. "Every time I spoke with Sana, she mentioned how thankful she was to have you here. I almost expected you to fly in with a cape!"

The lawyer's words surprised Kausar, and she glanced over at her daughter, who was gathering her belongings from a bailiff. Perhaps she had served some purpose, after all, beyond the domestic. The thought cheered her. After the disastrous events at Imran's *poorsa*, she had almost convinced herself she had blown her best chance at helping.

"What happens now?" Kausar asked Jessica. The lawyer wrinkled her brow, thinking.

"Sana has a curfew and will have to check in with an officer regularly, but she can work and continue as before. It will take a while for the trial date to be set. In the meantime, I suspect the prosecutor will offer a deal. Depending on what they come back with, I might counsel Sana to take it."

"She would go to jail?" Kausar asked, appalled.

"It might be the best option, Aunty. Murder trials are long, drawn-out, exhausting affairs. Families go bankrupt trying to fight the charges. They sell their homes, lose their jobs, and ignore their friends, trying to clear their name—and at the end of it, they don't have much of a life to return to."

"But my daughter is innocent," Kausar said. Sana approached them, Hamza trailing behind.

Jessica patted her hand. "That's for the jury to decide now, I'm afraid." She turned to Sana, and after hugging her client, assured them all she would be in touch. Then, with another cool nod at Hamza and a smile for Kausar, she let the family enjoy Sana's negotiated freedom.

The first thing Sana did when she returned home was take a long, hot shower. Downstairs in the kitchen, Hamza opened the fridge, looking for food. When he turned around, Kausar was waiting for him.

"Where were you really, the night Imran was murdered?" she asked. She was tired of playing games with this man.

An ugly expression suffused Hamza's face. "I thought you said your piece the other night. I can never do anything right."

"That is the question, Hamza *beta*," Kausar said softly. "Can you?"

Hamza swore, and the amiable mask he had worn in the courthouse for the judge, and for the undeniably attractive Jessica, slipped. He edged around Kausar and turned to face the sink, hands gripping the counter.

"You're right, I wasn't out of town on business when Imran was murdered. I was here, in the city. But I promise I wasn't anywhere near the store. That Detective Drake already made sure of my alibi. Not that I have a motive, unlike my dear *wife*." His words were bitter, and Kausar wanted to throw a pear at his head, except none were at hand. She made a note to do a grocery run.

Sana came down then, breaking their stalemate, wary eyes traveling from Kausar to Hamza. "Lunch?" she said with a forced brightness. "I'm craving Hakka."

Fatima texted shortly after the takeout arrived.

You're right. I was careless and impulsive. I hope you can forgive me, because this morning I called Parveen. She knows who you are, and she wants to talk. I promise to behave myself.

Looking between Hamza's sulky face and Sana's far-off expression as they silently shared Hakka noodles, chili beef, and Manchurian chicken, Kausar texted back. *Pick me up from the plaza. I have a few people I need to talk to first.*

F*izza had explained the concept of bubble tea, or boba, to* Kausar a few years ago: fruit juice or milk tea, mixed with chewy tapioca balls or flavored jelly. Kausar had compared it to *falooda*, the milky South Asian drink loaded with basil seeds and vermicelli, flavored with rose syrup, and topped with nuts and ice cream. When a bubble tea store opened up in North Bay last year, Kausar had tried it with May. Neither was a big fan.

Now, as she stepped into the small shop, she was greeted by an employee who looked no older than Maleeha. She wore a loose hijab, large earrings visible beneath the fabric, and a necklace with her name spelled out in Arabic—Nimra. Kausar asked to speak with the owner, and the young girl called to someone in the back.

"You're in luck—he's usually not here," Nimra said. She busied herself arranging fruit and other toppings. "Do you want to order something while you wait?"

Kausar asked for a plain milk tea and watched the girl expertly mix her drink, finishing by placing the cup beneath a machine that stretched hot plastic over the top in an airtight seal. "Were you working the day Imran was killed?" she asked.

Nimra shook her head, earrings flying. "I was at school. I only started here a few months ago. Though, honestly, when I found out who was murdered, I was low-key happy." The girl paused, her face flushing, and cast an anxious glance in the direction of the storeroom. "Don't tell him I said that."

Kausar paid for her tea before reaching for an oversized straw with an angled end to puncture the lid. She wondered why Nimra was so concerned about her boss overhearing. Everyone else in the plaza seemed to nurse a healthy dislike for Imran. "May I ask why you felt that way?"

Nimra shrugged. "Imran would come around sometimes. Usually when I was the only one here, me or Rita, that's my co-worker. It was weird."

"He made you feel uncomfortable?" Kausar asked.

Nimra's eyes moved to the backroom door once more. "Umm, sort of," she said quickly. Then, in a low voice, added, "There are a lot of kids, teenagers, who hang around. He used to stay for a while, not talking to anyone. He just . . . watched."

A look of understanding passed between the two women. The more Kausar learned about Imran, the less sorry she felt that he was gone. "If he made you uncomfortable, you should have told your boss," Kausar said.

Nimra made a face. "That wasn't an option."

Kausar was about to ask why when the door to the back office opened and Mubeen stepped into the store.

"This is the aunty who wanted to speak to you, Mubeen," Nimra said, and Kausar blinked at him. Mubeen ran the bubble tea shop in his father's plaza? It was hard to square the self-absorbed, opportunistic young man she had spotted at Imran's *janazah* and again at his mother's house, with this fact. She never figured Mubeen for a business owner.

Dressed in an expensive shirt and pants artfully rolled up at his ankles to reveal expensive Italian loafers, Mubeen seemed more like someone who would turn up his nose at a bubble tea shop, not run one. He was a good-looking man, she acknowledged—his features symmetrical, hair in a stylish fade—but there was a selfish cast to his mouth, confirmed when he didn't bother looking at her. She was just another older woman from the neighborhood, and his tone was dismissive when he addressed her.

"Sorry, Aunty, we don't sell chai, only milk tea," he said, voice flat. He turned to go, but Kausar waved her drink in his face.

"Quite delicious," she said. "I was hoping to speak with you about something else, actually. It's about your father, and this plaza."

Nimra's eyes grew wide at this, and she looked more carefully at Kausar.

Mubeen shrugged. "We can talk in my office. Bring me a mango slush," he called to Nimra.

"Sure thing, Mubeen," the young girl said, flashing a quick eye roll at Kausar.

Mubeen's office was a tiny space, and as she took a seat in the plastic chair jammed in front of a small desk, Kausar made a quick inventory of her surroundings. It was less chaotic than either of Imran's offices, but also curiously devoid of any personal details. She recalled what Nimra had said about her boss not being around very often.

"If you're here to convince me to keep the plaza, my mind is made up. I know Mr. Jin sells the best Chinese broccoli or okra or whatever, but you'll just have to get it from the Superstore like everyone else." Mubeen made a big show of leafing through his mail while he talked, not bothering to make eye contact. Kausar noted most of the envelopes were bills, addressed to him and not the store.

"So, you have decided to go with Ahmed at Silver Star Holdings, then?" Kausar asked, and Mubeen looked up at her, brow furrowed.

"How did you—" he started.

"Or have you managed to convince Patrick Kim to increase his offer? From my conversation with him a few days ago, he seemed quite eager to buy the plaza," she said.

Mubeen dropped the mail, abandoning any pretense at disinterest, she noted with some satisfaction, and scrutinized Kausar.

"Do I know you?" he asked.

"I was at your house giving your mother *poorsa* yesterday, *beta*. I believe it was shortly after you insulted aunties in general, and apologized to me in particular," she said.

He snapped his fingers. "*Plenty taken*. That's what you said to me. Who *are* you?"

Kausar smiled brightly. "I rather think we are beyond simple introductions, Mubeen. But not, I hope, beyond productive conversations. You're in debt."

"I am?" Mubeen seemed to have trouble following the conversation. Clearly all the brains had gone to his sister.

She motioned towards the stack of bills on his desk. "Creditors only send paper bills these days when they're angry at you." Kausar had no idea if this were true—she always paid her bills on time—but a red flush crawled up Mubeen's neck, and she assumed her guess had been correct. He swept the envelopes into a drawer and glared at her. She stared back placidly. Kausar was enjoying herself, she realized. It was fun to toy with Mubeen and watch him splutter.

"If you're not going to tell me who you are, what do you want?" he demanded.

"I wanted to warn you about Ahmed. The deal he is offering is not to be trusted."

Mubeen leaned back in his chair, scoffing. "What do you know about commercial real estate?"

"Not much. But I do know about mortgage fraud," Kausar said evenly. Mubeen's angry flush had crept up to his face now.

"My dad trusted Ahmed, they were in business together," Mubeen snapped. "I don't know who you think you are—"

"What sort of business?" Kausar asked, but Mubeen only scowled.

The door to the office opened, and Nimra entered, holding a mango slush for Mubeen and another milk tea for Kausar. She set both down before murmuring something in Mubeen's ear. His eyes widened as he stared at Kausar, and she realized the jig was up. Nimra must have realized who she was or asked one of the shopkeepers—her money was on Luxmi, the plaza gossip—about a desi woman in her fifties asking questions. With an apologetic glance, Nimra scurried out, and to Kausar's surprise, the young man started to laugh.

"You're Sana's mother," he said, and it wasn't a question. "Do you think I had something to do with my dad's murder, because I was eager to inherit all of this?" He spread his hands wide, taking in the tiny office, and presumably the rest of the plaza. "Let me guess. You're trying to investigate on your own. All you need is a magnifying glass and a Sherlock Holmes hat." He smirked.

"It's called a deerstalker," Kausar said coldly, but she knew she had lost the upper hand. "There's a lot of money in real estate in Toronto. People have been killed for less," she said evenly.

Mubeen cocked his head. "Plenty of money, and plenty of drama. It was bad enough my dad forced me to open a business here. He wanted me to follow in his stupid footsteps. But he picked the wrong kid. Anjum was the one who was interested. I only wanted to be left alone. After the plaza is sold—and no, I won't tell you to who—I'm moving somewhere warm with my hard-earned money. My sister and mom can take their share and figure things out for themselves."

"The only reason you can move somewhere warm is because of the money you'll get when you sell your father's plaza," Kausar said.

All the anger seemed to have left Mubeen, and he shrugged. "I was going anyway. This place is cursed. It never made my dad happy. He always wanted more, and he never knew when to quit.

That's what killed him in the end, even if it *was* your daughter who held the knife. I don't want any of it."

"What do you mean?" she asked, but Mubeen had reached his limit.

"You can pay Nimra for your second drink up front," he said, dismissing her.

The young girl waved away her card at the cash register, looking remorseful. "I'm sorry. Mubeen isn't the best boss, but he isn't like his dad, and I was afraid you were going to get him in trouble," she said, shamefaced.

"I quite understand," Kausar said. Nimra had loyalty, which she could appreciate, even though it made her job more complicated.

Nimra looked relieved. "I like your daughter. She let me borrow one of the *salwar* suits from her store once for a party. I don't think she killed Imran, but I don't think Mubeen did, either. He just doesn't have it in him."

Kausar silently agreed. Something Mubeen said came back to her now: that Imran had chosen the wrong kid to place his business hopes on.

"What about his sister, Anjum?" she asked the young girl.

Nimra shrugged. "Mubeen told me once that his dad should have offered her a store instead of him, and that she was always jealous. I guess his parents are traditional or whatever and figured Anjum would get married and leave the family. Except she's still single."

Ahmed had implied Anjum's engagement was imminent when they spoke, but was marriage what Anjum even wanted? Even Mubeen acknowledged his sister should have been given a bigger role in the family business. Had her jealousy over this favoritism for her dim-witted brother boiled over into rage? Lisa had admitted to hearing Imran argue with a woman the night before he died. What if that person were Anjum, and not Sana?

She wondered what Parveen would have to say when they met later today. Now that her identity was revealed, anything could happen—from being thrown out of the house again to an unpleasant confrontation. Thoughts whirling, she made her way towards the computer repair shop to finally meet the elusive owner.

CHAPTER 22

The cell phone and computer repair shop was crowded, the front jammed with dusty cases for iPhones and Androids, charging cords, wireless Bluetooth headsets, and other accessories, leaving only a narrow alley to the counter, where a petite white woman sat on a stool behind a computer. She had short, dark hair, brown eyes, and a plain face with overly plucked brows and a friendly expression. The name tag on her collar read *Deanna*.

Kausar took in the store with a sweeping glance as she made her way to the counter. "I have a question about my cell phone, and I don't want to keep bothering my grandchildren," she said, matching Deanna's smile. "I tried to come by a few days ago, but the store was closed."

The shop owner reached for a set of tools, and Kausar handed over her phone. "My hours were a bit erratic last week," Deanna said, apologetic. "My daughter was sick, and I didn't have anyone to watch her at home. That's the bonus of running your own business—I can close the store if I need to. I don't mind telling you, I was happy not to have been here."

"I heard the landlord was murdered," Kausar said. She was

glad Deanna at least seemed more forthcoming. "Did you know him?"

Deanna shook her head, her dark hair falling over her brow as she bent over Kausar's phone. "I haven't been here that long, only a few months, and I'm actually closing the store soon. I only met Imran when I first moved in."

"Business hasn't been good?" Kausar asked.

Deanna hesitated. "I took over the lease from another person, but there isn't as much demand as I thought in this location. Except for the grocer, this plaza isn't as busy as it was before the pandemic. Now that Imran's dead, his son will likely sell. That's what I heard, anyway."

"I'm sorry business has not been as you expected. Where did you hear that Imran's son wanted to sell?"

"Just around," Deanna said vaguely. "I don't really know any of the other business owners, but customers talk. At least they caught the person who did it. I can't believe it turned out to be one of the shopkeepers, Sana-something," Deanna said. She leaned closer, her breath minty from gum. "Personally, I think the police might have rushed the investigation."

Kausar made her eyes wide. "Why would you say that?" For someone who claimed to be uninterested in gossip, Deanna was eager to share her theories with a stranger. Perhaps it was lonely in this empty store.

Deanna shrugged. "I mean, why would someone with a unit in the plaza want to kill Imran? It doesn't make any sense." Her gaze was guileless when she looked at Kausar. "Have you heard anything in the neighborhood? The aunties always seem to know what's really going on, according to my mom."

Kausar watched the other woman, considering. There was something artificial about this conversation, as if she were the one being interrogated. "Everyone is very concerned," she started.

"I'd be terrified if I lived nearby," Deanna agreed. "Any popular theories?"

"I did hear that Imran might have got himself into some trouble," Kausar said, watching Deanna for a reaction, but her expression remained neutral. "A friend said there were late night deliveries and cars in the parking lot after hours. Did you notice the same thing?"

Deanna nodded slowly in agreement. "Did your friends note down any license plates? That might be useful, if they reported it to the police."

"I doubt they'd be comfortable speaking to the police," Kausar said. "Not many people in this neighborhood are."

Deanna hummed a noncommittal sound. She had removed Kausar's phone cover while they talked. She turned off the power, without bothering to ask what the issue was, and sprayed the device with compressed air before removing the SIM card and putting it back. She restarted the phone and handed it back to Kausar.

"All clean. Just some dust buildup. Service is on the house for you, Aunty, but please do come back if you want to treat your grandkids. I can set them up with the latest iPhone for a good price."

"I thought you said the store was closing?" Kausar asked.

"Can't hurt to do a little more business while I look for a new location. I'm thinking maybe in the west end," Deanna said.

Kausar turned her phone over in her hand, thinking. Deanna had put on a good show, moving those tools around nimbly, but she doubted the woman knew more about cell phones than she did. "Thank you for getting the dust out, but actually, my issue was a strange text message I received."

"One of those scam ones? I hope you didn't give away your banking details. The CRA won't come to your door, I promise," she said, referring to a well-known Canada Revenue Agency scam that targeted seniors. Why did everyone in Toronto seem to think she was so much older than she was?

"It was more of a personal message. Do you have any idea how to find out where an unwanted text was sent from?"

"Spam calls are from throwaway numbers, most of the time," Deanna said, putting her tools away.

Kausar noticed two photographs tacked to the wall: three young girls, no older than ten. The eldest, a dark-haired girl, wore a watchful expression. "Your children?" she asked, nodding at the photo.

Deanna glanced at the picture. "They keep me busy. Do you have children?"

Kausar nodded. "Also grandchildren. Teenagers can be challenging."

"I was a trial to my mother at that age," Deanna agreed. "Kids are up to all sorts now. You wouldn't believe the stories I've heard coming out of the local high school."

"You seem to know a lot about what is happening in the community," Kausar observed.

Deanna shrugged. "People talk to me."

Kausar studied the picture again. "It must be challenging, navigating two different cultures," she said. When Deanna looked blank, Kausar elaborated. "I'm sorry, I assumed your husband was desi." When Deanna continued to look confused, she added, "South Asian, I mean."

Comprehension dawned on Deanna's face. "Oh, yes, my partner is from India. It can be difficult, but I do love spicy food."

Kausar's cell phone beeped with a message from Fatima. Her friend was waiting in the parking lot.

"It was nice to finally meet you, Mrs. Khan," Deanna said. Kausar took one last look around and then left, with more than one aspect of the conversation troubling her.

Parveen's chai was not nearly as good as her daughter's, but to Kausar's relief, Anjum was not home. She was happy she wouldn't have to spend the visit worrying about being thrown out again, or that Anjum would make good on her threat to call the cops. Kausar could picture the annoyance on Ilyas's face if she were forced to ask him to spring her and Fatima from jail.

In contrast, Fatima seemed completely at ease; she praised the tea and even spoke warmly of Imran with a straight face. Her friend was a natural at deception, Kausar thought with admiration.

Fatima had been quick to apologize in the car during the drive over, and the friends had now made up. Kausar had even told Fatima about her strange conversation with Deanna, though neither of them could figure out what the shopkeeper's angle was. In Parveen's sitting room, Fatima was as good as her word and was behaving herself.

"I thought we could eat lunch together," Fatima suggested now. They had brought more food today; no doubt, Parveen's fridge was full to bursting at this point, but it would have been rude to show up empty-handed. The containers of biryani, raita, and a vegetable korma smelled delicious. "I'll set the table, while you chat with Kausar." With a meaningful look at her friend, Fatima disappeared into the kitchen.

Parveen was dressed in another dull-looking *salwar kameez*, this one brown with light embroidery around the neck and sleeves, with a light beige *dupatta* draped casually around her shoulders. She looked to be in her late forties, perhaps ten years younger than Kausar, with large, placid brown eyes and full cheeks that made it clear Anjum favored her mother. But where Anjum's prettiness was paired with a shrewd intelligence, her mother appeared passive and delicate. Kausar wasn't sure how to start, but to her surprise, Parveen spoke first.

"I was happy when Fatima called. When Anjum told me what she had done, throwing you both out, I was angry. I wanted to talk with you. You know, when that detective said they arrested Sana, I told him she wasn't at fault," Parveen said in Urdu. Her voice was soft, the words timid. For an instant, Kausar felt a wave of relief, but then Parveen's next words dashed the feeling to shreds. "A woman would not stab a man. Women are too weak."

"I don't think that's true," Kausar started to say, but Parveen waved away her protest.

"Most women would use poison, or ruin another's reputation. I did the same after my *ammi* died. I was fourteen years old when my father brought home a young girl and said she was my new mother. I filled his ear with poison until he got rid of her," she said proudly. "He paid her off and she went, along with her little brat. 'Not my brother,' I said to her. 'No part of you could ever be my family.'"

Kausar stared at Parveen. Was Imran's widow boasting about convincing her father to throw out a dependent young woman he had impregnated? Clearly, she had misjudged Parveen. The woman wasn't meek at all.

"That story does not paint you in a very good light, Parveen," Kausar said quietly. "You have a stepbrother somewhere who knows you ruined his mother's life."

Parveen seemed surprised at this. "My life has not been easy. I thought you of all people would understand."

Kausar blinked in surprise. This conversation was already heading straight off the rails. "I'm not sure I do," she said.

"I heard about you, even before this sad business with Sana," Parveen said, her expression almost dreamy. "When my parents married me to Imran at eighteen, I thought I was marrying a rich man. His family drove to our home in a Mercedes. But his father wanted Imran to earn his keep and treated him like any other tenant in the plaza. We struggled for years. Then he died, and Imran got everything. And now I have everything." She looked slyly at Kausar. "Just like you."

Kausar inhaled sharply. "We're nothing alike."

"You were married to an old man, too. He died and now you're rich. The best a woman can hope for is to become a comfortable widow." She tilted her chin in the direction of the kitchen, where Fatima was plating the food she had made. "Her husband died and left her with nothing. She had to take a job caring for other people's children, just to feed her own." Parveen wrinkled her nose at the thought. "Better to live with a bad man until your luck turns. Yes?"

Kausar considered this. "Are you saying Imran was a bad man?"

Parveen's eyes shone with a dark intelligence she had kept banked till now. "All men have evil in their hearts. It is because they aren't used to waiting, not like women. Imran was no different. He was never satisfied with what he had. He always wanted more."

Mubeen had said something similar. Was Parveen trying to tell her something? Kausar thought about Imran's friend Ahmed and the shady business Nasir suspected he was engaged in. Mubeen had also let slip that his father had been in business with Ahmed. She needed to know more.

"Perhaps our daughters won't have to wait the same way we did," Kausar suggested, hoping to goad the woman. "They have more options, and less expectations."

Parveen shrugged. "What has changed? Now women are expected to work outside the home and inside, too. The men haven't changed, they only expect more. I warned my daughter. When Anjum marries, at least she will know better."

"I didn't realize she was engaged. When is the wedding?"

Kausar asked. They were veering wildly from the purpose of this visit, and time was running out. Fatima couldn't stall in the kitchen forever.

"Once Anjum accepts the proposal I brought her. She knows what will happen if she refuses this one as well," Parveen said. There was menace in her words that made Kausar's skin prickle.

"What will happen?" Kausar asked, almost afraid for the young woman.

Parveen picked up the mug from the low table in front of her and took a dainty sip. Kausar had been so engrossed in the conversation she had nearly forgotten about the tea. "Imran didn't leave a will. As his wife, my name is on the title for the plaza. If Anjum wants to inherit her share, she will do as I say. It is what her father would have wanted—for his daughter to marry a respectable man from a good family."

"What about your son, what does he have to do to keep his inheritance? Mubeen wants to sell the plaza," Kausar said.

Parveen seemed surprised at this question. "Mubeen doesn't have to do anything. He is the boy, he will marry later. As for the plaza, I never liked it, better we get rid of it now. So long as we don't sell to that Patrick Kim." She leaned closer to Kausar, and her breath was sour. "Better to keep the business among our desi *log*, and not those Chinese."

"He's Korean Canadian," Kausar said sharply. Parveen was starting to make her angry, but the woman didn't seem to notice or care. Instead, she waved Kausar's words away, as if the details didn't matter.

"Once Anjum is married, I will move back to Pakistan. I have family there. Canada is too cold. Why did you stay here?"

Kausar had lived in Canada for almost forty years; this was home now. "My daughter and grandchildren are here," she answered shortly. She was struggling to keep a lid on her growing frustration. "You don't seem terribly upset about your husband's death, Parveen. I can't help but wonder why you invited me over?" This certainly was not the grieving widow act that Parveen had put on at the mosque or in front of the rest of the community.

Parveen regarded her with limpid eyes, but this time Kausar was not fooled. "I was curious to meet the mother of the woman who murdered my Imran."

"You said you didn't think Sana did it," Kausar said, her heart beating fast.

Parveen shook her head. "I said I didn't think she was at fault," she corrected. "Imran had a way of making people very angry, and I know he hurt others. He even upset Mr. Jin and fought with the man who runs the computer repair shop."

"You mean the woman who runs the repair shop," Kausar corrected. She was certain Deanna was the sole proprietor.

"What do women know of computer and phone repair? That is a man's job," Parveen said.

Kausar fought the urge to roll her eyes. A thought occurred to her. If Parveen could be so blunt, so could she. "Where were you, the night Imran was killed?" she asked.

The smile Parveen threw her was wolfish. "At home. Anjum was with me, of course. Do you know that detective, the white man with the thin lips? He did not even bother to ask. Once he had settled on your daughter, no one else would do. The *goras*, they think us quite harmless, don't they? What can a desi aunty accomplish, after all?"

Kausar stared at Parveen, feeling sick to her stomach. This visit was a mistake. Imran's wife had spent the entire conversation toying with her like a bored cat would a mouse, and she had learned nothing useful for Sana. She was starting to feel sorry for Anjum and to understood why Mubeen wanted to take his share of the money and run.

"I'll just check on lunch," she said, needing a break. When she poked her head inside the kitchen, Fatima was nowhere to be found. She heard a toilet flush, and her friend emerged from the bathroom, wiping her hands. Catching sight of Kausar's expression, Fatima mouthed, *That bad?* Kausar nodded, and, reaching for a stack of plates, and grimly set the table. The sooner they could leave, the better.

The women ate in awkward silence, punctuated by Fatima's cheerful observations about the weather and neighborhood gossip. When they rose to leave, Parveen had one final shot for Kausar.

"You should take the grandchildren away, when Sana goes to jail. It will be difficult for them to live here. Everybody knows already what their father has been up to." The accompanying smile was a poisonous dart. Kausar looked from Parveen's face to Fatima's suddenly stricken one.

"What does everyone know?" Kausar asked, though somehow, she already suspected the answer.

"Hamza is living with another woman, in the west end of the city," Parveen said. "I'm sure Sana knows, too. Wives always do."

In the car, a shamefaced Fatima confirmed the rumors. Reaching for her phone, she scrolled to a WhatsApp group, clicking on an image posted months ago.

In the photo, Hamza had his arm around a young woman with blond hair and blue eyes, lips painted a flirty red. They were laughing, pushing a grocery cart together. In another picture, Hamza was kissing the side of the woman's head, and Kausar felt a sudden rage fill her veins.

"One of the women from this WhatsApp group, her daughter lives in Mississauga. She saw them together," Fatima explained with some hesitation. "I would have told you sooner, but I didn't want to heap more trouble at your feet."

"Sana knows already," Kausar said, remembering the arguments she had overheard, the contempt with which her daughter and Hamza treated each other. Since she had arrived in the city, she hadn't observed them share a bedroom once.

"There's more," Fatima said, and her voice was hesitant. "I should have told you. But I hate gossip, and you were so upset the last time we met."

"Tell me, quickly," Kausar said.

"When this picture was shared on the group, a few of the women said that Sana deserved it. Because she hadn't been a faithful wife, either."

"Between her store, the girls, and Hamza never helping out, Sana would hardly have had time to cheat!" Kausar said hotly.

"That's what I said. Then someone from the group sent me a picture, privately." Fatima's fingers flew over the screen, and she turned it to Kausar, who caught her breath.

It was a candid shot. Sana sat on a park bench, her head thrown back in laughter, hair loose around her face. She was wearing the same colorful tunic she had worn when Kausar arrived, part of her new collection. Which meant the picture had been taken in the last few months.

Seated beside her, an expression of longing and love clear in his eyes, was Ilyas.

CHAPTER 23

Kausar had forwarded both pictures to herself, and she stared at them now as she sat in the sitting room, flipping back and forth. Her shock had first turned to anger, and now confusion. That Hamza was dishonest was no surprise. But was Sana guilty of . . . something? In the picture, she was seated beside Ilyas. Unlike Hamza and the mysterious blond woman, Sana and Ilyas weren't cuddled together. And yet the expression on Ilyas's face and the outright joy on her daughter's hinted at a deeper story. Did Sana still have feelings for her first love? Was Ilyas in love with Sana? If so, why had he stood silently by while she was arrested? What a mess this was all turning out to be.

She dialed May, but her friend didn't pick up, so Kausar busied herself tidying the main floor. Sana was upstairs taking a nap, her exhaustion manifest in the pile of shoes by the door, dirty dishes in the sink, and mail on the sideboard. When her cell phone rang, Kausar jumped on it.

"Goodness! You sound out of breath. Have you taken up jogging?" May's teasing voice was a balm to her nerves, and Kausar quickly went to her room, closing the door shut behind her.

"Hamza is cheating on Sana with a blond woman, Sana might be cheating with Ilyas, I was thrown out of Imran's house, his son runs a bubble tea shop in the plaza, and—" Kausar started, her words tumbling out in a torrent.

"Hey, wait, slow down," May said in a soothing tone. "Why don't you start from the beginning. But first, is Sana home?"

Kausar assured her friend that her daughter had been released on surety and the reminder calmed her down somewhat. Sana was fine, for now. Quickly, she filled May in on what had happened in the last few days. Once she was done, her friend was silent, thinking.

"Toronto certainly is exciting," May said finally with a laugh.

"I think it's the Golden Crescent that's exciting," Kausar said. "I'm not sure where to go from here, or even if I should. Jessica warned me: Now that Sana has been formally charged, my actions could prejudice the case to the judge and jury."

"You're simply talking to people. That's not a crime," May protested.

Kausar recalled Parveen's strange comment about Detective Drake's dismissal of her as a suspect. "What could I possibly know? I'm a simple immigrant woman."

"Hey, watch it, that's my best friend you're talking about," May said, concern in her voice. "Are you okay? I'm starting to worry about you, Kausar. It's been a traumatic week."

"Has it only been a week since Sana first called me?" Kausar asked dully. "It feels as if I have been here for months."

"It's called exhaustion, friend," May said. "I think it's time to think of the bigger picture. Sometimes when you have too much information, it's impossible to wrap your head around it. There's a reason murder boards are popular, you know. All the shows and internet detectives have them."

This elicited a smile that broke through her dark mood. Kausar pulled the yellow floral notebook from where she had hidden it under her mattress since learning Maleeha had so easily looked through it. So much had happened in the last few days, she hadn't had time to be diligent about updating her notes. Turning to a fresh page, she started to list everything she had learned, talking aloud to May as she wrote.

"Hamza admitted he's lost most of their money. That includes Sana's inheritance, I think."

"Do you think Sana knows?" May asked. "I doubt he would still be living in the house with her if she did."

"Unclear," Kausar said. She made a note in her book to ask Sana; she could do it at the same time she asked about her relationship with Ilyas. She wasn't looking forward to either of those conversations. "I'm also not sure whether Hamza lost money in Ahmed Malik's scheme or through bad investments in crypto. Or both."

"Never invest in a product you don't understand. You taught me that," May said.

"Nasir thinks Ahmed has been dabbling in mortgage fraud, where he dupes investors into giving him money that he pretends to put into real estate on their behalf," Kausar said.

"The depths people will lower themselves to in order to make money never ceases to amaze me," May said. "But more importantly, did you take a picture of Nasir? I taught you the selfie trick!"

Kausar laughed. "You're shameless."

"He sounds dishy. Variety is the spice of life, Kausar—and I know how much you like spicy food. Your eyes need to eat, too."

"Moving on," Kausar said with a smile. Her friend always knew how to lighten her mood. "There is some definite dysfunction in Imran's family. The son, Mubeen, is the clear family favorite, despite not doing much to deserve the role of golden child, other than being a boy. His sister, Anjum, is resentful of this and has put herself forward again and again as a successor to run the plaza, only to be shot down by her mother."

"That Parveen sounds like a piece of work. Reminds me of

my ex-mother-in-law," May remarked. "Sweet as pie when she wanted to be, but she could shoot a man dead at twenty paces using her death glare."

"Parveen made it clear she holds the purse strings. Her name is on the deed to the plaza, and she said she would only give Anjum her inheritance if she married whoever she picked out."

"For a woman so unhappy in her own marriage, she seems keen to force the same fate onto her daughter," May remarked.

"It happens that way sometimes. The same difficulty you experienced is pushed onto the next generation because you don't know any better," Kausar said.

"I think Parveen does know better. I think she's just a bitch," May said frankly.

"*May!*" Kausar said, scandalized by her friend's profanity.

"My granddaughter Lexi has been using some colorful vocabulary," May said, and Kausar could picture her friend's mischievous grin.

"I thought Lexi was three years old?"

"She's precocious, just like her grandmother," May said. "But back to your case. What else do you have?"

It *was* actually starting to feel like her case. "I did manage to take a few pictures of papers and files when I snooped through Imran's office in the plaza, and again at his home," she admitted.

"Talk about burying the lede!" May said. "Share the pictures, and I'll see if I spot anything. Fresh eyes and all that."

Kausar forwarded the pictures to her friend, running through the rest of her discoveries in her head. "I suppose the other big news is that Mubeen implied his father was working with Ahmed on some sort of business."

"And you agree with Nasir, you think this Ahmed person is what my oldest granddaughter would call *sus*," May said thoughtfully. "Perhaps you should pay him another visit. Take Nasir along with you."

"You really want that picture," Kausar said, smiling. Though talking to Ahmed again was a good idea. "What should I do about Hamza cheating on Sana, and her possible relationship with Ilyas?"

May hummed, thinking it over. "I think Sana is too smart not to know what her deadbeat husband is up to. In any case, he's not a priority right now. As for Ilyas . . ." she trailed off expectantly.

"No, I don't have a picture of him," Kausar said tartly. "He also has not responded to my message about the threatening text I received."

"In that case, tell Sana to dump him immediately," May said.

"I'll add it to the list of things I need to talk to her about," Kausar said dryly.

"I know things feel dire, but your progress so far has been marvelous," May said, admiration in her voice. "I think you might be the most talented detective I've ever met." She didn't add that Kausar was the only detective she knew.

Kausar referred to the notebook. "I have a few more lingering questions," she said, writing as she spoke. "Firstly, I realized what else was bothering me about my conversation with Deanna—how did she know my name? She called me Mrs. Khan in her store, and she seemed to know an awful lot about what was going on, though she told me she doesn't talk to the other shopkeepers and hadn't been around last week. Secondly, Parveen also mentioned that Imran was once a tenant in the plaza, though no one has brought that up before. And finally, who was the computer repair person Imran argued with at the plaza? Parveen was sure it was a man, but the store is run by Deanna now. Oh, and who broke the window in Sana's storage room?"

"To be honest, I don't see how the answers to any of those questions will help you find Imran's killer," May said.

"Neither do I," Kausar admitted. "But I still want to know."

"There's my girl. Curiosity reignited. You just let your pilot light go out for a second."

"You know, modern furnaces don't have those anymore," Kausar said.

"That's a shame. They make for a great metaphor." May's voice turned shy. "I have a theory, too. Less about the murder, and more about Hamza's behavior, and Sana's store. Since you told me it looked like they were having pretty big marital problems even before you knew about the affairs, I looked up divorce law in Ontario. We live in a no-fault province, meaning assets are divided equally between spouses. Sana has been a stay-at-home parent for most of her marriage, which means Hamza would have to pay a lot of spousal support. But if she had a source of income, and an asset such as a store . . ."

"Then Hamza wouldn't have to pay as much spousal support," Kausar said grimly. "In the meantime, since they are still married, he can borrow money against a communal asset. I wouldn't be surprised if he applied for another loan using the store as equity. He's deeply in debt. Good thinking, May."

"Would you say I'm the Hastings to your Poirot?" May asked. "More than your new friend Fatima?"

"Technically, I knew Fatima before I met you," Kausar said. When May squawked, she rushed to add, "Poirot would have figured it all out by now. I still have a rogue's gallery of suspects."

"My money is on Imran's widow," May said. "She admitted she would stay married to a bad man and wait until her luck changed. Maybe she grew tired of waiting and decided to do something about it?"

"Except Detective Drake ruled her and Anjum out already, as he never spoke to them again after their first inquiry. If I bring her up to Drake, he will only think I'm trying to save my daughter. The 'It's always the spouse' theory and all that," Kausar said glumly.

"Hmmm, I suppose you're right. What about the sale of the plaza? Any news on that front? Is Patrick Kim still in the running?" May asked. "I wouldn't mind a picture of him, either. Add that to your list of things to do."

"You have a one-track mind, May," Kausar said, laughing. "Are you putting together an album of Golden Crescent's finest?"

"I don't judge your hobbies, you don't judge mine. Also, is there treasure hidden in the basement of that plaza? I don't understand why everyone wants it so badly. You said there hardly seems to be any customer traffic," May said.

"I've been wondering the same thing," Kausar agreed. "What's so special about a rundown plaza in the Golden Crescent?"

"I think you have quite a few leads to follow, Detective Aunty," May said.

Talking to her friend had been therapeutic. Her exhaustion was dissipating, and she felt capable and inspired once more. She thanked May.

"Are you kidding? This is the most fun I've had since you helped nab the serial essay plagiarist at my school. The look on his smarmy sixteen-year-old face when he realized he had been outwitted by an old Indian lady!"

"Who are you calling old?" Kausar said, grinning. "I'm just starting my second act."

K*ausar had every intention of confronting Sana, but her* daughter didn't emerge from her room for dinner. When the girls went up to check on their mother, they reported that she was fast asleep. Hamza was not home, again, though neither Fizza nor Maleeha commented on the fact. After a simple dinner of *dal*, rice, and a vegetable curry, which the girls ate without any complaints, Kausar announced she needed to clear her head with a walk. With a meaningful glance, Maleeha offered to join her. It was time to meet with Brianna.

It was late April, and the weather remained erratic; Torontonians knew they weren't safely out of winter's cold embrace until next month. Kausar pulled her wool jacket close to her body, though beside her, Maleeha only wore a hoodie, impervious to the weather as all young people seemed to be.

"Brianna told us to meet her in the parking lot of the plaza," Maleeha explained, breath fogging in the dark. "She called it her office."

"Has she rented a unit?" Kausar asked, but Maleeha only shrugged. As they walked in silence, Kausar wondered how to bring up the cash she had found in her granddaughter's room. Maleeha would be angry she had snooped, of course, and might refuse to explain. Still, she should take advantage of the fact that they were alone together. She was about to speak when Maleeha turned to face her.

"Did Dad tell you about Carrie?"

Kausar stopped walking, taken aback by the abrupt question, though an uneasy feeling started in her stomach. The image of the blond woman in Hamza's arms flashed in her mind, and her fingers closed over her phone. "Who is Carrie?" she asked carefully.

"The woman he's seeing. I was the first one to find out. About the affair," Maleeha said, her voice jerky. She wasn't looking at her grandmother but staring at the ground. "I found texts and . . . pictures. On his phone."

For a moment, Kausar was shocked into silence, both at Hamza's indiscretion and her granddaughter's burden. "*Beta*, I'm so very sorry," she said, eyes welling with tears. "You never should have seen that."

Beside her, Maleeha angrily wiped her own eyes. "He kept

coming home late. Mom didn't seem to care. She's been so busy with the store and trying to make it a success. I noticed that even when he was home, he was always on his phone. I knew his password because he never changed it from when we were little. So, one day when he forgot his phone in the living room, I read his texts. I took screenshots of everything with my phone. He's disgusting," she said, her voice breaking. "I hate him for what he did. For what he's doing." They stood on the sidewalk, the dark houses around them the only silent witness to Maleeha's grief.

Kausar's heart hammered in her chest. She should have been here, she thought wildly. Perhaps she could have helped her daughter with the store or helped with the children. Instead, she had stayed in North Bay while her granddaughter and Sana suffered. She felt sick.

"I told him that if he didn't tell Mom, I would." Maleeha looked mutinous, as if daring Kausar to disagree.

"That was brave," Kausar said quietly.

"He tried to deny it. He laughed, at first. But when I showed him the screenshots, he started to cry." Maleeha's eyes were back on her shoes, while Kausar's gaze remained fixed on her granddaughter's beautiful, vulnerable face. Maleeha's skin was flawless; she had Sana's pointed chin and strong nose, Hamza's full lips. Beautiful and fierce, with a forceful, loyal heart. Kausar pulled her granddaughter to her then, and Maleeha slumped into her arms.

"It's all my fault," Maleeha whispered into Kausar's shoulder.

"None of this is because of you," Kausar said firmly.

"He told her the next day, but he kept me out of it. Mom thinks he confessed because of a guilty conscience, not because I forced him to do it," Maleeha said, wiping her eyes.

"Perhaps that is for the best," Kausar said gently. "Your mother would have carried the guilt of your knowing longer than her sadness over Hamza. I suspect your parents have not been happy for some time. But that is not your fault, *beta*. Your job is to live your life, and to love the people who are worthy of you. Okay?"

Maleeha looked at her grandmother. They were both nearly the same height, two petite women with the same brown, knowing eyes. "I'm glad you came, *Nani*."

"I only wish I had come sooner."

"'The best time to plant a tree is twenty years ago. The next best time is today,'" Maleeha quoted. "My history teacher told us that. It's supposed to be an ancient Chinese saying or whatever, but he said it's one of those idioms of no fixed origin. Most quotes are misattributed. Did you know that?"

"I did not," Kausar said. She could tell that her granddaughter had said as much as she was ready to about the situation, and she didn't want to push her for anything she wasn't ready to give. She glanced at her phone. "It is nearly ten. Brianna will be waiting."

They approached the parking lot, which was empty tonight save for a few cars. A faded blue Corolla was tucked into the corner, far away from the front of the plaza; Maleeha went to the driver-side window and knocked. Brianna had clearly been dozing; she rolled down the window, wiping her mouth.

"Nice nap?" Maleeha asked, and Kausar was amazed at how quickly her granddaughter had recovered from her bombshell confession only a few moments ago. She herself would be mulling over the part Maleeha had played in Hamza and Sana's marital breakdown for a long, long time.

The doors were unlocked, and Maleeha indicated that Kausar should take a seat on the passenger side, while she slid into the back seat.

The interior of the car was full of fast-food wrappers, the passenger side loaded with files and papers, which Brianna passed to Maleeha. "Welcome to my mobile office," she joked. "You good, M?"

Maleeha nodded, and Brianna turned to Kausar. "Oh damn, Aunty, I remember you. Pretending to be an innocent bystander that first day. You got me good, respect." She high-fived an amused Kausar.

Maleeha looked from Kausar to Brianna, confused. "You met already?"

"Your *nani* has been on this from the jump," Brianna said. "What can I do for you this fine evening?"

"Have you been camped out here since the murder?" Kausar asked.

"I come here some nights, to see what's happening and get some thinking done. I'm working on something big."

"Are you certain you're not a journalist?" Kausar asked, and Brianna threw her head back and laughed.

"I told you before, Aunty, I'm an activist. I'm all about that community grassroots organization. Maleeha knows what's good."

In the back seat, Maleeha shifted, uncomfortable with this assertion. "Did you really turn down university scholarships?"

Brianna shrugged. "Listen, I know how to play the game at school. They aren't giving away those marks for free. I worked hard, I was attending those Zoom classes and paying attention when everyone else was sleeping through class in their pajamas. But, like, what was it all for? The climate is going to shit—sorry, Aunty—people like me will never afford a house in this city, our economy is spiraling, and cabbage costs ten dollars. I'm not going to waste another four years on school. I want to see change in my lifetime. Know what I mean?"

Kausar smiled at the young woman's energy. She certainly had the charisma and passion to inspire others. No wonder Maleeha had called her a legend. "What do your parents think about this decision?"

"Dad's an activist, too, always has been, so he supports me. Mom thinks I've lost my mind. She made me defer the uni acceptances instead of sending them a nicely worded 'eff you' like I wanted." She rolled her eyes.

"What are you looking for in the parking lot?" Kausar asked, changing the topic back to the matter at hand.

"Lot of cars have been seen here late at night. Like, way more than are ever here during the day. I'm on the trail of a story, and I think it will be big. Might even be big enough to stop Imran's family from selling the plaza."

Playing devil's advocate, Kausar asked, "Why not let the sale go ahead? The plaza is old and in need of extensive repairs. I don't think the family is willing to put in the work. Why do you care what happens here?"

"Because whoever takes over, they're going to rip it all down and build condos no one who lives here can afford, which will start gentrifying the neighborhood until even those who have lived here for generations are priced out." Brianna's hand clenched on the gear shift, her face tight with frustration and anger. Clearly this was a topic she cared deeply about.

"This neighborhood is made up of eighty percent immigrants," Brianna said. "We have over three dozen languages spoken in Golden. We've got educated people living here, except they got those degrees overseas, which for some reason means they don't count in Canada. People have to work two or three jobs just to make ends meet. They—we—deserve a chance. It's happening all over the city: Working class and working poor, newcomers, first- and second-generation immigrants, even middle-class people, we're all being pushed out because of corporate greed. If they knock out the Golden plaza, that means they're coming for the rest of the neighborhood, too. If we let it happen, none of our families will still be living here ten, fifteen years from now." Brianna stared at them, arms crossed, daring both Maleeha and Kausar to disagree.

"Who's 'they'?" Maleeha asked.

Brianna turned back to the plaza. "That's what I'm trying to find out," she said grimly.

Kausar thought about her own family; without her and Hassan's wealth as a safety net, her daughter and grandchildren would have to pay the price for Hamza's poor financial decisions. Then she thought of Siraj, who had been nearly wiped out after a divorce and who had to rebuild in a suddenly very expensive city. Toronto had been a city filled with opportunity and promise when she and Hassan first settled here. Things felt very different to young people like Brianna.

"How do you mean to do that?" Kausar asked. "At the moment, you seem to be napping in an empty parking lot." She tried to make the query sound gentle, but the young woman bristled.

"I'm following my instincts. I'm following the money. And for some reason, multiple people want to spend a lot of money on this place. Being here is better than doing nothing."

"The questions you're asking, it could be dangerous. A man was murdered here a week ago," Kausar said. The idea of leaving this smart, passionate woman alone in a parking lot bothered her tremendously. She hadn't forgotten the way Cerise was harassed, simply for walking home after dark. Or what had happened to Ali years ago.

"Imran's murder was just the frosting. I want to see the whole cake, Aunty. And don't worry, I'll be careful." She took out a spray bottle. "Homemade pepper spray. Got my dad's scotch bonnet in there mixed with some water. Now, I have a few questions for you. I recognize game when I see it. Do you know who gets the plaza?"

Fair was fair, and Kausar was willing to share information with Brianna. "Imran's widow, Parveen, is the title holder, and she is leaving it to her son, Mubeen, to handle. The daughter, Anjum, wants to keep it. Patrick Kim, who runs Platinum Properties, wants to buy it, but he told me that another company, Silver Star Holdings, has put in a competing offer."

Brianna typed notes on her phone, but she paused at this. "Did you say Silver Star Holdings?" She looked thoughtful. "Thank you, Aunty. That's good to know. Be easy."

Dismissed, both Kausar and Maleeha exited the car and turned towards home. Something had eased between the two women, the confidences and their shared detecting bringing them closer than ever. Kausar squeezed her granddaughter's thin shoulder. "What will you do now?" she asked.

"Go home and do my homework," Maleeha said, her smile flashing white in the dark. "If I want to be a legend like Brianna, I need to put in the work."

Now would be the perfect time to ask about the thousands of dollars hidden in the cardboard box in Maleeha's closet, but Kausar was loath to ruin the easy camaraderie between them. Maleeha truly wanted to help figure out what had happened, and Kausar wanted to grow closer to her granddaughter. Still, there could be no relationship without trust. She opened her mouth to ask, when her phone started ringing. It was Ilyas.

"Where are you?" he asked roughly when she answered.

"At the plaza." At his long sigh, she added, "With Maleeha."

"That doesn't make me feel better. You two shouldn't be anywhere near that place at night." Before Kausar could ask why, Ilyas continued. "I'm calling because I looked into that anonymous message you received. It took me a while because I was busy with a few other cases."

"Don't tell me it's from a bot number?" she asked, recalling Deanna's guess. But surely Ilyas wouldn't have called this late if the number had been untraceable. A low thrum of fear and worry began to vibrate through her body.

"You need to come to the station right now," he said, voice grim. "The message you received came from Imran's cell phone."

CHAPTER 24

Kausar walked Maleeha home and gently rebuffed her attempts to tag along to the station. Ilyas had sent a car, and though the patrolwoman behind the wheel was not chatty, the radio was turned to the CBC, so Kausar didn't mind. She debated whether or not to text Sana, but in the end decided against it. Sana was likely still asleep. Better to find out what was happening first, before adding to her daughter's worries.

Ilyas was sitting at his desk in the open-plan office, surrounded by files, a cold cup of coffee at his elbow, when she was waved inside. He stood up when she approached, relieved to see her. "Thanks for coming in. I was worried when I realized why the number looked familiar," he said.

It was strange to see him now that she knew about him and Sana. Kausar took a seat on the chair in front of his desk. "I assumed Imran's cell phone had been by his body."

Ilyas shook his head. "It's not public knowledge, but we never found it. It wasn't in his office, not that anyone could find a thing in that mess. Drake didn't think it was important because . . ." he trailed off, embarrassed.

Because they had Sana at the scene and her fingerprints on the dagger and all over Imran, Kausar silently finished for him.

In a quieter tone, Ilyas asked, "How is she?"

Kausar considered. "Tired. Sad. Worried. This has been difficult for everyone. Especially when there are complicated personal feelings involved." She looked hard at him, and Ilyas flushed. He asked for her phone and carefully placed it in a bag, handing it to the officer who had escorted Kausar inside.

Ilyas waited until the officer left before he shifted awkwardly. "Sana and I . . . we're not . . . I didn't mean to . . ." He closed his eyes briefly. When he opened them, his expression had softened. "I never forgot her."

"Even though it was you who broke her heart?" Kausar asked.

Kausar hadn't been brought up to speak freely about romantic entanglements. She knew when her children had crushes, of course: In grade one, when Adam complained bitterly about his class rival, she suspected there were other feelings involved, later confirmed when she spotted him walking hand in hand with the girl in the playground. Ali had fallen in and out of love regularly, mooning after girls until his older brother gave him pointers on the fine art of pretending indifference. Sana, in contrast, had been more discreet. When they were children, it was obvious Ilyas was smitten; but it was equally clear Sana only ever thought of him as her brothers' annoying friend. Things shifted in high school, when Sana and Ilyas started to spend more time together. When Kausar's busybody friends had carried home tales of Sana and Ilyas alone in the park, she had said nothing. She trusted her daughter, and she trusted Ilyas.

Then Ali died, and everything fell apart.

Kausar never knew the particulars of what went wrong between Sana and Ilyas; she had been too consumed by her grief to take stock of anything else. She only knew that Ilyas had ended things, and she had comforted Sana as best she could at the time. When her daughter had met Hamza and married him within the year, Kausar had assumed the matter settled. But it was difficult to move on from a first love, clearly.

“We were too young,” Ilyas started, his voice low. “We broke up before I left for university, and the next thing I heard, she was engaged.” He was lost in memories now. “My job keeps me busy. I always wanted to make detective. When my mother’s health started to decline, I joined the Toronto force, to be closer to her. The day I moved back into the neighborhood, I bumped into Sana. It was like no time had passed at all, and we just . . .” He ducked his head, suddenly shy. “This is weird, talking to you about this.”

“Perhaps if we had spoken more openly when you were both younger, it might have prevented heartbreak,” Kausar said. She considered her words. “Or perhaps not. You have both grown up and learned.”

“I care about Sana, and I always will. But she’s still married to Hamza. She has kids. And now . . .” Ilyas trailed off.

“It would help if Sana were not sent to prison for the next twenty-five years,” Kausar agreed dryly. “I don’t understand how you could stand by and watch while she was arrested, if you felt this way.” She tried to keep the censure from her words, but Ilyas couldn’t meet her gaze.

“I suppose I thought it would be better if I were still on the case, instead of standing on the sidelines with no power,” he said in a low voice.

“You’re in a difficult position,” Kausar said. “But you’re not the one who had their life turned upside down. Which brings me back to the text message. How could someone have sent it from Imran’s phone?”

“There are two possibilities,” Ilyas said, relieved to be talking about something other than Sana’s arrest, and the role he had played in it. “The most obvious is that someone has Imran’s phone and used it to send the message. The second is that they cloned his number. In either case, the person knew your personal history and the best way to scare you."

"I was scared at first," Kausar admitted. "Now I'm more confused."

"We're checking your phone, to make sure there isn't any malware installed and see if we can figure out where the message was sent from. We should have it back to you before you leave the station, and let me know immediately if you get another text. Right now, it's just a waiting game."

"There's nothing more you can do?" Kausar asked, disappointed.

"This isn't the movies, Kausar Aunty. Investigations take time and resources. I had to call in a favor to the IT desk to get them to even look at your phone tonight. Besides, I have a feeling you've been busy yourself." The look he shot her was knowing, an allusion to her late-night meeting at the plaza parking lot.

"Sana told me to stay out of it," Kausar admitted. "But I can't simply stand back and watch things unravel. Not again. Sana's lawyer, Jessica Kaur, says the Crown has a strong case."

Ilyas looked around him, making sure they were alone. "The crime scene contained a fair amount of evidence on Imran's body and on Sana's clothing. Plus, the dagger came from the window display, and there's the argument one of the shopkeepers overheard between Sana and Imran the day before the murder. Not to mention the security footage we suspect she erased. Sana has made it impossible for us to verify her story, and she's also the only one involved with a criminal record."

"I'm ashamed to have to ask you this, but what did she do to get a criminal record? I asked her, but she wouldn't tell me. I wasn't the parent I would have liked to have been for her at the time," she said, and Ilyas hesitated.

"It happened a few weeks after Ali died," he started slowly. "She heard a rumor that someone in the neighborhood was responsible for the hit and run. We found out later it was just a coincidence, that the kid had been in an unrelated car accident on the same day, and in any case, the damage to the car wasn't on the side that hit Ali. I tried to hold her back, but she was out of control and she went at him with everything she had. There was no lasting damage done, but the boy's parents pressed assault charges. She's lucky the judge was sympathetic to the circumstances, her state of mind, and her clean record."

"I'm glad you were there," Kausar said. In the fog of grief and despair after Ali's death, entire days had gone by without her realizing, but she still couldn't believe that she had missed all of this happening.

"Adam and Siraj were there, too. If that kid *had* done it, I don't know what would have happened, what we all might have done." He swallowed. "I decided to join the police that day. I wanted to do something to help bring justice to families like yours."

The junior officer was back again, holding Kausar's phone in the plastic bag. She handed it to Ilyas, who stood to walk Kausar out.

"Take care of yourself, *beta*. When all of this is over, I hope you will visit," she said, accepting her cell phone at the entrance to the station.

"Inshallah," Ilyas said, his smile wistful. "I'd love to, but I'm not sure Sana will want to see me again once all of this is done."

"You have been friends for a long time," Kausar said, thinking of the picture on her phone—the naked yearning in Ilyas's eyes and her daughter's joy.

He kept those eyes fixed on the ground now, his shoulders hunched as he walked Kausar to the waiting female officer who would drop her back to Sana's house. "Look, I know you don't think very highly of Detective Drake. But something tells me he isn't completely happy with the investigation," he said, voice low so they weren't overheard. "To be honest, I think this text has him wondering if we have the right person. The evidence is solid—Sana has dug herself quite a hole—but I think the loose ends are really bothering him. If Sana were the guilty party, why would you be getting threatening texts telling you to stop asking questions?" When Ilyas met her gaze, his expression was almost pleading. "Now, I would never encourage someone to conduct a rogue investigation, but . . . maybe there's something more to be done."

Intrigued by his words, Kausar had plenty to think over on the drive home, and a plan started to formulate.

M*aleeha was reluctant to provide Kausar with Cerise's* home address the next day.

"But why do you need it?" she asked again, simultaneously packing her lunch, checking her phone, and eating cereal. The marvels of youth and eye-hand dexterity, Kausar thought. Fizza had left early for basketball practice.

"I want to visit her grandmother," Kausar repeated.

Maleeha's mouth was set in a stubborn line. "Cerise and I haven't talked in over a year. Maybe they moved."

"Please don't be difficult, *jaanu*," Kausar said, trying not to snap at her granddaughter. "I can always ask Lisa for it if you don't give it to me." Sana was sleeping in again, and Kausar was starting to worry. Her daughter had been a ghost since being released from custody, occasionally floating downstairs to make herself a cup of chai and barely talking to anyone save for a faint smile and hug for the girls. Kausar could recognize the symptoms of depression, but this appeared more like exhaustion and shock. She made a mental note to have a longer talk with Sana—and with Jessica for an update on the next steps in their defense strategy—when she returned from Cerise's home. Speaking of which—she raised an eyebrow at Maleeha, who sighed but rattled off an address.

The morning was chilly when Kausar set off for Beatrice's home, only a fifteen-minute walk away. She buried her hands in the pockets of her wool coat as she walked, deep in thought. Beatrice might not be home, of course, but she could leave a note. They had both grown up during a time when neighbors would routinely drop by without calling first; she hoped this visit wouldn't take Cerise's grandmother by surprise.

The family lived in a small townhouse complex south of the plaza, each home boasting a tiny driveway, a small patch of lawn, and a recessed garage. Beatrice's family had the end unit, and the border of the driveway was adorned with pretty flowers just starting to bloom. Kausar rang the bell, and Beatrice, her hair in a silk bonnet and wearing fuzzy pink slippers with a matching robe, answered the door. The initial suspicion on her face transformed into a friendly smile when she recognized Kausar.

"Mrs. Khan! You must be psychic. I baked you that pound cake and was going to bring it by tomorrow. Come in, come in."

Kausar had grabbed a box of peppermint tea from Sana's cupboard, not wishing to show up empty-handed, and Beatrice put the kettle on as she bustled around the tiny galley kitchen, keeping up a stream of chatter.

"I was just telling Cerise I've let too much time pass since we met. You must have wondered where my pound cake was. I don't like to make a promise and not keep it. Yesterday was my day off, and I sat down to do some baking. Coconut cake in the fridge already, and a nice pound cake for you. No, you take that home for the girls and your daughter, we'll eat some of that coconut cake now. Lisa keeps too many sweets in the fridge. I always warn her she's going to get the diabetes like I did, hit me at forty-eight and she'll be the same unless she watches out."

Beatrice placed a pretty mug painted with a bright pink dahlia in front of Kausar, along with a generous slice of coconut cake, before settling down across the small wooden table with her own portion. "Now we can have a proper chat. I don't have to get ready for work until noon, and you saved me a trip." Her smile pulled at the edges. "How is Sana? I heard about the arrest. Police got it wrong, as usual."

"She's back home now, *Alhamdulillah*," Kausar said.

"Thank God," Beatrice echoed. "Hope you found a good lawyer?"

Kausar nodded and took a sip of the tea. It was hot and sweetened with honey, the peppermint astringent and sharp, a nice contrast to the creamy coconut cake.

"Lisa sells this cake at her store. It's a big hit, a family recipe," Beatrice said with approval at Kausar's healthy bite. "Mine is better, of course. She's always after me to bake it for her, but who has the time?"

"It isn't easy to run your own business," Kausar agreed. "My Sana is always so busy and worried."

Beatrice nodded in understanding. "I heard she was having some trouble finding steady customers. Her stock is beautiful, but expensive."

Kausar was surprised; she hadn't known her daughter was having trouble. She had simply thrown that out there to sympathize with Lisa, but now it seemed obvious.

"In Golden, most people can't afford a lot of the extras lately. Not saying Sana's inventory doesn't deserve top dollar, but for many families, it's hard to buy groceries some weeks, let alone a pretty dress. I hope you don't mind my saying so," Beatrice said.

"Things seem more difficult now than when I lived here," Kausar agreed.

"Even Lisa has been thinking of closing her spot. Though she has her own reasons, of course."

Kausar seized the chance to discuss Lisa. "I was hoping to talk with your daughter before she went in to work. I wanted to ask about the argument she overheard between Sana and Imran, the day before he was killed. The police are using that to justify motive." Ilyas's discreet hint last night, along with Sana's listlessness, had led to another sleepless night while she contemplated her next move. Despite what she had decided on during her conversation with May, speaking to Lisa now felt like a priority. The overheard argument between Sana and Imran was a small piece of evidence, but a landslide could start with a single loosened pebble, Kausar reasoned.

"She went to the store early today," Beatrice said, then glanced at the calendar tacked up on the wall beside the table. "Lisa said she heard an argument the night before Imran was murdered? That's strange, I could have sworn she wasn't there that day . . . let's see, Imran was murdered last Tuesday, so that argument would have been the day before . . ." Beatrice squinted at the calendar, standing up to look more closely. "Yep, I was right. Lisa wasn't at the shop that day."

Kausar tried to hide her surprise. "She seemed confident about what she had heard when we spoke last."

Beatrice shook her head. "Impossible. Lisa had a doctor's appointment on that Monday. I remember because she asked me to cover for her behind the counter, but I couldn't find anyone to take my shift. She'd been waiting months for a specialist appointment, and there was a last-minute cancellation. She had to close the store that day."

Kausar sat back, coconut cake half eaten on her plate. "That means Lisa couldn't have overheard the argument between Imran and Sana."

"She was thinking of some other time, maybe. Besides, that man was always picking fights. He even made that sweet Mr. Jin angry. There were so many altercations in that plaza, they'd be easy to mix up."

"But Luxmi told the police Lisa overheard them the day before he was killed," Kausar said.

Beatrice sighed. "I don't mind sharing that my girl has been struggling lately, Mrs. Khan."

"Please, call me Kausar. What do you mean?"

"She's tired all the time, forgetting things. I wouldn't be surprised if she forgot her own name one of these days. I heard her on the phone with her friend the other week, and she was talking about selling the store and opening a food truck. You can control your own hours a bit more that way. Sounds just as unstable as running your own shop to me, but she knows her business."

"A food truck might be a nice change," Kausar said, her mind processing. "She could take it to festivals or cater events."

"Not sure where she'll get the money to set up a food truck. Lisa's smart like that, though. Wouldn't be surprised if she already had a plan mapped out. If the plaza is sold, she'll be ahead of the curve now."

"She's lucky to have you," Kausar said.

"Your daughter is lucky to have you, too," Beatrice added. "So is the neighborhood. I haven't forgotten your kindness to Cerise."

"Did you find out what she was doing that night?" Kausar asked.

"She told me she went for a walk. That girl hates walking, not when she can run. No, I bet she was out there to meet her boyfriend. *Martin*." Beatrice wrinkled her nose. "I told her he was trouble, but she said he's good to her. Her mom doesn't know. She's got enough on her plate." Beatrice hesitated, before continuing. "Besides, Lisa and I, we didn't always get on when she was younger. I never liked the boys she hung around, and when she married, I didn't come to the wedding. She didn't tell me when she was having problems with Cerise's dad, either, not until it was too late. I try not to judge now, but I have a feeling that

Martin is a bad sort. I told Cerise the same, but she only laughed. I worry about telling Lisa in case it reopens all those old wounds."

"I suppose everyone has a Martin in their past," Kausar said with a smile.

"Never held with that opinion. No need to make your own bad mistakes when you can learn from others."

"I married when I was not much older than Cerise," Kausar confessed. "I never had the chance to make those sorts of mistakes. Sometimes I wonder if I missed out."

Beatrice looked at Kausar for a moment, then threw back her head and laughed. "Perhaps you're right. I suppose there was a young man in my past, a long time ago, who was good for a laugh and not much else. I like you, Kausar. You're honest." The older woman looked as if she were trying to make up her mind about something.

Kausar decided to encourage her. "I try to be. I hope you feel you can be honest with me?"

"I do," Beatrice said firmly, making up her mind. "Though I hate to pile more troubles at your door."

"Is it about Sana?" Kausar asked, but Beatrice shook her head.

"Cerise told me something about Maleeha, and I've been turning it over in my mind ever since. The girls used to be close, up until last year. But Cerise told me Maleeha's changed. She sees her hanging around in the hallways when she should be in class. The school calls home with this sort of thing, of course, but they don't do much more than that, not when there aren't any other issues. She also said Maleeha's been hanging around with a different crowd. These new kids, Cerise called them 'shady.'"

"What does that mean?" Kausar asked.

"Means they're trouble. Maybe into more than the usual high school mischief. I'm not trying to stick my nose in, but I thought you should know." Beatrice's expression was grim, but Kausar thanked her just the same.

On the walk home, hands full of pound cake and a few slices of coconut cake, Kausar's thoughts churned. Lisa had been so sure she had overheard Sana threaten Imran the day before he was found dead inside her store. Had she lied, or simply made a mistake, as Beatrice insisted? And now, equally troubling, was Maleeha. What was her granddaughter up to at school? Considering what Maleeha had been dealing with at home—the weight of Hamza's secret and her unwarranted guilt over her parents' estrangement—her behavior was easily explained, though no less troubling. She still hadn't asked Maleeha about the cash hidden in her closet, either.

She'd have to ask her granddaughter about it all when she got home from school. But in the meantime, she needed to ask Nasir for a favor. It was time to pay Ahmed another visit.

CHAPTER 25

At home, Sana was lying listless on the couch when Kausar returned, though the sweet treats made her smile.

"Where did you go last night?" she asked. Even her voice sounded exhausted, and Kausar didn't want to add to her stress—but not talking openly with each other had landed them in enough trouble already.

Briefly, Kausar explained about the threatening text message and her late-night visit to the police station, though she left the side quest to the plaza out of the narrative for now.

By the time she was done sharing, Sana's eyes were wide and scared. "Ilyas is sure that the message came from Imran's missing phone? Mom, this is serious. Whoever has the phone probably killed Imran."

"I know, *beta*. I am being careful, I promise. Here, have some coconut cake."

Sana waved away the slice and stood up. "*Ammi*, I told you to stop asking questions. I'm in enough trouble as it is, and now you're being threatened by a killer!"

"If anything, the text I received helps your case," Kausar said. "Why would you threaten me? And how would you have been able to send the text? You were being held by the police when it came through."

But Sana was pacing now, her movements jerky and nervous, hand playing with her loose, messy braid. She looked like she needed to take a shower, though Kausar was hardly about to suggest it, in her agitated state. "Maybe Hamza could come back to keep watch at night. He could sleep on the couch. If there's someone out there threatening you, this impacts the girls, too."

Kausar took a deep breath. Her daughter had brought him up, and mindful of the pictures on her phone, she spoke. "Are you going to tell me what is happening with you and Hamza?"

Sana stopped her pacing to look at her mother. She must have recognized something in Kausar's steady gaze, because her shoulders slumped. "Hamza and I are getting divorced," she said quietly. "Though you probably suspected as much."

"I'm so sorry, Sana. Is there nothing to be done?" Kausar asked.

Sana shook her head. "He cheated on me, Mom. It wasn't the first time, either. I shouldn't have held on for as long as I did. But we have a life together—house, kids, everything all tightly wound up. Even after he confessed to the affair, he begged me to change my mind. When I wouldn't, he went back to his latest girlfriend," she said bitterly.

"I thought you were happy," Kausar said gently. "I'm sorry you did not feel you could talk to me about this."

Sana sank back to the couch, fingers playing with the fringe of a cream-colored blanket. "I wasn't ready to let go. We had built a life together. I mistook being busy for happiness for a long time. Looking back, we never should have married." Sana looked at her mother. "You were right about that."

"I didn't want to be," Kausar said. She took no pleasure in her daughter's words. She hadn't realized her muted objections to the marriage all those years ago had made an impression on her Sana.

"At first, we were fine. Maleeha was born a bit sooner than we planned, but she was a joy. Except Hamza was working all the time, and I was home with her by myself. I joined a few mom and baby groups, but those first few years were tough. We started fighting. Hamza was traveling, and even when he was home, he was distracted. I suspected there was something going on with a coworker, but he denied it. When Maleeha was four, we talked about separating. Then I found out I was pregnant with Fizza."

Kausar listened to this story with her heart in her throat. She'd had no idea what Sana had been going through. Her daughter never said a word during her brief visits to North Bay, or during their conversations on the phone. She asked if Hassan had known.

"He helped with the down payment on our house, remember? He thought it might help, if we didn't have to worry about money. He thought Hamza might work less so we'd have more time to work on our relationship."

Kausar wanted to cry at this revelation. Hassan had always been there for all of them, and in that moment, she missed her husband deeply. "Did it help?" she asked.

Sana nodded her head slowly. "With Fizza and Maleeha, our family felt complete, and it was nice not to worry so much about money. But it turned out to be just another distraction. The truth is, we were never a good match. Hamza wanted a wife who was more glamorous, more social. He's always been more focused on appearances than anything else, and he spent too much money in an effort to move up the social ladder. I wanted someone who was home more, who wanted to pour their energy into our family. By the end of last year, even before I found out about *her*, we both knew things were over between us. That was before I found out about all the money he lost."

That answered a question Kausar had been loath to bring up. “Did he tell you about his bad investments?” she asked.

Sana shook her head, cheeks flushed in anger. “I had to snoop through his papers and online records to find out. He cleaned out our savings. Thank God I used some of the inheritance from Dad to start my own business. I’m not sure I’ll be able to keep the store, but at least I can sell the inventory and start over.” There was such sadness in her voice that Kausar took a seat on the couch next to her, even as she was relieved Sana knew the true state of affairs, such as they were. Her daughter was no fool.

Kausar had known a few women who had divorced, women her age whose husbands had been tyrants, or abusive. But from this story, it seemed that Hamza and Sana had simply been unhappy, and then allowed that unhappiness to fester unchecked. Her first instinct was to wonder if they could have worked harder to fix things. But looking at Sana’s miserable face, she knew that voicing those thoughts would burn the tenuous truce between them. She reached out and squeezed her daughter’s hand.

“You deserve better, *beta*. When this horrible business with Imran is far behind you, I hope you will find your own happiness,” she said. The surprise and relief that flitted across Sana’s face made Kausar’s heart clench. Their relationship had been a careful dance of one step forward, one step back, but she hoped her presence now was starting to mend the gulf. “Perhaps that happiness might include Ilyas?” she added.

Sana’s face clouded immediately. “What do you mean?”

Kausar held up her phone, showing Sana the picture of her with Ilyas that Fatima had shared. “I know you two were close when you were younger,” Kausar began. “I also know he hurt you deeply, after Ali passed. People are saying—”

But Sana was having none of it. Her eyes blazed as she threw her arms wide. “*I don’t care* what people are saying! I’m tired of everyone acting like my life is theirs to judge. No matter what I do, it's never the right thing. First there's pressure to get married. Then to have a child. Then another child. And why haven't I had a son yet? Have we bought a house? How much money does my husband make? How much jewelry do I own? Why did I open a business, and why are the prices at my store so high? How dare I try to carve out my own life? I can't win, because the game is rigged and I'm stuck." Sana was breathing hard now beside her on the couch, hands shaking in fury.

Looking at her daughter's angry, beautiful face, Kausar felt a wave of love so all-encompassing, it took her breath away. But any move she made to embrace Sana would be taken as pity and condescension. Kausar looked down at her hands, so similar to her daughter's.

"I didn't mean to make you feel I was concerned about the gossip. I just meant, do you still have feelings for Ilyas, even after everything? Because he seems to really care about you," Kausar said. She wasn't sure if she meant the arrest, or the long-ago breakup. A tiny shift in Sana's eyes answered her question, but she rose from the couch and left before Kausar could ask anything else.

Kausar offered to meet Nasir at Ahmed's office, but he insisted on picking her up.

"The drive will allow us time to strategize," he said. It was early afternoon, and she was aware he had taken time from his busy law practice to help her, though he assured her it beat writing memos and reading email.

"What did your intern Razia think of you leaving early to help me?" Kausar asked when she had settled inside his Mercedes S-Class, the interior quietly luxurious.

"What she doesn't know won't annoy her," Nasir said, smiling. "Actually, I took your hint. She is now primarily working with my less devastatingly handsome partner Adeel. He's known as the desi Jack Black."

Kausar laughed. "Mr. Black is quite the charmer. Women love a man who can make them laugh."

"I make you laugh," Nasir said, eyes on the road.

"Yes, you do," Kausar agreed. Their brief shared glance was heated.

"Shall we run through the plan?" Nasir said with a half-smile on his face. She nodded.

I *was surprised when my assistant said you wanted to speak* to me." Ahmed's voice was muffled, and Kausar craned her ear closer to her phone to hear. Nasir's voice was clearer, of course—the speaker was closer to him.

"Yes, I've had some time to think over what we spoke about. I'd like to know more before I commit, but you're right. This red-hot real estate market won't last forever, and if we want to build generational wealth, we must strike now."

Kausar grinned at her friend's smooth delivery, just as they had practiced. She was seated inside Nasir's comfortable car, the windows cracked slightly for air circulation, listening in on a conversation happening inside Ahmed's office several stories above.

"We are not playing at spy craft," she had explained to Nasir when laying out the plan. "You will simply call me before you begin your meeting with Ahmed and make sure the phone is set to speaker, so I can hear what he says. No need to buy any fancy listening devices."

"But I have Amazon Prime," Nasir had coaxed. "Same-day shipping."

"No," Kausar said again. "The simplest plan is always the best."

The men were inside Ahmed's office now. "I'm a little unclear about how all of this works," Nasir said. There was the tinkle of cutlery and the sound of a teacup being placed on a saucer.

Kausar could picture Ahmed leaning back, the smug expression on his face, and her hand itched. It was probably better she had elected to stay behind.

Their initial plan had involved her accompanying Nasir, but they both agreed that Ahmed would speak more freely if she weren't there, given his condescension and dismissal of her as an older woman on her last visit. She trusted her friend to steer the conversation; Nasir understood the stakes for her family. If they could figure out what it was Ahmed and Imran were working on together, it might provide a lead for Detective Drake to pursue. Kausar clung to what Ilyas had hinted, that the detective wasn't happy with Sana as the main suspect, despite the overwhelming evidence of her guilt.

"Once you join our venture, I can provide more details. But for now, let me keep it hypothetical," Ahmed started. "People are recommended to me on a discreet basis, and after we establish a relationship, I tell them about the sort of work I do, and the returns I've managed to secure in the past. They usually beg me to invest their money for them. Most people don't really know what to do with their money, you know? And the promise of quick growth can be quite tempting. Some of them even decide to take out a reverse mortgage on their home and press the proceeds into my hands. That's where you come in. Once I obtain the capital, you help me sprinkle it around. Panama is great, and there are a few other friendly banks in other places. You'll get paid, plus an extra bonus for being discreet, and everyone is happy."

Nasir hummed, thinking it over. "What about the investor? Are they happy?"

Ahmed chuckled. "For a time, yes." Kausar bared her teeth at the phone. He was describing a pyramid scheme, where every new investor's capital was used to placate the previous one, except the so-called returns were built on a tower of sand, ready to topple at the slightest shift of the wind. Ahmed really was the worst.

"Why do you want me in on it?" Nasir asked. "Seems like the fewer people you have involved, the fewer you have to split the profits between."

"People trust you," Ahmed said, and Kausar noted his reasonable tone, his subtle flattery. She guessed Ahmed was quite good at convincing people to do as he wanted, once he had decided they were worth his time. "You have a certain reputation in our community. With your name attached, my business will grow, and so will yours. Believe me, we can't lose."

"Can I ask where you put the money?" Nasir said, and Ahmed chuckled again.

"This will only work if you stay in your lane. Don't ask too many questions, and I'll do the same. It's called *plausible deniability.* I'm sure you're familiar with the term." The condescension fairly oozed out of him, Kausar thought in disgust. "We run on referrals, so it will only be a few clients at a time. We like to stay exclusive. It makes our clients feel as if they are part of a special club."

A club where the reward was bankruptcy and ruin, Kausar thought. No wonder Hamza had been so easily taken in; he craved being part of anything exclusive. Kausar leaned forward, mentally urging Nasir to lead the conversation towards Imran.

"I could use the extra income. I've been meaning to expand my practice, and I need a lot of capital, more than I can get from a bank," Nasir said. "But before I agree, could I talk to someone you've worked with in the past?"

Ahmed's voice seemed to grow wistful. "Ever the good businessman you are, asking for references. I used to have a partner, someone who knew the community and who would send new clients my way, but he died recently. It was quite a blow to the operation."

"I'm sorry to hear that." Nasir's voice was a rumble. "In that case, I take it your partner was Imran, from the Golden Crescent Plaza?"

"How did you guess?" Ahmed sounded surprised, and a note of suspicion entered his voice.

"Great minds must think alike, because he also mentioned something to me in passing, once," Nasir hurried to explain. "He said if I wanted to make a good return on my investments, I should come to you at Silver Star."

His ego suitably stroked, Ahmed sounded mollified. "Imran was good at picking people out. I'm not surprised he and I had the same idea to approach you. If we decide to take this further, you'll have to keep this just between us. This is . . . coloring outside the lines of my job description at Silver Star Holdings."

"I'm not sure I understand," Nasir said, but Kausar did. This confirmation of her suspicions chilled her.

"This is a side hustle, if you will. My job at Silver Star is more straightforward. The people who own the company would not be happy if they knew about my other income stream. If they found out, I would have to make a quick exit."

Kausar inhaled sharply. Sana had mentioned that Silver Star Holdings was a legitimate business, with a board. It would make sense if Ahmed had been growing his "side hustle" by using Silver Star's name to lend legitimacy. If Ahmed had swindled Hamza out of his life savings like this, why would Hamza then send Kausar to him for financial advice?

"So this enterprise of yours is not affiliated with Silver Star," Nasir clarified. "I ask because it is common knowledge that Silver Star Holdings wants to buy Imran's plaza."

Ahmed sighed. "Yes, I gave Mubeen our latest offer a few days ago. I'm confident he won't sell to Platinum Properties. Their CEO, Patrick Kim, is too soft, in any case."

Kausar wasn't sure what Ahmed meant by that statement, but Nasir must have determined it wasn't important, because he moved on.

"You're brave to strike out on your own," Nasir said to Ahmed.

"To be honest, my talents were being wasted here, though we share a common vision. I'd like to keep things amiable with my employers. They're not the sort of people I want to upset, hence the need for secrecy. Lawyers are good at that. What do you say, Nasir? Are you ready to make some real money?"

The men shook hands, and then, as Kausar had instructed, Nasir casually brought up Sana.

"It must have been terrible, losing your partner like that. Do you think that Sana person is the one responsible for your friend's murder?" he asked. "I knew her when she was younger; her father was an old friend. I was shocked when I heard about her arrest."

As Kausar suspected, Ahmed was eager to gossip now that the business side of the conversation had been concluded. "Who can say? Though I wouldn't be surprised. I met Sana's mother recently, you know. She seemed clueless." Ahmed laughed. "Her son-in-law was one of the first people Imran sent my way. One of the unhappy clients," he said, and Kausar could tell he had leaned close now, because his voice was both confiding and loud. "When Hamza boasted to me how rich his mother-in-law, a recent widow, was, I made him a deal—if he convinced her to invest, I would wipe his slate clean."

Kausar leaned back in shock. She had suspected that Hamza was desperate, but not that he would put her directly in the path of a predator like Ahmed. She could hear the strain in Nasir's voice as he fought to feign calm. "How clever of you," her friend said.

"I did warn Hamza that real estate was a volatile investment." Kausar could picture Ahmed's wink. "He knew what he was signing up for, or at least, he thought he did." Ahmed's laugh was cruel, and despite everything, she felt some sympathy for the hapless Hamza. Fraud relied on the victim's shame at being duped. "In any case, I hope Imran's killer is brought to justice. Murder is bad for business. It brings too much unwanted attention. Our business is best done after hours, you understand. It will be worth your time, I guarantee it, Nasir."

The men spoke for a few more minutes, and by the time Nasir returned to the car ten minutes later, Kausar was bent over her floral notebook, writing furiously.

"I feel like I need to take a shower," he said with a grimace, before starting the car and maneuvering out of the parking lot. "I confess it was fun, even without the spy equipment. Any time you need a sidekick, let me know. Did you manage to capture the conversation?"

Kausar nodded, holding up the small recorder she had brought along.

"Ahmed is a stupid man. It's hard to believe people trust him with their money," Nasir said.

"They're usually duping themselves. He preys on people's greed," Kausar said.

"People like Hamza. I'd like to take your son-in-law to a secluded place and teach him a lesson," Nasir said grimly.

"My soon-to-be ex-son-in-law," Kausar corrected, and Nasir sent her a searching glance.

"I thought it was interesting that Ahmed seemed genuinely scared of his boss at Silver Star Holdings finding out about his side hustle."

"Do you know who runs the company?" Kausar asked, and Nasir shook his head but promised to look up the title when he returned to his office.

"I'm sure you've thought of this already, but if Hamza were angry at Imran for getting him involved with Ahmed . . ."

"The police checked Hamza's alibi. He was with his girlfriend in the west end of the city on the night in question," Kausar said quietly, and Nasir whistled. "On the other hand, Ahmed made it clear that Hamza was a referral from Imran. There could be more than one angry investor with a vendetta. There is also the possibility that Sana found out what Imran had done and confronted him herself," she added, with some frustration. No matter what she did, all her questions either led to more questions—or back where she had started, at Sana's door.

They lapsed into silence for the rest of the drive back to the neighborhood, but when Nasir parked on Sana's driveway, it was with the air of a man who had something else entirely on his mind. Kausar's heart sped up when he met her gaze. She had a feeling she knew what he was about to say.

"I know you returned to Toronto under unhappy circumstances," Nasir started. "Despite that, I've enjoyed spending time with you. Far more than I anticipated. And I have always enjoyed your company, Kausar." His smile was tender, warm eyes searching her own. She wasn't sure what he saw in her expression, but his words grew bold. "You and I are old enough to know not to waste each other's time. Kausar, you have always been one of the most beautiful and fascinating women I've ever known."

Kausar wasn't sure how to respond. "Thank you, Nasir. Your business cards are quite correct—you are as good looking as you are smart."

But Nasir was not easily distracted by a joke this time. The look in his eyes was open and vulnerable, and something in Kausar's gut tightened. Part of her wished he would stop talking, while another part was eager to hear what he had to say.

"I've always been your admirer, but something has changed

in you lately," Nasir said, his voice rough and intimate. "As if a light has switched on, making you burn even brighter."

"I've enjoyed spending time with you as well," she started, stumbling over her words. Kausar had never been in this position before, and she wasn't sure how to proceed. Yet her words were true—Nasir was funny, attractive, kind, and hadn't asked much of her. He was the perfect friend—though if she were being honest with herself, she had known from the start that he wanted more.

"I've been on my own for a long time now," Nasir began, and Kausar felt her heartbeat accelerate. "I know how to be alone. But I turn fifty-three next year, and I'm ready to imagine a different life for myself. I was going to wait before I broached the subject, especially with everything else in your life, but I confess I am not a very patient man. Not when the prize is you." He met her gaze. "I don't need an answer or a commitment. I only want to ask a question: Can you imagine a future with me?"

Silence stretched between them, taut and tense, and she couldn't speak. He must have understood her hesitation, because he nodded sadly.

"I understand," he said softly. "I shouldn't have spoken."

"You are good to me," Kausar said slowly. "It's just that I have never been on my own before, free to live entirely for myself. Believe me, Nasir, if there was anyone I could say yes to right now, it would be you."

He reached for her hand then, slowly enough that she could stop him if she wanted. Kausar watched as he placed a single kiss on the center of her palm. "It would be a shame to dim a light you have only just discovered," he said softly. "I've always known you would do great things. If you ever see a future that includes me, I'm here. In the meantime, call me anytime you need a friend."

She walked to Sana's door on unsteady legs, mind whirling with new possibilities.

CHAPTER 26

Fizza was parked in front of the television with a snack when Kausar let herself inside the house, and she informed her grandmother that Maleeha and Sana were in their rooms. After texting Fatima with a request, Kausar went to her granddaughter's room, hesitating before knocking once and opening the door, ready to confront Maleeha.

Part of her felt elated at Nasir's confession. She had always liked and admired him, but she wasn't looking for romance, even though the two of them made a lot of sense. Perhaps if things were different, she might have even answered yes to his question. But she had a murder to solve, and relationships with her daughter and granddaughters to fix. She hadn't been lying when she told Nasir that she craved her freedom, as well. Living life on her own terms, following her own whims, was intoxicating, and she wasn't willing to give it up just yet.

Her granddaughter was sprawled across her bed scrolling on her phone, but she greeted her *nani* with a smile. "Brianna texted today. She thinks you're cool," she said, putting her phone away and sitting cross-legged on the unmade bed.

"She is a most interesting young woman," Kausar said, taking a seat on the swivel chair in front of Maleeha's desk. A padded corkboard was decorated with pictures, and she examined them now.

"Where did you go today? Any new leads?" Maleeha asked, moving to stand beside her.

Kausar considered her options. After what her granddaughter had shared about Hamza's affair, she felt closer to her than ever. However, Maleeha had also lied about where she was going the other day, and Beatrice's warning about skipped classes and bad company was worrying. This conversation would not be easy.

She began by sharing a few details about Ahmed's shady dealings, and Imran's dysfunctional family relationships.

Maleeha's face lit up. "If Ahmed and Imran were working together to rip people off, I bet there are a load of people who wanted one or both of them dead. You should tell the cops."

Kausar hated to burst her granddaughter's hopeful bubble. "I would, except I suspect your father was one of the people duped by Ahmed and Imran. If anything, I fear it would add more fuel to the fire of evidence against your mother," she said gently. "Sana is still the primary suspect, I'm afraid."

Maleeha slumped. "So, my parents are broke because my dad lost all our money to a con man, and he can't be bothered to be here for his daughters or his wife because he's off with another woman," she said. "And my mom might still go to jail for twenty-five years. Things just keep getting better."

"I know this is disheartening, but everything new that we learn will get us closer to the truth, and I won't give up," Kausar said. Now was the time to bring up the money Maleeha had stashed away. She glanced at the closet, where she spotted the cardboard box peeking out. "I also wanted to talk to you about something else."

Maleeha flopped back on her bed. "I knew it," she announced to her ceiling.

Kausar sat next to her on the bed. "What do you know, *beta*?"

"You talked to Cerise's mom about me, right? Listen, Lisa used to be chill, but she's been mad ever since Cerise and I had that argument last year over Martin. He was flirting with me, and maybe I flirted back, but Cerise totally flipped. Mom stayed out of it, but Lisa didn't and got involved. I wouldn't trust anything she said."

"It was Cerise's grandmother I spoke with, not Lisa. Beatrice is worried about you. Have you been attending class regularly?"

Maleeha sat up, her face set in a petulant pout. "People need to mind their own business." Kausar couldn't help but think she sounded just like Sana. "Yes, I've been going to class. Why would I go to school just to skip?"

"Perhaps you are being influenced by others who are leading you down the garden path," Kausar suggested.

Maleeha blinked. "Our school doesn't have a garden." She frowned. "Is that what Cerise said? Adam, Nicole, and Malik, they used to be her friends, too, but they like me better and she's jealous. Besides, she got Martin in the end. She's too busy to hang with us now so I don't know why she cares what I'm doing."

Beatrice had mentioned Cerise's unsuitable boyfriend. This sounded like typical teenage drama, unrelated to Sana's current predicament. Maleeha continued, aggrieved. "The teachers always pick on them. It's not their fault. They don't need school anyway, they have their own thing going on," she said.

"What sort of thing?" Kausar asked, filing away the names of Maleeha's other friends.

"Reselling clothes, drop-shipping, that sort of thing. They asked if I wanted in. I mean, what good did school do for you, or Mom, or Ali *mamu*? The wrong people keep making money. Just look at Imran and Ahmed—they're robbing people and nobody is doing anything about it! Brianna is right, we have to find our own way. The old ways don't work anymore."

Kausar had no idea what reselling or drop-shipping was, but she understood her granddaughter's frustration. Was that the origin of the money in Maleeha's closet? It was time to find out. "Could I ask you something else?" Without waiting for an answer, she headed to the closet and reached for the cardboard box. Her granddaughter was by her side in an instant. Maleeha ripped the box from her hands, holding it protectively against her chest, her eyes blazing.

"You had no right to look through my things." Malecha was seething, but there was a trace of panic in her voice.

"I know, it was wrong of me," Kausar said. "But you are not being honest, either. You don't have a job, and yet you have thousands of dollars in cash hidden in your closet. You lied to me about studying in the library, and you enter and leave the house without anyone noticing. Don't try to deny it. I have witnessed your little cat feet with my own eyes on at least two occasions. I am worried that Beatrice and Cerise are right, that you are involved in something dangerous. Will you talk to me about it?"

Maleeha was frightened, and she jerked her head no. "I can't," she whispered. "Please don't tell Mom, it's not . . . please don't ask me to explain. You'll only make things worse."

Kausar looked at her trembling granddaughter and wanted to envelop her in her arms. "Let me help you, *beta*," she said.

"You can't. *Nani*, I want you to leave my room. Now." Maleeha was shaking so hard now, she seemed about to pass out. Kausar knew that pushing any further would only lead to tears or a denial.

She wanted to push, to demand to know what her granddaughter was up to, to grab the box of cash and march into Sana's room and . . . do what? Her daughter was barely functional, and Maleeha was clearly terrified. The question was, what or who was she scared of? She needed to think. "Of course, *beta*," she said instead. "We will talk later, inshallah."

She heard Maleeha's whisper from outside the door. "I made everything worse."

Kausar didn't look back at her granddaughter, but her voice was firm. "We will make it better together. I promise."

I *don't understand. Why didn't you insist she tell you what's* going on?" May said on the phone. "Maleeha is obviously mixed up in something serious, something dangerous."

"Perhaps," Kausar said. She had checked in on Sana after leaving Maleeha's room, before making her way to her own and shutting the door. Her daughter was sleeping, and Fizza was still in front of the television. "But she is not, I think, in any imminent danger."

There was silence on the other end as May absorbed what Kausar said. "You know what happened."

"I have a strong suspicion, that is all," Kausar said.

"Who did it? You have to tell me. I've been thinking about it all week, and I can't narrow it down at all."

"Plenty of people have motive and opportunity," Kausar agreed. "Including my own daughter, I'm sorry to say."

"That reminds me, I was looking over the pictures you took from Imran's office. Did you notice anything strange about them?" May said.

Kausar put her on speaker and flipped through the pictures rapidly, zooming in on the ones from Imran's office in the plaza. "It's a mess," she said.

"A disaster," May agreed. "Except for the desk."

"I noticed that, too, but I didn't think much of it," Kausar said. Zooming out, the clean desk looked like an anomaly.

"Chronically disorganized people don't have one spot they keep clean, not unless they're filming social media videos. I can't imagine Imran with a TikTok."

Kausar tried to magnify the files neatly stacked on his desk but nothing came into clear focus.

"It almost looks like someone came into the office and cleaned the desk for some reason," May remarked. "As for the files and the pictures from that notebook, I can't make any sense of them. But one thing is for sure—Imran was hiding something. Nobody writes in code like a child playing at spies if they're innocent. It's not good business."

Kausar's phone buzzed with a call on the other line, and she told May she had to go. The request she had texted Fatima had come to fruition, and her friend was waiting on the driveway to take her to another meeting.

"Detective Aunty is on the hunt!" May said cheerfully. "And don't think we're done talking about Nasir. I can't believe he asked you out, and you still haven't sent me his picture!"

A*njum was already seated inside the independent coffee* shop when Kausar and Fatima arrived, her hands wrapped around a large mug. Fatima joined the line to order, motioning Kausar towards the young woman at the table.

"I was surprised you agreed to meet with me," Kausar said, settling into the booth.

Anjum looked tired, and she wasn't wearing any makeup, but this didn't detract from her beauty. She wore another *salwar kameez* today, this one forest green with white embroidery around the neck and cuffs. Sana would approve. "I was curious," she said. "My mother said you visited the other day, despite my warning to stay away."

"How is your mother?" Kausar asked.

"She's half-packed and ready to move to Pakistan as soon as the plaza is sold and the money distributed. I can't wait for her to leave." Anjum's tone was flat, no inflection in her voice.

Kausar wasn't surprised. Parveen seemed a demanding and mercurial mother at the best of times. "She told us your marriage was imminent. That your inheritance depended on you agreeing to the match she found for you," she said, watching Anjum closely. Fatima joined them at the table, placing a tea in front of Kausar before taking a seat beside her and sipping at a fruit drink.

This comment got a reaction from Anjum. The young woman rolled her eyes. "Yes, I have to fulfill my manifest destiny and marry who she says, when she dictates. I'm surprised my parents didn't have marionette strings surgically attached when I was a baby, the way they want to run my life."

Kausar was surprised at the young woman's candor; she had been sure Anjum would refuse to talk. Her surprise must have shown on her face, because Anjum snorted. "Since you seem to make a habit of snooping no matter what I threaten, I thought I'd save you the trouble. A woman your age should conserve her energy," she added snidely.

Kausar and Fatima exchanged a glance, eyebrows raised. The gloves were off, clearly. "That's thoughtful of you, but I'm not in danger of toppling into my grave just yet," she said mildly.

"Fatima Aunty said you had information you wanted to share," Anjum said, impatience creeping into her voice.

Kausar glanced at Fatima. They had discussed a game plan in the car. "Have you found your father's cell phone since he passed?"

Anjum shook her head. "Since you're asking, I assume you know the police didn't find it with his body. Have you checked among Sana's things?"

Kausar ignored the dig. "I thought you might have access to it remotely. Imran might have asked you to keep track of his passwords. I know many parents need their children's help staying organized with technology." She tried to make this sound casual, but Anjum's eyes narrowed with suspicion. The idea had come to Kausar last night.

"So what if I did?" Anjum asked. "Let me guess, your granddaughter set up your phone and she has your passwords?"

Kausar let her silence be taken for agreement. "It must have been frustrating, having to take care of your parents, but being denied any autonomy over your own life. To be overlooked again and again, and watch your brother given the responsibility you knew you could handle."

Anjum shrugged. "You're not very subtle, are you? I see you, but you're not wrong. My mother never wanted me to go to university. Dad thought it was a waste of money, too. Why educate a girl when she will only get married and stay home with her children? They wanted Mubeen to get all the academic honors, but he couldn't be bothered to attend class half the time. Not that it mattered. My parents wanted us to play the roles they set down for us."

Fatima and Kausar exchanged another look, remembering their own conversation on this topic, the cultural expectations that had dictated their own lives.

"My parents are traditional," Anjum continued, and Kausar realized that the flat neutrality in her voice was actually a well-steeped bitterness. "That's a polite way of saying they're sexist and refuse to update their ancient views. In some families, no matter their faith, culture comes first—and in my family, girls come last. In the end, my grandfather paid my tuition and Mubeen's, too, which Dad thought was only fair."

"Because your father was upset at being treated like any other tenant in the plaza?" Kausar asked.

Anjum blinked in surprise. "You're aware he had a store there? It was years ago. I know Mr. Jin doesn't talk, so it must have been Luxmi. They're the only old-timers left at Golden."

Kausar shrugged, and Anjum leaned back against the booth,

now lost in memories. "I grew up in that plaza. Some of my happiest memories are running around with the other shopkeepers' kids. But my dad, who ran a dry-cleaning business, hated every second of it. He thought it was beneath him, as the son of the owner. My *dada* wanted him to learn the ropes, to be a tenant before he became the landlord. Now Dad is making Mubeen do the same thing, except he just wants . . . wanted . . . to keep him under his thumb." Anjum laughed, and the resentment was clear. "Not that anyone offered *me* a storefront."

"Is that what you wanted, to run your own business?" Kausar asked.

"Nobody much cares what I want," she said shortly. "I'm going to marry the entitled dillweed my mom picked out, and divorce him the minute my inheritance money comes in. And then I plan to never talk to anyone in my family ever again." Two bright spots of color bloomed high on her cheeks, and her eyes shone with anger. "I'm done putting my life on hold to make others happy."

"Good for you," Fatima said. These were the first words she had spoken since she joined them. Kausar remembered what her friend had said at her house, before Sana was arrested.

She repeated them now. "A woman's ambition is always limited by her circumstances."

Anjum pondered this. "That's true," she murmured. "Both of you are different from how I imagined."

"We could say the same of you," Fatima said. "Your outside does not match the inside: You dress in *salwar kameez*, make chai, and play the demure daughter, but you have a rebellious streak, and an escape plan."

Anjum shrugged again, taking a long sip of her drink and eyeing them over the brim. The anger that had flared a moment before now cooled into curiosity, but there was still a spark of wariness in her gaze.

"Have you given up on running the plaza yourself?" Kausar asked.

"It's out of my hands," Anjum said. "Not that I had any say to begin with. My father would never listen to me. He would rather lose everything than admit he was wrong."

"Your brother said Imran was never happy with what he had. He told me that unhappiness killed him in the end," Kausar said.

"I think it was your daughter's knife that did that, actually," Anjum said sharply.

"Or perhaps it was the natural outcome of the business he was conducting with Ahmed Malik," Kausar said. Beside her, Fatima stared. She had not had time to fill her friend in on the latest development. But she had a hunch that even if Anjum hadn't been consulted on what her father got up to, she was not unaware.

The young woman shifted, averting her gaze. "Ahmed has been trying to buy the plaza for a long time for Silver Star Holdings," Anjum said, carefully nonchalant, and Kausar knew her hunch was right.

"I'm not talking about the property deal," Kausar said. "I'm talking about the side hustle Ahmed had going with your father, bilking investors through an elaborate mortgage fraud and pyramid scheme."

Beside her, Fatima gasped in surprise. "What? Siraj was talking only yesterday of investing with Ahmed Malik."

This comment gave Kausar pause, but her attention returned to Anjum, who now resembled a trapped animal.

"I don't know what you *think* you've uncovered, but it has nothing to do with me," Anjum said.

"I'm wondering how much you knew, and if you were angry at your father for what he was doing. If—or rather, when—his scheme was discovered, your entire inheritance would be at risk from creditors or seized by the authorities. You have just told us you're willing to marry someone you don't love to get your share of the money." Kausar was taking a gamble here, and she wasn't sure how it would play out—whether Anjum would laugh, throw her drink in her face, or storm out. "What else might a person do to escape a life they don't want?"

A dark, secretive light flashed for a moment in Anjum's eyes, before she hid it with the expertise of long practice. "You're making a lot of assumptions, Kausar Aunty. You're shooting in the dark because your daughter is in trouble. Is this really the best you can come up with?" She stood up and gathered her bag. "It's time you stop playing detective and accept the truth—Sana is guilty, and she is going to jail."

Kausar stared at the table after Anjum left, Fatima fretting beside her.

"Do you think Anjum is responsible for her father's death?" Fatima asked.

"I thought it the most likely of several possibilities," Kausar said. "Now I'm not so sure. I'm missing something vital."

"When did you find out about Ahmed's pyramid scheme?" Fatima asked. "I have to warn Siraj not to invest with him."

"I didn't know Siraj was in a position to invest money," Kausar said, recalling her initial thought. Anjum's words ricocheted in her mind: *Sana is guilty.* Was she right, and had this all been for nothing? Was Sana's current listlessness a sign of her guilt?

"Ahmed promised him double- and triple-digit returns. Siraj asked to borrow money from me. He wants to buy a house. I need to call him," Fatima said.

The women were quiet on the ride home, Fatima distracted when Kausar thanked her for the company. In the kitchen, Sana was chopping vegetables for a simple stir fry. She looked better than she had for the past few days, and the relief Kausar felt at this normal activity made it easy to chat with her about inconsequential things.

That night over dinner, Fizza kept up a running commentary

about her latest basketball game—they lost, but she scored half a dozen points, including a three-pointer—while Maleeha picked at her noodles and avoided Kausar's gaze. As the meal drew to a close, Sana's phone pinged with a notification. She read the message, and her face drained of color.

"What is it?" Kausar asked, alarmed.

Maleeha fixed fearful eyes on her mother. "Is it Dad? Where is he?"

Sana was already up, wiping her mouth and striding towards the door. "It's Mr. Jin. He's in the hospital. Someone set fire to his store."

CHAPTER 27

Kausar updated May over text. Her friend's response was immediate. I don't like this. Mr. Jin kept his mouth shut and he was still attacked. Be careful.

Sana had left right away last night, leaving the girls in Kausar's care. Maleeha wanted to go with her but had been persuaded to stay back. The only reason Sana had been called was because her unit was near Mr. Jin's, and Sana's store had sustained some damage along with Imran's office, though they were lucky that a passerby had called 911. The fire had been contained quickly, and Mr. Jin taken to the hospital. The plaza was once again the center of an investigation by the police, and this time by the fire department, too.

Kausar's phone pinged and she glanced down, expecting another concerned message from May. Instead, it was from the same unknown number as before—Imran's old cell, she now knew. Her pulse quickened as she read the message.

Your daughter is next. Stop asking questions.

Kausar's blood ran cold. *Who are you?* she typed with frozen fingers.

She didn't have to wait long for a response. *This is your last warning.*

Kausar stared at her phone. She felt a tentative hand warm on her arm, and she looked into Fizza's worried brown eyes, so similar to her own. "*Nani*, are you okay?"

"Only wondering where your mother is right now," Kausar answered.

Her younger granddaughter had volunteered to help clear the table after dinner, while Maleeha was upstairs—she really did have a math test tomorrow, she'd promised.

Fizza now hollered for her sister to come downstairs. When Maleeha joined them in the living room, Fizza reached for her sister's phone and navigated to the Find My app. "Mom is still at the plaza," she confirmed.

"That lets you know where she is at all times?" Kausar asked. Her heart was starting to slow to a normal pace once more; this second message, so soon on the heels of Mr. Jin's attack, had shaken her badly.

"Mom made me install it on my phone so she can track me, but it works both ways. I can track her, too," Maleeha explained with the ghost of a smile. "I used to be able to track Dad, but he disabled his location a while ago." Kausar and her granddaughter exchanged a knowing glance: *Around the time his latest affair started.*

"I want a cell phone, too," Fizza said, returning the device to her sister. "I don't mind being tracked."

"You don't go anywhere, dummy. And when you do, you get dropped off like a baby," Maleeha said to her sister.

"I'm not a baby," Fizza said, indignant. She moved from the kitchen to the couch and reached for the remote to turn on a show, while Maleeha disappeared back upstairs to her room.

Kausar stared down at her phone. She should tell Ilyas right away about this latest threat, as he had requested. But as she read over the hateful message, her fear was overtaken by fury. How dare this stranger terrorize her and threaten her family? Without thinking, she opened the message and responded:

Ali is dead, but his mother is no fool. We will talk when I find out who you are. We both know that I am close.

Three dots appeared and disappeared, appeared and disappeared, but no response arrived. Satisfied, Kausar turned her phone off and waited for her daughter to return. She would pass the message along to Ilyas, but she wouldn't worry anymore about a coward who hid behind their phone.

When Sana returned, she assured Kausar that her store and the others had only sustained minor smoke damage. The bulk of the damage had been done to Mr. Jin's store—and on the old man himself. Mr. Jin had been badly beaten, though luckily the same passersby who had called 911 had also managed to scare off the attackers.

"You shouldn't have gone by yourself tonight," Kausar said, her heart in her throat. "There is a killer loose, and now this. The events might be connected."

Sana smiled sadly. "I have no one else to rely on now."

"You have me," Kausar said stoutly.

Her daughter hugged her. "I don't know what I would have done without you this last week," she whispered.

"Promise me you will be careful," Kausar said.

"Only if you promise the same thing. You haven't stopped asking questions, have you?" Sana asked.

This wasn't the right time to let Sana in on all that she had learned, and so she only nodded. "I suppose I'm not very good at listening to others," Kausar said. Her daughter only sighed in response.

They made plans to visit Mr. Jin at the hospital in the morning and went to bed.

Maleeha *insisted on coming with them the next day,* and the women arrived at Scarborough General Hospital, with its distinctive cylindrical redbrick ward, as soon as visiting hours started. Mr. Jin was happy to see them—and even happier to accept the Tupperware filled with basmati rice and chicken korma curry that Kausar had made that morning.

When Maleeha shyly passed him a small bouquet of daisies from the hospital gift shop, he grinned, then winced in pain. There were lacerations all over his face, and he struggled to sit up, clutching at his ribs. Still, he didn't complain, and he didn't want to talk about what had happened. Mostly he was upset the store would be closed for the next few days, worried how his customers would cope. His patience fueled Kausar's anger. Who could possibly want to hurt this kind, harmless man? She would find out, she vowed.

"Mr. Jin *saab*," she started, using the Urdu term of respect, "I know you have already spoken with the police, but they don't know the community as you do. There's been so much trouble at the plaza lately, and I can't help but think it's all related. Do you know who did this to you?"

Mr. Jin hesitated for a moment, then shook his head. "It was dark," he said, his voice a croak. "And it happened so fast. Thankfully, someone managed to chase them off. The police came quickly."

Kausar thought for a moment. "Do you think this attack is related to Imran's death?" Again, Mr. Jin hesitated. But then he nodded slowly. Kausar continued, keeping her voice gentle. "I want to see justice done. I want to help my daughter. Mr. Jin, do you know anything that can help me?"

Mr. Jin closed his eyes at this question, but when he opened them, a determined expression was on his face. "I never want trouble. My customers depend on me. The food prices, they are so high. People can't afford to eat. I've been selling at a loss these last few months, to try and help. But I can't keep doing that, so what *can* I do? If I close the store, the way my children want, where would my neighbors, people I have known for decades, seniors trying to live off their pension and old age security, buy their groceries? Ever since my Cynthia died, the house is empty," he said, referring to his wife. "My store makes me happy."

He was silent for a moment, taking time to breathe and gather his energy. Talking had tired him out. Shooting her mother a warning glance, Sana reassured the older man they could talk later, that he should rest now, but Mr. Jin shook his head stubbornly. "I should have told you what I saw sooner," he said quietly, looking at Kausar. "When you first came to the store. But I was afraid."

"Afraid of what, Mr. Jin *saab*?" Kausar asked softly.

"The people who come at night. The ones who take everything away."

Kausar and Sana looked at each other, baffled. What could he mean? Perhaps Mr. Jin had a concussion. Not wanting to put any more stress on him, Sana gently changed the subject and offered to help supervise the cleanup of the store, until he was better. Behind them, Maleeha excused herself and left the room, and Kausar followed, needing air and time to think over Mr. Jin's cryptic words.

Outside in the hallway, she spotted a familiar-looking tall man emerge from the elevator. What was Patrick Kim doing here?

He startled at the sight of her, echoing her thoughts. "What are you doing here?"

"Visiting Mr. Jin," Kausar explained. One of the puzzle pieces floating in her mind suddenly clicked into place as she took in his handsome face, with its sharp features and full brows, so similar to . . . "The same as you," she said slowly. "Mr. Jin is your father. Isn't he?"

Kausar and Patrick sat next to each other in the empty *waiting area reserved for families. As he spoke, she mentally berated herself for not realizing the truth sooner. Some investigator she was—the resemblance was obvious now, not only in Patrick's features but also in his calm manner.

"Korean naming conventions put the last name first," Patrick explained. "My father's name on his birth certificate is Kim Su-Jin. When he moved to Canada forty years ago, they thought his last name was Jin. When I was born, my parents set it right for me. There was always lots of confusion at parents' night in school," he said wryly.

"Ahmed said you were soft," Kausar said, almost to herself. "He knew the real reason you wanted to buy the plaza—it was for your father. You had no intention of knocking the building down to build condominiums."

Red tinted Patrick's cheeks now. "I grew up here," he said simply. "My parents worked hard. They put me and my sister through school. I found some success. After Mom died, my father and I drifted. I had no idea his business was suffering. When I found out, I wanted to do something. He's a proud man and would never take a handout, so I looked for another way to help."

"Do your investors know your real motive in pursuing the Golden Crescent Plaza?" Kausar asked. She was touched by Patrick's thoughtfulness, and watching the tall businessman squirm at being caught out was entertaining.

"The plaza is a good investment," Patrick protested, before matching her smile. "Though I'll admit it also has a special place in my heart, for a lot of reasons."

Kausar contemplated Patrick for another long moment. She had been foolish, she realized now. The signs and clues had been there all along. "I think I understand it now," she said softly. "I've been going about this entirely the wrong way. But the picture has been turned the right way around."

Patrick was puzzled. "What picture? Are you all right, Mrs. Khan?"

Kausar stood, swaying slightly as more and more of the puzzle pieces slotted into place, making her dizzy. "Your actions were motivated by love, not money," she said. "Your father has been lonely, and he needs you now. Never try to hide the things you do for love."

Patrick was still clearly confused but also touched by her words. "Thank you, Mrs. Khan. I've realized the same thing. What is money for if you can't help the people who mean the most?" He hesitated. "You won't tell my father about the sale of the plaza, I hope?" he added, a trace of anxiety in his voice.

Something wordless passed between them, and Kausar shook her head. "No, though I think you should."

S*ana found Kausar in the waiting room, and Maleeha* joined them a few moments later. The women drove home in silence after dropping Maleeha off at school.

"I hope you're being careful," Sana said abruptly, eyes on the road. "When you're doing . . . whatever it is you've been up to. If something happened to you, too, I'm not sure I could take it."

"Of course, *beta*," Kausar said, accepting this for what it was—her daughter's tacit consent for her investigation. Ironic, because she sensed she was near the end now. The thought made her sad; it was hard to believe that she had only been in the city for a week. Her life here somehow felt more real and vital than the life she had been living in North Bay.

As much as she missed May, and her small, quiet house in her small, quiet life in North Bay, the Kausar she was in Toronto felt more alive and invigorated, more like herself than she had in decades. Pain and grief had caused her to flee. She was starting to realize that Imran's murder came down to the same thing—pain, grief, and misplaced love. She discreetly swiped at her eyes.

Sana slowed as the car approached the house. "Were you expecting guests?" she asked, indicating a trio of women clustered by the porch. Squinting at the small group, Kausar smiled. Without waiting for her daughter to stop the car, she opened the door and swiftly made her way up the drive, towards Fatima, Beatrice, and May.

"I couldn't stay away," May said. "I made plans to drive down after you told me about the fire and the attack on Mr. Jin."

Fatima and Beatrice nodded; they had heard the news as well and wanted to make sure their friend was okay. This time, the tears were harder to hide. The affection and love she felt for her friends was all the motivation she needed to finish what she had started. She opened the front door and invited them inside for tea and snacks, before returning to the driveway where Sana was gathering their bags and carefully locking the car.

"I know you're guilty," Kausar said to her daughter. "Give me one day to prove your innocence."

Sana straightened, furrowing her brows. "That doesn't make any sense, Mom."

"Please. I need to do this for you. I *know* I can do this for you," Kausar added.

"Dad really underestimated you, didn't he," Sana said now, and a new note—one of speculation and something else—entered her voice.

The two women stared at each other as if they were truly seeing each other for the first time in years.

"I have a confession to make," Sana said, sounding almost shy. "When I called you that morning after I was taken to the police station, it wasn't only because I had your number memorized." Sana's stare communicated something she couldn't bring herself to say. "I will always trust you to do the right thing for me and my family. No matter what happens next, I want you to know that."

CHAPTER 28

"There are two of you now?" Ilyas said, leaning back at his desk at the police station. "I'm not sure I can handle this."

May looked from Ilyas to Kausar. "He's quite handsome," she conceded. "I forgive you for not using the selfie trick. A picture wouldn't have done justice to that smile. I can see why Sana likes him."

Ilyas sat up straight. "You told her about that? Is nothing sacred . . ."

Smiling, Kausar pulled up a second chair for her friend, before taking a seat. "Now that the formalities are out of the way, I need some help."

"What else is new," Ilyas muttered. "You know, I have other cases. I already looked into that Ahmed Malik person at your suggestion. Turns out he skipped town. Not even his wife knows where he went. If there was a connection between him and Imran, we can't do anything about it until he surfaces."

Kausar turned this over in her mind. Perhaps his conversation with Nasir had put the wind up, for some reason. She remembered Ahmed had said he would have to make a hasty exit if Silver Star Holdings found out about his side hustle. She would have to ask Nasir if he had looked up who owned the company, though she might wait a few days. Things felt a little tender between them right now.

She thanked Ilyas for following up on her lead, and then launched into the purpose of today's visit. "When I bumped into you outside the house my first night here, you warned me the neighborhood was not as safe as it used to be," she said to Ilyas. "What did you mean?"

Ilyas seemed surprised at this line of questioning. Clearly, he had expected more wild theories and requests for assistance. "Just what I said. Golden used to be safe, but that's changed recently."

"Why?" Kausar pressed.

Ilyas looked bewildered. "If I knew why people committed crimes, I'd be a sociologist, not a cop."

"That sounds more useful," May put in, and the handsome officer sent her an irritated glance.

"Who are you, again?"

"My best friend, May, visiting from North Bay," Kausar explained. "Why was Cerise being harassed by an officer that night in front of Sana's home?"

Ilyas was starting to get annoyed now. "I don't know what you're asking me, Kausar Aunty."

"Not too bright. The pretty ones usually aren't," May observed, and Ilyas glared at her.

"Setting aside systemic racism and the over-policing of Black people, did Officer Colin stop Cerise for any particular reason?" Kausar asked, like a teacher encouraging a recalcitrant student.

Awareness dawned, and Ilyas nodded. "You're talking about the car thefts. I'm sure you've noticed everyone is careful about their cars in the city. We actually handed out free Faraday pouches a few years back, to prevent would-be car thieves from cloning key fobs from outside a house. There's been a significant spike in auto thefts all over the province, but Toronto is the worst. Organized crime is behind it, of course. They target specific neighborhoods, and for the past year or so, Golden has been a hot spot."

Kausar recalled the pouch where Sana kept her keys, as well as the way Fatima was careful to park her car in the garage. Everyone seemed to know someone who had had their car stolen from their driveway, and discussions about how to prevent theft had surrounded her since she had stepped foot in the city. "Why is there a rise in this type of theft? I would have thought a car would be difficult to sell without attracting attention," Kausar said.

Ilyas moved some papers around on his desk, thinking before he spoke. "They don't only sell them here. There's a market overseas for cars, and a tidy profit to be made shipping them in cargo containers from North America. Cars are stolen from residential driveways, mall parking lots, literally anywhere. Big cities like Toronto are a hub, despite the fact that we have video surveillance everywhere. Distinguishing marks like registration numbers are changed, new paperwork created or bought. Within a short window, the cars are on their way, ready to be sold in another country."

"That's terrible!" May said. She seemed genuinely shocked. North Bay had its share of crime, but so far, the plague of car thefts had left the community alone.

Ilyas shrugged. "It's seen as a victimless crime. Owners file an insurance claim, they get some money and buy a new car. Sometimes the new car is stolen, too, a few months later. The worst part is, these organized crime rings recruit high school kids to steal the cars. If they get caught, it won't ruin their lives or go on their permanent record, because they're all underage." Ilyas's lips were set in a thin, disapproving line. "But that doesn't mean it's harmless. Some of these kids keep getting into trouble or wind up in jail later. Not to mention insurance premiums in the province have skyrocketed for the average driver, as well as car prices. Nobody wins except the criminals responsible."

"You thought Cerise might be trying to steal a car?" Kausar asked.

"Constable Colin said she was acting suspicious," Ilyas said, and the skepticism in his voice was clear. "I think she was just walking home. He should have left her alone. But yes, we had received complaints about young people loitering in the area and were on high alert. Three cars were stolen from nearby homes the week before Imran was killed, another one this week."

Kausar remembered what Brianna had said about the cars in the parking lot at night, the ones that were gone in the morning. Mr. Jin had said he was afraid of *the people who come at night*. He said they take everything away. Kausar knew already that Mr. Jin felt protective of the Golden Crescent community. He must have felt powerless over what was happening in his neighborhood, but hesitant to talk with outsiders.

Both Ahmed and Mubeen had described Imran as someone who was never happy with what he had. Even Anjum admitted that her father thought being a tenant was beneath him. Imran thought he was entitled to more money and power. What if he had made a deal with the wrong people, allowing stolen cars to be temporarily stored in his plaza parking lot? In return for a cut of the proceeds, of course. Had he asked for more money from the wrong people, or threatened to reveal what was happening in his plaza to the police, and been murdered for his trouble? The more Kausar thought about it, the more it made sense.

But what did this have to do with Sana and her store?

Another thought occurred to Kausar: What if her daughter was in on it, too? Was that really why she was at the store so early the day she found Imran's body? She dismissed the idea immediately. Sana might have been eager to make sure her store was a success; she might have known that her marriage was crumbling and that she would need another source of income soon. But she would never put her family in danger by becoming involved in criminal activity, at least not on purpose.

She realized Ilyas and May were both staring at her.

"Care to share?" Ilyas asked dryly.

"I'm trying to put the pieces together, Ilyas," Kausar started, her mind churning furiously. "From what you have said, the police are aware of the spike in car thefts in the Golden Crescent. Surely, you must have looked into reports of strange activity in the plaza. Which means the police had their own suspicions all along." A horrifying realization was unfurling, one she could hardly bear to contemplate, yet all evidence pointed in that direction. The expression on Ilyas's face all but confirmed it—he seemed to be bracing himself for her next words.

"You knew the Golden plaza was being used as a drop-off point for stolen cars all along. Didn't you?" Kausar asked, though it wasn't a question. Her palms were sweating, and she felt her heart begin to beat fast again, this time with a rising rage. "Has the plaza been under police surveillance this entire time?"

Ilyas shifted uncomfortably. "I can't answer that," he said.

Kausar's tone was hard now, unflinching as she stared him down. "This entire time, you *knew*. You *knew* organized crime had their hooks all over that plaza, yet you and Detective Drake arrested my daughter anyway. How could you do that to Sana?"

May looked from Kausar to Ilyas and back again. "What am I missing?" she asked.

The briefest trace of guilt flashed across the young officer's face before it was replaced by bland professionalism. "We're certain the two incidents are unrelated . . ." he began.

Furious now, Kausar stood up. "Then let's keep our investigations that way," she said tightly. "I'll end my inquiries the way I started them—alone."

She stalked out, not listening to Ilyas's protests and explanations, blood roaring in her ears even as her mind jumped ahead, forming conclusions, figuring things out, more and more puzzle pieces sliding into place. May rushed to keep up behind her. In the car, a tight-lipped Kausar explained her thinking.

"Ilyas all but confirmed that the police have had the Golden Crescent Plaza under surveillance, likely for months. I think Imran was playing a dangerous game. He suspected or knew the police were keeping tabs on the plaza as the hub for a stolen car ring, while at the same time allowing . . . let's call them his unsavory 'business partners' . . . to use his parking lot for temporary storage of their stolen vehicles. Perhaps he asked these same business partners for more money, maybe he tried to blackmail them, or perhaps they realized he knew about the police surveillance. Either way, that's what got him killed. He was trying to play both sides."

May looked at her friend. "What does that have to do with Sana?"

"Nothing," Kausar said grimly. "The police are only going through the motions of arresting her. If they come out and admit they set up a sting operation in the Golden Crescent Plaza, it would ruin a bigger operation, one they've been working on for months. They always had their eye on the bigger prize: the organized crime that is behind the widespread car thefts in the city. They're using her as a distraction, as a scapegoat, so they can continue with their surveillance of the plaza."

"Are you saying the police don't really think Sana is guilty?" May asked, shocked. "They let her think she was their prime suspect this entire time, to protect another ongoing investigation?"

Her friend was outraged, but Kausar's anger was about to go nuclear. She slammed her hand down on the dashboard, startling her friend. "I should have known something was wrong from the start. They initially said Sana was a flight risk, but then she was released on my surety without any trouble. Ilyas encouraged me to keep digging and asking questions. He even told me that Detective Drake was not happy with Sana as lead suspect. Ilyas knew, all this time."

The friends sat in silence for a moment.

"But then . . . who killed Imran?" May asked tentatively.

"That's just it," Kausar said grimly. A picture was starting to emerge, the details clearer the longer she stared at it. "Despite everything, despite their surveillance, they don't know. But I think I've finally figured it out. I just need to prove it."

CHAPTER 29

Kauser went with May to the plaza, for one last check. The shell of Mr. Jin's shop lay gaping like an open wound, windows shattered and the smell of roasted vegetables and burnt plastic permeating the air. Inside, empty bins had been stacked to the side, and a scattering of limes lay on the floor. A dozen or so neighbors were picking up debris, sweeping the floor, and putting the store to rights, while others prepared to board up windows until new glass could be ordered and installed. The storefront looked bereft without the familiar face of Mr. Jin greeting customers with his usual stoic nod, but the sight of the neighborhood showing their appreciation for their favorite grocer was touching.

"People say Toronto is unfriendly. I guess it depends what part of the city," May observed.

"This is a good place to live, in some ways," Kausar agreed. They would have stopped to offer their services, but they had more pressing matters to attend to, the sort that would ensure the Golden Crescent Plaza remained safe in the future.

Inside, Lisa was helping coordinate the team of volunteers. When she spotted Kausar, her expression immediately turned wary. She spoke to one of the people milling about, before joining the women outside.

"I can't imagine who would do this to Mr. Jin or his store," Lisa said, indicating the storefront, after Kausar had introduced May.

"All of this could have been prevented," Kausar agreed.

They lapsed into a strained silence, each contemplating the senseless act of destruction that had kneecapped a local establishment many families relied on. Who knew how long it would take for Mr. Jin to be up and running again, after he recovered from his attack?

The expression on Lisa's face was resigned, and she indicated for Kausar and May to follow her. Once inside her store, Lisa began closing the blinds and indicated for Kausar to begin. She didn't mince words.

"Your mother told me something interesting when I visited your home the other day. She said you had to close the store the day before Imran was murdered, for a doctor's appointment."

Lisa's hand slowed. "I might have. One day feels very much like another, in a job like this. I'm sure you understand what it's like to be a busy mother."

Kausar and May exchanged a meaningful glance. She had hoped Lisa would be forthcoming, considering they all knew why she was here. "I imagine the week your landlord was murdered might be a memorable one. Why did you lie about overhearing an argument between Sana and Imran the day before?"

"I did hear them argue!" Lisa shot back, her tone high and insistent.

Kausar took a deep breath. "I just want the truth, Lisa. Enough damage has been done already. Will you be brave and share what really happened?"

Lisa bowed her head, breathing hard, and the women waited. When she looked up at Kausar, her eyes were bright. "You don't understand the stress I've been under. Imran was no help at all, and he knew I was desperate. I'm glad he's dead."

May patted Lisa's hand. "It will be a relief to unburden yourself, dear. Better to tell Kausar than the police, I think. Not that we would ever give you up, but they might have questions for you."

Lisa took a deep breath. "I know you spoke with my mother. You know I lied about overhearing the argument the day Imran died. I did hear Imran arguing with someone, but it was later that night, and it couldn't have been with Sana. I watched her close her shop and leave when I returned to the plaza after hours. I needed to go somewhere quiet after my specialist appointment, somewhere I could think." Lisa's hair was coming loose from the scarf she had tied over her braids, and she reached back to tighten it now.

"Why did you lie?" Kausar asked.

"Patrick asked me to," Lisa said, and her lip trembled. She sank to the stool by the door. "Nobody knows this next part, not even my mom. I was diagnosed with lupus a few months ago. My symptoms are getting worse, and it's been hard to pretend everything is all right. When I first found out, I went straight to Imran and told him I needed to break my lease. With the hours I keep, I couldn't run the store anymore. He refused. He wouldn't even let me sublet, like he did with Siraj's store. He suggested I get my daughter to help out after school. But I won't have Cerise here without me."

Kausar absorbed this. She had a feeling she knew why Lisa refused to have her young daughter at the store without her—the same reason why Nimra was uncomfortable at her shop when Imran dropped by. "I'm sorry to hear about your diagnosis. It sounds like you have had a very challenging few months. When my Hassan found out he had pancreatic cancer, I remember he walked around in a daze for weeks."

The women were silent, lost in thought. May broke in. "Sorry, I'm not clear, what does this have to do with Sana?" she asked.

Lisa stared down at her hands. "This is the part I'm not proud of," she admitted. "Before you condemn me, remember how you felt right after your husband's cancer diagnosis, and then add the complication of being a single mother who has never worked any job outside restaurants, okay?" She waited until Kausar nodded before she continued.

"When word got out about Imran's death, Patrick called me. He knew I stayed late most nights at the shop to do prep for the next day, and he wondered if I had overheard anything in Imran's office the night before he died. I said I had, that Imran had been arguing with someone. He asked if I knew who it had been, and I said yes. He asked me to keep quiet about what I had overheard, because he didn't want any scandal associated with Imran's death. At the time, I thought the death was an accident, that maybe Imran tripped and hit his head."

"But you didn't tell the police," Kausar said. "Luxmi did."

Lisa half smiled. "I don't like talking to the cops if I can help it. But I knew Luxmi wouldn't be able to help herself. Telling her was as good as telling them." She hung her head. "I told Luxmi I had heard Sana argue with Imran. I didn't realize it was murder, and I figured that if they had found Imran in Sana's store, they'd be questioning her anyway, so it wouldn't make much difference. And it was petty and wrong, but I was also still a little mad at Sana for how she reacted when our daughters were fighting. I never would have done it if I knew the sort of trouble it would land Sana in, but that's the truth."

May gasped in shock. "You implicated Sana because you were angry about a fight between your daughters?"

Lisa hung her head in shame.

"Why didn't you speak out when things became serious for my daughter?" Kausar asked sternly. She knew Lisa had been guilty of something, but this story made her angry.

Lisa spoke in a low voice. "I never believed she did it, so I thought the police would eliminate her from their inquiries quickly. Patrick wasn't happy that I implicated Sana, but he asked me not to say anything. He promised he would let me out of the lease, once he bought the plaza. He even said he would invest in my food truck. I would still get to cook, but I could take days off when I wasn't feeling well. I know what I did was wrong. I'm so ashamed of myself. I haven't been sleeping, and I wanted to make things right. I would have spoken up if Sana went to trial, I swear it."

Kausar looked at Lisa's tear-stained face, and her pity swallowed her anger. "It's not too late to make things right. You should call Officer Ilyas and tell him the truth."

The young woman slumped in her stool, but she accepted this judgment meekly. "Can you forgive me?" she asked. "I've made myself sick over this. Especially after what you did for Cerise."

"It is not my forgiveness you need, but rather Sana's. I'll leave that for her to decide." Kausar hesitated. "I understand you were under a lot of pressure and that you wanted to make sure you would have a way to provide for your daughter and take care of yourself. I'm sorry Imran put you in the position to have to make those hard choices."

Lisa nodded. "I know we shouldn't speak ill of the dead, but I'm glad Imran is gone. He was a horrible person."

"That seems to be the universal consensus," Kausar agreed. "Did he get on with *anyone* in the plaza?"

"The only tenant he was nice to was Deanna, who runs the cell phone repair store," Lisa said thoughtfully. "She's the newest, so maybe she hadn't figured out that he was the worst. I saw them talking a lot."

"You said Imran allowed Siraj to sublet his store. I didn't know he had a business in the Golden Crescent Plaza. His mother told me he had to sell after his divorce," Kausar said.

"Imran was sexist and racist, too. He let the male shopkeepers get away with more than the women. Luxmi always complained that he charged her more rent than he did Mr. Jin," Lisa said, sounding bitter. With some effort, she softened her tone. "I did feel badly for Siraj. I know what it's like to be in a tight spot financially. After my divorce, I had to move back in with my mother, too. I let him do all the deliveries for my restaurant. He's a good guy."

Kausar filed this information away. "What do you know about Deanna?"

"She's friendly, always chatting with the other shopkeepers and curious about the area. I think she grew up outside Toronto. To be honest, I think she tries too hard to be liked."

"She must be busy with her three children," Kausar said casually.

Lisa seemed surprised. "She never mentioned them to me. But people can be private about their families, I suppose." She wiped her eyes and put her hand out for Kausar to shake. "I'm sorry again about the trouble I brought into your life. It hasn't been an easy few months for me, but that's no excuse. Are we okay?"

Kausar accepted Lisa's hand with only a beat of hesitation. In the grand scope of things, the young woman's crimes had been petty and driven by a fierce protectiveness. Unlike Imran, she deeply regretted her actions and would be unlikely to repeat them. They shook hands, and the relief on Lisa's face was practically beatific.

"That was amazing!" *May said as they walked to the other* end of the plaza. "I'm sweating through my jacket. How did you know Lisa would come clean like that?"

Kausar shrugged. "She had no reason to hide anymore. I don't think she wanted to, anyway."

"What's next?" May asked.

Kausar turned to face her friend. "I have a plan, but I will need your help to execute it. I do have a favor to ask of you."

"Name it," May said.

Kausar looked towards the cell phone repair store, which looked empty. She was pretty sure Deanna was in there anyway. "Can you take Sana out for coffee today?"

May looked perplexed. "I thought I would stay by your side and help with questioning the suspects. It's fun to be the muscle in your interrogations."

Kausar looked at her petite, blond friend, with her oversized T-shirt, leggings, and crocs, and repressed a smile. "As terrifying as you are, I need you to do this for me."

May agreed with only a little bit of grumbling and was soon on her way, leaving Kausar to confront Deanna alone.

"Another cell phone emergency?" Deanna asked, opening the door with a faint smile and ushering her inside.

"If it were, I doubt you would be able to help," Kausar countered. "I just spoke with Officer Ilyas. He mentioned the operation would be wrapping up soon."

At least Deanna didn't insult Kausar by playing dumb or feigning confusion; she knew her cover was blown.

Kausar continued. "I had my suspicions when you took my phone and only blew some air into the SIM card slot, especially since I hadn't even told you what the problem was. Even I know that's not how you fix anything."

A faint smile creased Deanna's mouth. "Always works for me," she said.

"Did Imran know all along, Officer Deanna?" Kausar asked.

Deanna shrugged, refusing to answer, but she didn't have to. "Was it because I called you Mrs. Khan? It was a slip of the tongue. I hoped you wouldn't notice."

Kausar nodded at the three girls in the picture taped by the counter. "I always notice. Also, you didn't know what the word 'desi' meant despite your supposed South Asian husband, plus you were very interested in your neighbors, and Lisa said you never mentioned your children."

Deanna closed her eyes. "I guess the neighbors do talk. Just not to me."

Kausar reached for the photo, asking for permission with a raise of her eyebrow. "Knock yourself out," Deanna said sullenly. She pocketed the photo and prayed that May had managed to convince Sana to leave the house. She needed it to be empty when Maleeha returned from school.

CHAPTER 30

Fizza was at basketball practice, with a playdate to follow, leaving Maleeha alone in her room when Kausar returned home. May had let her know she'd convinced Sana to grab a coffee nearby.

You've got at least an hour. Can't wait to hear all about your latest scheme! May texted.

Things still felt awkward between Kausar and Maleeha, but time was running out. Her granddaughter needed to let go of her fear and hesitation; Kausar was the same way and understood her thinking. She was willing to provide the push—she just hoped Maleeha would trust her grandmother enough to finally confide in her about what was really going on. But first, Kausar had to set the scene.

After ensuring Maleeha was in her bedroom, she worked quickly. First, she grabbed a spray bottle and sprayed her face and neck with water. Next, taking a kohl liner, she darkened the shadows under her eyes. Finally, she positioned herself in the foyer, where sound traveled best in the house.

She reached for the coat stand, heavy with jackets and an assortment of scarves and bags, and yanked it down, hard. It landed with a pleasing crash on the tile floor. When she heard footsteps hurrying down the stairs, Kausar quickly arranged herself underneath the stand and adopted a dazed expression.

"What happened?" Maleeha asked, her face pale at the sight of her grandmother sprawled on the ground.

"I was just putting some things away, when I felt dizzy," Kausar said, wheezing slightly. "I tried to steady myself and reached for the coat stand. It fell on top of me." She rubbed her head, wincing in what she hoped was a convincing manner.

"Are you hurt?" Maleeha asked, worried.

"No, no . . ." Kausar answered. She squinted at her grandchild. "Sana, can you get me some water?"

Maleeha blanched. "I think you have a concussion. We need to get you to the hospital."

"I'm fine, Sana," Kausar insisted. She moaned quietly and put a hand to her head. "But the doctor did say if I had another episode, I should go straight to the emergency department."

Maleeha's voice crept higher. "*Nani*, it's me. Mom's not home. I cannot handle this right now. I'm taking you to the hospital."

"Sana isn't here to drive us," Kausar said weakly. "We'll have to take the bus. Perhaps you can carry me? I hope there are no delays in the bus schedule . . ."

"We can't take the bus like this!" Maleeha exclaimed. Then she bit her lip, thinking. Kausar watched her granddaughter's eyes flick to the Faraday pouch by the door, where Sana stored her car keys.

"If anything happens to me, promise you will take care of your little sister," Kausar said, her voice faint. "Why is it so hot in here?" She wiped at her forehead, where the water she had sprayed earlier was starting to dry. Maleeha made up her mind and reached down to help her grandmother to her feet.

"Let's go," she said grimly. "Ambulances take too long when they get a call from Golden. I'll drive you."

"If you insist," Kausar said weakly. She edged her feet into shoes then feigned a dizzy spell while her fifteen-year-old granddaughter, who was too young to even apply for a learner's permit in the province, guided her to Sana's car and expertly started the engine, reversing neatly out of the driveway. Maleeha kept her eyes fixed on the road ahead, muttering under her breath when they stopped at a red light, but was otherwise entirely self-assured behind the wheel.

Kausar couldn't help but admire the confident way her granddaughter handled the car, easily changing lanes and keeping pace with traffic. She waited for another red light before she spoke, in a different voice than the one she had used to terrify her granddaughter. "Who taught you how to drive?"

"Dad," Maleeha said. Her gaze flickered to Kausar, and what she saw made her eyes narrow in suspicion. She was no fool. "When I was thirteen. He said I was a natural, but that I shouldn't tell Mom. In hindsight, that might have been a red flag."

Kausar absorbed this. She knew Maleeha had always been closer to Hamza than Sana. His betrayal must have devastated her. Kausar laid a hand on Maleeha's arm. "*Beta*, maybe you should pull over to a side street. I think we need to have a little chat."

Maleeha was starting to cry now, tears welling in her eyes. She knew the game was up, but instead of remonstrating Kausar for the elaborate stunt she had pulled, she was shaking with the effort of holding herself together. "You weren't really hurt," she said, her voice muffled and thick.

"When you hurt, I hurt," Kausar said, and Maleeha started sobbing. "Let me help you. None of this is your fault."

"All of it is my fault!" Maleeha cried. "If you only knew—"

"Did you kill Imran?" Kausar asked.

Maleeha stared at her grandmother. "No. I swear. I didn't touch him."

Kausar kept her gaze locked on her granddaughter's face. "But you saw something," she said.

A part of her wanted to be wrong, to have all her deductions up to this point lead to nothing. But then Maleeha nodded and burst into a fresh round of tears, and the roiling feeling in the pit of Kausar's stomach turned to cold understanding. She had been right all along.

Kausar held Maleeha while she cried, stroking her hair and crooning comforting, nonsensical words until the girl hiccupped into silence. Then Maleeha, in a halting voice, told her everything that had happened. When she was finished, Kausar cupped her granddaughter's face and made her a promise. "I will fix everything, *beta*. But for now, do you think you can drive us back home? Of the two of us, I think you have had the most recent practice."

CHAPTER 31

It was May's idea to host a dinner party and invite everyone involved in Imran's murder. "The detective always gathers the suspects into the library to reveal the murderer!" she said, an excited gleam in her eye. When May got an idea in her head, it was hard to dissuade her.

"I always wondered why the suspects showed up when summoned, and without a lawyer, too," Kausar mused.

May snapped her fingers. "Good idea. Invite Jessica Kaur. And of course, your dishy lawyer friend Nasir. You might as well invite Fatima, too. I want to check out my best friend competition. We hardly spoke earlier today."

Kausar laughed, nodding amiably. After Maleeha had driven her home, and after her granddaughter had calmed down, they talked for a long time in the driveway. To her relief, Maleeha had agreed to let her grandmother handle next steps. Which so far involved making dinner and then making small talk with the family and May, all while her mind churned furiously. May was staying with them, and after the kitchen was clean and the girls and Sana had gone up to bed, the two friends lingered in the sitting room, talking in low voices.

They both agreed that things were falling quickly into place, though her friend's mention of Nasir gave Kausar pause—she wasn't sure how to proceed on that front. May immediately picked up on her hesitation.

"We're too old to play games," she said now. "And you're too young to give up on this second chance at love."

"Who said anything about love?" Kausar protested. "You're the one who told me to enjoy my second act."

"You should call him. Tell him you miss him," May teased.

"Absolutely not," Kausar said. "Though he might have some information, about the real owners of Silver Star Holdings."

"Whatever you want to call it," May said, winking. Her expression turned thoughtful. "I'm proud of you, Kausar. You've had an incredibly hard time of it, first with Ali, and then with Hassan. When you first told me about returning to Toronto, I was worried about you. I had to stop myself from driving down every day, to make sure you were okay. But you surprised me."

"I've surprised myself," Kausar admitted.

"You always had this gift, an ability to see beyond the surface. Now you can finally share it with your loved ones and your community. No matter what happens next, I'm happy for you."

Touched, Kausar hugged May tight. "Thank you for always cheering me on."

"You do the same for me," May said. "Now, back to the case. Are you going to tell me who killed Imran? I know you've figured it out."

Kausar shook her head and tried to look mysterious. "According to your detective shows, I'm not allowed to unmask the killer until the very end."

"How about a hint?" May wheedled. "Poirot always gave Hastings a fair shot."

Kausar considered this. "What turned the tide for me was when I realized Patrick was Mr. Jin's son," she admitted.

"Patrick is too handsome to be a killer," May said. "Right, Detective Aunty?"

Kausar tilted her head in acknowledgment, but refused to be drawn in. "It was more what I realized at the hospital. I had been looking at Imran's murder from the wrong angle entirely. Think about why the storage room window in Sana's store was broken. Why Imran's cell phone was missing. I realized that everyone involved has been keeping a part of themselves hidden. Once I looked beyond their facades, I could see the truth."

May sighed dramatically. "You're as opaque as Sherlock, and as vague as Poirot. I suppose I should be happy you're not making fun of my intelligence. I always thought those two great detectives were quite mean to their sidekicks."

"You're hardly my sidekick," Kausar protested. "We're partners."

"Except one of us knows whodunnit, while the other is left to wait like everyone else," May groused.

Kausar smiled. She knew May actually enjoyed the suspense of a drawn-out reveal. What her friend really wanted was to organize the murder mystery party of her dreams. "You win," Kausar said. "Let's host a dinner party."

May clapped and hooted, before looking around guiltily. Everyone in the house was asleep.

"I don't know how we will convince everyone to attend," Kausar said, her mind already thinking ahead to meal planning, and how she would bring Sana around to this plan. Yet the more she thought about it, the more the idea appealed. It seemed fitting, somehow. They all deserved to know the truth—for better, and for worse.

"That part is easy," May said, grinning. "Just tell everyone you have an update on the investigation and that the price of admission is dinner. Promise a show, and nobody will be able to resist. Trust me."

The invitation list was easy: Mubeen, Anjum, Ilyas, Patrick,

Hamza, plus Jessica Kaur, Nasir, and of course Fatima, Maleeha, and Sana. Before the women retired to bed, they had the entire party planned out. The stage was set, and Kausar had only to light the final match. Her stomach turned over at the thought, and she silently made a *dua*: *Please, God, let the truth unravel as You will.*

M*ay's idea to pique everyone's curiosity turned out to* be correct: Nobody could resist the promise of a secret revealed. When Kausar called and texted the invitations the next day, after first clearing it with Sana, she was surprised at the barrage of immediate acceptances. Only Patrick demurred, citing his father as an excuse. Mr. Jin was still in the hospital, but Kausar promised it would be worth his time and that she would make up a care package for his father if Patrick joined them. As for Ilyas, Kausar told him that he owed her.

Her hand shook when it was time to call Nasir, the last person on her list. To her relief, his tone was as warm and friendly as ever when he picked up, no trace of accusation or hurt.

"Kausar! I was hoping you would call. I promised myself I would give you space, but I was about to break down and dial your number."

"It's only been two days," she said.

"And yet it feels like two months. I suppose I've grown accustomed to having you back in my life. In whatever way you wish to be," he added.

Kausar felt her face color. May glanced at her from the couch, where she was finishing her morning tea. She made kissy faces until Kausar walked away.

"I was wondering if you had a chance to look up the owners of Silver Star Holdings?" she asked.

There was the sound of a mouse clicking and Nasir's deep

voice humming in her ear as he opened a document on his computer. "I looked it up yesterday, and I'm afraid the information was inconclusive. An anonymous numbered company holds the title. I traced that company back to another company, and another one behind it, and so on. The usual nesting doll arrangement you find in large corporations."

"Is that suspicious?" Kausar asked.

Nasir considered. "It could be entirely innocent. Or it could be a way for the company owners to hide their identity. We would have to do more digging to find out, and that would take time."

"Thank you for looking into this for me," Kausar said.

"It was my pleasure," Nasir said. "Truly."

She believed him. He had shown himself to be a good friend to her, willing to step in when she needed help, capable of thinking quickly on his feet. Most important of all, he had not tried to stop her from following her instincts. In that moment, she felt grateful for having Nasir back in her life and reluctant to let this momentary awkwardness stand in the way of what she hoped would be a true friendship—and maybe more.

"I'm having a dinner party—" she started, and Nasir interrupted.

"I'll be there. What time, and what can I bring?"

And just like that, Kausar felt her breathing ease. With Nasir and May by her side, she knew she could pull this off and that she would have backup in case anything went terribly wrong.

W*ith May's help, she spent the day cooking chicken* biryani, *dum kheema*, a vegetable curry, and a simple *kheer* rice pudding for dessert. Both Fizza and Maleeha wandered into the kitchen and offered to help stir pots but wandered away once they grew bored. As for Sana, her exhaustion had returned, and she spent the day sleeping.

Ilyas and Hamza arrived at the same time, and their awkward interaction set the tone for the evening. The men had never been friends—Hamza arrived in Sana's life just as Ilyas had left it, and they were nearly polar opposites, as evidenced by their choice of gift: While Hamza had brought a large, showy bouquet for Kausar, Ilyas quietly placed Sana's favorite chocolate on the kitchen counter. Hamza also tried to pretend that nothing was wrong, but when he went in for a hello hug, Kausar neatly sidestepped. Even May only held out the tips of her fingers for Hamza to shake. At least Ilyas knew better than to assume he was out of the doghouse—he nodded shamefacedly at the two women before quietly taking a seat at the dining room table, which had been set for a dozen people with the use of an extended folding table.

Fatima arrived next and immediately got to work in the kitchen, helping to transfer food to serving dishes and chatting amiably with May. Patrick followed soon after, and Mubeen arrived with his sister, and then Jessica. Nasir was last, and he brought a tray of mango lassis to share, with a wink for Kausar, causing May to nearly swoon.

When a wary Sana finally joined the group, followed by Maleeha, the strangest dinner party in the history of the Golden Crescent got started. The guests milled about the kitchen, holding plates of appetizers, the conversation flowing from the weather (very cold for this time of year) and latest scandal at the mosque (a bake sale gone awry) to a short-lived conversation about the Maple Leafs' chances at the Stanley Cup (highly unlikely; Go Leafs Go). When dinner was ready to be served, Kausar directed everyone to join her at the table. Fizza had already taken her food upstairs, uninterested in the gathering once Kausar had offered unlimited time on her phone as an alternative.

Finally, after chai was served and each guest had helped themselves to the *kheer*, Kausar rose from her position at the head of the table.

"Thank you all for coming today, and for indulging me. You have all been very patient."

She could see Ilyas trade glances with Patrick, clocked the smirk on Mubeen's lips and the shuffling among the gathered guests as they calculated how soon they could make their excuses and leave. Kausar took a deep breath, and with a careful *bismillah*, started.

"Many of you knew my youngest child, Ali. He was murdered by a hit-and-run driver when he was fifteen years old, and his killer was never found. When Sana told me she was under suspicion for Imran's death, and was later arrested for his murder, I realized I had to help. I had to discover the truth. To atone for my failure to help my son."

A few expressions of sympathy were sprinkled among her guests now, along with a rising sense of discomfort. No one wanted to think about what had happened to Ali, the senselessness of her family's loss, the open wound that had yet to heal.

"I've asked you here because a man is dead, killed in a frenzied attack for an unknown reason. I am confident I know that reason now. You see, from the beginning, Imran's murder was entwined with family, love, and misdirection."

Kausar's eyes glittered as she looked around the assembly. May flashed her a thumbs-up. Patrick, Ilyas, and Anjum had their eyes fixed on her. Hamza and Mubeen wore near-identical smirks on their faces, but Maleeha looked miserable. For her part, Sana kept her gaze on her full dessert bowl; she hadn't eaten much during dinner, either. Only Nasir nodded in silent encouragement; his look said, *I'm here with you.* Also, *I have a getaway car if we need to make a quick escape.*

"I spoke with many people about Imran's character. He was not popular. He was an angry man, a cruel man, and he ruled over the Golden Crescent Plaza like a tyrant." She cast a glance around the assembly. A few guests were shifting uncomfortably.

"Why did you call us here?" Anjum asked, her tone challenging. "Great food and all, but this is starting to feel a bit cringe."

Mubeen laughed. "I'm enjoying myself," he said. "It's not like I have anything to hide."

"You each knew some of your father's secrets," Kausar said to them. "As a result, each of you have much to hide."

Mubeen protested, while Anjum's expression grew resigned. She must have known Imran's financial fraud would be exposed eventually, even if he was not there to face the consequences. At the other end of the table, Ilyas and Jessica Kaur leaned forward.

"Imran's cruelty took many forms. He pushed Anjum away and insisted Mubeen follow in his footsteps, knowing he had no interest or competency in running his own business," Kausar said. A squawk from Mubeen was soon silenced. "When his long-time tenant Lisa asked to break her lease for personal health reasons, Imran denied her. He wouldn't even allow her to sublet—yet he allowed another tenant to sublet to Deanna."

"Everyone knows Imran was a jerk, Mom," Sana said. She was exhausted and drained, her beauty hidden behind dark circles under her eyes, her hair lanky and face pale. "This isn't a referendum on his character."

Kausar ceded the truth of these words, and after exchanging a glance with Nasir, placed a voice recorder at the center of the table. "No, but his character does provide possible motives for the killer. What most people didn't know was that Imran was involved in a long-running fraud, one responsible for stealing the life savings of his friends and acquaintances." She pressed play.

Ahmed's voice was clear: "*Most people don't really know what to do with their money, you know? . . . Some of them even decide to take out a reverse mortgage on their home and press the proceeds into my hands. That's where you come in. Once I obtain the capital, you help me sprinkle it around.*"

Kausar looked around the table at the assembled guests, each one listening intently. She caught Hamza's eye, and he looked away.

"I used to have a partner . . . who would send new clients my way, but he died recently. It was quite a blow to the operation."

Nasir's voice caused the party to look at him in surprise. *"I take it your partner was Imran, from the Golden Crescent Plaza?"*

"How did you guess? . . . Imran was good at picking people out."

Anjum reached across and pressed stop on the recorder. Beside her, Mubeen was pale. "We'll lose everything once that gets out. We won't even be able to stay in the neighborhood."

"My own family was impacted by the con Imran and Ahmed were running. Hamza admitted as much to me," Kausar said, her voice relentless.

Hamza couldn't meet anyone's gaze, but he jerked his head in affirmation. "By the time I figured out I'd been taken for a ride, the money was gone. I blame myself."

"That's a first," Sana said. Her lips were in a tight line. "I'm glad you signed a prenup. Now I can sue you." Across the table, Kausar caught the smirk on Jessica Kaur's face.

"At first, I thought the murder was a revenge killing from an unhappy investor," Kausar continued. "Either Hamza, or Sana, or perhaps another 'client' of Imran's who wanted to get even. Except Hamza has an alibi for the night Imran died, and why would another unhappy investor strike now, when they could have tried to get their money back through legal channels?"

Uneasy murmurs rose and fell at these words, and Kausar waited a beat before continuing.

"Then there was the plaza itself, which had multiple competing offers. It made no sense—why would a wealthy, successful property developer like Patrick Kim focus on the Golden Crescent Plaza, despite other—arguably better—properties available?

Then I learned Patrick had grown up in this neighborhood. None of the original business owners at the plaza remained, so there was no one left to recognize Mr. Jin's eldest son."

Patrick, his color high, nodded. "I wanted to help my father. The store was his life. It barely makes money anymore, but it's important to him."

"But you weren't only motivated by filial piety," Kausar said.

"It's also a good investment. Land in Toronto is always a good bet," Patrick added. His cheeks were tinged red now, and he tried, and failed, not to look at his fellow guests. At one guest in particular.

Kausar smiled kindly at Patrick. "It has been hard for you." She turned to Anjum, who was statue-still now. "For both of you."

There was a sharp, collective inhale. Kausar continued. "Sana's initial arrest was bolstered by a story from Lisa. She claimed to have overheard an argument between Sana and Imran the night before his death. Except Lisa admitted to me that she lied about the identity of the woman arguing with Imran. She also said Patrick Kim initially asked her to keep quiet, even offering to help break her lease and finance her new food truck business when he bought the plaza. Why would he do that? There had to be someone he was trying to protect." Kausar was stern now, and Patrick motionless. Kausar had decided to keep Lisa's more petty motives in initially blaming Sana out of the narrative; the past was done.

"It's true," Anjum broke in, her voice strained. She glanced at Patrick, her expression at last naked, her love for him finally on display for everyone to see. "I was at the plaza that night. I asked my dad, once again, to accept our relationship. Patrick and I were going to marry, no matter what, but I didn't want to break with my family entirely. He said—" Here, her voice broke slightly, until she recovered. "He said I would marry Patrick over his dead body. That the wedding would kill him."

Patrick's chair overturned, but he didn't pay it any attention as he made his way to Anjum. He took her in his arms, and she buried her face in his shoulder. After a moment of silence, with Patrick's arms circling her waist, she added, "I'm done living my life for a family that has shown me no care or consideration." She met Mubeen's gaze. "If you want a relationship with me, you'll have to put in the effort and be respectful of my choices. I told Mom the same thing. I won't be bought, blackmailed, or coerced by anyone, not anymore."

Mubeen scoffed at his sister's words and Patrick made a motion to stand up, but Kausar waved him back to his seat. "You will turn out just like your father if you continue this way," she said to Mubeen, her words sharp. "You're doing it already: bulldozing over your sister's wishes, manipulating your mother, accepting power as if it were your due. You know nothing of finance, and yet you insisted on selling the plaza to Silver Star Holdings because Ahmed flattered you, and because you didn't like the way Patrick looked at your sister. You need to grow up."

Mubeen was shocked at this reprimand, as if no one had ever spoken to him this way. His sister buried her smile in Patrick's shoulder, but Jessica Kaur's sharp bark of laughter cut the tension, and a few others chuckled. Mubeen stood up, glaring at the company.

"I'm out of here," he said. "I thought this would be good for a laugh, but you're all dull company."

"You are welcome to leave," Kausar said, her tone icy. "Or you can stay and listen respectfully, if you wish to know who killed your father. The choice is yours."

After a moment, curiosity won out, and Mubeen resumed his seat, not meeting anyone's gaze. Kausar glanced at her daughter. Sana was pale, and the look she threw her mother now was desperate, beseeching. Kausar ignored it, her voice steady as she continued.

"Nimra, the young woman who works at Mubeen's bubble tea shop, told me that Imran frequented the store after school hours, when many teenage girls were also around. She said his behavior made some of them uncomfortable. She spoke much more highly of the way you treated her, Mubeen," Kausar added with a nod. "Lisa told me that when she asked Imran to break her lease, he encouraged her to bring her daughter to work, and she refused to do so." She turned to Sana, who was gripping the table tightly now, a light sheen of sweat on her brow.

"Maleeha used to help you at the store, didn't she?" Kausar asked gently. Sana nodded, the motion jerky. She cast her eyes around the table until she met Maleeha's gaze. Kausar's granddaughter was pale, but she nodded at her to continue. She knew what was coming; they had discussed this at length.

"Imran dropped by frequently when you came to the store to help your mother," Kausar said, and Maleeha nodded. "Sana noticed his attention. She warned him off."

"One time, I left Maleeha in the back room sorting through inventory." Sana's voice was hesitant. "When I happened to check on her, Imran was there, too—I guess he'd come through the shared entrance—and Maleeha looked trapped. He'd backed her into a corner and was looming over her, hardly allowing any space between them." Sana spoke in a monotone. "Maleeha told me it wasn't the first time he'd gotten too close and made her uncomfortable. I was so angry. I told him that if he ever touched Maleeha or even came near her again, I would kill him. He died a few days later. I wonder if I had willed it to happen."

"Even you cannot levitate a blade into a man's chest all on its own," Kausar reassured her daughter. She cast a look at the assembly, and her gaze stopped at Hamza.

Her son-in-law's eyes were wide and he gripped his dessert spoon tightly. "Did Imran hurt you?" he asked Maleeha.

His daughter didn't meet his eyes. "He never touched me, but I just . . . it made me feel so awful. I hated the way he'd look at me and talk to me."

"If that bastard wasn't dead already, I'd tear him apart with my bare hands." Hamza's anger had him breathing hard.

May hastened to fill Hamza's glass with more water and patted him on the shoulder, murmuring soothing words. She knew how to deal with emotional outbursts from her time as a teacher, and she motioned for Kausar to continue. Hamza might have been a terrible husband, but he loved his girls, Kausar thought, as she watched him struggle to regain his composure. She turned back to the rest of the guests; she had their full attention now.

"I will say it once more. From the start, nothing about this murder made sense. Close-knit communities are always like this. There are so many threads to untangle, and everyone's lives are tightly wound together. The police knew all this, knew there were many connections and possible suspects, and yet they quickly homed in on one, and arrested Sana. Law enforcement often gets things wrong—except they usually do not do so on purpose." Ilyas started to protest, but Kausar raised her hand. "The person I blame for all of this sits before you." Kausar rested her gaze once more on Sana. Her daughter looked terrified.

"From the start, it has been clear that only one person could be responsible for Imran's murder," Kausar said softly. The silence was heavily pregnant with anticipation. "Occam's razor is at play here. When all other possibilities have been eliminated, what is left, no matter how unlikely, must be the truth." She paused to take a quick breath.

"The truth is, my daughter Sana is guilty. She stabbed Imran."

CHAPTER 32

Pandemonium. Maleeha jumped to her feet, crying out. Ilyas rose to his, too, eyes pinned on Kausar. *I hope you know what you're doing,* his look seemed to say.

"What are you saying, Mom?" Sana asked. Her voice was wooden, eyes darting around the assembled group as if planning her escape. Kausar reached out a steadying hand, reassuring her.

"You are guilty, Sana," she said gently, "of stabbing Imran with the ceremonial dagger from your window display. Though you are not, I think, guilty of his murder." She let this statement quiver over the assembly before adding, "You are only guilty of something else—of trying to protect your daughter."

All eyes swiveled to Maleeha, who was now openly sobbing.

"What did Imran say to you?" Kausar asked Sana gently. "When you came into the store and saw him dying beside your cash register. What were his last words?"

Sana's words were inaudible. She cleared her throat. "He said, *Your daughter did this.*"

Kausar sat back, nodding. "I thought it must have been something like that. Maleeha was there that night at the plaza. You had proof."

Sana continued, as if something had loosened within her.

"Maleeha had been acting strangely. I thought she might be in trouble, having more issues with her friends, or acting out because she knew Hamza and I were making plans to separate. I knew something was wrong. When I saw Imran bleeding out in my store, I panicked. Then he accused her, and my only thought was to protect my daughter."

Maleeha jumped in. "He was lying! How could you believe him?"

Kausar nudged her daughter on. "What really took you to the plaza that morning?"

"I woke early, and when I walked past Maleeha's room, I saw the door was ajar. When I pushed it open, I realized she wasn't in her bed." Sana's voice grew quieter with every word.

Kausar picked up the thread. "You could see her location using the Find My app and saw that she was not at home. She was at the plaza—inside your store, in fact."

Sana said nothing, but the look she threw her mother was plain. *Stop talking*, it said. *Say no more.*

But Kausar was relentless. Silence had led them here, and the only way to clear her family's name was to make a spectacle nobody could sweep under the rug, with as many witnesses as possible. Sunlight was the best disinfectant, after all.

Making sure Ilyas and Jessica were both paying attention, she said, with great deliberation, "Sana went to the plaza for Maleeha, but she found Imran instead. She heard Imran's last words and decided there was only one thing to be done." She took a quick breath, bracing herself.

"Sana framed herself for the crime."

Stunned silence, a sharp intake of breath, and then a babble of voices broke out once more. Kausar held up a hand, and the group quieted immediately. She ticked off points on her fingers as she spoke. "Sana cleaned the trail of blood leading from her store to Imran's office, and even tidied his desk, the sole clean spot in the room. She had the idea to replace the real murder weapon—I suspect a regular blade of some sort—with the ornamental dagger from the window display. That was why only her fingerprints were on the weapon. She even shattered the window in the storage room and made sure the store was in disarray, pulling things to the ground, to muddy the scene further. Finally, she erased the security footage, which no doubt showed Imran staggering into the store from his office, where he had been grievously wounded."

"Why would she do that when it could prove her innocence?" Anjum asked, just as the doorbell rang, disturbing the silence. May rose quietly to answer.

Kausar kept her eyes on her daughter. "She erased the footage, not because it implicated her, but because it *didn't*." Sana flinched, the movement an admission as clear as a confession. "Sana reasoned that Maleeha likely would not have been calm enough after stabbing a man to have thoroughly cleaned up after herself. Sana decided to provide overwhelming evidence that she had done it, so the police would not look further and find something her daughter left behind. That would be preferable to the alternative—her daughter's arrest. When Lisa told Luxmi, who subsequently told the police, that she had overheard Sana arguing with Imran the night before his murder, Sana didn't contradict the story. In fact, she told me it was true. Anything to cover for Maleeha."

Behind them, May returned from the kitchen, but she wasn't alone.

"I didn't kill Imran!" Maleeha cried. Her hair was in disarray now, tears streaking down her face. Sana went to her daughter, putting her arms around the girl and swaying back and forth. The glare she shot her mother was devastating.

"I know you didn't, *beta*," Kausar said calmly. Her gaze traveled around the guests at the table, one by one, until it finally settled on the new addition to their party. The man carrying a black insulated delivery bag from Lisa's roti takeout. "But you did," she said to Siraj.

It was Fatima's turn to cry out, but her son silenced her. "I don't know what you think you know, Kausar Aunty, but you're dead wrong." His glance flicked to Maleeha, who shrank away. The unease in the room had spiked up. There was more to the story, and Kausar continued.

"I started to suspect that Siraj was more deeply entwined in this business at Hassan's death anniversary," Kausar said. "When Maleeha came downstairs at Hassan's memorial, she was fine until she looked across the room. Not at her father, as I had initially assumed. She loves Hamza, despite everything. No, she was unhappy to see someone else—Siraj. Unhappy is not the right word, actually. She was terrified." Here she turned to Ilyas. "Ilyas told me a wave of car thefts had been terrorizing the Golden Crescent neighborhood. The criminal organization responsible recruits underage children to steal cars and bring them to a central location, where they are picked up and prepared for sale overseas."

Like at a tennis match, everyone's gaze moved from Kausar to Ilyas, who confirmed what she said.

"In fact, 42 Division suspected the Golden Crescent Plaza was the main hub of this organization," Kausar said. "They were so eager to uncover those responsible for the car theft ring that they set up an undercover operation. They even had an officer play shopkeeper, right in the Golden Crescent Plaza. Although I have to say, Deanna might not have been the right pick for a cell phone repair shop," she added.

She had been keeping an eye on Siraj as she related this next part of the story, and watched as he slowly worked through the puzzle, arriving at the same conclusion she had. His eyes flicked once more to Maleeha, but this time, her granddaughter looked determinedly away from him. Kausar smiled. She had him now, and Siraj knew it.

Meanwhile, Ilyas shrank in his seat. "No one else was available," he muttered. He caught Sana's scathing glare. "We had reason to believe the plaza was being used as a drop location for automative thefts. Sana's arrest was . . . strategic," he explained.

The hurt and betrayal was clear on Sana's face, but it was Jessica who spoke up, and she was furious. "I will be contacting Detective Drake in the morning. This is unconscionable."

"Sana *did* just admit to interfering with a crime scene," Ilyas shot back, before looking sheepish again. "I'm sorry," he said to Sana. "I wanted to tell you."

Kausar pulled out the photograph she had borrowed from Deanna and placed it on the table. "The cell phone repair shop used to be your store," she said to Siraj. "Parveen said a man used to run it, and this man would argue with Imran. Your mother told me you work odd jobs now, that you had to sell your store. But you didn't sell it—Imran let you sublet it. He knew your store was only a front for the people you really worked for, the ones behind the car thefts, and a lot more besides. You thought Imran let you sublet because he wanted to stay in your organization's good graces, but really, he had been approached by the police about what was going on in the plaza, and he thought he could work both sides."

Fatima was sobbing quietly this entire time. She spoke now, her voice heavy with tears; betrayal and anger were etched like scars across her face. "How could you do this to my family, Kausar? Or did you bury your heart in Ali's grave?"

Siraj went to his mother and put a comforting arm around her shoulders. "I'm sorry, *Ammi*." Then he turned to address the rest of the party. "After my divorce, I needed a way to get on my feet again, and Imran and I came to an agreement about my store. We parked our merchandise in his plaza, and in exchange for a fee, he turned a blind eye. But he was starting to get greedy. He wanted an in with our organization. He demanded to be paid more, and he wasn't above playing dirty. He threatened to sell the plaza and cut us off completely. He thought owning the plaza gave him leverage—and when he pushed my boss, they made it clear they weren't going to let the plaza go. That night, I warned him they didn't take kindly to threats, and things reached a boiling point. He attacked me with a knife. In the struggle, I grabbed the knife from him and—it was an accident, I swear it."

Kausar's voice was hard. "You left him to die. You took his cell phone so he couldn't call for help. That's why he was in my daughter's shop in the first place. The store was a mess because of Sana's actions, but no one asked *why* Imran was inside her store. The police wanted to keep public suspicion on Sana for their own reasons, and they kept their investigation to the surface level only. The only reason things went as far as they did is because Sana implicated herself so strongly."

"I don't understand. Why *was* my father in Sana's store?" Anjum asked now. Her face was pale, as if she were reliving Imran's death all over again, and Kausar's heart went out to her. Despite their complicated relationship, Anjum's loss was very real.

"He was looking for a phone," Kausar said gently. "Sana had a landline, right at the front of her store. It was knocked over, found right beside his body. He wanted to call 911. He wanted to live."

"I took his phone because I needed time to get away," Siraj said. "I dropped it outside the store. I didn't take it with me, the police could have easily tracked it."

"I didn't see a phone on the ground when I arrived that morning," Sana said, wrinkling her nose in confusion.

"What about the attack on my father?" Patrick asked Siraj, a barely controlled tremor of rage in his voice. "Was that you, too?"

Before he could respond, Fatima turned to Kausar, and her voice was broken. "You lost your son, and now you want everyone else to suffer the same. Siraj, stop talking, I will get you a lawyer."

N*o one thanked Kausar for the meal.*

Instead, the guests filed out silently, maneuvering around Fatima's sobbing form. Ilyas read Siraj his rights, before calling the station. When the other officers arrived and Ilyas explained the situation, Sana was arrested alongside Siraj. Kausar wasn't surprised; her daughter had interfered with a crime scene, and the police would need to take statements and figure out what had actually happened. For real, this time.

In the end, Kausar was left with May, Maleeha, and Fizza, who had rushed downstairs when the commotion started and still didn't understand what was going on. May made Fizza some hot chocolate and coaxed her back upstairs, promising to explain everything.

The kitchen was a disaster, dirty dishes and pots and leftover hostess gifts abandoned on the table and counter. It would take a long time to clean it all up, but then, Kausar was used to picking up other people's messes.

"She did it for me. She framed herself to save me," Maleeha said. Her granddaughter hadn't moved from the table, not even when Sana was taken into custody for the third time in eleven days. Kausar took a seat beside her.

"Most parents would do anything to protect their children," Kausar said. She hadn't forgotten the last detail of Imran's purloined cell phone. Siraj claimed he had dropped it outside the store. If he were telling the truth, who had picked it up and sent Kausar those threatening messages? She had been so sure it was Siraj, but now she was beginning to wonder.

"Sana opened the store for you and Fizza," Kausar said. "She knew her marriage to your father was over. She wanted to be able to support herself on her own. Perhaps that is why you decided to steal cars, too."

Maleeha looked mortified. "I was angry. At both my parents. When my friends at school said there was a way to make money fast, I went along with it. I know it was stupid, but it made me feel like I had control over something in my life."

Kausar wrapped her arms around her granddaughter. "Sometimes our rage and hurt pull us in unhealthy directions."

"Is that what happened to you, after Ali died?" Maleeha asked, her voice muffled against her grandmother's shoulder.

Kausar pulled back from Maleeha. "For a long time, I forgot myself. My anger and sadness made me forget the people around me. Like your mother, and Adam, and even Hassan. My grief almost drowned me. I didn't ask for help, either, which made everything worse."

Maleeha's breathing had steadied now, her tears wrung out in a cleansing torrent. "I think I did the same thing," she admitted.

The two women were silent for a long moment, each wrapped up in their thoughts. "You are lucky Siraj decided to keep you out of the story. He must have realized there was no point in adding threats and intimidation to his criminal charges," Kausar said.

"I was so scared of him," Maleeha said in a small voice. "I worried he would hurt me, or worse, come after Mom or Fizza. I knew what he was capable of doing to keep his real business operating."

Kausar held her granddaughter close, remembering what Maleeha had confided in her the day she had tricked her into driving—about what had really happened the night Imran was murdered.

Maleeha had arrived at the plaza in the early morning hours with another stolen car—only her second or third, she hastened to assure her grandmother. She went to Imran's office as usual, where Siraj was waiting for her and the other teenagers he had working for him.

Except that night, Maleeha heard raised voices in the office. She recognized Imran and Siraj, fighting about something. Frightened, she ran to her mother's unit and hid. Except a few minutes later, Imran staggered inside and collapsed right by her.

She had tried to help, she told Kausar. She had tried to stanch the flow of blood with a scarf she had been wearing, but was scared off by the sound of another car pulling up near the store—Siraj's reinforcements, she assumed. She later realized it was her mother, summoned by the silent alarm and worry over her daughter.

Except when Sana arrived at the scene, she jumped to the wrong conclusions and made everything worse.

"Is that why you asked to help with the investigation?" Kausar asked Maleeha now, stroking her hands through her soft hair.

Maleeha shrugged. "You kept asking questions, and I worried it would all come out, that I would go to jail. I was scared."

Kausar put her arm around her granddaughter's thin shoulders, and Maleeha leaned against her, solid and warm. "It is better it has all come out, *beta*. Believe me, silence is far more dangerous."

They sat cuddled together for a long moment. Then Maleeha asked, in a small voice, "Are you going back to North Bay?"

Kausar didn't even hesitate. "Yes, *beta*." Maleeha's shoulders fell, and Kausar continued. "It will take me a few weeks to pack, before I return. My place is here, with my family. If that is okay with you?"

The smile that split her granddaughter's face felt like the sun breaking through clouds. "That sounds good to me," Maleeha said, and rested her head on her grandmother's shoulder.

CHAPTER 33

*It felt strange to be back in her bungalow in North Bay, an inver-*sion of her actions from only two weeks ago, when Kausar had sat in this same living room and answered the phone call that would change the course of her life.

The room hadn't changed. The same Agatha Christie books were stacked on her coffee table, and she was surrounded by the same drab furniture she had chosen when she first arrived in the tiny town seventeen years ago. She felt Hassan's presence here more than anywhere else; he was with her in every room of the house, in the decor and paintings and kitchen utensils they had picked out together: stable, solid, and unchanging. The only thing that had changed was her—she was no longer running from ghosts.

In the end, Sana had spent another night at the police station being questioned, and had then been charged with mischief and interfering with a crime scene. Serious offenses, but unlikely to land her with jail time. Jessica was already speaking to the prosecutor about a deal to drop the charges. In exchange, Sana would promise not to sue for wrongful arrest.

Ilyas had done them all a favor by admitting an undercover operation had been in progress at the Golden Crescent Plaza when Imran was murdered. The fact that he had conveniently made this confession in front of a dozen witnesses helped Jessica's argument. Kausar wondered if he had done it on purpose, as a mea culpa for his role in Sana's arrest. Even so, she wasn't sure her daughter would ever forgive Ilyas for his betrayal.

For her part, though she was sure Detective Drake would never admit culpability, Kausar was positive Sana's arrest had been a smokescreen to buy time to catch the bigger fish—the criminal organization responsible for the car thefts in the Golden Crescent neighborhood, and likely across the province. With Siraj's arrest, the Toronto police had a major breakthrough. All along, Sana had simply been at the wrong place at the right time to take the blame.

The fact that she had willingly tried to take that blame to spare her daughter made the case easy for Detective Drake.

All of which meant that Sana was home in time to share a final cup of chai with her mother the next afternoon, before Kausar left for North Bay with May. Both mother and daughter needed time to process the events of the last twelve days, and while their relationship was on the mend, they were both too used to dealing with their feelings alone.

Now May passed her a roll of sturdy tape to seal up the last of her boxes. "Are you going to sell the house?" she asked, looking around. Since she had returned to North Bay with her friend, Kausar had been a whirlwind of activity, clearing out a decade and a half of possessions in a week. The speed with which she had accomplished this revealed the truth: that she had never fully invested in her life here. She had been living a half-life since Ali's death, trying desperately to convince herself she was whole.

"I'll keep it, for now," Kausar said. "This community means a lot to me, and I'll be back. Maybe the girls would enjoy spending part of the summer here." She paused. "In the meantime, if your Jenny needs a place to stay . . ." she trailed off delicately. In the midst of her own drama, she hadn't followed up with May about her family troubles.

"You really don't miss anything," May said. "Jenny's leaving her husband. You were right, she's pregnant again. The IVF took, but the strain was too much for them. She says she'd rather be a single mom than stay in a loveless marriage."

"Jenny can stay here as long as she likes," Kausar said. "I insist."

May hugged her and said her daughter would be in touch. "Do you plan to move in with Sana?" May asked, and Kausar shook her head. She hadn't discussed her plans in too much detail with her daughter, but she was pretty sure that if they tried to cohabitate, there was a high chance of another homicide.

"I will stay with them for another few weeks, to help Sana put the house up for sale. She wants to stay in the neighborhood and will look for a smaller house once her separation is finalized. I will buy a small place in the Golden Crescent. Close enough to visit. Not close enough to be underfoot."

"What about Sana's store?" May asked.

"She wants to keep it, despite everything. I told her I can help until she gets back on her feet." Nasir had predicted Imran's estate would be held liable for the role he played in Ahmed's mortgage fraud, and victims, in addition to Hamza, were already starting to come forward since the case was publicized. Litigation might last for years, though, and in the meantime, Sana had bills to pay, and an expensive divorce to navigate.

The next year or so would not be easy for Sana, and Kausar resolved to be there for her family. She wondered what would happen to Parveen and Mubeen, now that their hopes for a quick sale of the plaza had been dashed. No doubt, they would be all right in the end, though they might be forced to use the profit of any sale to pay costly legal bills.

"Maybe I'll come down to visit," May said.

"I would be disappointed if you didn't. The condo I'm looking at purchasing has a guest room," Kausar said. She smiled at her friend. "I wouldn't have been able to do any of this without you, May." The friends knew this was an ending, of sorts, but also a new beginning for the next chapter.

"There's one thing I still don't understand. Who was behind the car theft ring? I can't picture Siraj as the mastermind, and he kept mentioning his boss," May said, busying herself with piling boxes closer to the door for the movers to pick up. "That was clever of you, to order food from Lisa's store. You laid the perfect trap."

Kausar bowed her head modestly. The idea had come to her when she remembered Lisa relied on Siraj for all her deliveries. "I believe Siraj when he said he killed Imran in self-defense, though he will have a difficult time convincing a jury of his peers. He likely became involved with a criminal organization when he was younger. His family went through a hard time after his father died. Fatima had to scrape together minimum wage jobs to pay the bills. He might have felt he had no other choice. The bigger question is, will Siraj turn on his employers?"

May sighed. "I can't help feeling sorry for him, and especially for Fatima."

Kausar recalled the look of devastation on Fatima's face, the venom in her former friend's voice. She hadn't wanted to hurt Fatima so soon after reuniting, and she regretted this most of all. But the truth had been inescapable. Perhaps, after enough time had passed, the two women might be able to talk, even if a continued friendship was now impossible.

"What will happen to the plaza now?" May asked.

"Once everything settles, I suspect Parveen and Mubeen will sell to Patrick. Whether they like it or not, he is about to become family. And he might be their only option, now that Ahmed has disappeared."

"Your strange dinner party did seem to be a sort of public

coming out for Anjum and Patrick," May said. "I think they will be happy together."

Kausar agreed. There was something about the couple that felt right. Certainly, they loved each other deeply. Patrick hadn't let go of Anjum for the rest of the night, and she had turned to him for comfort again and again. She remembered that Anjum had described her childhood in the plaza, running around with the other shopkeepers' children—including Patrick—as the happiest time of her life. She wished them both well.

"Speaking of being happy together . . ." May raised a questioning brow. "Your Nasir is delectable. Does he have a brother?"

Kausar laughed, shaking her head. Nasir had called the day after the dinner party, and they had talked for a long time. Since her return, they had been texting nearly every day. For now, that was enough.

"At least the car thefts will stop in the neighborhood," May said. "Whoever is in charge will lay low for a while, before they set up somewhere else. Did you know Canada has the highest number of car thefts in the world per capita? I read that online," May said. "The thing I keep coming back to again and again is Imran's cell phone. Siraj said he dropped it outside Sana's store, but Sana didn't see it when she arrived soon after. If not Siraj, who sent you those threatening messages?"

Kausar had thought about the threatening messages for a long time, and still had no idea who had sent them. She hadn't received any more after standing up for herself, so perhaps the matter was laid to rest.

May reached for the tea she had prepared for them both, which had now grown cool. She made a face and took both cups into the kitchen to warm them up. When she handed Kausar her mug, May threw her friend a knowing look. "You've got a taste for it now, don't you?" she asked, pride and sadness mixed in her question.

"For what?" Kausar asked, sipping her tea. It was weak, and heavily sweetened. She needed to teach May how to make a proper cup of chai before she left, as a parting gift.

"For solving crimes. I tease you about being Detective Aunty, but you only proved me right. I think the title suits you," May said. She raised her mug in a toast. "To your second act. May it be full of mystery, intrigue, and redemption."

The two friends' eyes met, and Kausar knew May understood there was another reason for her return to Toronto.

As much as she looked forward to mending her relationship with Sana, and to watching her granddaughters grow, another part of her finally felt strong enough to confront Ali's death. The ghost that had chased her from Toronto had finally beckoned her home, and she was ready to accept the challenge. God willing, she would help her youngest child find peace.

Once she had settled in, Kausar would begin, and she would not stop until she found out what really happened the night Ali was murdered. She drained her tea and set it on the side table. There was work to be done.

ACKNOWLEDGMENTS

I've always wanted to write a mystery, and I can't quite believe I'm here, writing the acknowledgments for a story that has lived in my head since 2017. Kausar Khan is my homage to community and second chances. May we all be enveloped by the former and gifted with the latter.

This book would not have existed without the insight, support, and inspiration of a few key people in my life. Firstly, all the stars and flowers to my editor at HarperCollins Canada, Jennifer Lambert: you have been a cheerleader for Kausar from the very start, and were it not for your enthusiasm, excellent advice, and constant support, this book would never have left my imagination to find life on the page. Thank you, thank you, thank you. Thanks also to my HarperCollins US editor, Caroline Weishuhn, who has been a champion for Kausar and her world. Your suggestions and edits have been magical, and I feel so lucky to work with you on this series!

Many thanks to my agent, Laura Gross, who loved Kausar and the Golden Crescent neighborhood from the very start, and who assured me it wasn't a terrible idea for a romance author to try her hand at mystery. Your confidence made me confident. Thanks also to my film and TV agent, Sean Daily. You always steer me right. Thank you for always staying calm and measured.

There is a team behind every book published. On the Canadian side, huge thanks to HarperCollins Canada publisher Iris Tupholme, as well as Cory Beatty, Neil Wadhwa, and Alice Tibbetts for sales, marketing, and publicity. Also thanks to Dori Carlson, Natalie Meditsky, copyeditor Catherine Dorton, and interior designer Renata De Oliveira. On the US side, many thanks to HarperCollins publisher Doug Jones and associate publisher Amy Baker, as well as Megan Looney and Rachel Molland for marketing and publicity, and to Michael Fierro. A big thanks to Olivia McGiff for the beautiful cover design!

Thank you to my writer friends, especially Ausma Zehanat Khan, who has patiently listened to every rambling thought I've had about this series for literally years. Many thanks to the writers who have generously blurbed or given my work a shout-out. You are all incredible and talented and I'm so very lucky to number among your company.

Thank you to my mother, Azmat, a lifelong fan of the genre. From *Columbo* to Agatha Christie to *Murder, She Wrote*, your passion for mystery laid the foundation for my own. Enormous thanks to my mother-in-law, Fouzia, who has devoured cozy mysteries for as long as I've known her. The best parts of Kausar were inspired by you, Umma.

As always, thank you to my husband, Imtiaz, my OG supporter, cheerleader, and forever my first reader. I'm thankful every day I get to walk through life beside you.

To my kids, Mustafa and Ibrahim—you can read this one, it's not a romance.

Finally, thank YOU, brilliant, wonderful reader—if you've followed me from my other novels, know that your support means everything; and if you're reading one of my books for the first time, thanks for giving me a chance. I am forever grateful for the gift of your time and attention. By the way, you look really pretty today.

Until next time,

xx, Uzma